# THE
# BOND
## THAT
# BURNS

# ALSO BY BRIAR BOLEYN

## BLOODWING ACADEMY

*On Wings of Blood*

*The Bond That Burns*

*The Wings That Bind*

## BLOOD OF A FAE SERIES

*Queen of Roses*

*Court of Claws*

*Empress of Fae*

*Knight of the Goddess*

## WRITTEN AS FENNA EDGEWOOD

### The Gardner Girls Series

*Masks of Desire* (The Gardner Girls' Parents' Story)

*Mistakes Not to Make When Avoiding a Rake* (Claire's Story)

*To All the Earls I've Loved Before* (Gwen's Story)

*The Seafaring Lady's Guide to Love* (Rosalind's Story)

*Once Upon a Midwinter's Kiss* (Gracie's Story)

*The Gardner Girls' Extended Christmas Epilogue* (Caroline & John's Story—Available to Newsletter Subscribers)

**Must Love Scandal Series**

*How to Get Away with Marriage* (Hugh's Story)

*The Duke Report* (Cherry's Story)

*A Duke for All Seasons* (Lance's Story)

*The Bluestocking Beds Her Bride* (Fleur & Julia's Story)

**Blakeley Manor Series**

*The Countess's Christmas Groom*

*Lady Briar Weds the Scot*

*Kiss Me, My Duke*

*My So-Called Scoundrel*

BRIAR BOLEYN

# THE BOND THAT BURNS

ONE PLACE. MANY STORIES

HQ
An imprint of HarperCollins*Publishers* Ltd
1 London Bridge Street
London SE1 9GF

www.harpercollins.co.uk

HarperCollins*Publishers*
Macken House, 39/40 Mayor Street Upper,
Dublin 1, D01 C9W8, Ireland

This edition 2025

1
First published in Great Britain by Briar Boleyn 2024

Interior images: Whitney Law at New Ink Book Services

HB ISBN: 9780008792190
TPB ISBN: 9780008792206
SPECIAL EDITION ISBN: 9780008804206
SPECIAL EDITION (EXPORT) ISBN: 9780008804572

Printed and bound in the UK using 100% Renewable
Electricity by CPI Group (UK) Ltd

For more information visit: www.harpercollins.co.uk/green

For the ones who love dangerous boys and even more dangerous dragons. Wings up, fangs out!

And to Ashley Stevenson, for her wonderful ideas— some of which appear in these pages!

# A NOTE ABOUT
# TRIGGER WARNINGS

Bloodwing Academy is a dark fantasy romance series with bully vibes. The series deals with topics that some readers may understandably find triggering.

A trigger and content warnings list may be found on the next page.

**Please keep in mind that reading the trigger warnings list will spoil certain plot elements.**

Avoid reading the trigger warnings list if you do not have any triggers and do not wish to know specific details about the plot in advance.

# TRIGGER WARNINGS

Abduction and Kidnapping
Blood and Gore
Blood Play
Child Abuse
Death and Loss
Dubious Consent
Emotional Manipulation
Graphic Violence
Harm to Animals
Injury/Threat to Animals
Mental Health Issues
Murder
Nonconsensual Mind Control
Physical Abuse
Power Imbalances
Psychological Abuse/Bullying
Sexual Assault (Threat of)
Strong Sexual Tension
Substance Abuse
Torture

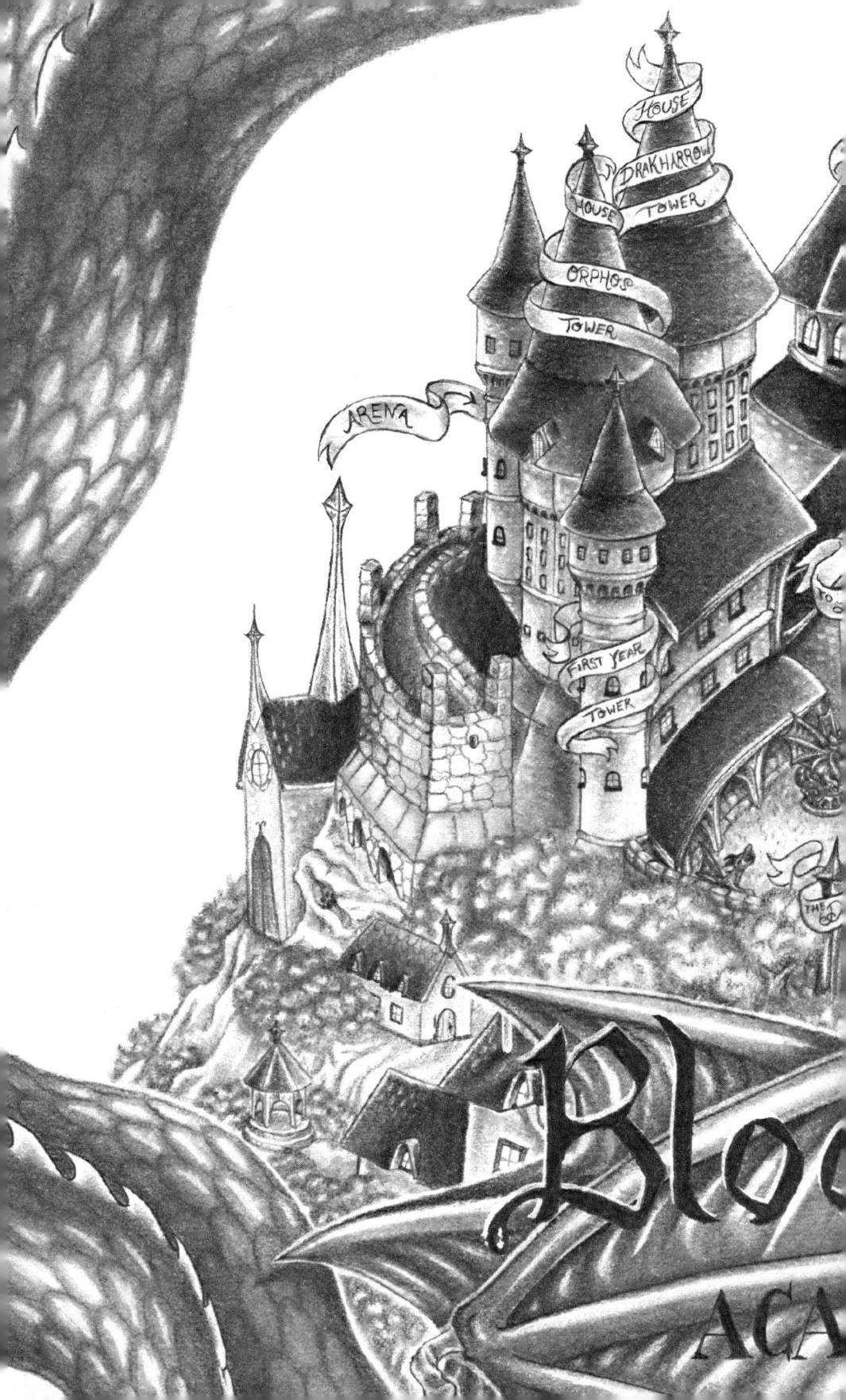

# Book 1

# MEDRA

*Bloodwing Academy*
*Last Days of Summerfell*

I'd spent my summer break in jail.

No, that wasn't fair to those who truly were imprisoned. My room in Drakharrow Tower wasn't a jail cell. But I *was* a prisoner. Still, at least my cell was padded. I had small luxuries. I had books. Food. Hot baths.

And I had not—yet—been beaten. Though, I knew Viktor Drakharrow would have liked to hit me very much. But I was getting ahead of myself. Days spent alone could do that to one. Sure, I had visitors sometimes. But not the ones I wanted.

The dragon. Nyxaris.

The moment he'd burst from the stone was one I'd never be able to forget. And the sight of him flying over Bloodwing? Everything had changed from that moment. I'd been playing a game of deception ever since. And I didn't see that changing anytime soon.

Yet the sorrow I'd felt these last two months over what I'd lost had little to do with dragons. And everything to do with Blake Drakharrow.

# MEDRA

*Two Months Earlier*

T he brief moments of silence after Nyxaris's departure felt like the calm before the storm. I could still hear his roar echoing in my ears. My heart was pounding. My body was still trembling. And yet, Nyxaris was secondary on my mind.

First and foremost was Blake.

He stood there, a few feet away from me, frozen like I was. Speechless like I was. But the look on his face . . . Shock, yes. But nothing else. He stared at me, unapologetic. Remorseless. No word of apology on his lips. He should have fallen to his knees and begged for forgiveness. But instead he just stood there.

Seeing him like that did something to me. Pushed all thoughts of the dragon from my mind. I opened my mouth, ready to erupt with fury a second time that evening. Nyxaris's roar would seem like nothing compared to mine when I was through with Blake-fucking-Drakharrow.

The stillness of the courtyard shattered. People flooded into the Dragon Court from every entrance. Students crowded in, filling the cloistered passages, peering at Blake and me where we stood amidst the rubble. I could see the excitement on their faces. In some cases, the fear. Was Florence there, somewhere in the crowd? What was she thinking? Had she been afraid when she saw Nyxaris's flight? I wanted to reassure her, to go to her. But before I could move, Headmaster Kim's voice rang out.

"All students will return to their dormitories at once."

There was a moment of hesitation. I saw indecision on students' faces. They wanted to be there, to see what happened next.

To my knowledge, our stern yet steady Headmaster Kim had never bellowed before. Now he did. "Perhaps you did not understand me the first time. *Now!*"

Students began to scamper out. Kim marched towards Blake and me. He was not alone. A group of older highbloods trailed behind him. I scanned their faces, my heart falling as I recognized Viktor Drakharrow, his red eyes gleaming as he looked at me with unmistakable greed. No, more than that—triumph. I half expected him to grab me and snatch me from the courtyard that instant.

Then I recognized the woman walking beside him. She was petite, slender-framed, with straight silver hair cut at chin-length. Her dark angular eyes looked at me with some wariness, but also with intelligence and curiosity. I knew her. I'd seen her portrait in the headmaster's office.

Natsumi Avari. Kage's mother. She was a member of Bloodwing's Board of Directors.

I scanned the highbloods around her. There must have been a meeting of the board that night. That's why so many were here. Not too often that a board meeting was adjourned by a dragon, I'd bet. I had only a vague idea of what a board of directors did. Helped to run Bloodwing somehow, I presumed. Was it a good thing that they were all here now, at this moment? Or a very bad one? I decided having more witnesses to whatever Viktor Drakharrow was about to do couldn't be a bad thing. After all, Natsumi was House Avari. She wouldn't just go along with whatever Viktor said.

I could feel highblood eyes on me. Sizing me up as if a wild animal had suddenly wandered into their midst. There had been a time I'd wanted them all to look at me exactly as they were now. As if I were someone to be reckoned with. Someone to be feared.

But now I knew that having all of this highblood attention on me was the last thing anyone should ever wish for.

There was a clatter and the sound of a heavy door banging as the last of the students cleared out. Headmaster Kim's face was grim as he reached us. He opened his mouth to speak.

"Incredible. Absolutely incredible." It was Viktor. He walked past Kim, coming closer to me than I liked. His red eyes met mine. He smiled slowly, his avarice palpable. I didn't smile back. "How did you summon the dragon?" he demanded, as if unable to wait a second longer to begin his interrogation.

I jumped. "I—" I started to say. But then everyone burst in.

"What exactly happened here?"

"What did you do?"

"How dare you!"

"Are you in control of it?"

"Where is it going? Where did you send it?"

"Can you command it? Tell it to return here at once."

"The dragon belongs to House Avari."

I looked at the speaker of those last words: no surprise that they had come from Natsumi.

Kage's mother looked at me calmly, ignoring the other board members and Headmaster Kim. "Let us not forget that. The dragon belongs to House Avari."

I opened my mouth to tell her that I was fairly certain the dragon believed he belonged only to himself. But in a flash, Viktor was beside her, his face close to hers.

"The dragon belongs to its rider," he hissed. "And the rider belongs to House Drakharrow."

To her credit, Natsumi didn't retreat. She held her position, gazing boldly back into Viktor's venomous red orbs. "I know you may be used to making decisions unilaterally within your own house, Lord Drakharrow. But this is a matter that must be settled by a tribunal," she said coolly. "In the meantime, make no mistake—House Avari stakes its claim. Nyxaris was and remains ours."

Viktor scoffed. "You may stake all the claims you wish. The rider is ours. She is mated to my own kin, my nephew. She rides for House Drakharrow. Good luck controlling a riderless dragon, Natsumi."

"Let's remember where we are. Who we are," Headmaster Kim interjected. "Let us maintain order. Lady Natsumi is correct, Viktor. This is a matter for a tribunal now. The other regents must be informed immediately of what has occurred here tonight."

"And just what *did* occur here tonight?" A tall highblood man stood off to one side, looking more shaken than the others. He stared at me from pale blue eyes, as if trying to conceal his fear from his more powerful peers.

"The tribunal will establish that, Lord Sylvain," Headmaster Kim assured him.

*Sylvain.* This must be Evander's father. Visha's future father-in-law.

Lord Sylvain clasped his hands together, twisting the rings on his fingers nervously. Lean and elegantly dressed, he wore a flowing tunic embroidered with white and red flowers. He took a deep breath. "That's not good enough. We all know the tribunal will take weeks to convene. If not months. Why, Lord Mortis is nowhere near Veilmar right now. He's visiting his family's estates, of which there are many. Who knows how long it will take to track him down?"

"We will find him," Headmaster Kim replied. "The tribunal will settle the matter."

"What are you really afraid of?" Viktor stepped towards Lord Sylvain, a sneer on his lined, pale face. "For it *is* fear that I see on your sniveling features, is it not, Sylvain?"

Lord Sylvain flushed. "How dare you."

"Perhaps Lord Sylvain simply requires reassurance," Natsumi Avari said smoothly, stepping farther into the little circle that had formed around us.

Headmaster Kim frowned. "What sort of reassurance?"

"I want the matter dealt with at once," Lord Sylvain snapped, looking at me. "Not weeks or months from now. The dragon is gone. But this girl—" he looked at me and frowned "—at least she may be contained."

"Me?" I burst out. "I'm not a threat to anyone."

Lord Sylvain glared at me. "Not a threat? Do you know what you have done, girl? Do you have even the faintest notion of what you have brought back?"

I opened my mouth to start to protest that I hadn't even meant to bring a dragon back. Then I closed it again. Would it really benefit me to tell the truth? To say it had all been an accident? Right now, Lord Sylvain was afraid of me. If I said I'd done all of this unwittingly, I'd look like a fool. Worse, I'd lose whatever edge I had. Better that they fear me than know the truth. That I was as powerless as they were when it came to controlling Nyxaris.

"I want her confined." Lord Sylvain was finally finding his confidence. "Chained. We cannot risk her doing it again."

"You really are a greater idiot than I took you for, Sylvain," Viktor snapped. "A great, bungling coward."

For once, I agreed with Blake's uncle. I took a risk. "I don't understand. Isn't this what you wanted?" I asked the question of all of them, but my eyes were on Viktor.

His eyes narrowed as he looked back at me.

"Lord Drakharrow, you wanted this to happen, didn't you?" I prompted. "Aren't the highbloods more powerful with dragons?"

"Dragons, yes," he snapped. "Plural. And you woke the wrong fucking one, girl."

I flinched. Viktor was thrilled a dragon now flew over Sangratha, yes. But like Lord Sylvain, I realized he was afraid, too, terrified that House Avari would wind up with the upper hand.

"I agree with Lord Sylvain," Natsumi Avari spoke up. "The rider should be confined until the tribunal."

I bristled. "I'm not sure my dragon would appreciate hearing that you all wish to place me under lock and key."

"Then, summon him here, rider," Natsumi said softly, meeting my eyes. "Bring Nyxaris back. Let us discuss this matter with you both."

"He has more important things to do than listen to highbloods argue," I said as haughtily as I could.

"Then, he has left your fate to us," she pointed out.

There was nothing I could say to argue.

"We will have answers for you all very soon. I promise you that," Viktor Drakharrow said, stepping in front of me and blocking me off from the others. "She is our rider. But you deserve answers as to what has happened. We will find out what she did and how."

"*She* has a fucking name, Uncle," Blake said. He reached for my arm, as if to pull me out of Viktor's circle of proximity, but I quickly took a step back.

"Don't you dare lay a hand on me," I snarled.

There was quiet. Everyone had heard me. Blake's face flushed red. Viktor slowly turned to look back and forth between his nephew and me. What he saw clearly did not please him, but he said nothing to either of us, simply turned back to the other highbloods.

"May we confine her to a room in the Drakharrow Tower, or would you rather she be placed in the dungeon, Lord Sylvain?" Viktor asked with deceptive courteousness. "Perhaps with only stale crusts of bread to eat. Shall we keep her in a weakened state, lest you feel more threatened?"

Headmaster Kim cleared his throat. "That's enough, Viktor. I believe what you've proposed should be to everyone's satisfaction. Keep her in Drakharrow Tower."

Viktor nodded, then turned to look at me. His red eyes seemed suddenly colder. "Still, there may be no need for any of this. You'll tell us exactly what happened. And you'll do it now, girl."

His thrallweave slammed into my mind and I cried out, sinking to my knees on the stones.

"I said you will tell us exactly what happened." Viktor Drakharrow's voice was like a whip, slicing through the air and cutting me to pieces.

I had never felt this kind of pain before. Invisible but brutal, he hit my mind with a force unlike anything I'd ever felt. I gasped, clutching my head, my vision blurring as pain pulsed behind my eyes. But he wasn't inside. He was an attacker at the gates. My walls were still up. I had not caved. Something fierce inside me fought back. I closed my eyes, clenched my teeth, my sweaty hands digging into the cold stone as I threw up barrier after barrier with every ounce of strength I had.

Still, Viktor's power crashed into me again and again. Suffocating, insistent, digging his claws of pain inside.

"Stop," I heard Blake shouting. "Uncle, stop this. Look at her. You're hurting her."

Dimly, I realized I was bleeding. Drops of blood trickled down my face. I heard some of the highbloods hiss and take a step back. The scent of my blood drew them in but also alarmed them.

Then, just when I thought I might break, a voice boomed across the courtyard.

"What the hell is going on here?" Professor Rodriguez stormed into the circle, his eyes blazing with fury. "Get away from her. This instant."

I forced my eyes open in time to see Viktor's face twist with irritation. He looked away from me, more surprised than angered. "Rodriguez."

His thrallweave attack faltered. I gasped, drawing in a long breath. I felt Blake's hand touch my shoulder, as if to help me stand, but I pushed it away without even looking at him.

"How dare you interrupt? How dare you even enter this place?" Viktor took a step towards Rodriguez and for a moment, I was frightened for my professor.

But Rodriguez didn't back down.

"This is a highblood matter," Viktor hissed. "You should not be here, blightborn. Get out."

Rodriguez's fists were clenched. I watched as Blake moved to stand behind the professor, his face ashen.

"I do dare," Rodriguez said, his voice low and menacing. He stepped farther into the circle defiantly. "This girl has given you precisely what you've always wanted, Viktor. She's made history here today—she's brought you back a dragon." He swept his gaze over the gathered crowd of highbloods. "And instead of thanking her, what are you all doing? Standing here and preparing to tear her apart like a pack of vultures."

Natsumi Avari stepped up beside Rodriguez and Blake. "He's right, Viktor. Besides, you know thrallweave can do lasting damage when used so forcefully. Do you want to keep your rider in one piece, or don't you?" I stared up at her, stunned, as she inclined her head. "On behalf of House Avari, I thank you, Medra Pendragon, for your service here today."

The words were double-edged and everyone there knew it. Still, I nodded.

An aftershock of pain rippled through me and I put a hand to my temples, then yanked it away in shock as I felt a sticky wetness. Blood.

Blake moved forward. "Here. Medra, let me . . ."

I ignored him and tried to push myself up with my own strength.

Rodriguez crouched down beside me. "Here," he murmured, his hands strong and surprisingly gentle as he helped me to my feet. "Take your time."

I nodded, swallowing tears of anger and frustration, leaning on Rodriguez as I slowly stood up. I could feel Viktor's eyes on me, his still anger pulsing towards me. But he made no move to cast thrallweave on me again. He didn't need to: he'd have me locked in his tower soon and could try again anytime.

"Very well, Professor," Viktor said, his voice dripping with disdain. "Let the rider rest tonight. She'll be confined in Drakharrow Tower to await the judgment of the tribunal."

Rodriguez straightened. "Fine. I'll escort Miss Pendragon there myself." Without waiting for an answer, he began to guide me away from the group of gawking highbloods.

I saw Blake begin to follow, then hesitate. Before he could

change his mind and come after us, Viktor approached him and put a hand on his arm. He turned to speak to his uncle and that was the last I saw of Blake.

Together, Rodriguez and I walked out of the courtyard, leaving the others behind. I felt a sense of relief settle over me as we exited, even though I knew it was temporary. The halls were quiet as we made our way through Bloodwing towards Drakharrow Tower.

"You did well," Rodriguez said as we walked. He glanced at me. "In truth, I can't believe you kept him out."

"Neither can I," I said bluntly. "I don't know how I did it. I thought he was supposed to be—"

"He is," Rodriguez cut in. He was speaking quickly. Too quickly. It was clear there were things he wanted to say and he didn't think we had much time. "Medra, the school shuts down for Summerfell tomorrow. All of the students will be gone and most of the professors. I usually stay, but . . ." He let the sentence hang there unfinished. He wasn't sure he'd be permitted to remain. "I'm not sure we'll have another chance to talk before the start of the next school year."

"You don't think they'll let you see me? Even to visit?" My heart sank. If there was anyone who could help me through this, it was Rodriguez.

He shrugged. "If it's up to Viktor . . ."

"He'll want to know how I shut him out," I guessed. "He'll be furious that you've been tutoring me."

A smile flickered over Rodriguez's face. "Let him be. It was Headmaster Kim's decision. And his indiscretion."

"He can't fault either of you for training me. You can position it as protecting me from the other houses," I suggested.

Rodriguez nodded.

"You know more about dragons than all of these people put together," I blurted out. "Did you know this would happen?"

He shook his head. "Not all of them. One man was there when dragons flew, long before tonight."

"Viktor?"

He nodded. "He's the oldest living highblood in Sangratha. Did you know that?"

"I'm not surprised," I said sourly. "He looks like the epitome of ancient evil."

Rodriguez smirked. "He's not particularly likable, is he?"

"He's a fucking monster," I spat. "And you don't have to hide your hate from me, Rodriguez. I know you do. Hate *them*, I mean." His face tensed up and I knew I'd said too much. Still, I had so many questions. I wasn't about to hold back now. "Why did the dragons disappear in the first place?"

"You mean you haven't learned that already in any of your classes?" Rodriguez said. It was clear he knew the answer.

"No. Or in the books you told me to read." I frowned. "They were written before the last dragon disappeared. Where are the others?"

"Others?" Rodriguez tilted his head.

"Books that were written about why the dragons disappeared. About how—" I said with frustration "—and what about the four stone dragons? How did they get like that? Obviously Nyxaris was under some sort of curse or enchantment."

Rodriguez nodded thoughtfully. "That seems like a reasonable conclusion."

"Oh, come off it," I demanded. "You knew. You knew all along. You wanted me to wake him. You wanted me to take that book."

Rodriguez's eyes were suddenly hawklike. "I never said that, Miss Pendragon. You stole that book from my office, as I recall."

"I borrowed it," I countered. "And I don't think you were really all that upset with me when I did. Maybe you wanted me to."

"Why would I want that? Why would I want the highbloods to get back their greatest weapons?"

"I don't know," I exclaimed. "Tell me. Because clearly there are reasons."

"Reasons you can't find in the history books I gave you? How fascinating."

"So we're going to dance around this, are we?" I shook my head in frustration. "Fine. Be that way. But there is a fucking dragon out there right now. Flying free. Because of me."

"So you did do it on purpose?"

"No!" I blurted out. "You know I didn't."

He studied me. "Yet you did it. A blood ritual of some sort. Why were you conducting such a ritual in the first place? Why take the book if it wasn't to awaken a dragon?"

"I had another reason. A good one," I said reluctantly. "Consider this an accidental side effect."

Rodriguez sighed. He seemed to be relaxing again a little. He ran a hand over his hair. "Look, there's too much to tell. So much it's too risky to share."

"If you can't trust me, who can you trust?" I demanded. "He was in my head, Professor. In my damned head."

Rodriguez looked fascinated. "Nyxaris, you mean?"

I nodded. "He speaks Classical Sangrathan. Did you know that?"

"And you do, too?" He shook his head. "I suppose we should be grateful, however you came to that knowledge." He looked at me curiously. "What did he say? Where did he go?"

"An answer for an answer," I said stubbornly. "How did the dragons disappear?"

"Some died of a plague."

"Like the one your grandmother couldn't save?" I guessed.

He nodded.

"And the others? Did they *all* die of a plague?"

"There's a lost history here, Miss Pendragon. A history of the dragons that the highbloods have purposely hidden. Even from one another."

My heart hammered. "How is that possible? How could a highblood hide something like that from other highbloods?"

"A question that it would be fascinating to pose to Viktor Drak-harrow. But I don't recommend doing so."

I scowled. *Fine. Next question.* "Why would those four dragons have been preserved like that? Enchanted? Why not keep them alive and use them?"

"That's a question beyond even my scope of knowledge," Rodriguez said. "Perhaps you ought to ask your dragon."

I felt a pang of guilt. "He's not my dragon."

"Did you try—"

"I read the book," I said quickly. "The part about bonding. Yes, I tried. I did everything I could remember. Everything I could think of to do at that moment." I glanced around. We were almost at the entrance to the House Drakharrow Tower. "But it didn't work."

"So he flew away." Rodriguez studied me. "Does he have any intention of coming back?" He held up a hand. "No. On second thought, don't answer that." He sounded tired suddenly. "Don't tell me. I don't want to know."

"Why?" I asked nervously.

"Because I have no idea how good my thrallguard really is. How well I'd hold up if . . ." He looked at me.

"If you were tortured." I bit my lip. "Is that what they're going to do to me? To get the answers they want?"

He sighed. "Do you really want an honest answer?"

I folded my arms over my chest and hugged myself. "This is going to be a fantastic summer, isn't it?"

He grimaced. "You have a few advantages. You can defend yourself with thrallguard. It might be enough. Not all of them will try to use it on you, but Viktor certainly will try again. He doesn't give up easily. Then, there's Blake."

I winced. "Blake is not an advantage."

"Whatever's going on with you two on a personal level, I don't really care. But he's still your archon. That hasn't changed. He can help you to some extent. I suggest you let him."

"If he even wants to," I said dourly.

Rodriguez ignored me. "You also have leverage. If you say you can control that dragon, they'll have to believe you. They can't risk not doing so. Especially if they can't break you to find out the truth." He threw up his hands. "Whatever the truth is. Again—"

"You don't want to know," I finished for him. "Right. I get it." I sighed and touched a hand to my temple. The blood had dried. "Why did I bleed when Viktor used thrallweave on me?"

"You were under an overwhelming amount of strain. Viktor is incredibly powerful. It's not completely unheard of. Thrallweave attacks can be painful, though usually the result is only a bad headache."

"Spontaneously bleeding just from strain?" I furrowed my brow. "Natsumi said it could do permanent damage."

"When used as a method of torture, yes. I have no doubt Viktor is experienced in that. But he'll need to keep you whole." Rodriguez touched my shoulder gently. "Look, we're nearly at the tower. What you need to do is hold them off until the tribunal can meet. Do you think you can do that?"

"I suppose it depends on whether they plan to torture me or not," I said bitterly. "How long will it be before the tribunal is held?"

Rodriguez hesitated. "From what I understand, Lord Mortis is away from Veilmar and House Orphos is dealing with some family matters. But I'm sure they'll want to have this settled before the start of the next school year."

I groaned. "All of Summerfell, really? Two months of waiting?" Two months of lying and bluffing.

"Eventually, that dragon is going to need to make an actual appearance." He ran a hand over his face. "Have you tried begging?"

"I begged. Believe me, I begged." And now Nyxaris was gone. I couldn't hear him in my mind. Did that mean I had no way of reaching him again?

"Best-case scenario, they'll agree you need to continue at Blood-wing and intensify your rider training. There might be pressure on you to repeat what you did before and try to wake another dragon."

"Absolutely fucking not," I said automatically. I could just imagine having to lie about *two* dragons.

"Good. I wouldn't suggest that. At least, not unless you get a tight control on Nyxaris." His concerned expression told me just how worried he really was.

"It was an accident," I reminded him. I thought of what he'd just said. "What's the worst-case scenario?"

"They decide to destroy you. Both of you."

I gaped at him. "What?"

Rodriguez's face was stony.

"That's insane. They just got a dragon back. Why would they want to destroy it?" I asked, feeling stunned.

"So that the entire kingdom doesn't devolve into infighting and civil war resulting in the loss of countless lives, especially blight-born ones? I'd say that's a pretty good reason," Rodriguez replied with discouraging coolness.

"Or they could just agree to . . . let bygones be bygones."

Rodriguez's lips twitched. "To let dragons be dragons, you mean?"

I nodded.

"You need to remember where you are, Miss Pendragon," he said, not unkindly. "In the heart of the lions' den."

"You mean the *vampires' den*," I muttered. "Which is so much worse."

He gestured ahead of us. "Speaking of highbloods, someone's waiting for you."

I turned to where he pointed and frowned. Blake leaned against the wall next to the entrance to the House Drakharrow Tower.

"Damn vampire speed," I muttered under my breath. He'd beaten us there, so he must have gone another route.

"I'll see her the rest of the way from here," Blake said, stepping forward.

Rodriguez nodded. "No Viktor?"

Blake shook his head. "But he'll be back."

"Of course he will." Rodriguez whistled. "Well, good luck, Miss Pendragon. Good night."

"I'll show you to your room," Blake said as Rodriguez walked away.

Before I could reply, he'd turned and I had to follow. Vampire speed . . . and very long legs. I picked up my pace. I didn't want to be there, and yet I couldn't help but feel a prick of curiosity as we entered House Drakharrow's privileged space. Come Autumntide, this was supposed to be my new home. Before the events of the evening, I'd even looked forward to moving into the tower. In one night, everything had changed. I wasn't merely a student or Blake's consort; I was once again his prisoner.

I'd only been in the tower one time, at the start of the first year, when I'd been wounded by Visha, and Blake had brought me to see a healer. Now I looked around me more carefully, taking in the grand stone archway carved with coiled dragons that led into the tower. The dragons' eyes glinted with rubies that reminded me of Viktor Drakharrow's cruel red ones.

Blake led the way into a large open hall that I assumed was the Drakharrow common room. Unsurprisingly, red and black were the accent colors here instead of the deep blues and soft grays I was used to in the First Year tower. Chandeliers of wrought iron hung above us. The walls were lined with dark wood paneling and decorated with ancient weapons and crests. Relics of battles fought for the glory of House Drakharrow, no doubt.

The room was a little foreboding, but I could see it being cozy enough with time. Right now, the space was empty, but a blazing fire roared in the massive stone hearth even though it was almost summer. Comfortable armchairs, sofas, and chaises, all covered in soft red velvet, were arranged in a variety of positions to facilitate study and conversation. Banners of deep crimson and black hung from the ceiling, proudly showing off depictions of red dragons or bearing the house motto, *Sanguine Vincti.*

*Bound by blood.* My lips twisted. The words seemed to mock me now more than ever.

Around the common room, students' chairs sat empty. A few were even overturned. Books and other possessions were scattered over sofas and tables. The room had clearly been abandoned quickly in everyone's haste to reach the courtyard earlier. Most of the students must have been in the midst of packing. Tomorrow morning they'd be returning home for Summerfell.

Blake led the way towards the stairway, pausing only briefly to snap at a few students who had snuck out of their rooms and were peering down curiously at us from one of the balconies. They vanished quickly at their House Leader's command, leaving an uneasy silence. Blake moved at a steady pace, his back straight and steely. I followed, hardly able to look at him without feeling a fresh wave of anger.

We reached a landing, and I noticed a door ajar with three faces peering out. Blake didn't even have to speak: the glare he shot the students was enough to send them scattering backwards with panicked squeaks. The door slammed and we were alone again. Blake's jaw tightened. He didn't look back or speak as we climbed another spiraling staircase. I watched his hand trail over the stone railing, carved like a dragon's tail, rubies embedded into the scales of stone. In some ways I had an intimate knowledge of that hand, those fingers. But that part of us was over.

Finally, Blake stopped outside a door. He opened it, stepping aside to let me walk in first. Lanterns had been lit and a small fire burned in the modest-sized hearth. The room was unexpectedly spacious, with a large canopy bed draped in soft red fabric patterned with dragon scales. Tall arched windows lined two sides of the room, overlooking the darkened school grounds and the sea beyond the cliffs.

I glanced over at Blake, arching a brow. "So, this is my cell."

Blake's lips twisted into a small smile. He looked back at me, his gaze holding something uncertain. "It was meant to be your room all along. You're just occupying it sooner than expected." He nodded towards the windows, gesturing to a wood desk already set with parchment and quills, then to the shelves lined with books. "I'd already had it prepared and waiting for you."

The room was elegant. Beautiful, even. The rug beneath my feet was soft and plush. Black, with a motif of gold, silver, and red dragons. I saw a wardrobe off in the corner, no doubt already stocked with clothes in my size, all in House Drakharrow colors. I should have been grateful it wasn't a dungeon. But no matter how elegant it was, it still felt like a cage.

Blake gestured to one of the walls that lacked a window. "You'll find my suite of rooms beside yours."

My lips twisted. *His and hers. How sweet.* "Wonderful," I said, in a voice that made it clear it was anything but.

Blake frowned. "There's a private bath through that door," he said eventually, pointing. "The windows let in a lot of light in the winter. You'll have a good view."

"Is that all?" I watched his face fall. "Are we finished?"

He was, without a doubt, still maddeningly attractive. The slight shadow of blond stubble along the angles of his jaw. His gray eyes that once made my breath catch. He looked at me now with an intensity that seemed meant to draw me in. But it didn't matter what he looked like: he'd proven he was the monster I'd known he was all along. The connection between us that I'd slowly been accepting had been severed. He'd taken something from me that could never be restored. Not just blood. Trust.

Blake cleared his throat. "Medra, I—"

"Don't," I cut him off, my voice chill and unyielding. "And I've already asked you not to call me that. We are not friends."

His face darkened. "You're still my consort."

That might have been true for now. But bonds could be broken.

"You can call me whatever you want. But it's meaningless. After what you did tonight, you're nothing to me." I stepped towards the bed, putting my hand firmly on one of the posts. "I'd like you to leave. Now."

I could see the flash of hurt, then the flicker of anger, before he schooled his expression. I understood. This wasn't how I'd imagined the night going either. We'd both have to suffer with disappointment. There was only one person to blame for it. And I was looking at him.

With a tight nod, Blake turned towards the door. I started to breathe a sigh of relief.

Blake paused. "We'll speak further tomorrow." Then he pulled the door shut behind him.

I gritted my teeth. The asshole couldn't bear to let me have the last word.

I heard a key turn in the lock and nearly laughed aloud. Well, I was alone like I'd wanted. Alone in a place that should have felt like home, yet where I was every bit the prisoner.

# CHAPTER 2

# MEDRA

Threenext day, I heard the key turn in the lock as I sat in a chair by the window reading. I was expecting it to be Blake, but instead Viktor Drakharrow marched in.

"Among blightborn, it's customary to knock," I couldn't help saying, as I put down my book and stood up.

He ignored me. His presence filled the room as he moved towards me. Cold. Oppressive. He had been alive longer than anyone else in the realm, yet there was nothing really *alive* about this man. He reeked of death.

I felt a shiver crawl up my spine as his gaze settled on me. "Does Blake know you're here?"

Viktor's lips curled into a faint sneer. He narrowed his eyes and before I could prepare myself, a wave of force slammed against my mind. I reached out for something to hold on to as my knees buckled, but it was no use. I fell to the floor, unable to brace myself. Pain pulsed through my temples. I clenched my jaw. The only thing keeping me conscious was the look of frustration on Viktor's face as he stared at me down on the ground. *It's not working,* I thought with triumph.

Rallying slightly, I threw up another blockade of walls. Once they'd been paper-thin. Now they were brick and mortar: I sealed every crack. I still wasn't sure how I was doing it, but I was determined. He would *not* get in.

Viktor's irritation turned darker. "A little blightborn bitch should not be able to keep out her highblood master."

"And yet look at me doing just that," I said sweetly.

His hand shot out and before I could move, my head spun to the side as he slapped me hard. My cheek throbbed. I could taste copper on my lips. "So which am I?" I asked angrily. "A blightborn bitch or the dragon rider you need? Either you value me or I'm worthless. Which is it?"

Viktor bent down, his voice dropping to a whisper. "Do you wish to be tortured, girl? Because, I assure you, I am more than capable. You are a consort in words only. You are not part of this family and never will be. I assure you, I will hold nothing back."

My pulse raced but I forced myself to hold his gaze, my mind scrambling. "Why not ask me the questions first? You might not need to bash your way into my mind or destroy my body."

"No, but I'd enjoy doing so," he murmured, his eyes flicking over me. It took everything I had not to visibly shudder.

Viktor stood upright, squaring his shoulders. He was shorter than Blake, I suddenly noticed. Yet there was nothing diminished about his presence: he was the most terrifying man I'd ever met. And considering my grandfather, that was saying a great deal.

"Fine. Let us try it your way. Tell me, how did you wake the dragon?"

I took a deep breath. My lies had to be perfect. Convincing. This man was not a fool. "It was an accident. I didn't mean for it to happen."

His eyes narrowed. "Be more specific. Surely you can recall something."

I shook my head. "Do you remember when the tremors started around the school?" I remembered he resided elsewhere. "Please, just ask the headmaster. He'll tell you all about it. I think that was when it began, months ago. This wasn't a recent thing. Nyxaris has been in the process of awakening for a while. But,"

I made sure to add, "Nyxaris believes I woke him. He thanked me for it."

"You spoke to the dragon?" Viktor demanded.

I nodded. "Mind to mind. Yes."

Viktor stared at me for a long while. "I will accept that pitiful answer for now. But it is greatly lacking. You will go over every detail that occurred leading up to the first tremor and you will come up with more. I will know how this happened. The answer lies in your mind, and I will have it. Willingly or unwillingly."

I nodded. What else could I do? "I'll try to recall more."

"Why was it the House Avari dragon that awoke? Why Nyxaris and not Vorago?"

I licked my lips, tasting the blood. "That's a good question," I said carefully. "I've been wondering that as well."

"You climbed atop the creature one day, so I am told." Viktor's lips curled with distaste. "Miss Pansera had you under her control then."

"Yes," I admitted. "She used thrallweave on me."

Viktor scowled. "Yet suddenly you are not so susceptible. Strange."

"The headmaster and my professors—" I was careful not to specifically mention Rodriguez but I knew Viktor would find out anyhow "—they all agreed it would make sense to tutor me in thrallguard. Like riders of old."

Viktor's face flushed. "The fools. I should have been consulted. Blocking me out should have been impossible."

I said nothing but the words sent a warm heat through me, as if they had been praise. So not many could block out Viktor? He wasn't used to being thwarted. Not for the first time, I felt a surge of gratitude that he had not been consulted before Headmaster Kim made his decision.

"You touched the black stone dragon. You mounted it."

I felt my cheeks redden. There had been absolutely nothing

erotic about what Regan had made me do that day, and yet the way Viktor said the words made my stomach turn.

"Perhaps that was all the connection that was needed," he mused. "A touch between rider and stone. So stupid. So simple."

Sure, that and a few drops of my blood and a ritual poem. I wasn't so sure Viktor was right about my touch being the key. After all, I had climbed Nyxaris long before doing the ritual. But let him think whatever he wanted.

Viktor's red eyes clouded as he studied my face. "Now, let us get to the heart of the matter. And do not think I will not know if you lie, girl. Can you control it? This creature you've woken from stone?"

Slowly, I pushed myself to my feet, drawing myself up and lifting my chin defiantly. "Yes. Nyxaris will return to me when I call. He is mine to command."

Viktor's eyes narrowed. "You think you can control a dragon? A child with no knowledge of real power?" He leaned in closer, and I remembered the blood on my lip. "Do you really think I'd believe such an audacious lie?"

My heart pounded but I held my ground. "It's the truth, Lord Drakharrow. If you want Nyxaris under your command, then you need me. I may not have full control yet—" I made it sound like an admission "—but with time, I *will* establish it." My pulse hammered with every word. "If you push me too far, though, he'll sense it. Are you willing to risk losing both of us?"

Viktor grabbed my chin roughly, forcing my face closer to his. "Let me be very clear." His voice had dropped to a whisper that sent a shiver through my bones. "If you fail to do what you've just promised, if you embarrass this house . . . I'll make sure your suffering is unending. Do we understand one another?"

My throat felt tight with fear, but my resolve hardened. This man was bluffing as much as I was. He needed me.

I pulled out of his grip and stepped back. "Keep your hands off me. I'm the only one Nyxaris will come back to. I'm the only one who can bring him to heel." I narrowed my gaze. "If you can't accept that, then kill me now, Lord Drakharrow, and watch your dragon disappear into the clouds forever."

Viktor's nostrils flared. He stepped forward and shoved me hard. With a gasp, I fell back into the chair I'd been sitting in when he'd arrived.

"If you plan to torture me, then just remember my dragon will know of it when he returns," I said boldly.

I highly doubted Nyxaris would care. What was it he'd said? Oh, yes: that he'd have scorched Blake and me if I hadn't happened to be the one who'd awoken him. The black dragon didn't seem of the particularly kindhearted sort.

"I'm not afraid to get the truth out of you, girl," Viktor snarled. "If I have to—"

"Uncle, there you are. I've been looking for you." Blake stood in the doorway breathing hard. His gaze immediately went to me. I could sense him taking in my disheveled state, the blood on my lips.

Viktor straightened, his hands falling back to his sides. "You're interrupting, Blake."

Blake didn't move, but I saw his jaw clench. "I'm sorry. I thought you wanted to speak to me. Well, I'm here now."

For a moment, I held my breath. Was it too much to hope my threats had gotten through to Viktor? Viktor looked down at me, sneered, then moved to the door. As his uncle crossed the threshold, Blake glanced at me briefly but said nothing, simply pulled the door shut behind him.

The key turned in the lock and I was alone again.

CHAPTER 3

# BLAKE

I stood rigidly as Viktor paced the opulent chamber inside the Black Keep. The heavy curtains were drawn, muting the sunlight and giving the room an oppressive glow. Viktor's long strides carried him back and forth across the carpet in front of the hearth, his hands clasped tightly behind his back. He was angry—didn't take a genius to figure out that much.

"She resisted me," Viktor said without preamble. "Do you even understand how rare that is?"

I shrugged. "She's stubborn, not special. I have no doubt in your ability to get through to her eventually, Uncle."

Viktor stopped mid-step, turning to face me with an icy glare. "Who gave her permission to learn thrallguard?"

"I wasn't privy to the meeting where it was decided," I said slowly. "But I would assume Headmaster Kim was involved."

Viktor gnashed his teeth. "That blightborn-loving fool. Did he even think to consult me?"

I highly doubted Kim harbored any undue love for blightborn. Or even for Pendragon. But I said nothing. I tilted my head slightly. "The riders of old were all trained in thrallguard, weren't they? Perhaps they simply based the decision on that precedent?" I only knew this because Rodriguez had told me. "Pendragon *did* almost die on her first day because of how susceptible she was, after all."

Viktor's lips curled into a sneer. "None of that would have occurred if you had kept your women in check. Don't lecture me on history I bore witness to, boy. Those riders were loyal to their houses. They knew the cost of disobedience. Does this one?"

My jaw tightened. "Thrallguard lessons won't make her untouchable. She's just a girl playing with fire."

My uncle's eyes narrowed. "A girl who woke a dragon, Blake. Do not underestimate her."

It seemed as if he were the one who'd already done that, but I held my tongue.

"She needs special handling," my uncle said, as if to himself. He glanced at me. "What I'd like to do is beat the answers out of her. I've never met a blightborn who could not be broken with the proper . . . persuasion. I could drag the truth from her lips with pain until there was nothing left but submission. But . . ."

I waited a moment. "But?" I finally asked cautiously.

His lips thinned. "She claims the dragon would know."

"Ah. That is . . ." I searched for the right word ". . . unfortunate. And do you believe her?"

"I don't know what to believe. It's entirely possible she can communicate with it, that much is not in question. We need that dragon. She's our only connection to it, as it stands now. The Avaris will try to thwart us every step of the way. We need her obedient. We need her compliant."

I decided not to mention there might be complications with that.

Viktor looked at me. "I want to know everything about this girl, Blake. What she knows, what she's hiding, and more importantly, what she can *do*. She's hidden things from us from the very start. She came out of nowhere. It's time we found out who she really is. You'll report to me regularly. I expect progress."

I tried to look confident. "Of course."

"For now, we'll proceed with caution."

Reading between the lines, I knew what that meant: he'd turn to torture as required.

"Do you miss Regan?"

The question caught me off guard. "A little perhaps. But she was disobedient."

A harsh laugh burst from my uncle's throat. "The irony. You dismiss one consort for disobedience while aligning yourself with another who defies us at every turn."

My lips quirked into a humorless smirk. "She won't defy us for long. I can break Pendragon, Uncle. She'll soon be loyal to House Drakharrow. Wait and see."

Viktor studied me. "If you fail, I will deal with her myself. It will not be pretty. I promise, you won't like the result."

"I understand."

"In the meantime, keep her pliant. The girl seems to think you care for her. Don't allow that to change. Blightborn are slaves to their emotions. That is their great weakness. Use it against her."

I nodded. "A wise suggestion."

Viktor frowned. "She attended the Wintermark Ball with Kage Tanaka."

I flinched. I hadn't thought he'd known about that. "She did. Probably because I hadn't asked her. Tanaka saw an opportunity and invited her. She said yes." I shrugged and tried to look nonchalant. "Does it really matter?"

"Having Kage as a rival has been good for you. We Drakharrows thrive on competition. But now you may have let that pup think he can get away with far too much. If he thinks to steal your consort out from under—"

"He won't," I interrupted. My hands curled into fists. The thought of Kage Tanaka luring Pendragon away. To his house. To his bed. "We're blood-bound now. I'll see him dead before that happens."

Still, it was not lost on me that I seemed to need Pendragon more than she needed me. Though, if she knew what my uncle had planned for her, maybe she'd be more willing to accept my protection.

"You need her to feed. What does she need from you?" my uncle demanded, astute as always.

"I'll remind her of her place. She's forgotten where she belongs. She's forgotten who holds the true power here and always will," I growled. "Kage will stay away from her. I'll see to that."

And Pendragon would sure as hell stay away from him.

"Do not kill the Avari. His house would retaliate and we are not prepared for a war."

*Yet.*

The word hung unspoken between us. But with a dragon flying over Sangratha, and the most powerful two houses prepared to fight for control of it, there was no doubt in my mind: war was on the horizon.

Viktor moved towards me, circling me slowly, like a predator assessing his prey. "You think you understand what you're dealing with, don't you, Nephew? The girl. The dragon." He let the words hang in the air, then leaned in. "But you know nothing, boy. I've seen what happens when highbloods underestimate riders. And the dragons . . . Well, they've always been more dangerous than we let anyone believe."

My brow wrinkled, but I tried to school my expression. "Of course. You know all of this firsthand, Uncle." It was a statement. I kept my tone respectful.

Viktor smiled. It didn't reach his eyes. "Let's just say some histories are better left in the past. Focus on your task. Leave all else to me."

He turned towards his desk, dismissing me with a wave of his hand. I left the chamber, the door thudding heavily shut behind me. For the first time, I found myself wondering what else had been buried when the dragons died.

# CHAPTER 4

# MEDRA

*Two Months Later*

Candlelight flickered across the stone walls of my room. It was a beautiful warm night, one of the last summer evenings. I could almost appreciate it. If I ignored the fact I was enjoying it from prison.

I moved to stand by one of the high-arched windows, running my hand over the crimson curtain that hung there, embroidered with black thread in swirling patterns that reminded me of dragon wings.

I tugged at my dress. Black wool, tight in the waist but loose in the skirt, with short sleeves. The skirt was cut at the knee and I wore tight black leggings underneath. The sleeves of the dress bore the House Drakharrow motto along each one, written in a beautiful script that stood out in red thread. Everything about the outfit felt suffocating. Once again, I was branded with the highblood mark. I touched a hand to my hair. I'd pulled the long red curls into a low braid, but a few loose strands were clinging to my skin. I pushed one of the windows open to let a cool sea breeze drift in. A little better.

The knock I'd been dreading came, but Blake didn't wait for an answer. The door simply opened and he strode right in, as if he owned not just the room, but everything within it.

He was every bit the highblood prince tonight: haughty and

devastatingly handsome. Over the summer, his pale gold hair had grown just past his chin, enough to sweep it back and secure it with a leather strip at the nape of his neck. The style suited him, baring the sharp angles of his face and lending him an air of authority. He'd taken to going a few days between shaving over the summer. He hadn't quite grown a beard, but the stubble did nothing to soften his features.

Now his lips curved into a sardonic smile and I glimpsed his fangs.

I'd set up two chairs by the fire, making sure to leave a foot of space in between. We'd done this before. Once a week, all summer. It was the only time I had to see him, thank the gods. My meals were brought to my room. A servant escorted me for walks on the grounds once a day. And after the first few days of trying to get me to talk, Blake left me alone. Our little feeding dates had become a regular pattern. But I wasn't planning on continuing this way forever.

I sat down in the high-backed chair and stretched my arm stiffly over the armrest.

"Well? Let's get this over with," I snapped.

Blake raised an eyebrow, but took a seat in the chair beside me, his movements slow and deliberate. He wanted this to take as much time as possible. He wanted to drag things out, provoke me. I gritted my teeth but said nothing, just stared straight ahead into the fire.

He took my wrist, his fingers curling around it with a surprising gentleness that only made me feel angrier. The warmth of his hand was jarring. His thumb brushed against my pulse and for a moment, I felt my treacherous heart stutter.

"This would be easier," he said, leaning towards me, his voice low, "if you'd stop pretending you hate it."

My head snapped towards him, fire flaring in my breast. "Don't fucking flatter yourself. If I could, I'd let you starve."

His grip tightened. Not enough to hurt, but enough to remind me of his strength.

"This doesn't mean I forgive you," I said, hearing my voice tremble slightly. "Or that I will ever, ever trust you."

Blake's gaze slid over me. "And this," he said, sounding at once bored and haughty as he lifted my wrist a little, "doesn't mean I care."

"How could you ever think I would want this?" I hissed. "Don't ever forget I wish I could just let you rot."

Blake froze, his lips hovering an inch from my wrist. "Oh, I won't forget, Pendragon. But we both know what would happen if you tried. You're not stupid enough to test me."

My lips curled. "Maybe I should."

"You won't," he countered, his voice a low growl. "Because you know exactly what would happen. I'd tell my uncle the truth—that you have absolutely no control over that dragon."

"You don't even know that for a fact," I retorted. "What makes you think Viktor would even believe you?"

He smirked. "Just face it, Pendragon. You're helpless without me. I'm your only hope at bluffing your way through this."

"That's what you'd like to think, isn't it?" I spat. "I think the first thing I'll have Nyxaris do when he returns is burn you to a crisp. No more feedings. Problem solved."

He laughed. "If you could have, you'd have done it already. So why haven't you? Because you have no control. And if Viktor finds out . . ."

I flushed angrily. "Why are you even still here? Oh, that's right. Because you *need* me. So get on with it. Drink, already."

Blake glared but didn't reply. Just lifted my wrist a little higher and moved his mouth to my skin. The bite was sharp. His fangs pierced my skin with practiced ease. Pain lanced through my arm, followed by the strange, nauseating pull of the blood leaving my body. Not for the first time, I thought of the girl at The Drained Rose. I shuddered. How could anyone ever find this pleasurable?

Blake paused, as if he had felt my tremor. I ignored him, staring at the fire and refusing to even look at him. Refusing to acknowledge the inherent intimacy of what he was doing to me.

When he finally pulled back, his lips were stained crimson. His lips were stained with *me*. He wiped the back of his hand across them languidly, clearly in no hurry.

"You make this so much harder than it needs to be, Pendragon."

"You think I care about making things easier for you?" I said sharply. "Next time, you'll drink it from a vial."

His face darkened. "I certainly won't."

"Why not?" I demanded, rising to my feet and grabbing a scarf to wrap around my wrist. I'd known he'd refuse. "Rodriguez said it can be done. I asked him. I'll draw the blood myself, and you'll—"

"No," Blake cut me off, his voice emphatic. "That's not how this works. I'm not an animal you can feed scraps to. If I have to endure this, so do you."

My blood was boiling. I wondered if I could actually burn him with my anger. If only it were that easy. "You're unbelievable. You've already taken everything from me. My blood, my freedom. Yet you act as if you're the one suffering, somehow."

"You think I wanted this? To be bound to someone who hates me, someone who—"

"You love it," I snapped. "I think you fucking love it. As if whatever you had going on with Regan wasn't just as toxic. As if someone like you even knows what it's like to really respect another person."

Blake stared at me, then shook his head stubbornly. "Whatever. You're boring me, Pendragon." He stood up and started to move towards the door, then paused. "Don't worry about the tribunal tomorrow. That's why you're really so upset tonight, isn't it? Everyone knows where you stand. You're House Drakharrow's. And you're mine."

My pulse spiked. "I don't belong to anyone."

His lips twisted. "You should stop lying to yourself. Everyone belongs to someone here. Even me."

"Maybe you should learn to stop seeing the world that way," I suggested. "Not everyone is just a possession or something to be used and discarded on a highblood's whim. Not even when it's your uncle."

"Maybe not everyone," Blake said softly. "But certainly you."

For a moment, I held my breath. Was he serious? "Do you even believe half of the horrible things you say?" I demanded, my voice trembling.

Something dark crossed his eyes. His gaze dropped to my wrist. "I believe you're wasting my time."

"Then, get the hell out," I almost shouted.

He smirked. "Don't lose any sleep over tomorrow. You'll make it through."

I clenched my jaw. Was that supposed to be a pep talk? Reassurance? Being reminded that I might make it through the tribunal only because of where I stood in relation to Blake and House Drakharrow was not comforting.

The door clicked shut behind him and I slumped back into the chair by the fire, cradling my wrist. For a moment I let myself imagine how it might have been. Without the weight of everything that had broken us. Blake's betrayal, the tribunal, the dragon.

But if Blake thought he'd come out the victor in all of this, he was wrong.

# CHAPTER 5

# MEDRA

T he day of the tribunal dawned cold and gray, as if the last pieces of summer had been sucked away overnight, skipping autumn, and going straight to the cusp of winter. I'd already decided on what I would wear the night before. I dressed quickly, running a brush through my hair and then leaving it in a cloud around my shoulders. My red curls marked me. There was no hiding who I was, so why bother taming it or toning it down?

There was a knock at the door. Headmaster Kim had told me he would be my escort to the Black Keep where the tribunal would be held.

It was time. I grabbed my cloak and pulled it on quickly.

Half an hour later, we stood on the isle of the Black Keep, inside the Tribunal Chamber. The chamber was farther within the keep than I had been before. Circular, with high stone walls, the chamber seemed to stretch endlessly upwards. A single, massive chandelier hung in the center of the ceiling, lined with hundreds of white candles. At the front of the room, elevated above the rest of us, sat the Tribunal Panel in a tiered wooden enclosure. Each panel member wore a long black robe, accented only with a subtle touch of their house colors.

There were eight tribunal members, but four may as well have not existed at all. Four were the regents of Sangratha—the four heads of the great houses. For all intents and purposes, they controlled everything. The other four were randomly selected from other noble but relatively minor highblood families. Only the four House Leaders held permanent seats on each tribunal.

In the very center of the chamber sat a single chair made of iron. It did not particularly encourage me to see the chair was bolted to the floor. Heavy chains dangled ominously from the armrests, making me wonder what kinds of people were usually brought before the tribunal.

I swallowed hard as Headmaster Kim led me down the main aisle towards the Tribunal Panel. Around us on either side in rising tiers were seated row upon row of highbloods. Onlookers to my trial. There seemed to be an excellent turnout. The room was filled to the brim and loud with the buzz of their murmurs, reminding me of a swarm of hungry wasps.

Across from the iron chair and to the left of the wooden enclosure that held the panel members stood a solitary podium. Headmaster Kim had explained on the way over that the highblood who had been appointed Arbiter would stand at this podium, overseeing the proceedings and acting as a neutral party. But the Tribunal Panel held the real power. Four held the most. And perhaps even two above all.

I scanned the room, my eyes going towards the Tribunal Panel and the people who would decide my fate today. Viktor Drakharrow sat in the front row, his crimson eyes glowing faintly as he watched me approach. He wore the customary black robes, only his had blood-red lapels embroidered with the Drakharrow motto to indicate his house. As if there would be any mistaking who he was.

To his right sat Lord Garrick Mortis, Catherine's father. I'd seen him once before, that first day in the Black Keep. Now I inspected him more closely. Lord Mortis was a towering figure. His broad shoulders and thick chest tugged at the seams of the black tribunal robe. His pale face was scarred, the mark of a blade slashing diagonally across his cheekbone to his temple. He looked back at me grimly from behind a thick silver beard. Everything about him radiated a tough, brutal authority. I suspected I would find no ally here. Lord Mortis's robes had white lapels and the Mortis house motto was inscribed on them in red: *Mortem Excito. I summon death.*

Next to him was seated an elegant petite woman. I knew this must be Kage's grandmother and Natsumi's mother-in-law, Lady Elaria Avari. Lady Avari's long silver-white hair was pinned up with jeweled combs, framing her heart-shaped face. Her dark brown eyes held a cleverness and warmth that Viktor's and Lord Mortis's both sorely lacked. This woman clearly missed nothing, calculated everything. Elaria's fingers were covered with rings set with diamonds and onyxes. Around her throat hung a heavy half-moon pendant made of silver that reminded me of the necklace Kage had given to me. She touched a hand to the silver lapels of her black robe, stroking the embroidered motto inscribed there: *Luna Sanguinea Surgit. Blood moon rises.* For the first time I wondered what exactly the significance of the moon was to House Avari.

I didn't recognize any of the four highbloods sitting in the second row so I skipped over them, moving to the last of the four front seats. A jolt of surprise passed through me. Lysander Orphos sat there. I'd no idea he was the leader of House Orphos beyond the walls of Bloodwing Academy. All of the other House Leaders were much older, formidable figures steeped in authority. Lysander, with his softer expression and delicate features, seemed distinctly out of place. Not because he lacked presence, but simply because he was so much younger.

The House Orphos leader's long silver-white hair was down in loose waves around his shoulders, falling over the purple silk of the lapels of his robe. I couldn't make out the motto written there, but I didn't need to. I'd seen it before, on the tapestries at Bloodwing. The Orphos motto was *Sanguis Somniatorum. Blood of dreamers.*

Lysander glanced at me briefly but then his eyes flitted away. I watched as he frowned, following his gaze to a young girl seated in one of the upper tiers of the gallery. Lunaya Orphos's skin seemed to radiate its own soft glow. Like her brother, her silver-blond hair fell in a sleek curtain, straight down her back. Her features were delicate, sweet, and almost otherworldly. An upturned small nose, soft lips curved in a dreamy, half smile, and wide innocent eyes. Lunaya's hands were clasped together in her lap, her head tilted slightly as she looked up at the man speaking to her.

I felt a prickle cross my skin as I recognized him. Marcus Drakharrow.

Blake's elder brother leaned over Lysander's sister, his muscular, hulking frame dwarfing her small one. To me, Marcus seemed to exude menace. But it was clear that Lunaya didn't see it. Instead, she smiled and blushed as Marcus said something and grinned down at her. I glanced back at Lysander. His hands gripped the armrests of his chair tightly. It was obvious he didn't appreciate Marcus speaking to his younger sister, especially when he couldn't be there beside her.

Headmaster Kim touched my arm as if to tell me to pick up my pace and I realized I'd been dawdling.

As we reached the iron chair in the center of the chamber, my heart sped up. I couldn't take my eyes off those iron chains. I glanced at Kim. He looked bored, if anything. Not as if he were about to chain me to the chair.

Taking a deep breath, I pulled off my cloak and hung it over the back of the chair, then sat down swiftly.

A ripple of excitement spread through the gallery as my arrival was noticed. Highbloods leaned forward in their seats, whispering to one another, their expressions ranging from curious to outrightly hostile as they peered down at me. I kept my head high and my hands in my lap, careful not to touch the chains.

Headmaster Kim stood awkwardly beside me for a moment. Then he cleared his throat and moved away. Apparently, his part in this little drama was over.

The Tribunal Panel rose above me, a wall of black-robed authority. Viktor's glowing crimson eyes burned into mine, angry as always, yet constantly assessing. I forced a small smile, determined not to reveal my unease.

I shouldn't goad him. I knew that. But it was impossible to resist. I moved my hands to smooth out the wrinkles in my skirt. Gray wool. I touched a hand to the collar of the shirt I wore tucked into it. Blue linen, the colors of a First Year student. *Not* the colors of a girl belonging to House Drakharrow—or to Lord Drakharrow's nephew. Was it my imagination or were Lady Avari's lips twitching in amusement as she looked me over?

I risked a glance behind me. In the first row of seats, I caught sight of Theo sitting next to Blake. His dark honey-blond hair fell around his pale face. When our eyes met, he smiled a small, encouraging smile. It was meant to reassure me, I knew, but the nervous set of his jaw betrayed him. Was Theo nervous for me, or for himself?

Blake seemed determined to ignore me, which was fine by me. He stared past me as if he were bored, slouched low in his seat, his long legs spread wide, his fingers tapping the armrests of his chair.

Movement drew my eye and I stiffened as a tall, slender figure rose from the crowd a few rows back. Regan Pansera. She sauntered across the floor towards the Tribunal Panel audaciously, hips swaying back and forth, looking as if she thought she owned the place. My gaze followed her as she ascended the short steps to the Tribunal Panel box. She wore a tight dress of pale lilac that hugged her body, showing off every curve. I watched as she bent over, purposely sticking her ass out so everyone in the audience had a great view. Then she leaned in close to Viktor Drakharrow, her lips moving in a whisper.

I couldn't hear what she said, but I didn't need to. The indulgent smile Viktor gave her said enough. Seeing Viktor smile like that—a real, genuine smile directed at Regan, of all people—made my stomach turn.

Regan giggled softly, then brushed Viktor's arm with her hand before stepping back down. I couldn't believe she'd voluntarily touched the creepy old man. She took her time crossing the floor, as if trying to ensure every single person in the room noticed her. As she passed by me, she slowed deliberately, her lips curling into a self-satisfied smile. I ignored her, refusing to give her the satisfaction of a reaction.

The low hum of voices in the chamber fell silent abruptly. I looked up to see a highblood man striding towards the podium. *This must be the Arbiter.*

My heart sank. *Shit.* I recognized him at once: Regan's father. Lord Pansera.

Dressed in the same black robes as the Tribunal Panel but devoid of any house markings, Lord Pansera stepped up behind the podium and fixed me with a cold stare, then struck the podium with the flat of his knuckles. The sound echoed through the chamber. "This tribunal will now come to order," he announced loudly.

I could feel all of the highbloods behind me turn their eyes towards the podium. What was Blake thinking right now? Did he have any real idea of what the outcome would be today?

"We are gathered here today to determine the rightful claim over the dragon known as Nyxaris and, by extension, the fate of the girl responsible for the creature's awakening." Lord Pansera sneered slightly as he said the word *girl*, as if I were nothing but a sour taste on his tongue.

He gestured towards the Tribunal Panel. "The esteemed members of our panel have been entrusted with determining the best course of action."

The most powerful people in the land and the ones least likely to have any sort of ability to be neutral would make decisions about a dragon who had shown he had absolutely no intention of listening to another highblood. But sure, it made perfect sense. After all, no one had ever claimed Sangratha was a fair or rational kind of place.

"We will begin by hearing the claims of the houses directly involved." Lord Pansera turned slightly, addressing Elaria Avari. "Lady Avari, you may state your house's claim."

Elaria Avari rose gracefully to her feet and stepped to the front of the box, placing her ringed hands on the wooden edge. Turning towards the crowded tiers of seats, she gave a small smile. "Honored citizens of Sangratha and members of the tribunal," she began. "House Avari's claim is both simple and undeniable. Nyxaris is a Duskdrake, a dragon bred and flown exclusively by House Avari in ages past. For generations, our house was steward to these magnificent creatures. Their legacy is tied to our own."

She paused, her gaze sweeping across the assembled crowd. "The dragon's awakening is no accident. House Avari has been selected to lead Sangratha into a new age. An age of dragons."

A shiver passed over me.

Lady Avari raised her arms theatrically. "Join us. Join Nyxaris. This dragon is ours by right of history, blood, and tradition." Then she inclined her head graciously and returned to her seat.

I thought Elaria's speech was a little presumptuous. But at least she hadn't suggested executing me.

A quiet murmur of approval from the gallery rose up from behind me. Lady Avari was certainly no Viktor Drakharrow. But it didn't matter if I liked her or not: she was staking claim to a dragon she had no control over. Like almost every highblood I'd met here, her arrogance was boundless.

Lord Pansera turned to Viktor next, lowering his head respectfully—something, I noticed, he had not bothered to do for Lady Avari. So much for neutrality. "Lord Drakharrow, state House Drakharrow's position, if you will."

I thought back to that first day in the Black Keep when Viktor had essentially sat upon a throne with the other three regents standing around him. Now he sat in the tribunal box, as if he were only their equal—not their superior. But it was all an act, wasn't it? He resided in the Black Keep, after all. He ruled this land in all but name.

And yet if House Avari was completely lacking in power, surely there would have been no need for the tribunal. Viktor would have been able to do whatever he wanted. So there was some hope left—if you could call it that. Some sort of a power struggle was obviously happening, even if it were behind the scenes. I had to admit, part of me was hoping to see House Avari show some real pull here today. But for now, I bit my lip as Viktor rose to his feet.

"My lords and ladies," he began. He smiled smoothly at the crowd, and I just about choked. I'd never seen him try to be charming before. "House Drakharrow's claim is equally clear, if not more so. Medra Pendragon, the lone dragon rider of Sangratha, is betrothed to my nephew, Blake Drakharrow, the Black Prince. This betrothal cements her allegiance to our house."

For the first time I wondered about the whole *prince* thing. If Blake was a prince, did that mean Theo was, too? Was Catherine Mortis considered a *princess* of her house? I remembered what Professor Hassan had said last year about the Era of Pretenders, where each of the four houses had tried to set up their own royal courts. Perhaps that was where the tradition of giving royal titles stemmed from.

I forced myself to focus on what Viktor was saying.

"By extension, whatever action Miss Pendragon should happen to take, whether intentional or not, reflects upon House Drakharrow." He let the words hang for a moment and I heard murmurs of agreement.

He turned his crimson gaze towards me, his expression inscrutable. "Miss Pendragon's bloodline is clearly that of a rider. The last known rider to exist in our realm. What an incredible thing, is it not?"

Again, the murmurs of agreement. Was he actually trying to get these people on my side?

"This rare and precious lineage binds her to the traditions of dragonkind. And as she is bound to my nephew Blake, her actions are inseparable from House Drakharrow's interests."

I clenched my jaw. Where exactly was Viktor going with this?

Viktor paused, letting his words sink in. "Therefore, it is House

Drakharrow's claim that Nyxaris awakened *only* because of Miss Pendragon's bond to Blake. A bond forged by blood and by tradition. Without the existence of that bond, there would have been no awakening."

I couldn't help it. I gasped aloud. Of course he'd take this route; I should have expected it. Viktor smiled down at me. To anyone else, that smile might even have seemed paternal.

"House Drakharrow's influence clearly extends to this remarkable event. And therefore, the dragon is ours by all rights, for so is its rider," Viktor concluded.

My body was trembling with fury. How dare he? How dare *they*? For surely Blake was a part of this. The dragon hadn't awakened because of Blake. If anything, it had awoken in spite of him. My mind raced as I fought to keep myself in check.

Lord Pansera turned to the assembly of highbloods as Viktor resumed his seat. "We have heard the claims of House Avari and House Drakharrow. We will now hear propositions for a resolution to this matter. Lord Mortis, the floor is yours."

The room fell silent as Catherine's father rose. He towered over the Tribunal Panel, his scarred face and heavy frame wafting pure highblood power. "Lords and ladies," he began, his voice deep and gruff, "honored members of the tribunal. House Mortis has always valued pragmatism above all else. For centuries, we have relied on reason to guide our decisions, ensuring our survival and prosperity. It is only after great deliberation that I present the position of my house."

He had been away when Nyxaris had awakened, making a tour of his estates. It sounded as if House Mortis had a great many properties. Had Catherine been with him? I wondered if Lord Mortis had consulted with his daughter before speaking today.

Garrick Mortis looked over at me and I sat a little straighter. "When this woman first appeared, I suggested she be executed or mated with a highblood to secure her allegiance and ensure her bloodline remained within our control. I believed it was the simplest solution and so I did not disagree with Lord Drakharrow when he proposed betrothing her to his nephew."

My stomach twisted. They spoke of me as if I weren't even a person, simply a bloodline to be used and preserved. I wondered when exactly the talk of breeding would start. I had to admit I was somewhat surprised it hadn't already. Now, there was a lovely thought: bearing Blake's children. Children who Viktor would no doubt try to use and manipulate for his own purposes.

Over my dead body. They were in for a rude awakening if they thought I'd ever allow it.

Lord Mortis paused. His scarred face tightened as if the next words were difficult to admit. "But I was wrong."

I froze.

"The truth is," he continued, "the dragons should never have been brought back. The power they represent is far too great for any one house to yield. For over a century, we have maintained a delicate truce."

I remembered what I had learned about the Dragon Wars and shivered. House Mortis had once allied with House Avari. Was Lord Mortis turning his back on his ally now?

"Add to that the risk of rebellion—" Lord Mortis cut himself off sharply, as if he had said too much.

*Rebellion?* I shifted in my seat, trying not to look eager at having heard the word.

But Lord Mortis was moving on. He gestured to me with a blunt motion of one hand. "The solution is clear. This girl must be destroyed. The dragon should be hunted down and destroyed with her. That is the only way to ensure such a vast power does not fall into the wrong hands."

The Tribunal Chamber erupted. *Death?* My chest tightened, my breath catching in my throat. Was that really going to be today's outcome? I glanced at Viktor Drakharrow. The highblood was practically shaking with rage. Evidently Lord Mortis's words had come as a shock to him, too.

I thought of my mother, trapped in the dagger I had left back in the tower room. I wouldn't even have a chance to set her free if they executed me after the tribunal today. Or would they give me a few days to prepare for my fate?

I risked glancing behind me. Blake was on his feet, his face a storm of fury.

"You're insane!" he shouted, his voice echoing off the stone walls of the chamber. I flinched.

Theo slowly stood up beside him, his face pale but his jaw set. He put a hand on his cousin's shoulder, his knuckles white. My gaze swept farther down the row. For the first time I noticed Kage. He sat beside his mother. Both were calm, poised. If either one was surprised or angered by Lord Mortis's declaration they weren't showing it.

As if he'd felt my eyes on him, Kage turned his head. His eyes met mine. He stared back at me, unshakable as marble and just as unreadable. His crescent-moon tattoo curled up the side of his neck, peeking out from just above the collar of the black tailored suit he wore.

Lord Pansera's voice cut through the din and for once I was grateful to hear it. "That's enough," he shouted, bringing the chamber back to a semblance of quiet. "Thank you, Lord Mortis, for establishing your house's position. Lysander Orphos will now speak for House Orphos."

Lysander rose from his seat. He adjusted the purple lapels of his robe, his expression serene and composed. I somehow doubted he planned to throw his weight behind Lord Mortis, but I realized I knew very little about Lysander and what he believed or didn't believe about blightborn or dragons.

When he finally began to speak, his voice was soft, yet carried easily across the room and was surprisingly firm. "Members of the tribunal and gathered highbloods. The awakening of the dragon Nyxaris has shaken the foundations of all our houses. But perhaps we are too quick to act, too desperate to control that which cannot be tamed."

I couldn't help but notice the way Lord Mortis was looking at Lysander—practically sneering. I remembered what Coregon had called House Orphos: *weak*. Blake had called them *weird*. But looking at Lysander now, I couldn't help but wonder if *reasonable* and *kind* should be added to that list.

Lysander's pale blue eyes swept across the chamber. "The dragon is awake, yes. But only one. This awakening does not signal the return of the dragons as we knew them." A little ironic coming from such a young highblood, but I took his point.

"There can be no breeding," he went on. "No resurgence of the species. Nyxaris is alone, an echo of the past. Not a herald of a new era."

I felt a twinge of sadness, hearing the black dragon spoken of that way. But Lysander was right.

"To stake a claim to one dragon, to tie Nyxaris to one house, would be folly," Lysander said, his voice calm but unyielding. "No house should wield such power over the others." He looked down at Lord Mortis. "Lord Mortis and I agree in that respect."

Lord Mortis nodded stiffly.

"We have kept the peace for over a century," Lysander continued. "House Orphos stood behind the Peacebringer and all that he represented. We stand behind his teachings even now. If we allow one house to rise above the others, it will lead to war."

Soft-spoken he might be, but Lysander's logic was cutting.

"As for our lone rider, Miss Pendragon," Lysander continued, his gaze moving to me, "I propose she be allowed to choose her own path. Whether that means remaining at Bloodwing Academy, remaining Blake Drakharrow's consort, or carving out a very different life for herself, she is not a tool to be wielded. She has awakened a dragon, yes. But that does not mean she belongs to any one of us. Let her lead her life as she sees fit."

There was a very long pause after Lysander returned to his seat. His calm presence, his rational words seemed to linger in the air, and it seemed for a few moments as if no one wished to break the tension. Either that or he had shocked them too greatly to be able to speak at all.

But then Lord Mortis exploded. He shot to his feet, his hands slamming down on the edge of the tribunal box. "Has the boy lost his mind?" he bellowed, his face flushing red with anger. "Let the dragon fly free? Let the rider do as she pleases? That is not how this works. Do you have any understanding of what is at stake here, boy?" Lord Mortis glared at Lysander, who steadfastly ignored him.

Meanwhile, I sat frozen in my iron chair, trying to absorb what was happening. Lysander had done the unthinkable: he had suggested I be allowed to choose my own path. The idea had become so foreign to me, so inconceivable, that I almost couldn't process it.

Viktor Drakharrow stood up and placed a hand on Lord Mortis's shoulder. "I'm afraid I must agree with Lord Mortis. This is not some game, young Lysander. This is about highblood power, about our survival. Your softheartedness will doom your house, but we will not allow it to doom the rest of Sangratha."

The crowd in the gallery had lost all sense of order. I heard jeers and shouting from behind me but did not turn. Lady Avari, I noticed, said nothing.

Lysander, to his credit, did not flinch under Viktor's or Lord Mortis's attacks. He simply folded his hands in his lap. He must have known his suggestions would be laughed at, but he had spoken anyway. He'd stood up for what he believed. Of course, the real question was, did the rest of House Orphos feel the same way he did or was he an outlier among them?

Lord Pansera looked a little desperate as he stood on the podium, slamming his palm down on the wood over and over as he tried to regain control of the room. "Order! This tribunal will come to order."

Finally, the ruckus subsided. Part of me longed to turn and look at Blake. He had reacted so strongly to Lord Mortis's suggestion.

But how had he reacted to Lysander's? The idea that I might belong only to myself and not to him or to his house must have seemed unthinkable to him.

Finally, I couldn't stand it any longer. I turned and glanced back at where Blake sat beside Theo. He looked dazed. Not angry. Simply . . . *confused*, if it could be called that.

Lady Avari rose to her feet, smoothing the skirt of her robe. "If I may, Arbiter . . ."

Lord Pansera looked at her with something like relief. "Lady Avari, certainly. You may speak."

I felt the crowd settle down a little more, calmed by this poised highblood woman. Her gaze swept the room, her dark eyes sharp and calculating. "My lords and ladies," Elaria began, "we have heard much today about claims and entitlements, have we not? But what we have yet to discuss is the rare opportunity that lies before us." Her dark eyes fixed on me. "The awakening of Nyxaris is not a calamity, nor is it a mistake. It is a chance. A chance to correct certain imbalances that have persisted for far too long."

I frowned, uncertain of what she meant.

Lady Avari paused, then gestured at Viktor. "Lord Viktor Drakharrow has, for years, consolidated power around himself and his house, to the detriment of the rest of Sangratha. The dragon's return is a sign that such unchecked attempts at dominance must come to an end."

Viktor was on his feet in an instant, his voice loud as a thunderclap. "This is outrageous! You overstep, Elaria—"

"Sit down, Viktor." Lady Avari's voice cut through his outburst like a knife. "You'll have your turn. But first you will hear me speak."

The room seemed to give a collective gasp as Viktor hesitated, his jaw tight, his eyes flashing crimson. Reluctantly, he sat back down, wearing the expression of a scolded schoolboy.

Lady Avari turned back to the crowd as though there had been no interruption. "It is clear to me," she said, her voice icy, "that

Medra Pendragon's fate was left in the wrong hands. She should never have been permitted to become betrothed to Blake Drak-harrow. That bond was forged under duress and with no consider-ation for the girl's well-being—or for the balance of power among our houses."

It was pretty clear which one of those was more important to Elaria, but I appreciated her at least pretending to care about my well-being. It was certainly more than Viktor had ever done.

Lady Avari's dark eyes softened slightly as she looked at me. "Consequently, I propose that Medra Pendragon be allowed to choose a new archon."

My jaw might have actually dropped.

"Someone who will better represent her interests and those of our collective houses," she went on.

"And you propose that archon be your grandson, Kage Tanaka, no doubt, do you, Elaria?" Lord Mortis's voice was dry and he made no move to stand.

There were ripples of laughter through the crowd, but they seemed good-natured. Lady Avari was clearly well-liked by many of her peers.

Elaria smiled. "I do, of course, Lord Mortis. Kage would be a fine archon for the rider and he has no other consorts."

My eyes widened. The room exploded into chaos.

I didn't have to bother turning around to know Blake was back on his feet. But before he could raise his voice again, Viktor's voice broke through the uproar.

"Impossible," I heard him shout.

The clamor of the crowd continued.

"Impossible," Viktor roared over the continuing chatter. "Ab-solutely impossible."

The chamber fell silent.

"What you propose is impossible, Elaria, and I shall tell you why."

My heart sank. I knew exactly what he was about to say.

"The bond has already been solidified. Their blood was joined. Blake feeds from the girl, she is his source. You demonstrate your ignorance and your complete willingness to disregard tradition in what you just proposed, Elaria, but I am not surprised." Viktor curled his lips disdainfully. "House Avari has always been fool-hardy."

Elaria bristled. "So it is true, then. The rider has been shackled to your nephew for his survival. How . . . unfortunate." She looked at me with something like genuine regret.

I risked another glance backwards. Not at Blake, but at Kage. He sat stoically in his seat beside his mother, his hands clasped together. Perhaps the only indication he was feeling something, anything, was the fact that they seemed clasped a little too tightly. The muscles in his neck over the collar of his black jacket twitched as he met my gaze.

What did Kage really want? I suddenly wondered. Did he want me? Truly?

As I turned back to the tribunal, Viktor's lips were turned up in a sneer. "Whatever fanciful ideas you might have, Elaria, they are irrelevant. The girl belongs to House Drakharrow."

Maybe it was the fact that he'd called me *girl* for the hundredth time. Maybe it was the fact that he'd said *belongs*. But something ignited in me.

I shot to my feet. "No."

I hadn't shouted. Even so, my voice easily cut through the room like a knife through butter.

"I don't belong to anyone."

You could have heard a pin drop. Or a drop of blood fall. All eyes were on me. Even Lord Pansera seemed shocked into speech-lessness at my boldness.

"You've all been speaking about me as if I'm not even here. As if I don't have a voice in any of this. But I do. If you're going to de-cide my fate, then at least give me the chance to speak for myself. I deserve that much." I took a deep breath. "And so does Nyxaris."

# CHAPTER 6

# BLAKE

I'd fucked up. A small part of me was willing to admit that. But only to myself. Say it to anyone else? Hell no.

A Drakharrow didn't make mistakes.

So, instead, I'd made things worse. Dug myself in deeper.

My eyes were fixed on Pendragon as she stood, her red hair trailing in a living flame down her back. Her voice defiant, her posture unyielding despite the scrutiny of every tribunal member bearing down on her. She radiated fury and courage in equal measure. For the first time in months, I wondered if I'd miscalculated everything. Underestimated just how stubborn she truly was.

I clenched my jaw, trying to push the thought aside. What I'd done I'd done at least partly for her. No, primarily for her. I'd saved her life, even if she didn't know it. Would she rather be mated to my uncle? Fed from by Viktor?

Drakharrows didn't doubt themselves. We didn't question our actions or apologize. Apologies were for the weak, for those who lacked the resolve to see their plans through.

All summer long she'd kept me at bay, treating me no better than some stray mutt she had to feed. What did she want, anyhow—for me to kneel? To beg? Maybe that's what she'd expected. Maybe that's what she thought she deserved.

I tamped down the part of myself that wondered if she was right. The idea made me itch with revulsion and discomfort. I shifted in my seat, forcing myself to look away from her. And my gaze landed on Tanaka.

Kage fucking Tanaka.

The other Bloodwing House Leader looked too calm, too composed by far, considering what his grandmother had just proposed. His expression gave nothing away, but my instincts flared. He *had* to have been involved. There was no way Lady Avari would have proposed such a scheme, otherwise. Kage probably suggested it himself.

Fury boiled low in my gut. Whatever this was between Pendragon and Tanaka, it had gone way too far. This wasn't jealousy. No. This was about the best interests of my house. About protecting the bond, the dragon. Not about Pendragon or whatever fucked up thing this was between us.

Her voice rang out, sharper now, and I forced myself to focus. She was still speaking. No, not just speaking. She was fucking *confessing*.

"I never wanted to be betrothed to Blake Drakharrow," she announced loudly.

I flinched.

"I wasn't given a choice. You were all there that day. And later? Blake tricked me when he forged our bond. He manipulated me, bonding me to him against my will and then by feeding from me without my permission."

I crossed my arms across my chest. I didn't bother to hide the shit-eating grin from my face.

*Good luck, Pendragon*, I wanted to call out. *Good luck complaining to a room full of highbloods about* permission *when you were a blightborn*. She'd lose the crowd's sympathy quickly. They generally didn't like it when blightborn played the victims.

I barely resisted the urge to shout *Grow a fucking backbone, Pendragon!* I decided it wouldn't go over well. Especially not with Theo. I snuck a glance at my cousin. He'd shifted away from me and was looking straight ahead. Clearly, he was pissed. I scowled. Well, fuck.

If my own cousin wanted to disown me after all I'd done for him, fine. I had other friends.

Finally, that idiot Pansera grew a pair and spoke up. "You will sit back down at once," Lord Pansera snapped.

"No, I certainly will not," Pendragon snapped back.

I frowned. Before the Arbiter could respond, Lady Avari spoke up.

"I, for one, would like to hear Miss Pendragon finish what she has to say," the Avari matriarch said smoothly.

I growled. Dammit. This was really happening.

Lysander Orphos was nodding in agreement. The fucking traitor. I couldn't believe what he'd dared to propose. Of course he'd be in agreement with the Avaris. "As would I," he announced.

Lord Pansera hesitated, obviously fuming and afraid of what my uncle would do to him later, but relented. "Very well. Speak but speak quickly."

Pendragon gestured to her clothing and my jaw tightened. She'd purposely scorned my house colors—I'd remember that. Yet another sign of her blatant disrespect.

Now she lied to everyone.

"I don't feel any affiliation with any house," she declared, turning slowly so all could see her in the First Year colors. "I chose to wear the colors of a First Year to this tribunal not as a sign of disrespect to House Drakharrow, but as a sign of my neutrality. Why should your only dragon rider serve *one* house and not all of you?"

I stiffened as around me, the room shifted with a murmur of surprise—and then, to my shock, with ripples of agreement. I saw several heads nodding thoughtfully. I glanced down at Viktor. His expression was impassive. But I knew my uncle too well. Beneath that stony exterior, he was seething. Pendragon had just dared to openly challenge the stacked cards of his control.

My eyes swept the room again, this time landing on Marcus. My older brother sat higher up in the gallery, beside Lunaya Oprhos, of all people. My brow furrowed as I caught the look of hatred etched on Marcus's face as he watched Pendragon. What was Marcus even doing sitting next to Lysander's sister in the first place? It wasn't like him to spend time in the company of anyone from Orphos; he'd never bothered to hide his derision for their house. Yet there he was, leaning close to the Orphos girl, whispering something that made her smile sweetly.

"When the dragon awoke, he spoke to me."

My attention snapped back to Pendragon.

"I promised myself to him in service, but he refused to accept me. Our bond is not yet complete," she declared.

I felt my heart twist slightly with unexpected pride. My consort had spoken to a fucking *dragon*. No one else alive could say that.

"You see, Nyxaris doesn't feel any obligation to any house," Pendragon went on.

I saw Elaria Avari tilt her head thoughtfully as she heard that little revelation. *Ha.*

"He doesn't recognize any of your claims. But perhaps, given time, I can help him remember the loyalty that once existed between dragons and highbloods. That's why you need me. I'm your only link to the most powerful creature in existence. Are you really going to let that slip away, by simply discarding me like Lord Mortis proposed?"

My emotions were a tangled web as I watched her. She was my source, a means to power. I'd saved her from Viktor. There was no way I'd let her be executed.

But there was more to it than that and I knew it. She stood there, commanding the attention of a room full of highbloods like no other blightborn in existence had probably ever done before. She was drawing their awe in the same way a dragon might have, simply by her sheer presence. Her sheer will.

I'd let myself start to care for her. I still couldn't take my eyes off her. But now? Part of me hated her all over again. For rejecting me. For rejecting my house. Maybe most of all, for rejecting the most primal, intrinsic part of my nature.

My fangs. My bite.

"I ask you for time," she went on. "Time to continue my studies. Time to learn, time to understand the bond between Nyxaris and myself. And I ask you for freedom. To be untethered from a mating bond I never wanted. To be free to make my own choice."

I nearly choked as the room fell into even deeper silence. I could feel my face heating from the humiliation. Fuck this. Fuck all of this. And most of all, fuck Pendragon. She wanted to be out on her own, did she? Maybe that could be arranged. Just not in the way she might hope.

Lady Avari was the first to rise. Her face was filled with quiet sympathy as she looked down at Pendragon and I despised her for it. "As far as anyone knows, child," she said gently, "there is no way to dissolve such a bond." She looked around the room. "But I agree with Miss Pendragon on all of her other points. She should be allowed to continue her studies—and be given time to bring the dragon's fealty back where it belongs."

I snorted—loudly.

"There is wisdom in her requests," Elaria concluded.

In *all* of them, in other words. I glared at the old woman. I watched Viktor shift in his seat, but before he could speak, Lord Mortis beat him to it.

He stood abruptly and pointed a finger at Pendragon, his voice growling in anger. "What proof do you even have that the dragon listens to you? You spoke to him, you claim? What evidence do we have of that? The dragon is gone." He gave a mocking laugh and a ripple of agreement spread through the room.

I shook my head. For a moment they'd been on Pendragon's side. Now Mortis had them swayed again. By the Bloodmaiden, my people were fickle.

"But no, it's worse than that," Lord Mortis bellowed, his deep voice echoing across the chamber. "What if she *is* talking to the dragon? For all we know, she'll tell it to turn on us. Just like the dragons of old."

I frowned, trying to recall that little bit of history and failing, as around me the crowd burst into an uproar, glimpses of fear on many faces as Lord Mortis's words sunk in.

Then, Pendragon's voice cut through the clamor. "You want proof, Lord Mortis? I'll give it to you. To all of you. Follow me."

# CHAPTER 7

# MEDRA

W hat am I doing? What am I doing? Silently, I kept chanting the words in my head as I led the way outside the Black Keep, trying to project as much confidence as I possibly could.

Outside the air was sharper. Cooler. The breeze had picked up and it bit against my skin as the entire Tribunal Panel and audience of highbloods followed me in a rustling tide of black robes and suspicious mutters.

My heart was pounding as I stepped out into the large cobblestone courtyard that lay in front of the Black Keep. Ahead of us lay the massive iron bridge that connected the island to the mainland and the city of Veilmar.

This had to work. It had to.

All summer, I'd kept my secret. Clung to this one hope. Kept a card tucked up my sleeve. A card I hadn't dared to play until now.

*Nyxaris?* I called to him through our connection. Silence.

*Nyxaris?* I tried again. *Are you there?*

There was no response. My heart was a drumbeat of panic in my chest. Around me the highbloods were stirring restlessly. Some were complaining of the cold and wanted to go back inside.

I tried again. *Please. If you're there, please answer me, O Great One. I beseech you.* I felt like an idiot, but I had no choice.

"She's bluffing," I heard Lord Mortis declare loudly. "Look at her, just standing there. She's making fools of us all. There's nothing here. Let's go back inside. I believe the rider's fate is clear. We'll put the matter to a vote."

"No," I exclaimed. "Please. Wait."

*Nyxaris, please,* I thought desperately. *Please don't do this to me. I know my life is insignificant to you, but I swear I'll keep my word if you help me. I'll do anything you want.*

Still, nothing.

I swallowed hard, trying not to meet anyone's eyes. Not even Theo's.

Something in the air shifted. A low, distant rumble arose, far above us. The sound grew louder with every passing second. Murmurs went through the crowd. The sounds became clearer and clearer until there was no mistaking what they were.

Beating wings.

Nyxaris's voice rumbled through my mind, deep and sardonic. *You sound desperate, little wingless one. Did you think I'd abandoned you?*

I sucked in a sharp breath. *You're not funny. You know that?*

His laughter was a growl in my head. Why did I have to get the dragon with the sense of humor? Would the other three have been like this?

*Oh, but I am. Look at you down there, surrounded by these tiny, pathetic creatures.* He paused, as if considering. *Perhaps I should make you all wait longer. Teach them proper humility.*

*No,* I said quickly. *Please.*

*Patience, young one. I have kept my promise.* He gave another deep rumbling laugh, as rich and deep as his scales.

This time I could hear him from the ground. So could everyone else. Gasps rippled through the crowd.

I tilted my head back, searching the sky. *There.* Silhouetted against the gray clouds, a dark shadow moved, cutting through the air with incredible grace. I wasn't the only one who had spotted the dragon. Screams broke out around me. One highblood man swooned against his partner.

Nyxaris circled high overhead, as if showing off—which he

probably was. The dragon's wings were so large they blotted out what little light pierced the overcast sky. He flew low, swooping over us, his wings nearly brushing the tops of our heads. The high-blood man who had been swooning crumpled to the cobblestones in a dead faint. Some of the highbloods were backing up. I saw a few run back inside the Black Keep.

*I am here. Satisfied?* Nyxaris's gruff voice said in my mind.

I didn't answer. My throat was tight as I watched him descend. Slowly, deliberately, he spiraled lower until he'd landed on the bridge. Around me there were gasps of awe.

*Showmanship, wingless one*, the dragon purred shamelessly. *It's an art.*

The bridge let out a worrisome groan.

My stomach clenched. *Yes, you're very impressive indeed. But is that thing going to hold your weight?*

Nyxaris snorted his amusement. *This bridge was built long before you were born. The ancestors of these people were not entirely incompetent.*

So he'd done this before, perhaps sat on that very bridge before. Who had his rider been then? It was hard to wrap my mind around how ancient he really was. I had so many questions. But I knew better than to ask.

"Look at that creature. The beast is an abomination," Lord Mortis growled from behind me, breaking the spell. His voice was shaking—from rage or fear or both. "The girl and the monster should be destroyed. We've indulged in this farce long enough."

I forced myself to ignore him, keeping my eyes on Nyxaris who crouched regally on the bridge, his molten gold eyes surveying the crowd with undisguised disdain. I glanced around at the highbloods, wondering if they could read Nyxaris's expression as well as I could.

Slowly, I turned to face them all, my back to the dragon. "Here is your proof," I announced. "Nyxaris listens to me. And if you let me, I can make him listen to all of you."

Nyxaris made a loud snorting sound from behind me. *In their dreams, perhaps.*

I winced, praying the highbloods wouldn't notice. But I didn't have to worry. Around me the crowd broke into more murmurs of amazement.

Things seemed to be going well, until Lord Mortis stepped forward. His boots thudded heavily against the cobblestones as he moved to stand next to me. "A parlor trick," he sneered, his face twisting with contempt. "The beast is just that—a beast and nothing more. A mindless monster."

Nyxaris gave a low rumbling growl deep in his throat, but Lord Mortis ignored him. The highblood House Leader turned to face the crowd. "This is not the momentous occasion you all seem to believe it is. The beast will split us apart and bring ruin to our kind."

*This one tries my patience*, Nyxaris complained.

*Please*, I begged silently. *Just be patient. I'll handle him.*

I took a deep breath, trying to think of how I could de-escalate the situation. Then I saw it: a glint of steel in the highblood's hand. A dagger. My breath hitched. I glanced to the side and caught sight of Blake moving through the crowd, his gray eyes locked on Mortis. He'd seen it, too.

I froze, torn. Was the dagger meant for me? Or would Mortis really be stupid enough to attack a dragon? I was unarmed. Besides, I couldn't make the first move even if I wanted to—not against a regent. It would be tantamount to suicide.

Mortis stopped at the edge of the bridge, glaring up at the black dragon. He had balls, I'd give him that. Wisdom, however, perhaps not so much.

"*You* are nothing but a relic," he spat at Nyxaris. "And *you*—" He jabbed his dagger in my direction, making no pretense of hiding it now. I heard gasps go up from the crowd. "You are nothing more than this beast's delusional herald."

*Move. Now.*

Nyxaris's command slammed into my mind. I shifted to dive away but before I could, an arm wrapped around me, and the world became a blur of motion. I hit the ground hard, the bulk of someone else beneath me. My heart thundered as I turned my head just in time to see Nyxaris unleash a torrent of flame.

Dragon fire wasn't like ordinary fire.

It was an overwhelming force, beautiful and terrible in equal measure. The fire that roared out of Nyxaris's open jaws was molten light, impossibly bright. Streaks of crimson and gold spiraled like living veins, radiating into the air like deadly ribbons. Witnessing it was like staring into the heart of destruction. A reminder of why dragons had once ruled the skies—and why Viktor Drakharrow wanted control of one so badly.

I supposed we were lucky Nyxaris was an experienced dragon. Showing rather impressive restraint, he directed his flames straight down at Lord Mortis and not into the crowd as a whole. Instantly, the highblood man was engulfed in the flames. His scream was sharp and brief, quickly drowned out by the crackling of burning flesh.

When the flames died out moments later, their fuel source had been utterly obliterated. Only ash and char remained of the man who had so arrogantly dared to approach a dragon.

I felt the body beneath me shift and quickly looked down. Kage Tanaka's dark eyes stared up at me. There was something to be said for vampire speed.

"You're safe," he announced, so matter-of-factly that it almost felt dismissive. As if he went around rescuing people from dragon fire every day.

Shakily, I pushed myself off him, my legs trembling as I turned to face Nyxaris. The dragon's gold eyes were fixed on me. Trying to ignore the still-smoking remains of Lord Mortis, I stepped towards him.

"Miss Pendragon!" Viktor Drakharrow's voice snapped across the courtyard.

I turned to see him marching forward. He stopped, staring down at Lord Mortis's corpse. I had no idea just how far dragon fire could reach, but perhaps Viktor did.

"Maybe you'd better keep your distance, Lord Drakharrow."

He scowled but, for a moment, looked uncertain.

Lady Avari's calm voice broke the tension. "Miss Pendragon, did you instruct Nyxaris to do that?" Her question sent a ripple through the crowd. I felt all eyes fix on me.

Soberly, I shook my head. "No. Absolutely not." I looked at the highbloods standing around her. "But this should make one thing very clear. Nyxaris is not bound by anyone's will. Not mine and not yours. He acts as he pleases."

*Very accurate,* Nyxaris rumbled.

I ignored him. I knew he hadn't killed Lord Mortis to protect me. Hell, he probably wouldn't have cared if I'd accidentally been burned to death in the flames. He'd just have found someone else to answer his questions.

"Lord Mortis insulted Nyxaris," Lady Avari observed.

I nodded. "He did. More than once."

Lady Avari and I looked at one another. "If I recall my history lessons," she said slowly, "one does not insult a dragon."

*Well, certainly not to our face. The man was a fool,* Nyxaris chimed in. *I'm surprised he'd lived so long.*

I took a deep breath. "Nyxaris says Lord Mortis was a fool."

There were murmurs from the crowd. I glimpsed Kage standing to the side of the bridge, his arms crossed over his chest. If he had any fear of Nyxaris himself, he wasn't showing it. Or perhaps his grandmother had simply taught him well. Blake stood in the middle of the crowd. He wasn't even looking at me; he was too busy glaring at Kage. I managed not to roll my eyes. If anything, he should have been grateful. If I'd died, his free blood meals would have gone up in smoke. I wondered what he'd have done then.

Someone was pushing their way to the front—Catherine Mortis.

She was dressed in a leather tunic and trousers in the red and white colors of her house, her silver hair braided into a coronet atop her head. Her eyes were gray like Blake's, I realized, but much paler, almost white. They settled on the still-smoldering remains

of her father. I watched her face but there was no crack in her gla-
cial composure. She lifted her eyes from her father's corpse and
looked at me.

I swallowed. "Catherine, I'm sorry for your loss."

Her gaze was sharp. "Thank you," she said simply.

Lady Avari cleared her throat softly, pulling my attention back.

"I have to go," I said, looking at Elaria.

Her colleague had just been burned to a crisp in front of her. Yet
despite this, Elaria Avari's eyes were calm. "Do you intend to return?"

I gaped at her. I had never even thought of not doing so. Now
I thought of how easy it would be to leave. Wasn't that what I'd
wanted from the moment I'd arrived in Sangratha?

I glanced across the sea, not at the city of Veilmar, but at the
other island to my right where Bloodwing Academy sat in a blaze
of dark crimson. I thought of my friends. Florence. Her mother, Jia.
Professor Rodriguez. Vaughn. Hell, I even thought of the fluffin,
Neville. If I stayed, I'd be able to see them tomorrow. What would
the highbloods do to them if I didn't return?

I drew in a shaky breath. "Yes. I'll come back. Soon."

I turned towards Nyxaris. I'd thought the tribunal would be the
hard part. But now that I looked up at the massive black dragon, I
feared I'd been wrong.

*Do not be afraid, wingless one. I will not drop you,* Nyxaris teased.

I wanted to tell him I wasn't afraid of flying or falling. But it
would have been a lie. Besides, my mind was suddenly too mud-
dled to say anything at all. Instead, I stepped closer and closer until
I could reach out a trembling hand to touch his side. The dragon's
scales were smooth and radiated a soft heat.

I looked up at his enormous height. *How am I supposed to . . . ?*

There was no saddle. No reins. Nothing to hold on to.

*Climb.* Nyxaris's voice was imperious and impatient. *You've come
this far.*

Right.

My fingers curled around a scale and I began my ascent. It was just like the day I'd climbed the black dragon in the Dragon Court. Except now Nyxaris was flesh and blood, not stone. I wasn't sure which was worse. His scales were certainly easier to grip now that he was alive. But the fact that he *was* alive was, well, fucking terrifying. At one point, I glanced down and immediately regretted it. The world below seemed impossibly faraway. It didn't help that we were on a bridge with the sea churning far below us. I swallowed hard and kept climbing.

Finally, I reached the ridge of his shoulders. I pulled myself up to straddle the base of his neck, my hands clutching at one of the spines that protruded from his back, and looked down at the highbloods. They must have thought I was mad. I was completely exposed. No saddle, no straps.

*I'm going to die, aren't I?*

*You are not going to die,* Nyxaris answered. *You will not fall. I will not allow it. I will not permit you to humiliate me in such a ridiculous way.*

I caught movement in the crowd. Blake had moved to the front. He stared up at me, his gray eyes wide with something like awe—or fear. Was he afraid for me? Or because of me?

Nearby, Kage stood watching, too. The look in his dark eyes was hard to decipher. Respect, maybe. Or amusement. I wasn't sure which.

"All right. Let's get this over with," I muttered aloud, my fingers tightening around the spine.

Nyxaris's wings beat powerfully as we lifted higher and higher into the sky. I clung to the spine I was holding for dear life. It was bony but strangely elegant, its surface glossy and black. The tip looked extremely sharp. I wasn't about to test it, though.

Below us, the Black Keep had turned into no more than a child's toy. Beside it lay Bloodwing Academy. The place I couldn't help still thinking of as home. The city of Veilmar stretched out along the coast. Its bustling streets were already too far away for me to make out the details of anything clearly.

Nyxaris angled his massive body and we soared out to sea. My breath caught as the endless expanse of water came into view. The waves looked so small. At this height, if I fell, even the water wouldn't save me. Death would be instant.

*Hold tight, rider.* Nyxaris's voice rumbled in my mind, dry with amusement.

"As if I had another choice," I muttered. My hair was whipping wildly in the wind, my cloak flapping behind me like a banner. I squeezed the spine tighter between my hands, my thighs clutching the dragon's sides.

*Did your riders ever use saddles?* I asked breathlessly.

At first he didn't answer. Then his reply came, clipped and begrudging. *Yes.*

*Really?* I pressed on, emboldened. *What were they like?*

Nyxaris's annoyance radiated through our connection. *Functional. Practical. Leather, reinforced with steel. Straps secured the rider. Of course, the weaklings fell, regardless.*

I gulped. Even with straps. I firmly forced myself not to look down again. I thought about how I might get a saddle made. Would they have to take Nyxaris's measurements? I tried to imagine that and nearly burst into hysterical laughter.

Nyxaris interrupted my thoughts, his tone sharp. *Do not mistake this for a recurring event, Medra Pendragon. You are here for one purpose.*

My stomach twisted. *I know. I know why you agreed to this. I haven't forgotten.*

*Then, begin,* he growled. *You owe me answers.*

All summer I'd managed to string him along, refusing to answer his questions until he promised to help me and only then. At first I worried he would simply go out and find someone else to help him. But evidently that wasn't as easy as it seemed or he'd probably have done it by now. Perhaps only riders could speak to dragons—another thing I'd have to ask Rodriguez about.

The books I'd read—well, scanned in haste—had been useless. Now I wondered if Rodriguez had purposely set it up that way. Obviously he kept the good ones to himself. He knew more than he let on, and he'd wanted to share only tidbits. Why? Until he knew if I was trustworthy?

Of the books I'd flipped through, one had been focused on mythology and lore. I now realized half of it was bunk. The other was pure history. Authored by a scholar who had clearly never interacted with dragons herself. She told stories secondhand, mostly of old battles and political intrigue between houses, barely touching on what it actually meant to be a rider. The last had been interesting but it was dense and mostly to do with healing. I'd read enough to use for my essay quotes, but hadn't gone through it cover to cover.

All of the books had been centuries old and none had included practical information relevant to my present situation. What I needed were books written by riders themselves. Or, better yet, by a dragon. I wondered if a dragon had ever had anyone ghost-write their biography for them. Perhaps I could be the first.

I decided another book was called for. *How to Speak to Dragons.* No, *How to Speak to Dragons Without Winding Up a Scorched Corpse.* Now, that would be useful.

I realized I was hesitating. I could feel Nyxaris simmering with impatience. *Did you really not know? That there were no other dragons alive when you woke, I mean?*

Nyxaris's silence stretched long enough that I began to wonder if he'd reply.

*I did not,* he admitted at last. *I sensed the world had changed, but I did not know how profoundly.* There was something raw in his tone. Grief. Though, he quickly masked it with irritation. *My memory is incomplete. Clouded. As though pieces of me were absorbed into the stone.*

*Foggy?* I asked, as gently as I could.

*No.* His tone was sharp. *Fragmented. Missing.*

I bit my lip, feeling a pang of sympathy for the creature beneath me. I had no illusions about his ruthlessness, but the idea of waking to such a harsh reality seemed cruel.

*Do you know how it happened?* I asked cautiously. *How were you made stone in the first place?*

*If I knew that, do you think I'd be here with you, asking you questions? You really are frustratingly ignorant, even for a young one,* the dragon snapped.

I flinched, then held on a little tighter as we dropped sharply. I'd upset him. *It must have been a curse of some kind. A powerful enchantment,* I guessed, after the silence had gone on for a while.

*Obviously,* Nyxaris replied grumpily.

*Don't you want revenge on whoever did that to you?* I asked curiously.

*Of course I want revenge. But they are probably long dead. Now, are you asking the questions or am I?* Nyxaris snapped. He was lying. But I wasn't going to press him. Not yet. *Tell me everything you know about what happened to my kind.*

And in that moment, something snapped into place. All that I knew was woefully inadequate.

Nyxaris's wings cut through the air as I searched my mind. We'd learned a little about the Dragon Wars. Everyone knew the war had been the dragons' undoing. But how? The books Rodriguez gave me hadn't been written recently enough to include the Dragon Wars. Professor Hassan's lectures had barely scratched the surface. She had spoken about alliances between houses, civil war, catastrophic losses. But she hadn't explicitly said *how* the dragons perished.

I glanced down at the sea, my stomach lurching at the height.

*So quiet.* Nyxaris's voice rumbled, tinged with annoyance. *Have I frightened you into silence? Tell me.*

I swallowed hard. *I learned about the Dragon Wars in a history class last year. My professor said the last of the dragons perished during that time. Some must have been killed in battle. One of my other professors said some died of a plague. But . . .*

*But what?* Nyxaris's voice lashed through my mind, demanding more.

I inhaled, trying to gather my thoughts. *But I don't know if anyone knows how your kind went extinct. Not precisely. Maybe I just haven't read the right books. Or maybe . . . Maybe no one truly knows.*

Nyxaris's growl reverberated through my skull, sending a shiver down my spine. *Are you saying your kind forgot* us?

For a moment I worried I'd offended him worse than Lord Mortis had. *No,* I said hastily. *Not forgotten.* I hesitated. *I mean they can't remember. Because the truth has been hidden.*

Nyxaris snorted. He didn't respond immediately. Instead, he banked left, tilting sharply.

I gasped, my heart in my throat, as we dropped down closer to the glittering surface of the sea.

*This is unbearable,* Nyxaris said finally. I could hear the desperation tinging his voice.

*I know. You deserve answers. You deserve . . .* I searched for the right words. *You deserve so much more than this. To awaken alone . . . I can't imagine how awful that must have been.*

He was quiet for a long time.

*No, you can't,* he said finally. *To be the last of one's kind—I am not sure it is a life worth living.*

A lump formed in my throat. *Don't say that. Please. I need you. I care about what happens to you.*

He snorted. *You care only about your own survival, young one.*

*No,* I said stubbornly. *It's more than that. Be patient. Let me search for more answers. I swear, I'll get some for you. One of my professors has books—very old ones. I'll look through them. He's helped me before. But if he doesn't, I'll find a way. I'll do whatever it takes.*

Silence.

When Nyxaris's voice returned to my head, it was low and commanding. *You owe me more than promises. Do not fail me.*

My throat tightened. *I'll keep my promise.* I hesitated. *And I want to thank you. You have my eternal gratitude for what you did today.*

Nyxaris's laugh was different from his usual rumble this time. There was something bitter to it. *You awakened me to serve your own needs.*

*That's not true,* I protested. *I didn't mean to awaken you at all. And I certainly wouldn't be bothering you if my life weren't on the line.*

For a moment, he was silent. The wind whipped around us. *You make promises so easily, little earth-walker. But words are fleeting. Tell me, then—what of the ritual? Even if it was an accident, can it bring back the others?*

I hesitated, the weight of his question hitting me like a hammer. *I don't know. I don't even fully understand how it worked. It wasn't planned.*

*Convenient,* the black dragon muttered. *You meddle with power beyond your comprehension. Yet now you think you can find answers for me.*

My frustration bubbled to the surface. *I will try. I swear that. But you need to ask yourself something. If it were even possible to bring back the others, is that something you'd truly want?*

I felt his wings falter for a fraction of a second. *Would I want it?* he echoed. *To see my kin again? To hear their roars? Yes, I think I would.* Then his voice darkened. *But would they be free? Or would this cursed world of highbloods snatch them away as it always did, chaining us to their wars and their greed?*

I still didn't see how the dragons had ever been brought under highblood control. But I assumed that had to do with the rider bonds—something Nyxaris had already firmly insisted he would not be allowing again.

*Did you fight in the Dragon Wars?* I asked tentatively. *Were you there?*

His silence was heavy.

*I do not remember.* His tone was stiff, almost pained. *I fought in many wars. They blend together in my mind.*

I sensed his growing frustration.

*It's all right,* I said soothingly. *We'll find answers together.*

He let out a low, guttural growl. *Something of me was taken when I was turned to stone. You spoke of revenge. Payment is required. A heavy loss has been incurred.*

I could sense his fury, his pain. *Once you struck fear into highblood hearts. They needed you, yes, but they must have hated you, too.*

*That is true,* he admitted.

*You can strike fear into their hearts once more, if we act together. Would you rather be hunted and pitied, or admired and feared?*

Nyxaris snorted. *Such simplistic thinking.*

*But it's true, isn't it?* I insisted. *If we work together, we can make them believe they control you—when you and I will know it's the other way around. I will help you. I promised. We'll find out who did this to you. It doesn't matter how long ago it was. Someone still alive must know something. We'll find your missing pieces, too.*

He didn't reply. I took that as an answer. And in that moment, I realized my relationship with Nyxaris was just like mine and Blake's: neither of us really wanted to be in it. We were trapped together.

So here I was, begging Nyxaris for small pieces of himself. Just like Blake had to do with my blood. Except, I told myself, Blake never begged.

What sort of person could turn a dragon to stone? What sort of person would *want* to?

The sun began to drop as we flew on in silence.

# Book 2

# CHAPTER 8

# MEDRA

Nyxaris left me on the bridge leading to Bloodwing Academy. I walked slowly through the exterior courtyard towards the great double doors leading into the school. When would I stand here again? I'd only left the academy a few times in my first year as a student—once to sneak out onto the beach for the bonfire party Theo had invited me to. That had been disastrous. Especially for Kiernan, the highblood Blake had killed. I'd also made it all the way to the city of Veilmar, following Blake through the secret tunnels that lay beneath the Dragon Court.

A shadow moved, stepping out of the twilight. Blake—he'd been waiting for me.

There hadn't been a verdict, I realized. Not before I'd left. Had the Tribunal Panel arrived at a decision? If they were going to execute me, surely they'd have sent someone other than Blake to bring me in. Or would they get him to do it? We both knew he was stronger than me. If he wanted to simply kill me, could he?

My heart started to pound. "What are you doing here?"

"I thought you might want to know what happened after you took off," he drawled, shoving his hands into his trouser pockets as he came towards me.

I tried not to look as scared as I felt. "I assume they figured out a way to break our bond after all and now I'm House Avari's. Should

I move my things to Kage's tower?" I was joking, but the look on Blake's face made me freeze.

"Don't," he warned. "Don't even joke about that."

I crossed my arms over my chest. "Why not? Because you hate House Avari? Or is it just Kage who bothers you so much?"

His jaw tightened. "You know why."

I took a step closer, my voice deliberately sharp. "No, Blake, I don't. House Avari probably wouldn't have forced me into a bond I never wanted. They wouldn't have treated me like some possession. At this point, I think I'd be happier there. Kage might actually show me some respect."

It was like striking a match to dry kindling. Too easy. In an instant, Blake was in front of me, moving with that terrifying vampire speed. Before I could even step back, his face was close to mine.

"Respect you?" he growled. "You think Kage would *respect* you? You think House Avari would treat you better? Grow up, Pendragon. They'd use you. Just like every other highblood house would, if they were given half a chance."

"At least it would have been my choice," I spat. "Don't you dare stand there and pretend to be any better when you fed from me without my consent and claimed me without even asking."

Blake's jaw clenched again, but he didn't back away. For a moment, the tension between us was unbearable. His eyes dropped to my lips, then flicked back up, and for one horrifying moment, I thought he might . . .

"For now, you're alive," he said finally. "The tribunal reached a verdict. You're staying at Bloodwing. Under House Drakharrow's oversight."

I let out a shaky breath, relief and frustration warring inside me. "No one listened to Lysander. What a surprise."

"Lysander is a fool who's going to get himself killed," Blake said derisively.

"No one listened to Lord Mortis either," I pointed out.

"Garrick Mortis." Blake shook his head. "Not quite as much

a fool as Lysander." He looked at me intently. "But maybe he was right."

"He wasn't right. Killing me would be signing your own death sentence," I snapped. "You need me, remember? I'm useful."

"Useful? Don't flatter yourself. You're an asset for now. Everyone wants to see how this plays out." He smirked. "After all, you claim to be able to control a dragon."

I lifted my chin. "Doesn't it make you want to run screaming like a little boy? The thought of all that dragon fire right at my fingertips?"

He laughed, clearly not intimidated. "It might, if I thought that anything that dragon did was done with you in mind."

I flushed. "Good thing I have you to protect me, then," I said bitterly.

His smirk widened and I hated how my pulse sped up at the sight of his lips, his face. "You survived your first year because I allowed it. Don't make me prove that to you now." He suddenly pushed his chest up against mine, shoving me backwards. His breath was hot against my ear. "Why don't you just fall in line, like a good little girl?"

My chest tightened with anger, fear, and something else I refused to give name to, and I shoved him, hard. He didn't budge, but it was still satisfying. "Fuck you, Blake. Go ahead. Show me what life would be like without you. I think it sounds too good to be true. But you won't, will you? Because then I'll see just how small your *power* really is." I laughed, trying to make the word sound like a double entendre and Blake reddened with anger.

His eyes narrowed. "I've been shielding you since the day you got here."

"Bullshit. You wanted me to fail," I reminded him. "You said you'd never mix your bloodline with mine, remember?"

"I . . ." He swallowed. "I think it's time for a reality check. You don't seem to understand the position you're really in. How precarious it is. If I step aside, you won't last a day."

I refused to be intimidated. After all, what was the worst that
could happen? He needed me alive. "I don't need your help, and I
certainly don't want it. I never did."

He chuckled arrogantly. "I'll enjoy watching you learn the hard
way."

"You're such a highblood bastard," I hissed.

"And you're a liar," he shot back. "You talk about breaking our
bond, as if it's even possible. And as if you'd really want that."

I was trembling. I stared back at him, hating the cruel satisfaction in his gray eyes. But worse than the anger was the flicker of
something deeper. Something that felt suspiciously like longing. I
crushed it mercilessly. "You think I'm bluffing?" I said, my voice
shaking with fury. "Believe me, I'm not. I'll find a way. And once
I do, I'll never look back."

Something passed over Blake's face—a crack in the mask. But it
was gone in an instant, replaced by an infuriating, mocking smile.
"Good luck with that," he said, stepping away from me. "Welcome
back to Bloodwing, Pendragon. I'll be watching."

With that, he turned and walked away, leaving me standing
alone, heart pounding and resolve hardening. I'd find a way to
break free of these unbearable chains. And I'd make sure Nyxaris
never bowed to House Drakharrow. Not now. Not ever.

At least what was left of the day improved from there. A present was
waiting for me in my room when I returned to Drakharrow Tower.

I stepped into the room and froze, my tension evaporating into
surprise.

Sitting cross-legged on my bed reading a book and looking as if
she'd been patiently waiting for hours was Florence Shen.

"Florence!" I exclaimed.

"Medra!" Florence jumped up, her long dark hair swishing as
she flew into my arms for a hug. "I thought you were never com-

ing back! They wouldn't tell me anything except that you were still at the tribunal."

I thought about where I'd actually just come from and decided it could wait. Florence tugged me over to the bed and I realized she'd made herself at home. Not only had she brought a stack of books—already studying ahead of the start of classes, no doubt—but a teapot and pair of mugs sat on my desk alongside a plate of pastries.

"I thought you could use some calming tea," Florence explained. "Though, it's cold now. My mother made it from a family recipe."

I smiled gratefully. "I'll drink it cold, I don't mind. It was very sweet of you."

"How did the tribunal go? I've been waiting and waiting here . . ." She trailed off and for the first time I realized how tense she was, what she must have thought as she sat all alone waiting to see if I'd ever come back.

"Everything is going to be all right," I said quickly. It was more or less the truth, at least for now. "They're letting me stay at Blood-wing. They're not going to execute me, if that's what you're worried about." The joke was supposed to be lighthearted but then I saw the look on Florence's face. "You've been sitting here for hours, haven't you? Wondering if I was coming back at all. Oh, Florence. I'm so sorry."

She bit her lip, a single tear sliding down her cheek. She brushed it away. "After last year . . ."

I nodded. "Naveen. I know."

"I can't lose anyone else," she said, her voice thick. "Not another friend."

We were silent for a moment. I knew we were both thinking of Naveen. We'd been as thick as thieves last year, the three of us. Now there were just us two.

Because of me. Because of what I'd done to survive.

But I wasn't going to let my darkness infect Florence's light.

I grabbed a sugar-dusted cookie, then sat down on the bed, pasting a smile on my face. "Let's talk about something else. How was your summer?" But before we could exchange more news, the door swung open and a pair of violet eyes peered in.

"I thought I heard laughing. Having a party? Can I join?"

Florence and I exchanged glances, then I grinned. "Come in, Visha."

Visha shut the door, then marched over and plopped down on the bed, running her hands through her hair. She'd let it grow out a bit over the summer, but kept one side fully shaved. I was fairly sure she could shave her head completely and still look stunning.

"So, I hear you had a sweet ride back to Bloodwing after the tribunal today," Visha said mischievously.

"Ride?" Florence looked back and forth between us. "What does that mean?"

I laughed nervously.

Visha's eyes twinkled at Florence. "She didn't tell you yet? Our girl rode a dragon."

Florence's eyes turned into saucers. "What? You did? Oh, Medra, that's wonderful! You've bonded with Nyxaris!"

I grimaced. "*Bonded* is putting it strongly. He hasn't burned me to a crisp yet."

"Bah." Visha waved a hand. "She's understating it. Our little rider doesn't like to brag. I mean, she did have him roast someone but it wasn't her."

I thought Florence was going to choke. "Roast someone? Who? When? By the Bloodmaiden, what did you do, Medra?"

I winced at the exclamation. "*I* didn't do anything, I assure you. It was all *him*."

Visha looked at me curiously. "So it really is true?"

"What is?"

She shrugged. "Well, at least half the school thinks you had your dragon slay Lord Mortis for you because he wanted you executed."

Florence shrieked. "What?" She glared at me accusingly. "You said they weren't going to execute you."

"They aren't," I said soothingly. "That was just . . . one small part of the conversation."

Visha snorted. "I mean, I don't think anyone is going to suggest it for a while. They're too scared shitless now."

"Oh, Medra," Florence moaned. "A *regent*? A House Leader? What did Catherine say?"

I shifted uncomfortably. "She didn't look exactly pleased. But she didn't demand we duel to the death either."

"Catherine will be fine," Visha said dismissively, sliding off the bed and going over to the plate of pastries. "She's probably thrilled. She just got a huge promotion, thanks to you."

"It wasn't me," I reminded her. "Nyxaris did that. Honestly, he nearly scorched me in the process and if he had, I doubt he'd have cared." I thought of Kage, flying out of nowhere to grab me. "Lord Mortis insulted Nyxaris. Apparently, that's in very bad form."

Visha cackled. "I'd say. What an idiot." She turned to face me, a cookie in one hand and a raspberry tart in the other. "You wouldn't believe the things they're saying about Mortis already. He's a laughingstock. If Catherine wasn't pissed at you before, she might be now." She tilted her head thoughtfully. "But again, she is the House Mortis Leader now . . . I mean, within Bloodwing and outside of it. She's a regent, so maybe she'll be grateful."

"Her father is dead," Florence said, sounding shocked.

"Yeah, and he wasn't an easy man to get along with. Now Catherine is free," Visha pointed out.

"Is that really it? The House Leader dies and their kid just steps up? That's how it works?" I asked curiously. "I had no idea Lysander was the leader of his house now."

Visha nodded. "That just happened over the summer. His uncle died, and Lysander was the next in line. I mean, it's not always the eldest child who inherits the spot. The leader gets to choose their heir. But Catherine was her father's."

So much power consolidated among so few people.

"I can't believe you rode a dragon and didn't tell me as soon as you walked in that door," Florence exclaimed. She threw up her hands. "So you're not bonded? Then, how does it work, exactly?"

I sighed and leaned back against one of the bedposts. "I'm not sure it does." I eyed Visha. If I kept talking, it would mean sharing some things I hadn't shared with anyone else. I trusted Florence completely. But Visha? Her friendship was newer.

The violet-eyed highblood caught me staring at her. "Do you want me to leave?"

"No," I said quickly.

She shrugged. "It's all right if you do. Just say the word. I'll get it."

And I knew she would. She'd just go. She wouldn't kick and scream about it like someone else might.

I thought of all that had happened between us since we met. She'd treated me like shit at first, then she'd saved me during the Consort Games. Of course, she'd done it because Blake had told her to. But she'd been decent about it; she'd tried her best to help. She really did seem to want to let bygones to be bygones. I still didn't know her very well. But there was something about her I'd come to like. She was blunt. Direct. Even harsh in a way. But I sensed I could trust her.

I took a deep breath. "Look, if I start talking, it might make it awkward for you. Blake doesn't know any of this—and I don't want him to."

Visha nodded slowly. "I get it. I'm not going to spy on you for him, if that's what you're worried about."

"But he's your House Leader," I said.

"And he's your archon," she pointed out.

"For now." I gritted my teeth. "A lot has happened since the last day of school."

We stared at one another. Then Visha smirked. "Don't worry, Pendragon. I know we're not at the sharing-our-deepest-secrets stage of our relationship yet. We haven't had enough sleepover parties for that. You can save all of your dragon bedtime stories for Florence."

I frowned, worried I'd really offended her. "That's not—"

Visha cut me off, her cocky grin widening. "Relax. I'm not going to pine away. I'm not cut out to be a tragic hero."

Florence giggled nervously, trying to break the tension. "Speaking of relationships, how are things with your triad, Visha?"

Visha's smile turned wolfish. She sat down near the hearth and leaned back against the stones with one knee propped up, looking like a complete rogue. "Oh, you mean the boys?" She waved a hand. "They're fine. Honestly, it's a miracle when they even notice I'm there."

"Uh, do they not . . . ?" I asked cautiously.

"Oh, they notice," Visha reassured me, her grin growing sharp. "I'm not one to tolerate being ignored for long. We saw each other a few times over the summer. My family's estate isn't far from Lucian's. Let's just say I had a very busy time reminding them why I'm the one who holds that particular knot together." She leaned back, putting her hands behind her head, her violet eyes gleaming with mischief. "But you know, a girl can't survive on two boys alone." She paused to roll her eyes. "Especially when they're obviously smitten with each other."

I thought of Theo and Vaughn. "So, they're allowed to . . . ?"

Visha laughed loudly. "We're all *allowed* to, it's only Blake's uncle who's such a prude. We can breed and still fuck other people. It's not a crime."

Florence leaned forward, her expression simultaneously shocked and interested. "So you like to . . . keep things interesting?"

"Of course." Visha grinned. "Let's see. I learned some swordplay from the brooding heir of the Adros family in Veilmar."

I snorted. "Swordplay. Sure."

She raised a hand to her heart. "I swear, there were swords involved."

Florence laughed and I grinned.

"To cut you loose from the bed after, maybe," I joked.

"Him, actually." Visha's eyes danced. "Then there was a sweet little thing on Lucian's estate who wanted me to teach her a few lessons."

"Always the teacher, never the student?" I teased.

"Oh, no, I go both ways," Visha said seriously. "There was Lady Callis of House Orphos who met me at her summer house for a few trysts. She thought she could tame me. Poor thing, she's back home with her triad now. Dull things the other two are, too."

Florence blinked. "Well, you've certainly kept busy."

"Life's too short, Shen." She eyed Florence up and down. "Especially for mortals like you. Might as well have fun while you can."

Florence blushed. "You're ridiculous."

"Stick with me and maybe I'll bring you along next summer. You look like you could use some excitement," Visha observed, looking at Florence's stack of books critically.

Florence's blush deepened. "I think I'll stick with my books."

"Books?" Visha looked appalled. "Where did you say you spent your summer?"

"I—I spent it here," Florence stuttered. She glanced at me. "At Bloodwing mostly. I helped my mother in the library. We visited some of my mother's family for two weeks but that was the extent of my travels." She shrugged her shoulders. "Pretty exciting stuff."

"I can't believe we were both trapped here and I didn't even know it," I said slowly.

"I tried to see you but no one was allowed in," Florence said miserably. "Not until today." She glanced at the door. "I might even have begged Blake."

"Blake?" I sat up straight. "Please tell me you didn't. He's dangerous, Florence. I think you should stay far away from him." I thought of something. "Please tell me you didn't—"

There was a loud knock at the door. I turned my head as it creaked open slowly. My heart had already started to pound. If Blake dared . . .

But it was Theo's face that appeared, wearing a charmingly sheepish expression. "Room for one more in there?"

Visha raised an eyebrow. "Since when do you even ask for an invitation?"

Theo grinned and shrugged. He stepped inside and held up a small, wriggling ball of orange fur. "I brought a date."

"Neville!" Florence exclaimed, leaping off the bed and rushing forward to take the fluffin from Theo's arms. The little creature barked—a high-pitched, melodic sound—and wriggled even more excitedly as Florence cradled him against her chest and made cooing sounds of affection.

"He was sniffing around the hallways," Theo said. "Clearly searching for his one true love."

I eyed the little fluffin. Neville had grown over the summer. He was no longer the tiny pup I'd found on the beach last year. His fur, once a soft reddish-orange, had deepened a little into a darker copper. The creamy white fur on his chest was fluffier than ever, making him look as if he were wearing a ruff of snow. His tail, bushy and almost as long as his entire body, swished back and forth with excitement as Florence fussed over him.

"He's huge now," I said, smiling. "Where has he been all summer?"

"Oh, someone's been feeding him." Theo eyed Florence. "And if it wasn't Florence—"

Neville's joyful reunion suddenly turned into chaos. With an excited yip, he wriggled free of Florence's lap and began to tear around the room like a whirlwind. His busy tail streamed behind him as he bounded from one corner to another, jumping onto the bed, then skidding across the rug. We all watched him with interest, even Visha.

"Is this what you've been dealing with all summer?" I asked, as I watched the fluffin zoom through the room and knock over a stack of books in his frenzy.

Florence laughed and shook her head. "Sometimes. My mother likes to say he's our worst library patron. I had to escort him out a few times."

"Your mother allows a fluffin in the library?" Theo said with interest. He held up his hands quickly. "I'm not going to tell anyone."

"She does love Neville, but *allow* is putting it strongly." Florence bent down and scooped up the fluffin as he tried to run past her. "That's enough, now, Neville." She carried him over to the bed where the fluffin lay down, panting.

"I think he wore himself out," I said, eyeing the little creature. "At least, for now." I looked at Florence. "So he's been living with you in the library?"

"I don't live in the library, Medra," Florence said, laughing. "My mother has a suite of rooms, and I stayed there with her over the summer. Neville would sleep over sometimes, but I didn't see him every day. He'd disappear sometimes. I figured he was roaming the castle." She purposely didn't meet my eyes. I knew we were both thinking of who Neville had probably been paying visits to.

Blake hadn't brought the fluffin to see me over the summer. And he hadn't snuck Florence in. Because he couldn't, or because he had chosen not to?

"I bet he's been sneaking into the kitchens," Visha observed. "Look at him! He's fat enough to roll."

"He is not," Florence said primly. "He's just putting on some winter weight. Like a squirrel."

Theo laughed. "Blake was probably feeding him, too. Neville's been sniffing around Drakharrow Tower since I got back. He's obviously at home here already. Look at him, he's practically glossy."

I frowned, thinking of Blake caring for the fluffin. It didn't square with everything else I knew about him. For a while, I'd believed Blake was capable of caring for something else besides himself or his precious house, but I'd been wrong.

Neville had worn himself out again. He collapsed in a heap at Visha's feet. The highblood girl gingerly stretched out a hand to rub his white belly. "He's so soft," she said, sounding surprised. "I've never petted one before."

I smiled. Finally, we'd found something Visha hadn't done already.

The room descended into quiet. Theo helped himself to some cold tea and passed me the other mug. Then he cleared his throat and looked at me hesitantly.

"So," he started, his voice carefully casual, "how are things going with you and Blake?"

The air immediately turned heavy.

Visha stopped petting Neville. Florence shifted uncomfortably in her position on the bed.

I didn't meet their eyes. "What do you mean?" I said, pretending ignorance.

Theo sighed. "I was there, Medra. At the tribunal today." He glanced at Visha. "You've probably heard?" The highblood girl nodded. "And Florence will get the short version eventually, I'm sure," Theo said, looking at my other friend. "It's all anyone's talking about. You woke a fucking dragon. And now you've asked for your bond with Blake to be dissolved."

"And everyone claims it can't be," I reminded him sharply. I looked around at each of them. I knew Florence was my friend. I wanted Visha to be. Theo, too. But two of them were highbloods. Their loyalties were . . . stretched. I weighed how much I should say. "Blake bonded with me without my consent. He gave me his blood before the Consort Games—and he didn't tell me what the real consequences of sharing blood would be. Then he drank from me, without my permission after Selection Day was over, there in the Dragon Court."

"Is that why the dragon woke up?" Visha asked, her eyes wide.

I shook my head. "No, I don't think so." I didn't feel like explaining there had been a completely different blood ritual much earlier than that.

Theo and Visha exchanged a look—one loaded with highblood understanding. I glanced at Florence. Her face was outraged. She was blightborn: she understood. Did they? The divide in the room suddenly felt as wide as a chasm.

"That's not unusual for a highblood," Visha said bluntly. "I mean, we don't usually take blightborn consorts. But archons can often do whatever they want. It's tolerated, even—"

"Stop," Theo interrupted. "It's not right, Visha. And you know it. It's not how things should be."

I wasn't sure if he meant the arrangement between consorts and archons, or blightborn and highbloods, or all of it. Visha raised one eyebrow but said nothing.

Theo continued, "You know, before Blake's father, things were worse for blightborn. Much worse. Now Viktor's working to undo everything his brother stood for."

"He was your uncle," I said quietly. "The Peacebringer, I mean."

Theo nodded. "Alexander Drakharrow."

"How did he die? Professor Hassan mentioned him in class but not the details." I'd been curious ever since.

Theo hesitated. "He basically disappeared. We were told he'd died, but I still don't know what happened exactly. Then his wife disappeared, too—Blake's mother, Desdemona."

"I thought she was in the Sanctum," I said, staring at him.

Theo shrugged. "Right. That's what everyone says. I haven't seen her since."

Visha yawned. "Not unheard of. Some of these older highblood ladies, they take their bonds very seriously. Too seriously, if you ask me."

"It was a love match," Theo said quietly. "Between Blake's parents, I mean. They were a pair, not a triad."

"Not unheard of," Visha acknowledged. "But restricting your-self to just one person?" She shuddered and we all laughed. It broke the tension for a moment.

Until I raised the temperature in the room again by asking, "What about uprisings? Have there been rebellions?"

Theo frowned. "Not that I know of. Why do you ask?"

"When I first arrived . . . in Sangratha, I found myself in a burned-out village. Everyone else was dead." The memory flashed through my mind. Smoke and ash. The stench of rotting bodies.

"Oh, that." Theo looked shaken.

"What?" I said sharply. "Tell us."

"It wasn't an uprising," he said reluctantly. "Not exactly. But some blightborn in that village were being . . . challenging." He held up his hands as my mouth opened. "I don't know what ex-actly that means either. But Viktor thought it was a big deal. He sent Marcus to handle it."

My stomach turned. "And Blake? Was he involved?"

All of those people. There would have been children among them.

Theo quickly shook his head. "No. Blake wasn't part of that. In fact, Marcus went too far." He eyed me sympathetically. "I guess you know what I'm talking about."

I felt Florence's eyes on me. "Everyone was dead," I said quietly, by way of explanation. "Nothing was left. The village had been completely destroyed."

"Marcus wouldn't even need to be ordered to do something like that," Visha said darkly. I remembered that Marcus had been a student at Bloodwing until the year before last. "He'd do it for the sheer fun of it."

"That's monstrous," Florence whispered, her face pale. "There were rumors about some blightborn murders in Veilmar. But I didn't think highbloods were involved."

I said nothing. My friend was still naïve in some ways.

"Well, most people don't," Theo said quietly. "That's the point. They're not supposed to." He gave Florence a strange look.

"Blightborn, you mean," she said, looking ill at ease.

Theo didn't reply. The room fell silent again. But this time it wasn't a comfortable quiet. The weight of the conversation hung over us like a storm cloud.

I'd missed my friends. But this division between us . . . If we weren't careful, it could split us in two. That was the last thing we needed. I took a breath. "What are your schedules looking like? Do we share any classes this year?" I hadn't even looked at my timetable. But I'd noticed it sitting over on the desk. Now I went to fetch it and handed it to Florence who had pulled out her own.

"Oh my goodness." Florence clapped her hands together and looked delighted. "Look at this! We have a class together."

I hadn't dared to get my hopes up that that might happen. I figured Blake would do his best to keep me as far away from House Avari as possible.

"We do?" I said, sliding onto the bed beside her. "Which one?"

Florence looked even more excited. "The Alchemist's Garden!"

I scrunched up my nose. "The what?"

"Rather poetic name for a class at Bloodwing," Theo observed.

"Isn't it?" Florence said happily. "It's co-taught by Professor Rodriguez and a visiting scholar, Professor Vasanti Allenvale. My mother was gushing about it. Apparently, Professor Allenvale is very famous. Half of the class will take place in the traditional classroom with Professor Rodriguez and the other half of the time we'll be out working in the greenhouse, learning about—"

"Plants?" Visha guessed. Visha and Theo stared at Florence as if she had two heads.

"Exactly," Florence said, beaming.

"It sounds fascinating," I said loyally. Visha looked as if she was about to snicker so I glared at her until she coughed.

Florence was continuing to scan my schedule. "You're also in some combat classes."

Visha perked up. "Which ones?"

"Let's see . . . She has Defensive Arts and Historical Strategy, one after the other. They're often taken together. Oh! I'm registered in the Strategy component of that class." For a moment, Florence looked excited. "Oh, wait, no. My class is at a different time."

"That'll be the section for House Avari students," Theo noted gently. "So you're in healing and strategy classes?"

Florence looked crestfallen for a moment, then she nodded. "Yes. I'm taking some of both."

"Plus some extra ones, besides?" I guessed. When she blushed, I knew I was right. "Basically, Florence is a scholarly genius," I explained to the others.

"Stop it," she said, flushing more fiercely. "I am not. I just have no problem spending all my time studying."

Visha was looking appalled again. But she shook her head. "When is Medra's Defensive Arts class?"

Florence checked the timetable. "Every second day just after lunch."

"That's the same section I'm in," Visha said with a grin.

"I'm in that one, too," Theo said, surprising me. "Blake's not," he quickly added.

It would be strange not to see Blake in a combat class, but it was for the best. The more I could avoid him the better.

"You have another class that looks interesting, Medra," Florence said, still studying the piece of parchment. "Historical Perspectives: Sangratha and Dragons."

Now it was my turn to feel eager. "That sounds interesting. Who's it with?" I hoped it would be Rodriguez.

But Florence shook her head. "It doesn't say." She paused. "You're in another scouting class with Professor Stonefist. Intermediate Combat for Blightborn."

I was surprised I wasn't in more classes tailored to dragon riders. But maybe they didn't have anyone to teach them. That would make sense.

"There are some gaps in your schedule," Florence said, scanning. "Maybe that's when they expect you to work with Nyxaris."

My heart sank. "Yes. Maybe." That would be a problem, if so. Or maybe the gaps were for extra thrallguard sessions with Rodriguez. I could hope.

I glanced at Theo. The mention of the scouting class had reminded me of Naveen. But also of Vaughn Sabino. "Do you have any classes with Vaughn?"

Theo shook his head. "No, but why would I? He's not in House Drakharrow."

"What?" I stared at him. "Yes, he is. He was selected into it. I was there."

"I remember that, too," Florence commented.

Theo crossed his arms over his chest. "He's not now. I had him moved."

"What?" I stared. "How? You can do that?"

Theo glanced at Visha. "Not normally, no. But I talked to Blake. Vaughn didn't want to be in Drakharrow. I knew he was hoping for Orphos, so Blake had Lysander take him."

"That's amazing," Florence exclaimed. "That was so kind of you, Theo."

Visha was staring at Theo oddly. "Very kind. Not very high-blood behavior."

Theo rolled his eyes. "Maybe I'm not a very good highblood. Are you?"

Visha shrugged. "I'm whatever the fuck I want to be."

"Then, you're lucky," Theo said, almost accusingly. "I can't be. But Vaughn . . ." He took a deep breath. "Vaughn can be whatever he wants. He has a right to be happy."

I was fairly certain that Blake had requested Vaughn for House Drakharrow because he'd been hoping to make his cousin happy. I wondered how Blake felt knowing his work had been undone. Maybe he was simply relieved that Theo planned to avoid Vaughn.

"Hopefully you and Vaughn can still see each other sometimes and talk," I said softly. "If you both want to, I mean."

Theo frowned down at the floor. "Right. Maybe." He looked

at the door. "It's getting late. Tomorrow's our first day. I'd better be going." He gave me a wistful look. "But it was good to see you, Medra. Outside the Tribunal Chamber and alive and well, I mean."

I came towards him and put my arms around his shoulders briefly. "You, too, Theo. I mean it. You're one of the good ones."

Someone punched me in the shoulder from behind. "Hey, I resent that," Visha complained.

"I wouldn't dare call you *good*," I teased.

She cocked her head at me. "Now you're getting the hang of it." She punched me lightly in the arm again. "See you tomorrow, Pendragon." She nodded to Florence. "Good luck, Shen."

"Thanks, Visha," Florence called, from where she was still curled up on my bed. Neville had jumped up and joined her. He looked up as Visha and Theo left, then put his head down on his paws sleepily.

"This little fellow needs a nap," Florence observed, running her hand over the fluffin's back. "He's still growing."

"He's lucky to have you as his mother," I joked.

She smiled. "Well, I'm his mother half the time . . ." She trailed off and I realized the implication that Blake was Neville's part-time father.

I sighed. "I don't want to talk about Blake." Or think about him being responsible for raising a tiny, impressionable fluffin, even half the time.

"Right. What about dragons? Can we talk about that?" Florence asked hesitantly.

"I'll give you the short version." Briefly I filled her in on how my relationship with Nyxaris was going—and how it wasn't.

"Well," she said cautiously, when I was finished, "at least Nyxaris seems open to some communication. That's fairly reasonable—for a dragon, I mean."

"He saved my life," I said bluntly. "And I won't forget that. I owe him."

"But can you keep this going over the year?" Florence asked quietly. "The charade, I mean."

"I don't know. I'm supposed to be a dragon rider. But I really doubt Nyxaris is going to suddenly agree to daily rides." I told her what he'd said about not even thinking about a saddle and she winced.

"No saddle, all right. Well, maybe he'll change his mind about a saddle *and* about bonding with you once you get him more information about what happened to him," she said.

"That's the hope." I sighed.

"You're tired," she said sympathetically. She slid off the bed and scooped up the sleeping Neville. "I'll see you in the morning. You might be in House Drakharrow but we can still eat together in the refectory, right?"

"Let them try and stop us," I said, smiling at her. I had another thought. "Look, what Theo said about Vaughn . . ."

"Yes?"

"Theo was able to get Vaughn transferred to another house even though he'd been selected into Drakharrow."

"Yes, that is unusual. Selection Day is supposed to be final."

"But it's not. Highbloods can do whatever they want," I said impatiently. "We already knew that. It should be no surprise."

Florence frowned. "So what's your point?"

"My point is I want you to talk to Kage for me. About having me moved to House Avari."

Florence's jaw dropped. "What? Are you serious?"

"Of course I'm serious. I could be with you and I'd be away from Blake. It would be perfect."

"But doesn't Blake have to, you know . . . feed?"

I shuddered. I hated thinking about him depending on me for blood. "Yes, but it's just once a week. We have an arrangement." I hoped he'd stick to it, even now. "He could come over to the Avari tower or I could come to him here. We'd figure it out."

"I don't think Blake would like the idea much, Medra," Florence said nervously.

"Leave Blake to me. But you broach the subject if you see Kage before I do, all right?"

Florence nodded anxiously. "I'll try my best. But Kage Tanaka and I . . . we've never really spoken."

"He's intimidating," I agreed. "I know." I sighed. "If you see him, mention it. If not, I'll try to find him tomorrow or later this week."

"You're so bold, Medra," Florence said, her eyes wide. "I'm not sure I'd be if I were in your shoes."

"Thank the Bloodmaiden you aren't in my shoes," I joked.

"I do," she said seriously. She bounced the sleeping fluffin in her arms a little and I heard Neville start to purr. "All right, I'm leaving now. Sleep well."

"You, too," I said, walking her to the door.

She leaned towards me, brushing her lips against my cheek. "I missed you over the summer."

"I missed you, too," I said, my heart suddenly aching. I'd been so lonely. I hadn't even realized just how lonely I'd been until I'd seen her. "Thank you so much for sneaking into the Drakharrow tower. That was very brave."

She looked proud of herself. "It was, wasn't it?"

"I love you, Florence," I said before I could stop myself. I blushed. "You're a dear friend."

She looked surprised for a moment. "I love you, too, Medra. You know that. You're my *best* friend."

I felt like my heart would explode. "No one's ever called me that before," I confessed.

"No?" Florence lifted her chin. "Well, then they missed out. You're an amazing friend." She grinned at me. "See you tomorrow."

The door clicked softly shut behind her. I stood there a moment, staring at it, the silence of my tower room encroaching around me once more. Florence's parting words still lingered. I'd never had a friend like her before. The words she'd used had settled in my chest like a glowing ember, warming places I hadn't even realized were frozen.

I'd lost so much when I'd arrived in Sangratha. I'd lost so much simply by virtue of being *me*. Back in Camelot, I'd been repeatedly told that my aunt Morgan and uncle Draven had loved me. But they'd been away for most of my childhood. There had been Crescent, but he'd never warmed to me. He'd tried to show me affection but deep down, I'd always known he saw me as too different to love.

A lump formed in my throat. Then there was my mentor, Odessa. She'd loved me. I knew that now, even though she hadn't been the kind to speak about her feelings very often. She'd died so I could live. Ever since I'd been born, people had been throwing their lives away so I'd survive. First my mother, then Odessa, then my aunt and uncle had nearly lost theirs. But I didn't need to be saved. I needed to be loved. Florence had taught me that. She'd already taught me so much.

I turned back to my room and went over to the edge of my bed. The sky was dark. Moonlight streamed through the windows, illuminating the dagger that lay on my bedside table.

I'd only spoken to my mother sparingly over the summer. There had been . . . changes in her. Some disturbed me. But I needed her now.

I picked up the blade, its weight familiar yet strange as always. *Are you awake?* I whispered.

A faint hum rose in my mind. Our connection was very different from the rumbling imposing presence that was Nyxaris. Then her voice came, soft and knowing. *Always for you, dear one.*

I exhaled slowly, sitting back down on the bed and holding the dagger in both hands. *I don't even know where to start.*

*The beginning is always a good place*, she suggested. *Or begin with what's weighing on you the most.*

I gave a tired laugh. *I just got back from the tribunal. I rode a dragon.*

I went through the events of the day, explaining in more detail than I'd given to Florence. I knew I'd tell my friend more tomorrow. But today, I hadn't wanted to overwhelm her—or add to her own burdens.

*The dragon frightens you*, my mother suggested. *He killed a man before your eyes.*

*Yes. No. Yes, but not because I think he'll hurt me. At least, not intentionally*, I amended. *It's . . . everything he represents. I don't know if I can be what he needs.*

*We are both new to this world. But despite that, it's clear the bond between dragon and rider was never meant to be easy. He needs you as much as you need him. Even if neither of you wants to admit it.*

I frowned. *Maybe. But this isn't like the bonds of old. There's no one else. No one to train me. Nyxaris doesn't want me as his rider. And he's so lost. So angry.*

There was a pause. *And what about you? Are you so very different? Are you not angry? Are you not lost?*

I winced. She was right, of course. I was drowning in fear and frustration. I felt trapped. So did Nyxaris. I felt alone. But how much more alone must he feel?

*At least I know why I'm angry and who I'm angry at*, I said. *He doesn't even seem to remember what happened to him. Or to the other dragons. I can't give him answers. I'm as in the dark as he is.*

*Then, find them*, my mother said.

I groaned. *It's not that simple and you know it.*

*It is if you make it so.* I could hear her growing impatient—with my limitations or with her own? *You have more resources than you realize. The dragon has memories. Even if he thinks he's forgotten, they could be locked within him even now. And, as you've already guessed, the highbloods are hiding truths they don't want you or any other blightborn to find. So search out those truths. Look everywhere.*

Her words hit me like a slap. *You think I haven't tried? The books Rodriguez gave me last year were worthless. He's as bad as a highblood, keeping his own confidence and not letting me in.*

*Then, make him tell you. Force the truth from him, if you have to.*

My grip on the dagger tightened. *And how exactly am I supposed to do that? He's my professor, Mother.*

*You have a dragon, Medra,* she reminded me. Then her voice softened. *You are stronger than you know. You have already survived what no one else could have. You are not alone.*

I stared down at the blade. Her words were meant to be comforting. But they only reminded me of how much was at stake—not just for me but for everyone around me. *Nyxaris asked me if I'd want to bring the other dragons back,* I murmured. *But I didn't know how to answer that. Would it even be right to try? What if the highbloods just enslaved them again?*

*How did they do that in the first place? You need to find out.* She paused. *Do you trust him?*

*I don't know,* I said honestly. *I want to.*

*Then, start there.* Her voice faded. She was gone.

I set the dagger down on the bedside table and lay back on my bed, staring up at the ceiling. Instead of stars, there was a red canopy over the bed, always reminding me of where I was.

This had started to happen more and more often. Orcades would be there one moment, gone the next. She was . . . less reliable. Her emotions swung sharply.

She'd put me off when I'd suggested we plan a way of setting her free. Now that we knew what had happened the first time thanks to the ritual, I think she was afraid for my sake to have me try again. But I couldn't stop thinking about it. She was fading. Changing. It was my fault. Just like Naveen. Both were my burden, my responsibility.

And so was Nyxaris.

Tomorrow I would start looking for answers. I wasn't a prisoner anymore. I was a student again.

# CHAPTER 9

# BLAKE

The common room of Drakharrow Tower was already filled with noise when I descended the staircase the next morning. The clamor of voices and laughter was like music to my ears. My territory. My house. My rules.

I strolled into the center of the room, turning heads, making sure my presence was noticed. A few of the newer highblood students glanced up and straightened, their eyes glancing over me nervously. Good. That was how it should be: respect through fear. It was a lesson I had been taught growing up. It was a lesson Pendragon had to learn, sooner or later, no matter how stubborn she was. I'd announced some changes this year. Now I saw the highbloods in my house had taken my recent orders to heart.

Thralls knelt at the feet of highblood students, their heads bowed, veins bared for feeding. Across the room, one of the more eager new First Years, a highblood named Laurent, sharp-featured and wiry, was feeding openly. As I walked past, he looked up at me, his mouth smeared with blood. Part of me was disgusted, but I hid my reaction. I chose not to use thralls, but I knew they were an accepted part of highblood life for almost everyone else.

I clapped him on the shoulder. "Enjoying breakfast?"

He smirked. "Always, House Leader."

"Excellent." I turned around slowly, scanning for my quarry. I'd told one of the Second Years to notify me as soon as Pendragon stepped out of her room. They hadn't, so I assumed she had yet to emerge. If she'd already left, I'd be very upset with that Second Year.

But then footsteps rang out from the top of the staircase. I lifted my head and there she was. She looked as if she hadn't slept much. Her fiery hair was more tousled than usual. But she was still carrying herself with that damned rebelliousness I knew all too well.

The room went quiet for a moment as everyone noticed her. The few blightborn students who'd been in the common room had quickly fled as they'd taken in the atmosphere, and I didn't really blame them. I wasn't about to allow anyone in my house to mess with them, but still, it was probably for the best that they didn't witness this next part.

"Well, well, if it isn't the dragon tamer herself," I called loudly, ensuring everyone could hear me.

Pendragon glanced down the stairs. For a second, her eyes widened in surprise. Then I watched as she took in the scene around me—with thralls scattered throughout the room and highbloods in mid-feed. Her lips tightened.

"Good of you to join us," I continued. "We wouldn't want you to be late for your first day of class." I saw her flush slightly: the dig had hit home. Not that I'd be stooping to any of Regan's petty tricks. No, my methods were going to be more . . . direct. "I was just explaining to everyone how impressive your dragon truly is."

She met my gaze. "Really? How surprising. Must have been a short conversation since you know nothing about him."

Nervous laughter rippled through the room and I scowled. "Don't sell yourself short," I said smoothly. "After all, it takes a very talented rider to drive a dragon away so quickly. What was it? One ride and he decided he'd had enough of you? Not that I can really blame him."

Laughter erupted. Laurent snickered obnoxiously. I made a mental note to keep an eye on him. He was trying too hard. Probably a spy for my uncle.

Pendragon didn't stop walking down the stairs, but her jaw tightened and I saw a flame spring to life in her eyes.

"I see you've trained them well, Blake. They laugh even when you're not funny," she said, as she took another step.

"Careful, Pendragon. That attitude won't serve you well here this year. Not in House Drakharrow. Not with me." I gestured around the room at all the highblood students. "You see, I've been generous so far. Feeding from you nicely. Asking politely. But that can change. Perhaps we should have our breakfast with the rest of the group from now on." I lowered my voice a little as she reached the bottom step and shot her a nasty grin. "Tell me the truth now. You'd like that, wouldn't you? Got a little taste of voyeurism and liked it, didn't you?"

Pendragon paled. She knew exactly what I was referring to. Only a bastard would mention it, but so be it: I'd be that bastard.

She didn't stop, heading for the door that led to the hall and to the rest of the academy.

"Oh, don't rush off." I moved swiftly to block her path. "We haven't even gone over the new rules yet. For instance, if you want to stay in my house, you need to start showing the proper respect. Kiss the ring, Pendragon." I held out my hand and showed her the Drakharrow ring I was wearing—a gold dragon eating its own tail. "Come on, now. It's tradition."

She stepped up to me, her chin lifting. "*Respect?* What a strange word coming from someone who thinks humiliation is an effective leadership tactic."

I leaned in slightly. "You have no idea what being under my command really means. But I'd be happy to teach you."

"Thanks, but I'll pass," she said coolly.

The tension between us was as hot as a flame. I could feel the others' eyes on us. They were eating this up. But this next part wasn't for their ears.

"Out," I barked abruptly, my voice echoing through the large room.

Around us students stopped feeding and leaped to their feet, grabbing books and bags. Laurent hesitated, but I glared at him and he hastily headed for the door. The thralls were last to go, but they soon scurried out, heading back to their quarters in the tower.

When the door shut behind the last of them, I turned back to Pendragon. "You know, I've been patient," I said. "More patient than you deserve."

She crossed her arms. "And here I thought you were just biding your time and trying to find a new way to ruin my life."

I ignored the jab and stepped closer. "Here's how this is going to work. You'll stay away from Kage Tanaka. In fact, you'll stay away from anyone belonging to House Avari entirely."

She laughed—a short, bitter sound. "You're serious? What are you going to do if I don't?"

I growled. "Don't push me. We have a balance going on right now. But that can all change."

"Balance? You mean when you take my blood? Right. That's really balanced. Completely normal. Just your average relationship." She shook her head angrily. "How about this? I'll talk to whoever I want to and I'll go wherever I want to and you'll stay the fuck away from me except when it's little doggy's feeding time."

I bristled with rage. "You think this is a fucking joke?"

She sobered. "I don't think any of this is actually funny, no, if that's what you're asking." She tilted her head. "Have you ever stopped to think about it, Blake? About what this so-called bond is doing to us? Look at you. Trying to control me when you don't even *like* me."

I opened my mouth, then closed it again.

"And being forced to feed from me. Why does it have to be like this? Why do we both have to be miserable?"

I snarled. "We don't have to be. This was your decision."

"You mean I could have just complied with your demands like a good little consort? Begged to come into your bed, just like Regan used to? No. That was never going to happen. Not when you acted like drinking me was your damned right." She shook her head almost sadly. "By the gods, look at you. You still don't even think you've done anything wrong, do you?"

I flushed. This wasn't going quite the way I'd planned.

"What if this bond isn't even real? Have you considered it? What if it's just another way for your uncle to pull your strings? If there's a chance we could end this, wouldn't you want to? Think of it. We'd be free." She was staring at me so beseechingly, so eagerly.

Her words hit me like a blow and for a moment I couldn't even respond. To hear her say the words out loud and to my face—it was almost unbearable. And then, all I could see was Kage Tanaka wrapping his arms around her waist as he pulled her from danger. His hands all over her as he danced with her at the ball. His necklace dangling from her slender throat as she walked through the school wearing House Avari colors.

"No," I said coldly. "I wouldn't."

"Then, you really are even more of a monster than I gave you credit for, Blake," she said, her expression turning to disgust. "I don't know what's worse. Thinking you're doing this because you're too scared of your uncle to do anything else. Or thinking you're doing this because you actually like torturing me."

"Oh, it's the latter. Definitely the latter," I said coolly.

The door behind us creaked open and Theo's voice broke the moment. "Medra!" Theo stepped into the common room, his gaze flicking back and forth between us uncertainly.

"Come on, Medra," he said, finally, jerking his head towards the door. "Breakfast is waiting. Visha and Florence are already in the refectory."

I clenched my jaw. Florence Shen. Pendragon's friend who was now in House Avari.

And Visha Vaidya? She was a Drakharrow through and through. The girl knew better. Hell, I was considering making her my second. Now she'd just jeopardized that. As for my cousin? Theo was blatantly ignoring what I'd told him to do. We'd have to speak again later.

Pendragon hesitated, her eyes lingering on me for a split second. Then she brushed past, leaving me standing alone in the middle of the room. No matter what I did, she slipped further and further from my grasp. And the truth was, it hurt so much I didn't know whether to hold on tighter—or just let her go.

# CHAPTER 10

# MEDRA

We were supposed to be meeting Visha and Florence in the refectory but once Theo and I were out in the hall, I stopped. "I don't think I feel up to breakfast. I think I'll just go straight to class."

"Don't let Blake get to you," Theo protested. "He's just . . ." He trailed off.

"Being an asshole? Like he usually is?" I watched Theo's expression of discomfort. "Look, I know he's your cousin, but—"

"It's not just that he's my cousin," Theo said quickly. "I know him. I know what he's been through. He's had a tough time of it, Medra. But despite that, he's stood up for me, time and again."

"Stood up for you to who?" I demanded.

Theo didn't answer immediately. But it was obvious. "Blake's been through a lot," Theo repeated stubbornly.

"I'm sure he has," I said, as gently as I could. "But he doesn't seem to have learned from it. He might be kind to you, but he doesn't extend that same kindness to others."

"You have to understand," Theo implored me. "Blake really believes you're his mate. You're his only consort now. He cast off Regan for you. You're his sole source. That kind of a relationship is everything to a highblood. He's completely dependent on you." He shifted awkwardly. "To know you don't want him back, that you'd reject him completely if you could . . . Well, it must be driving him mad. Especially a protective highblood male like Blake."

"*Protective?* I think you mean *possessive.*" I shook my head. "My relationship with Blake is so toxic. I didn't want to be tied to your cousin, Theo. I didn't want to hurt him. But I didn't get a choice in any of this. You say Blake's feeling desperate? Well, so am I. And I'm going to do everything in my power to try to end this for both our sakes."

"If Blake finds out he'll go nuts," Theo said miserably.

My lips twitched. "More nuts?"

Theo grimaced. "You haven't seen anything yet, believe me. Besides, Medra, what's the point of going down this road? You heard what everyone said at the tribunal. It's impossible."

"Well, your people also thought the dragons were gone forever, didn't they?" I pointed out. "And that turned out to be false. So when they tell me bonds can't be broken, forgive me if I don't pay very close attention."

Theo smiled slightly. "Fair, I guess."

I wanted to point out that Theo wasn't the one who had to hold weekly feeding sessions with Blake. But I realized I was encroaching on some vulnerable territory. Highbloods were prickly about the idea of blightborn not *wanting* to be fed from. It was almost as if it hurt their feelings or something. Even Theo, who was so progressive in most other ways, seemed to still have at least some of this mentality.

"I'll see you in the refectory later, okay? Maybe at lunch." I touched his shoulder and forced a smile. "Good luck today."

He nodded and then slouched away, still looking morose and reminding me of Naveen a little. Except Theo's hair was perfectly styled and he wore expensive, tailored clothes. And he was a highblood, of course.

I wondered who Theo had fed from this morning. He was looking a little paler than usual. Did he space his feedings out like Blake did, waiting as long as possible? Did he dislike using thralls like

Blake had claimed to? I wasn't sure these were things I should ask. But I was pretty sure I needed the answers if I was going to try to develop a real friendship with Theo and Visha.

I made my way through Bloodwing's halls, purposely skirting around the Dragon Court. I wasn't ready to see that place again so soon. The thought of the remaining three stone dragons still sitting there frozen made my skin crawl. So, instead, I took the cloister path, walked to the end of the arched tunnel and pushed through a side door that led outside. I breathed in the sharp, salty air of the island. The morning sun was beginning to break through the clouds, casting a soft glow over the rocky cliffs and grassy slopes surrounding the castle. Everything was still green and vivid. The leaves hadn't begun to change color yet.

It felt strange to be leaving the castle to attend a class. I walked slowly down the pebbled path towards the greenhouse that lay nestled at the base of the hill. As I grew closer, I eyed it curiously. This was the nearest I'd ever come to the greenhouse, though, of course, we could see it through various windows from inside the castle. Up close, the building was larger than I'd thought, with an arched roof and a beautiful glass-and-iron frame. The structure looked surprisingly delicate for such a functional building.

The breeze whipped at my cloak and I pulled it around me. I'd chosen my outfit with practicality in mind. My fitted black trousers were tucked into knee-high boots, perfect for the muddy, mossy hillside. Overtop I wore a thick soft black wool sweater—free of House Drakharrow insignia. I'd torn off the house motto patch that morning. It had left a slightly frayed spot, but no one had noticed so far. I'd worried Blake might, but I needn't have been concerned: he'd been too busy bullying me that morning to notice what I was wearing.

A crowd of students were already gathered around the greenhouse. I saw Florence. She stood near the entrance, holding a stack of books, her face lit up with excitement. It gave me pause to see her in black and silver and not the blue and gray First Year colors.

But she was in House Avari now. Considering how Blake had acted that morning, maybe it was for the best. I wondered how she'd fare with Kage as her House Leader.

"Medra!" Florence called, spotting me. She waved enthusiastically and came towards me, juggling her stack of books.

"How did you beat me here?" I asked her. "I thought you were having breakfast in the refectory."

"You weren't there so I came here instead. I didn't want to be late for my first class," she said, beaming. "I can't wait to see what we'll be working on with Professor Allenvale. My mother says she's brilliant. She's written so many treatises on alchemical applications in battle."

I smiled at her enthusiasm. "I'm glad one of us is excited."

She tilted her head, her smile faltering. "What about you? You don't have to be worried about Regan this year and there's no chance she'll be in a herbology class. But is everything else all right?"

"I just came from a bit of a run-in with Blake," I admitted. "But don't worry about it. I'll tell you about that later. Let's just focus on class for now."

She nodded, but her concerned expression lingered on me and made me wish I hadn't said anything. One of us should have a good first day and I wanted it to be Florence.

I looked around, scanning the faces of our fellow classmates. To my surprise, we were a mix of blightborn and highbloods from all four houses. I even spotted another familiar face: Lunaya Orphos. She stood near the edge of the group, her straight silver-blond hair hanging around her shoulders. She'd fixed her gaze dreamily on the greenhouse like she was peering into some other world.

Before I could decide whether or not to say hello and introduce myself to Lysander's sister, a cheerful, melodic voice broke through the chatter. "Good morning, everyone!"

A woman was approaching. I assumed this must be Professor Vasanti Allenvale. The professor's arms were full of parchment scrolls and herb clippings. She even had a potted plant precariously balanced on top of everything. Our instructor was younger than I'd expected. She was also a highblood, which surprised me as she was co-teaching the class with Professor Rodriguez. But then, Rodriguez seemed to get along with some of his highblood colleagues at least some of the time—such as Professor Sankara.

Professor Allenvale's long hair was pulled back into a practical braid. Smudges of dirt streaked her robe which were trimmed in the purple and gold of House Orphos. A pair of round gold spectacles perched at the tip of her brown nose, giving her an air of sunny disarray. I glanced at Florence and grinned to myself as I saw her pushing her own, black-rimmed glasses self-consciously up the bridge of her nose as she watched the professor.

But the most surprising thing about Professor Allenvale was the color of her hair. When she turned and I could see her braid more clearly, I noticed that the long strands were streaked with purple and green highlights. I blinked. I'd never seen a highblood with dyed hair before. It seemed so out of place at Bloodwing where tradition loomed large over everything. But the more I thought about it, the more I wondered why students didn't do it more often.

"Well, it's so nice to see you all—and on time, too. Pardon my tardiness. I hope you're all ready for a wonderful term together," the professor said brightly, adjusting the scrolls and other items in her arms. "Let's not waste any time, shall we? Follow me inside the greenhouse and I'll show you where the magic happens." She beamed at us. "Well, figuratively speaking. Alchemy is mostly a science, after all."

"But there is some magic to it, isn't there, Professor Allenvale?" Florence asked eagerly, as she hurried up to the professor and lifted the potted plant out of her arms. "Here, let me help you with that."

"Thank you so much, Miss—?"

"Shen," Florence said, beaming back at her. "Florence Shen. And it's an honor to meet you, Professor Allenvale."

"Ah, yes, you must be Jia's daughter. What a lovely woman.

An incredibly helpful librarian. Why, when I was working on a new paper for publication this summer on the synergistic effects of herbal compounds for wound salves, her insight was invaluable. I can only imagine how proud of you she must be. Professor Rodriguez mentioned to me that you were on a healer's and a strategist's path." Professor Allenvale tilted her head. "Your timetable must be very full."

Florence flushed with pride. "Thank you, Professor. Though, I'm not sure I'll be able to keep up the double course load for much longer. But it's just so hard to choose one specialization."

"Well, perhaps this class will help to sway you," Professor Allenvale said, her eyes twinkling. "Now, tell me, Miss Shen, what do you think of magic's role in alchemy? Necessary or simply supplementary?"

Florence didn't hesitate. "I think that magic can enhance alchemical results but is rarely required. Understanding the natural properties of herbs and how to properly combine them is the foundation. Magic is a bonus."

"An excellent perspective," Professor Allenvale said. "I like to think alchemy is a science first and foremost, grounded in experimentation and study. Magic can amplify its potential but some of the best alchemists I've ever known had little to no magical ability."

Considering how little aptitude for the arcane Professor Wispwood had been able to detect in me last year, I was encouraged to hear this.

From the other side of the group, a soft voice chimed in. "And perhaps," Lunaya Orphos said dreamily, "alchemy also teaches us to appreciate the magic that is inherent in nature itself. Some things don't need to be enhanced. They already hold more power than we could ever hope to understand."

Florence was nodding thoughtfully beside me. "That's a good point. I'm still very new to alchemy, but already it seems as if it can sometimes feel like uncovering secrets rather than creating something new."

Professor Allenvale clapped her hands together happily. "I couldn't have put it better myself. Beautifully put, the two of you. Alchemy is indeed a delicate dance between discovery and creation."

They'd lost me a little but I was thrilled that Professor Allenvale was so kind—and so appreciative of Florence's sharp mind.

Allenvale was looking around at the rest of us. "Now, let's put some theory into practice. We'll start by forming groups. Let's see, I think I'll have you in groups of three. I'll assign you so we can ensure a good mix of skills and perspectives." She scanned the group, her eyes landing on where I stood close to Florence. "Oh! Hello there. Red hair." She beamed. "I suppose you must be Miss Pendragon."

"Yes," I said, a little nervously.

"Excellent. You'll pair up with Miss Shen." Her eyes flicked over to Lunaya. "And Miss Orphos, would you care to join them?"

Lunaya drifted towards us, a sweet smile on her face. "I'd be delighted."

"Wonderful." As Professor Allenvale organized the rest of the students into groups, I exchanged a glance with Florence. I wasn't quite sure what to make of Lunaya, but she certainly seemed agreeable enough—especially for a highblood. There was something about the girl's presence that was sweet and calming.

Professor Allenvale clapped her hands to get our attention. "Your first task is to familiarize yourself with three key plants we'll be working with this term. Please choose a table. At each one, you'll find some samples of mirthleaf, shadowroot, and emberfern. Each one has unique properties that form the basis of a great number of restorative concoctions. I want you to observe them, study them, take some descriptive notes, and prepare to share what you've gleaned with the rest of the group in a few minutes. Some of you may have had personal experiences with these herbs already so I invite you to share those insights."

As we moved towards our worktable, I leaned close to Florence. "Her hair is amazing. Is that a House Orphos thing?"

Florence looked thoughtfully at our instructor. "Well, sort of. Professor Allenvale usually teaches at a university in the Sable Isles. Most of the students who go there are from House Orphos. And apparently things are less formal there. A little more open."

I glanced at the professor and her purple and green streaks. "That must be nice."

We approached the table where small pots of the assigned plants waited.

Not for the first time, I wondered how and why I'd really wound up in this class. I was thrilled to be with Florence, of course, but I wasn't on a healer's path like she was. I wasn't sure how any of this would apply to dragon riding. I had a moderate interest in herbalism and botany, and I'd received decent marks in Professor Rodriguez's Restoration class. But I'd been surprised to hear The Alchemist's Garden was on my timetable.

I eyed the potted plants curiously. Mirthleaf had delicate, feather-like leaves that shimmered faintly, as if they'd been dusted with gold. The plant's scent was slightly citrusy.

Florence leaned in, touching a leaf gently. "This one is used in energy restoratives, isn't it?"

"Yes," Lunaya agreed. "But it's also an antidote to certain poisons if distilled properly."

I looked back and forth between the two girls, already impressed. They seemed to know a lot about alchemy. I wasn't sure what I could bring to the equation. "Why don't I be our notetaker?" I offered quickly. My handwriting wasn't as nice as Florence's, but I figured it was one way I could contribute to the group. I quickly scribbled down everything they'd said about mirthleaf and then glanced at the next pot. Shadowroot was very different. The plant had dark, almost black leaves with a faint bluish sheen to them.

"This one doesn't exactly scream *healing*," I observed, half expecting them to tell me I was wrong.

Florence grinned. "You're right. It's a tricky one. Shadowroot can be toxic in large doses, but it's a critical ingredient in remedies for frostbite."

I studiously wrote down what she'd said.

"It's said to grow best under a new moon," Lunaya added suddenly. "My house sometimes uses it in dreamweaving potions."

I stared at the highblood girl. Was she supposed to be telling us this?

Florence looked fascinated. "That's right. You're in Year Two now, too, aren't you, Lunaya? And since you're a highblood, you'll be taking House-related magic courses."

Lunaya nodded slowly.

"What's your magic course called?" I asked, curious.

"The Veil and the Mirror," Lunaya replied, soft-spoken as always. I couldn't imagine this girl ever bellowing. I wondered what Blake would make of her. "It involves exploring the meaning of our dreams and searching for portents in the world around us."

"Your house motto is *Blood of Dreamers*, right?" I remembered. Lunaya nodded.

"But what does it mean, exactly?" Florence asked, looking as curious as I was. "Can you really control what you dream?"

"Many of us learn to do so. That part is quite simple," Lunaya replied. "It's stepping into the dreams of others that's more of a challenge. That and conjuring dreams of the future."

"Dreams of the future?" I said sharply. "Can you really do that?"

"I'm not sure if I have a true calling," Lunaya said, reverting back to her dreamy attitude. "But my professor says I have a knack for deciphering portents. I suppose we'll see in time."

I thought of the other three houses. I knew House Drakharrow specialized in blood magic. As I'd already managed to do some blood magic of my own last year with my mother's help, I wasn't too impressed with the concept. It was unpredictable, powerful, and dangerous as far as I was concerned. But still, I wondered what exactly the blood magic courses entailed.

"House Avari specializes in magic to do with shadows, illusions, and other kinds of manipulations," Florence observed. "Of course, since I'm not a highblood I won't be able to take those courses." She sounded almost disappointed.

"And House Mortis?" I lowered my voice. "Are they really . . . necromancers?"

"They learn to manipulate the dead, yes," Lunaya said complacently. "But most of these magical courses are irrelevant."

"Irrelevant?" Florence sounded almost offended. "Is any knowledge really irrelevant?"

"Most of our houses specialized in battle magic that could be used against one another and that was amplified by our house dragons," Lunaya continued as if she hadn't heard Florence. "Sangratha is at peace, so the magic is mostly theoretical. Some of it hasn't been actively used in centuries. I'm not sure my professor can even practice half of what he talks about. But the theory is fascinating, to be sure."

"I can only imagine," Florence said enviously. She sighed. "Well, shall we move on? This plant isn't going to talk about itself."

"Emberfern," Lunaya said, reaching out a hand to brush a leaf. "Careful. The sap can burn you if you're not protected."

"Good to know," I muttered, keeping my own hands away from the plant.

"Though, you've ridden a dragon," Lunaya said, looking at me with a small smile. "So I suppose you're not afraid of fire."

"It's used in tinctures to treat hypothermia," Florence said. She cleared her throat and I remembered I was supposed to be writing this down. I scribbled quickly. "And in salves to stimulate circulation. But it can be volatile, so it's often paired with mirthleaf to stabilize it."

"House Drakharrow would use it on their dragon riders," Lunaya said suddenly. "When prepared correctly, it was said to be able to amplify courage and strength."

I thought about what Blake had told me about the Infernus

dragons. How their flames were the fiercest but they were prone to volatility, making them dangerous to handle. Is that why House Drakharrow riders needed such a concoction?

As I finished writing down what Lunaya had said, she turned to me. "Medra, I wanted to tell you how happy I was that you weren't executed."

The comment was so sudden, I almost dropped my quill. Beside me, Florence froze. I had the sudden impulse to laugh.

"Um, thank you, Lunaya?" I managed to say. "That's very kind of you. I'm glad I wasn't executed, too."

Beside me, Florence made a choking noise, but Lunaya didn't seem to notice. "My brother and I were both very relieved. Lysander said what he could during the tribunal, but he knew no one would listen to him. It makes us both happy to see you back at Bloodwing. Alive."

For a highblood, her words were so genuine, so guileless. I found myself smiling at her. "I appreciated what Lysander said at the tribunal very much. Your brother didn't have to stand up for me, but he did. It means a lot."

"Lysander believes in doing the right thing, even when it's hard or goes against tradition," Lunaya said simply. "And so do I."

There was a moment of silence as we looked at one another.

"Well, um, I've finished my notes." I glanced around. "I think Professor Allenvale is about to begin."

As the professor began to call upon each group in turn, surveying us for our observations, I couldn't help but wonder just which highblood traditions Lysander and Lunaya were ready to discard.

"Hungry, are we?" Florence asked with a laugh, as my stomach rumbled.

Our class had just ended and all of the other students were streaming back into Bloodwing.

"Starving," I moaned. "Nothing good ever came from skipping breakfast." Not to mention I hadn't even grabbed a cup of kava.

She laughed. "Thought you would be. Here, I grabbed this from the refectory buffet table." She pulled a parcel wrapped in brown paper from her schoolbag. "I thought we could have a picnic outside." She looked at me sympathetically. "No kava, though."

"That's all right. I'll swing by after classes and grab a mug . . . or two," I said, smiling at her. I unwrapped the parcel she handed me to reveal fresh brown bread, mellow orange cheese, slices of ham, and a cup of berries. "Perfect."

We ate lunch on a flat rock overlooking the churning sea. The waves below crashed against the rocky shoreline. Seabirds flew overhead. The sun was out and it soon became so hot I shrugged my cloak off and sat on it instead. I didn't want to go back inside. I lay back on the rock, thinking about Lunaya and Lysander Orphos.

Florence sat cross-legged, flipping through one of her books. "It's nice out here, isn't it?"

"Yes. Let's live on the beach and never go back to Bloodwing," I grumbled.

Florence hesitated. "Is Blake really going to try to make your life worse?"

"Oh, definitely," I said immediately. "He seems intent on it." I glanced at her, trying to decide whether to tell her about the scene in the Drakharrow common room that morning. But the last thing I wanted to do was make her worry about me more. The rhythm of the sea filled the silence.

"What class do you have next?" Florence asked finally.

"That history class. You're really not in it?"

She shook her head. "But I'll walk you there. I know my way around the castle better than you do."

I'd learned a lot last year, but she was right. And the history class was listed as being in a new location I didn't think I'd visited before.

A little while later, Florence left me at the bottom of a winding staircase. No other students we'd passed had been going this way.

I was the only one at the bottom of the stairs that supposedly led to the cliffside wing where Historical Perspectives would be held.

I made my way up the stairs and emerged into a narrow corridor. A single door, reinforced with iron, stood at the very end. I pushed it open and stepped into a strange classroom unlike any I'd seen before. The room was semicircular and the far wall was entirely open to the sea beyond. Tall roughly hewn red sandstone pillars were all that separated the classroom from the jagged cliff's edge. A breeze swept through the space, rustling papers on the desk that stood off in one corner.

Professor Amina Hassan stood behind the desk, her back ramrod straight, her cane gripped tightly in one hand. Her expression was as severe as ever as she looked at me.

"You're late," she snapped, tapping her cane against the stone floor as she walked towards me. "Sit down."

I knew I was a few minutes early if anything, but I didn't bother arguing. There were low stone benches arranged in rows and I took a seat on one. I glanced around, realizing the room was still empty. And if I was supposedly late . . .

"Where is everyone else?" I asked.

"There is no one else. This is a private session."

I stiffened. "A private session. Why?"

"You're a very privileged girl," Hassan said, her lips curling in a way that told me she thought I was spoiled and arrogant. "Lord Drakharrow has arranged this class for you. He believes you require special instruction."

I felt my stomach drop. "How kind of him. But I really don't think that's necessary."

"That's not for you to decide," Professor Hassan said.

"But—"

"Headmaster Kim has approved your course of study. Would you like to take it up with him?" she snapped. "Or perhaps you'd like to return to the tribunal?"

"The tribunal?"

"Yes. It's my understanding that Lord Drakharrow had your timetable approved by the other members of the Tribunal Panel. They all agreed this course was essential for a dragon rider of Sangratha." She smiled thinly.

I knew when I was outnumbered. Balling my hands into fists in my lap, I watched as Professor Hassan began to pace back and forth across the cavern-like room.

"This class is to teach you the history and purpose of dragon riders. To ensure you understand your place in the hierarchy of our world. Riders have always been subordinate to highbloods. You are a tool, Miss Pendragon, and so is your dragon."

My jaw twitched. "I don't think Nyxaris would agree with that assessment."

Hassan narrowed her eyes. "Nyxaris is an animal. He is an asset. He exists to serve. As do you."

"He's not a tool. He's intelligent—wiser than we are. And he doesn't serve anyone," I shot back.

Professor Hassan gave a tight-lipped smile. "If that is really true, you will find yourself in a great deal of trouble this year, Miss Pendragon. You *will* learn to control him. To command him according to highblood wishes. That is your duty as a rider."

She moved to stand by one of the sandstone pillars. "The tribunal—and by extension, the four regents—expect you to prove your worth to them this year. You are here not simply to learn but to show results. You are here to show them that your dragon can be controlled. Do not forget it was you who made that claim in the first place."

With a sinking feeling, I knew she was right. I'd done it to buy time. Could my time be up already? "I thought the tribunal had already made their decision. My life was spared and I was to attend Bloodwing again."

"Yes, but their decision was not an end but a beginning." Hassan's lips twisted. "Do not delude yourself, Miss Pendragon. You are still under intense scrutiny."

My heart hammered. She was blatantly admitting they were spying on me now?

"Failure to meet the tribunal's expectations will have serious consequences," she finished.

"What kind of consequences?" I asked warily.

"For one," she said, her voice hard, "your freedom. It is conditional. If the House Leaders feel you are not making adequate progress with Nyxaris, your movements will be restricted once again. You will be confined to your quarters. Your access to anyone outside House Drakharrow will be limited. You'll be allowed out only for essential reasons."

I tried to force myself to stay calm. "What exactly are they expecting me to do?"

"You'll demonstrate you have control. You'll summon the dragon when you are commanded to do so. You'll practice and execute specific maneuvers."

Military ones, no doubt. I could only imagine where this would lead. If they had their way, I'd be a tool to hunt and kill and so would Nyxaris.

"Not to mention teaching the dragon to demonstrate the proper submission," Professor Hassan went on.

I did *not* see that going over well.

"You'll prove that the beast obeys you." Hassan's cane struck the floor for emphasis. "Your first public evaluation has already been scheduled for next month. You'll be expected to showcase a number of maneuvers which are of strategic importance. I suggest you start preparing immediately."

I stared at her. "And if I can't?"

"Can't? You can't afford that possibility, I assure you. Understand this, Miss Pendragon. The tribunal spared you because you represent potential. They want to see if that potential can be harnessed for the good of the realm. If they cannot get results by using the carrot, then they will turn to the stick."

"What the hell is that supposed to mean?" I demanded.

Hassan's smile was scathing. What a horrid woman: she was enjoying this. "Do I really need to explain it? Do you think your friends will be immune to punishment if you fail? Little Florence Shen, for example. A brilliant pupil. But do you believe she is untouchable? Do you want her to end up like your friend Naveen?"

I froze. Naveen's face flashed in my mind. The way his entire essence had been distorted into something twisted and monstrous. The awful moment when I'd been forced to kill him during the Consort Games. My stomach churned.

"He failed and so did you," Hassan said bluntly, dismissing my pain and Naveen's life. "Mr. Sharma could not meet Bloodwing's high standards. If you think the four great houses would hesitate to make another example of one of your friends, you are gravely mistaken."

I felt dizzy. I gripped the stone bench with both hands. *Florence.* They wouldn't. They couldn't.

Professor Hassan took a step closer and leaned towards me. "Your defiance endangers everyone who associates with you."

I couldn't help it. I looked up at her, hoping for some measure of understanding. "But, Professor, Nyxaris isn't just some instrument to be used. He's an intelligent creature, just like you or me. He has more wisdom and experience than any of us, including you and Lord Drakharrow."

Hassan's eyes flashed. "Careful, Miss Pendragon."

"But it's the truth," I said, barreling on. "You're asking me to force him into obedience—as if I even could. He's not a weapon. He's not our property. I'm not going to treat him like one just to make the tribunal happy. Have you forgotten what happened to Lord Mortis?" Maybe that's what the tribunal needed to be reminded of.

"You insolent child," Hassan hissed, her voice trembling with fury. "You dare to mention Lord Mortis to me? As far as I am concerned, you ought to have been executed for his death. You believe you're above centuries of tradition? That your feelings or those of that beast's outweigh the will of our masters? You are lucky to still be alive."

I knew she believed every word she said. I tried to breathe slowly. "I think that we need to be patient and treat Nyxaris with respect. It's easy to preach obedience when you've never had to earn it. Nyxaris isn't a mindless creature we can order around. But then, I guess that's something you wouldn't understand, is it?" The words were out of my mouth before I could stop them.

We stared at each other.

"You ungrateful little brat of a girl," Hassan spat. Her hand was shaking on her cane. "You dare to lecture me? As if you have any idea what it means to serve. To truly sacrifice for the greater good. You think your precious dragon sets you apart, makes you special? All it makes you is dangerous. You are a loose cannon in a world that needs order!"

I flinched but didn't reply.

"I have spent my life proving myself worthy of the highbloods' trust," she continued, her voice trembling. "I didn't stumble into power. I earned what I have. Every moment, every opportunity."

I felt a twinge of guilt. She was right that I hadn't earned what I had. But I refused to back down. "So what you're saying is that you've earned the right to let them use you." The words slipped out, sharp and cutting.

Hassan's eyes widened with disbelief, then narrowed with rage. "You arrogant little whelp," she hissed. "You think you can lecture me on loyalty? You know nothing."

"I understand more than you think," I shot back. "I woke up in a burned-out village your precious highbloods had destroyed. I saw Naveen die because he'd done nothing worse than fail a few courses at this fucked-up school. And now you're telling me they'd threaten Florence, an innocent girl, and that sits right with you? You think she'd deserve that? That's cruelty, not sacrifice. Look at you, defending it."

Hassan's composure cracked. "The world *is* cruel, Miss Pendragon. Those who survive do so by aligning themselves with those in power, not by defying them. If you insist on waging this futile little rebellion of yours, you'll be crushed and so will everyone you care about. I'll be happy to stand on the sidelines and watch."

She moved towards the door. "I'll make my first report to the tribunal. When they decide your fate, you'll have no one to blame but yourself."

The door slammed shut behind her and I stood there, staring at it, my heart pounding. I'd just burned a bridge with Professor Hassan. Was our private class over before it had even begun? I'd made things harder for myself. Harder for Florence. For everyone I cared about. I couldn't let what had happened to Naveen happen again. Not to Florence. No matter what it took, no matter how much groveling I had to do, I couldn't let my friend pay the price for my rebellious tongue.

But how could I prove control over Nyxaris when he'd barely speak to me?

I turned towards the open sea, watching the sun on the horizon. If I wanted to keep Florence safe, I needed to do what the tribunal wanted. And if I wanted Nyxaris to cooperate, I'd need leverage. Something that would show him I was trying to find the answers he needed. Something I could use to gain his trust. I needed it before the tribunal's patience ran out.

# CHAPTER 11

# MEDRA

My head was pounding from the disaster that had been my history class with Professor Hassan. All I wanted was a steaming mug of kava to wake me up. The thought of the strong, black liquid—maybe with a hefty teaspoon of sugar or two—sent a pang of longing through me. I had to start researching dragon history in the library that very night and kava might be the only thing that would keep me going.

I'd just rounded a corner on my way to the refectory, already picturing the way the mug would feel in my hands, when a group of students suddenly blocked my path. I blinked slowly. They were all blightborn. Their stiff postures and narrowed eyes struck me as unusual. Something was wrong.

"What's happened?" I said immediately. "What's wrong?"

When none of them answered, I shrugged and moved to step around them. But one of the students moved to block me, a tall, burly boy with dark brown hair that curled over his ears and a small scar that stood out against his pale cheek. His broad shoulders and clenched fists gave me pause. He looked as if he were ready for a fight.

"Excuse me," I said cautiously. "Is something wrong? Are you all right?"

"All right? You've got some bloody nerve asking that," he said, his voice low.

I looked at the other students, unsure what to make of this boy's hostility or theirs. "What are you talking about?" I asked as gently as I could, genuinely confused.

One of the other students standing behind him, a pretty girl with tightly braided black hair, stepped forward, her lips twisting in a sneer. "You really don't know?"

I was starting to get annoyed. "No. But perhaps you could enlighten me. Either that, or please get out of my way."

The tall boy took a step closer. Too close for comfort. "What about the fact that you woke a dragon? A damned dragon. For them!"

I froze. "For them?"

"The highbloods," he snapped. He looked around nervously as if making sure none were around. He lowered his voice a little but kept going. "The same ones who used dragons to crush anyone who dared to stand up against them. The same ones who kept our people in chains. Now you've gone and brought their ultimate weapon back." He shook his head as he looked down at me in disgust. "You're a traitor."

The other students nodded in agreement, clearly just as resentful towards me as the boy was.

What was going on here? After what I'd learned last year, I hadn't thought such rebellious talk was even possible. After that night in the Sanctum when I'd witnessed the ritual, I'd made Blake confess that the blightborn were being manipulated. Kept compliant by an insidious form of highblood magic, similar to thrallweave.

Part of me was kind of impressed. These blightborn students had spirit and I admired that. But they were also going to get themselves killed if they weren't careful.

"Look," I said, keeping my voice low and trying to be patient. "You have to be careful with what you say or you're going to get yourselves into trouble."

"Is that so?" the boy sneered.

"Yes, look at where you are," I hissed. "Besides, I can assure you, Nyxaris doesn't belong to the highbloods."

"Doesn't he?" the girl with braids scoffed. "They'll make sure he does soon. And then how many of us will he kill with you on his back? You'll have blightborn blood on your hands in no time. Unless someone stops you before it's too late."

I stared at her, reeling at the implications of what she'd just said. Did I really have to fear my own people now? I was half-fae, but I'd always felt aligned with the blightborn. There were no fae in this world and I was half-mortal, after all.

I held up my hands in an effort to keep the peace. "I understand why you're upset, but you have to believe me. I don't want to hurt any blightborn and I have no intention of doing so."

The burly boy cut me off with a harsh laugh. He was starting to get on my nerves. "Your intentions don't mean a thing. You've just made it easier for them to keep us under their boots."

I opened my mouth to respond but I could see the tensions in the group were rising fast. The blightborn students' faces were tense with anger and fear.

"End her," I heard one student mutter. I could see some were clenching and unclenching their fists, shifting on their feet. They were nervous and tense and looking for some sort of solution. They wanted their fear to go away.

They wanted *me* to go away. I wondered just how far they were ready to go to make that happen.

"What's going on here?"

The voice came from behind me, calm but commanding. Every blightborn head snapped towards the sound.

I turned to see Kage Tanaka standing in the hallway. His coal-dark eyes swept over the group, taking in every detail. He seemed as composed as always. But there was something about the deliberate stillness of his stance that made it clear he didn't need to raise his voice or make a single threat to command respect—or fear.

"Fuck," I heard the burly boy mutter. His gaze dropped to the floor.

The other blightborn students seemed to be deflating. They shuffled backwards awkwardly. Only the tall, burly boy and the girl with braids remained, their stances still defiant even under Kage's gaze.

"This doesn't concern you, Tanaka," the tall boy said suddenly, surprising me with his boldness.

Kage raised an eyebrow and came slowly to stand by my side. His beautiful lips curved in a humorless smile. "Really? Because it looks to me as if you're threatening the rider. As House Avari has a stake in Miss Pendragon's safety and that of her dragon, I think what you're doing concerns me quite a bit."

The girl with the braids stepped forward, her voice shaking a little but still stubborn. "This is a blightborn matter."

"Wrong," Kage snapped. His gaze lingered on the girl, then shifted to the others. "Some of you are in my house, aren't you? That makes your behavior *my* responsibility. And I don't tolerate insubordination."

Some of the students looked as if they wanted to bolt. I had no doubt Kage would remember every face.

"Please," I said, my voice low. "Let's defuse the situation, not escalate it."

Kage glanced at me. Then he gave an almost imperceptible nod.

"You don't understand what it's like for us," the broad-shouldered boy burst out. "You don't understand what this means for blightborn." He pointed a finger at me. "She's a traitor to her own kind."

"Your kind?" Kage sniffed. "The rider's always been one of a kind, if you ask me. But you're right, perhaps I don't understand. But here's what *you* don't understand. If you attack Miss Pendragon, if you so much as touch her, there will be consequences that you won't walk away from. Do you understand me?"

The boy muttered something under his breath, then nodded stiffly.

Kage looked over the group, his expression stone-cold. "Leave.

All of you. If I see anything like this again, you won't be dealing with just me next time. This sort of thing won't be tolerated in your houses—or at Bloodwing. Move along."

The girl with the braids was the first to turn and hurry away. The others followed her lead, some with nervous glances back at Kage. The tall, burly boy was the last to leave, his face still a mask of resentment.

Kage watched them go, then turned to me. "I've made a note of their houses. I'll report the incident to the other House Leaders. They'll be punished. Have no doubt about that."

"No," I said quickly, putting a hand on his arm. "No. Please don't do that. I don't want them punished."

Kage looked down at me, surprise in his eyes.

"I appreciate the gesture, but you didn't have to do that," I said.

"Yes, I did," he said evenly. "And you're welcome."

I grimaced. "I suppose I owe you a few *thank-yous* at this point."

"Well, who's keeping track?" He grinned suddenly and I almost gasped. His face was transformed. I'd noticed Kage rarely smiled, and when he did it was a calm smile, carefully controlled. Now he looked almost mischievous. He took a step closer towards me, his presence commanding, yes, but not overwhelming or threatening. Unlike Blake, who seemed to need to dominate every space he entered with the sheer force of his will, Kage's strength lay in the quiet control he radiated. He tilted his head, studying me. "Why didn't you want them punished? You'd be well within your rights to demand it."

I shrugged awkwardly. "Because they're scared. And they're not wrong, are they? I don't know all of the details of dragon history, but clearly their parents or grandparents must have told them something and it wasn't good. The highbloods haven't exactly given them a reason to feel truly safe either, have they?"

Kage's expression remained neutral, but I caught a glimmer of amusement in his eyes. "You're an interesting contradiction, aren't you, Medra Pendragon?"

"What do you mean?" I asked warily.

He moved and the torchlight hit his face, illuminating the sharp angles of his cheekbones, the perfect symmetry of his handsome face, the distinct contrast between his pale highblood hair and his obsidian eyes. I had to admit, Kage Tanaka was a stunning man. Different from Blake, yes. No less attractive in his own way.

"You speak as if you're one of them," he observed, his voice carrying a hint of curiosity. "And yet, you're not. You're the rider of a dragon. The only one in all of Sangratha. You're not like them. You're not like me. You're not like anyone."

I stiffened. "Maybe I carry parts of all of you. Why does there need to be such a division between us, anyhow?"

Kage shrugged. "I didn't write the rules. But you and I both know those with power always rise to the top." His expression became more contemplative. "You should be more careful. You have no idea what your dragon's awakening has set in motion."

I frowned. "What do you mean by that?"

His eyes scanned mine, as if deciding how much to share. "My grandmother has a theory. She believes the essence of magic in the world has shifted with Nyxaris's awakening. It began the moment he stirred."

I tried to process his words. "Shifted how?"

He gestured to the now-empty hallway. "You saw what they were like just now."

"You mean that shouldn't have been possible?" I guessed, taking a risk. "Not with the compliance magic the highbloods use to control blightborn. To keep them in line."

He nodded. "There are many justifications for its use. Some say it makes the blightborn happier, more content with their lives."

I opened my mouth to heatedly argue the point, but he held up his hand.

"I'm not saying it does," he said. "But something has certainly changed." He glanced around. "You've seen it for yourself. The students just now, they're proof of it."

I thought of the rebellious looks in the students' eyes when they'd confronted me. The raw anger. Their fearlessness. It was dangerous—and not just to me. To themselves. "So what happens next? Why would this be happening just because of Nyxaris?"

Kage shrugged, the movement fluid and full of his customary grace. "When highbloods had dragons, there was no need for compliance spells. The fear the dragons inspired was more than enough. But . . ."

"But what?"

He hesitated. "Those were more ruthless times. Dragons and highbloods fed freely—on anything they desired."

My heart sped up. *Dragons?* "That's horrible."

"Horrible, yes. But effective. And now? The world remembers. The magic remembers. The balance is shifting."

"You think things will go back to the way they were?" I asked, horrified.

"I don't think," Kage said, his voice steady, "I know. Something has changed. The world is adjusting to your dragon's presence."

I felt a chill. "What does that mean?"

He looked at me. "You know what it means."

If the highbloods couldn't count on magic to control the blightborn; if they only had one dragon—and one they couldn't count on, at that; if the blightborn decided to rise up, to rebel against their place in the order of things: violence would follow. And that would be disastrous for the blightborn population especially.

Kage's expression was almost sympathetic. "You're more dangerous than you know—to everyone. Highbloods, blightborn, even yourself." He straightened. "But you don't have to figure it all out alone." His lips curved into a slow, inviting smile.

I swallowed hard. "I don't?"

"Of course, that all depends."

"On what?"

"On trust. We both have our secrets, don't we, Medra? Truth is earned."

For a moment, neither of us moved. The space between us seemed to fill with an invisible charge. This wasn't the raw, tumultuous heat I'd sometimes felt around Blake, dangerous and explosive. This was different. More controlled, but no less intense. There was a push-and-pull between Kage and me, a question that always seemed to hang in the air between us. Waiting for an answer neither of us seemed ready to give.

Finally, Kage stepped back, breaking the spell. "You should go and get your kava before the refectory runs out for the day. You need your strength."

"Kage," I called after him as he turned to leave.

He paused, throwing a glance over his shoulder.

"What if your grandmother is right? What if the compliance magic keeps weakening?"

His expression darkened. "Then, I guess we'll all have to decide who we want to be in that new world. And who we want to stand with us."

Before I could reply to that, he was gone, his long strides carrying him away down the hall.

I stared after him, my thoughts in a tangled knot. It took me a moment to realize he'd known where I was going, knew I wanted kava. He'd been watching me. For how long? And why? What other details about me had he figured out?

Kage wasn't like Blake. He was even more of an enigma. He didn't demand my obedience. He offered something else. Something more tantalizing, more dangerous: choice. And the thing that both thrilled and unsettled me was that I suddenly wasn't sure what choice I wanted to make.

CHAPTER 12

# BLAKE

The Drakharrow common room was full and humming with life, just the way I liked it these days. But this evening, I sat brooding in my usual chair by the fire. The laughter of the others was grating on my nerves. Around me, students sprawled lazily on the floor, some of them feeding from thralls, their fangs pressed into willing necks. I watched the thralls, taking note of how blissed-out they looked, lost in their euphoric haze. All brought on from their enjoyment of the bite.

I clenched my jaw and forced myself to look away. I hated watching them feed. Not because I disapproved—this was the way it should be after all, though I'd never been one for thralls—but because it reminded me of my own predicament.

"Something weighing on your mind, House Leader?" Laurent asked, with a cocky smirk. The skinny highblood traced the neck of the thrall seated beside him with his fingers and the girl shuddered with pleasure.

"No," I snapped. I crossed my arms over my chest and shifted in my chair, letting the sharp edge of my tone warn Laurent not to press the matter.

But Laurent was an idiot. He didn't scare easily, even when he should. He leaned back, his smirk widening. Did he think he was ingratiating himself to me? What a fool. "You're hungry."

I shot him a warning glare. "Mind your fucking business."

Laurent shrugged, clearly enjoying teasing me in front of his fellow students. "You could always join us. You don't have to hold back. Or is the House Leader above such indulgences?"

I growled, not holding anything back as I shot forward towards him and grabbed him by the neck. The look on his face was priceless. I tossed him on the ground and he scrambled to his feet, his face white as a sheet. I pointed to the door and Laurent raced towards it, not bothering to say good-bye to the girl he'd been feeding from.

I sat back down, my hands tightening on the chair's armrests. Tossing Laurent had felt good. But I could still feel my tension building, hunger clawing at the edges of my control. It wasn't like I'd ever been reckless with my feeding. I'd always prided myself on my restraint. I'd only used sellbloods, the way my father had taught me, no one who might be unwilling. It was a matter of honor— Drakharrow honor. Honor my uncle knew nothing about. What would my father say if he could see me now? Or Viktor, for that matter?

My jaw tightened. I was trapped. I hated this. Hated the sight of others feeding while I sat here like a neutered beast, chained to Pendragon's rules: once a week, in her room, on her terms. It was humiliating.

A faint coppery tang of blood lingered in the air from the thralls. It only served to make my hunger worse. But it wasn't their blood I craved.

I leaned back, closing my eyes for a moment, remembering. Pendragon's blood was intoxicating. Unlike anything I'd ever tasted. So rich, so potent. The first time I'd fed from her, the rush of power had been almost overwhelming, igniting every nerve in my body with fire and strength. Her blood had something to it that no sellblood or thrall could ever hope to match. She was smooth and sharp as a blade, sweet and explosive with heat all at once. Each time I fed, I was left wanting more. Each time, I left feeling unstoppable. Like her blood could make me invincible, if only I could get enough of it. But the high didn't last. It never did.

I sighed restlessly. I wasn't due to feed from her until tomorrow. In the meantime, I could feel my patience fraying and my restraint slipping. How much longer could I keep this up? How much longer could I survive like this when every cell in my body screamed for me to find her and take her now?

Thank the Bloodmaiden that my uncle and Marcus hadn't found out about my situation. Marcus would laugh his head off at first. But then he'd do something drastic. He always did.

They'd blame me—but they'd also blame Pendragon. They'd be furious at her for keeping me on a leash. They'd want me to take steps, violent ones, and I wasn't about to go there. I wouldn't lay hands on a woman. At least, not one who wasn't already actively attacking me. And especially not my own consort. Pendragon was still mine to protect. That hadn't changed. At least, not in some ways.

I grimaced. I felt like I was starving. But no one would ever see me crack. I'd sooner set myself on fire than show weakness like that.

The door opened and Regan swept into the room, her silver hair falling in perfectly arranged waves, her House Drakharrow insignia embroidered meticulously onto the bodice of her red form-fitting dress. She spotted me and I saw her eyes light up with determination as she crossed the room.

I suppressed a groan.

"Blake," she said, smiling sweetly as she looked down at me. "We need to talk."

I wouldn't even meet her eyes. "No. We don't."

Her pretty lips thinned. She placed her hands on her hips, swaying slightly towards me. I knew exactly what she was trying to do. It wasn't going to work. "You're making a mistake, Blake. You're already regretting casting me aside, aren't you?"

"I don't regret anything," I said flatly, staring into the fire.

Her lips thinned petulantly. "Look at you. Pining after her. She doesn't even want you, does she? You threw me away for a blight-born girl who thinks she's too good for you." She tossed her hair over her shoulder. "You're pathetic, Blake. I should be laughing at you right now."

"Yeah?" I said, trying to sound bored. "So why aren't you?"

Because she didn't dare. Well, that, and she still wanted me. It wasn't just my ego talking. I could smell her from here.

"You're throwing away an alliance that could strengthen your house," she hissed. "You need me."

I looked up at her, finally meeting her eyes. "If I needed you, you'd still be part of my triad—and in my bed. I don't need you or want you, Regan. Now, go."

Her face flushed with anger, her composure slipping once and for all. Muttering furiously, she turned and stalked away, the high heels of the ridiculous shoes she wore clicking sharply against the stone floor.

I leaned back in my chair, feeling exhausted. Everything about this day was driving me crazy. The noise, the feeding, Laurent's stupid smirk, having to talk to Regan. Most of all, my constant, gnawing hunger.

My gaze fell on a curvy highblood girl sitting on a sofa nearby. I stared at her appreciatively. Her dress was short and had slid up her thighs, revealing long swaths of bare golden skin. The dress clung to her figure in all the right places, emphasizing her hips and ample breasts. She caught me looking at her and bit her lower lip, giving me a flirtatious smile.

Fuck it. Fine. If Pendragon wanted to act like I didn't exist, then two could play that game. I beckoned to the girl. She practically skipped over, sliding onto my lap with a breathless giggle.

The girl's body was warm and inviting. She pressed her breasts against my chest. "Need some company, my prince?"

There, now that was the proper deference. That was the kind of attitude I should be able to expect from my consort. I ignored the part of me that said it was also too easy. Boring, really.

Instead, I grabbed the girl's chin without responding and tilted her face up to kiss her, hard. She moaned softly and I felt a surge of satisfaction. I wasn't a monster. I could still please a woman. She tangled her hands in my hair, shifting more closely against me eagerly.

But something was wrong. It wasn't enough. *She* wasn't enough.

The problem was, I was a hunter. I needed the thrill of the chase. I needed a challenge.

And there was no one more challenging than Pendragon.

The door opened, and I glanced up. Pendragon stood in the doorway. She hadn't noticed me yet. She was holding something in her hands. I sniffed the air—kava, a big mug of it. Her long red curls tumbled over her shoulders. Her expression was relaxed. There was a soft smile on her lips. The look on her face made my blood boil. Just seeing her so content while I sat there, pining for her blood like a fool.

Jaw tightening, I pulled the girl closer and thrust my tongue down her throat, making her moan again—more loudly this time. There. That had gotten Pendragon's fucking attention.

She met my gaze, her eyes unreadable. Then her eyes went to the girl sprawled on my lap with her skirt hiked up, practically bare-assed. I cupped the girl's bottom, pulling her more firmly against me.

"Oh, Blake," she gasped. "Yes." She wriggled against me. "You wanna come up to my room?"

I looked back at Pendragon and saw her expression twist with distaste. That was fine. I'd take it. Disgust was basically jealousy's sister, after all.

I kissed the girl again, this time with deliberate intensity, closing my eyes and really taking my time about it. She melted against me with a happy sigh. This was probably the best day of her life. I didn't even know her name, but what did it matter?

I peeked my eyes open. Pendragon was gone. Instantly my mood soured.

I stood up and the girl on my lap slithered to the floor in a heap with a gasp of surprise. She started to protest but the look on my face stopped her.

I growled. Loudly. Around me, heads turned, but I didn't give a damn. None of them—not one—could give me what I really needed. I stomped up the stairs to my room.

Pendragon wasn't supposed to be able to walk away from me so easily. Turn her back on me like I didn't even matter. But the problem was, she just had. I knew she'd do it again, too. Over and over.

# CHAPTER 13

# MEDRA

I sat on the bench at one of the House Drakharrow tables in the refectory, stirring my oatmeal absently. Across from me, Visha tore into a loaf of bread, buttering slice after slice with abandon. I glanced at the entrance, hoping Florence would appear. Finally, I gave up. I needed to vent to someone. I knew it was a risk talking to blunt-as-a-brick Visha, but I went for it.

"He's insufferable, you know that?"

"Who?" Visha asked, speaking around her mouthful of bread. "Blake? What's he done now?"

"I walked into the common room last night and there he was with some girl draped all over him and his tongue halfway down her throat, right in front of everyone."

Visha's lips quirked into a smirk. "You mean Camilla?"

"I didn't ask her name," I muttered, stabbing my bowl of cold oats with the spoon as if they'd personally offended me.

"I only know because everyone's talking about it. Regan's pissed, of course. She still thinks Blake belongs to her." Visha eyed me. "Camilla's been sniffing around Blake since last year. Curvy, big doe eyes, dumb as a rock—a classic pick. He was probably just trying to make you jealous."

"That sounds about right," I said, frowning as I remembered the image of the girl sitting on Blake's lap, wriggling her ass all over him. The picture was burned into my brain.

Visha leaned forward, resting her hand on her chin. "The real question is, why does it bother you? Don't tell me you actually care what Blake does. Are you jealous?"

"Jealous? Of course not," I snapped, feeling my cheeks heat up. "I couldn't care less what Blake does—or who he does it with."

"Good." Visha sat back, grabbed an orange from a bowl and started peeling it.

"Good?" I asked cautiously.

"Right. Then, there's no problem. It's good you're not jealous."

I narrowed my eyes, pretty sure she was being sarcastic. "I'm just pointing out how ridiculous he is. One moment he's lording it over me like he owns me, body and soul, and the next, he's—" I stopped. I could hear myself, whiny and petulant. Visha was right. Why did I care? I shouldn't have been jealous. Yet clearly I was. And it was driving me insane.

"Letting off some steam with a willing lackey?" Visha shrugged. "Sounds like Blake. At least," she corrected, "the old Blake. I mean, Blake before he and Regan were forced together. And before you came along."

"I don't care," I insisted. "It's just . . . so vulgar. That's all. It was in poor taste. He's the House Leader."

Visha grinned, her white teeth flashing. "Sure, Pendragon, whatever you say. You know, if Blake is really open for business, maybe I'll give it a go."

I nearly choked. "You?"

"Sure. He's hot, right?" She shrugged. "I bet he's even hotter between the sheets. I like to try new things. You know that."

I stared at her, trying to wipe away the new image that had sprung into my mind of Blake lying naked on a white bed sheet, his arms folded behind his head as he gave me a cocky grin. "Yes, but . . ."

Visha snapped her fingers at me. "You have a serious problem, Pendragon."

"Oh?" I said, a little coldly. "And what's that?"

She laughed loudly. "You damn well know what it is. You *do* care. You need to make up your mind. Either you want him or you don't. Stop stringing him along."

I gasped. "Stringing him along? I am not stringing him along, Visha."

"To a highblood, you are. You're his source. You'll barely give him blood—and he wants more than blood from you, doesn't he?" She gave me a knowing look that made me blush. "Yeah, he does. I thought so. I don't know exactly what went on between you two last year, but he liked you enough then to cut Regan out of the triad, to stand up to his uncle, to call me in to save your ass during the Consort Games." She paused. "Shall I go on?"

"Please don't," I said sourly. "Next you'll be making him sound like a great guy."

She laughed again. "You could do worse than Blake. I mean that."

"He's controlling and possessive and vicious," I said. "He doesn't ask permission. He just takes what he wants."

Visha rolled her eyes. "Do you know how many girls here want a highblood exactly like what you've just described? Blake is what he's been trained to be. If anything, he's less vicious than he should be. He's gotten a little soft lately, to be honest." She looked at me consideringly. "And I think you're to blame."

"Me?" I glared at her. "Soft? Trust me. He's not soft. If anything, he—"

"Good morning!" Florence chirped, sliding into the seat beside me. Her dark hair was pulled into a neat braid. She set a tray down that she'd already filled at the buffet and eyed my untouched porridge. "You're not eating, Medra? What's wrong?"

"I'm eating," I lied, picking up my spoon. I wrinkled my nose. The food was cold. But I shoveled it in, determined not to make Florence worry or stuff her satchel with snacks on my behalf.

Theo dropped onto the bench beside Visha and tossed an apple up in the air. "You two look cozy," he remarked, glancing between Visha and me. "So, what are we talking about?"

"Blake's love life," Visha said, with a wicked grin. "Without Medra."

Florence's eyes widened. "Oh!"

"It's not a topic," I said firmly. "We're not discussing it."

"That's right," Visha said perkily. "Because Medra's not jealous."

Theo looked at me and grinned. "Oh, I see how it is."

Florence looked confused. "You do?"

Theo nodded. "Medra's not jealous."

Florence looked more confused.

"That's right," I snapped. "I'm not. And we're not talking about this anymore."

"That's right," Visha said innocently. "We're not talking about the girl who Blake was tongue-fucking in the common room last night."

Florence's eyes became wide as saucers.

"Visha!" I exclaimed. "That's . . . inappropriate."

Theo snickered. "You mean, in front of the children?"

Florence looked offended. "I'm not a child, Medra. You can speak about whatever you want in front of me." She colored. "I might not be the most experienced one in the bunch, but . . ."

"Oh, we'll change that, don't you worry," Visha said smoothly, causing Florence to color even more deeply.

"Yes, well," Florence said, flustered. "I have a lot of work to get through this year. I'm not sure I'll have time for any romantic entanglements."

"Entanglements don't have to take very long, Florence," Visha said sweetly.

Theo laughed. "Leave the poor girl alone, you vulture."

Florence changed the subject, much to my relief. "Medra, have you seen the assignment Rodriguez posted for Alchemy? We're supposed to—"

But she was cut off mid-sentence by a loud, drawling voice.

"Well, well, what do we have here?"

I froze. Blake stood at the end of our table, a smug smirk on his face. A cluster of House Drakharrow students flanked him, including a tall, skinny boy who looked thrilled at the prospect of whatever havoc Blake was about to cause.

Theo straightened up beside me. "Morning, coz."

Blake ignored him completely, his gray eyes fixed on me. "Funny," he said, his voice dripping with mockery. "I could have sworn this was a House Drakharrow table." He swept a hand upwards towards the banner hanging over us. "Yep. Red and black. House colors."

Theo frowned. "It is. We're—"

"And yet," Blake cut in smoothly, his gaze sliding to where Florence huddled beside me, "I see an outsider. Strange. I wasn't aware we were running a charity for outcast Avari."

"She's not an outcast," I said sharply. "She's my guest. There's no rule against it, is there?"

Blake smiled nastily down at me. "Oh, but there is. House Drakharrow tables are for House Drakharrow students. Not for outsiders." His eyes gleamed with malice as he leaned in slightly. "And certainly not for traitors."

"Traitors?" I shot back. "What the hell are you talking about, Blake?"

He crossed his arms. "Let's start with your behavior as my consort. You've done nothing but undermine me since day one. Or what about the way you fraternize with Avari students instead of supporting your own housemates?" He looked at the Drakharrow students standing on either side of him. "Tell me, everyone, do you feel supported by our dragon rider?"

Almost in unison they shouted out, "No!" The skinny boy beside Blake looked especially gleeful.

I grit my teeth. "This is bullshit. Maybe I should be questioning *your* loyalty, Blake. You're the one who's done nothing but humiliate me at every turn."

The refectory had gone silent. Every eye seemed to be on our table. Beside me, Florence seemed to have shrunk in on herself.

Miserably, she twisted her hands in her lap under the table. Theo looked thunderous, holding himself very still. Even Visha, usually unflappable, was looking distinctly uneasy.

Blake let out a low laugh. "Oh, Pendragon. Humiliation implies you don't deserve everything I dish out to you. But let's be honest. You've brought this on yourself. Sitting here, parading your little rebellion with your Avari friend."

I couldn't take it anymore. I slammed my hands down on the table and stood up. Florence winced and jumped. "Florence is my friend. That's not going to change no matter what house she's in and you know that. If you think for one second I'm going to let you bully her—"

"*Bully?*" Blake interrupted, putting a hand on his heart. "I'm simply enforcing the school rules, Pendragon. Something you'd understand if you had even an ounce of house pride. Or, you know, school spirit."

"Enough, Blake," Theo said suddenly, his normally easygoing voice steely. "This is ridiculous. Florence isn't hurting anyone by sitting here. And Medra—"

But Blake's hand shot up, silencing his cousin with a glare. "Ah, Theo. Always eager to defend the helpless blightborn, aren't you? Disloyalty deserves consequences. But if you're so concerned, why don't you get up and join them? That goes for you, too, Visha. Pick your side and stick with it. Either you're with her or you're with me."

Theo looked stunned. My heart hurt looking at the betrayal on his face. "You're asking us to leave? Because we'd dare to defend a friend?"

Blake's face was cold. "I'm not asking. If you can't respect your House Leader, you can find another table. Easy enough."

Visha stood abruptly, fixing Blake with a disdainful glare. "Gladly. If you're going to make an ass of yourself and our entire house, I'd rather not be associated with you."

For a second, Blake looked furious. Then his face turned hard.

Theo hesitated for a moment, then stood up slowly. He cast one last look at Blake, imploringly, but his cousin's expression didn't soften.

"Come on, Florence," I said softly, touching her shoulder. "Let's go."

Florence didn't have to be asked twice. She stood up with a choked sob, grabbing her tray. I swore to myself then and there that I would make Blake Drakharrow pay for humiliating my dearest friend. Florence didn't even wait for me, she just started moving down the main aisle, her head down. I started to follow her.

"You're welcome at my table." The voice was calm and firm.

I turned towards the House Avari head table where Kage Tanaka had risen to his feet. He stood tall, his white-blond hair shaved on the sides, gathered into a neat ponytail at the back of his head. Everything about him projected a soldier's bearing, not a noble son's indulgence. His dark eyes fell upon me as a hush fell over the refectory.

Kage gestured to the bench beside him. "Come. There's room," he said simply. He leaned down to speak softly to a girl seated beside him. She quickly nodded, then gestured to the students beside her and they all slid down without a word.

A lump formed in my throat. I felt a strong urge to look back at Blake, but I resisted. Instead, I squared my shoulders and marched towards Kage's table, touching Florence on the elbow as I came up beside her to make sure she followed. Theo and Visha were behind us.

Kage's eyes met mine as I approached. I saw unexpected sympathy there. And something grounding that made me feel, just for a moment, that I wasn't alone in the chaos Blake kept stirring up.

"Sit down," Kage said. But it was an invitation, not a command. He gestured to the open space beside him. "I hope you'll find the company more agreeable here."

"I'm sure I will," I murmured as I slid onto the bench. Florence sat down beside me, looking nervous. Theo and Visha looked even more uncomfortable than she did. I smiled at them reassuringly as they took the remaining spots.

Kage resumed his seat. He surveyed his table with the same calm authority that had silenced the room earlier. "House Avari welcomes guests. I trust that's not a problem for anyone."

His tone was light, but carried weight—enough to remind everyone around him who was in charge.

I finally glanced back at the Drakharrow table. Blake was still standing at its head, his hands flat against the table, leaning forward. His pale, sharp-featured face was twisted in fury. For a moment, I thought he might storm across the room towards me. But instead, he clenched his jaw and stalked out of the refectory. I turned back to find Kage watching me.

"You handled yourself well," he said quietly, leaning in toward me.

I'd only been this close to him once before. That night at the ball when we'd danced together. The memory was mostly a blur. Blake had dominated that night—like he seemed to dominate everything. But now I looked at Kage carefully and really tried to take him in. I was sitting close enough that I could smell his scent, a smoky, woodsy aroma that reminded me of pine and cedarwood. Light enough not to overpower, yet with an earthy warmth.

"Thank you," I said. "You saved my skin once again." I glanced around me. "And not just mine," I said, lowering my voice. "Florence . . ."

"I'll be keeping an eye on her, don't you worry." He smiled encouragingly. "She's safe in my house. She's earned her place here."

I looked at him with gratitude. "She certainly has. You have no idea how hard she works."

He laughed a little. "Of course I do. Why do you think I wanted her in Avari?"

I stared at him. For a moment I'd forgotten he'd made sure Florence would be selected for his house.

"Maybe this is a good opportunity," I said slowly. "I've been meaning to approach you. I wanted to talk to you about something."

Kage raised a brow. "Oh?"

I lowered my voice a touch. "Yes. Can you get me moved to House Avari like you did with Florence?" I'd surprised him. He hid it well, but I could tell.

"That would be . . . difficult," he said finally.

"But not impossible," I said quickly. "Not for you. Your grandmother is a House Leader. I'm sure together you and she can arrange anything."

Kage looked amused. "She's certainly a formidable woman."

"I have no doubt," I said.

"But even my grandmother has limits. House selections only happen on Selection Day, you know that."

I glanced around. "Blake had someone transferred from Drakharrow into Orphos. After Selection Day was over. I know this for a fact."

"He must have arranged it with Lysander," Kage said, looking thoughtful. "But that's unusual."

"Could you . . ." I hesitated. "I don't know, talk to Blake? Convince him, somehow?"

Kage's expression of amusement deepened. "When it comes to you, Medra, I don't think anyone could persuade Drakharrow. Not even that dragon of yours."

"That's not a bad idea," I said lightly, trying to hide my disappointment. "I'll ask Nyxaris to talk to him."

Kage laughed. "You're certainly something. Who knows, it might even work."

"Don't you want me in your house?" I pleaded. "I thought we'd work well together."

Kage sobered. "I think we would, too."

"Then, maybe we can make this happen. I'm desperate. I have to get away from Blake."

Kage narrowed his eyes. "Has he harmed you?"

I swallowed. "No. Not like that. He fed from me without my consent at first. But since then, we've sort of come to an arrangement. He doesn't like it . . . but it works."

"You're his only source. Your bond . . . it's deepened." Kage shook his head.

"And you don't want me because of that," I said miserably.

"It's not about that. It's about Blake not wanting to let you go. More than that, not being able to. No wonder he's so volatile right now." Kage glanced over at the Drakharrow table. "It reminds me of something."

"Of what?" I asked.

But Kage just shook his head. "Look, Medra. My grandmother would have moved heaven and earth to help you if that bond hadn't tied you to Blake."

"I didn't choose that bond," I said, gritting my teeth. "I'd break it if I could."

Kage's expression softened. "I'll help you anyway I know how. I'll try talking to Blake, if you want me to."

"Yes," I said eagerly. "Anything. Maybe if you talk, one House Leader to another. I know he respects you."

Kage nodded thoughtfully. "He's changed since his father died."

"You've known him that long?" I said. "I hadn't realized."

"Of course. Kids with parents in powerful positions . . ." Kage shrugged. "We get dragged along. Even when we don't want to."

I wasn't sure if he meant when they were children . . . or even now, when it came to other matters. "Right. I can only imagine."

Kage stood up. "Classes are starting soon."

I nodded. "Thank you again," I said, a little stiffly.

"You're welcome at my table anytime, rider. You and your friends. Drakharrow or not." He glanced around the room. "I see change coming. And I'm not the only one." I watched as his gaze landed on the table where Catherine Mortis sat. She was watching us steadily, her eyes icy.

Kage leaned down, lowering his voice so only I could hear. "Don't let Blake push you around, Medra," he said softly. "You're a challenge. For all of us. A challenge we might need."

There was something in the way he said it—calm, certain, and full of perception—that sent a shiver down my spine. Before I could reply, he straightened up and was gone.

I stared after him, then turned back to my friends. They were rising to their feet, grabbing their bags. I trailed behind them as we left the refectory, Blake's stormy image forcing its way back into my mind.

He was hotheaded, unjust, a bully. He was unpredictable, volatile, like a fire that couldn't decide whether to warm you up or burn you alive. And yet, I'd still felt a strange disloyalty sitting at Kage's table, asking him to be my safe harbor in the storm of Blake's fury.

# CHAPTER 14

# BLAKE

The courtyard was already filling up when I arrived. The sounds of weapons clashing in warm-up routines sounded as I stepped into the open-roofed training yard. It hadn't taken much to get transferred into this section of Defensive Arts, just a bit of sucking up to Professor Sankara. Perks of being a House Leader.

As a Fourth Year, I had some empty spots on my timetable, so I'd very kindly volunteered to help Sankara out with supervising the Defensive Arts class—out of nothing but the goodness of my tender heart, of course. I'd earn some extra credit and I'd get to keep an eye on Pendragon. After that morning, I wasn't about to let her out of my sight for long. I needed to remind her where she really belonged.

Leaning casually against the stone wall, off to one side, I watched as she finally entered, flanked by Visha and Theo. I scowled. What were they? Her personal bodyguards? Pendragon didn't even notice me at first. She was too busy laughing and chattering with them. The sight of her sent a twinge of irritation through me. Her red curls caught the sunlight streaming in from overhead in a way that made my heart quicken. Even her stupid freckles had somehow become attractive to me, scattered across the pale skin of her cheeks like perfect little embers. She was dressed in simple black training gear, the form-fitting fabric outlining her athletic frame.

I narrowed my eyes as I noticed that nothing she wore bore the Drakharrow insignia. She'd removed every patch, every bit of embroidery. She'd purposely damaged house property.

I saw more than one pair of male eyes following her and at least one girl stopped what she was doing to gawk. But Pendragon didn't even notice the attention. She was oblivious. In her own little world, apart from the rest of us. It set my teeth on edge. Evidently she'd rather spend more time with Kage Tanaka than with her own house.

But no matter how much she fought it, she was mine. My consort. My source. If I let her, she'd continue humiliating me. Her dangerous streak of disloyalty would have consequences for us both. My uncle was still a threat to us. It went against everything my father had taught me, but I had to do this. Pendragon had to learn her place, just like everyone else: it was for her own good. So I'd toughen her up a little. Eventually, she'd break and toe the line. Maybe it would even help her with her dragon. They both seemed to have issues with being overly willful. Pendragon couldn't bring that dragon to heel unless she was following the rules herself, now could she?

I stepped into the center of the courtyard and called out, "All right, everyone, listen up."

Pendragon's head snapped toward me. I almost laughed at the look of shock on her face.

"Professor Sankara has a board meeting so he's running late," I said, addressing the class. "He may show up towards the end of class, but until then I'll be leading today's session." I met Pendragon's eyes. "As a Fourth Year, I've also volunteered to help out this term." I grinned. "So get used to seeing me around."

A few students laughed. Most of them had seen me step in for Sankara last year and knew what to expect. Theo cast a wary glance in my direction. I thought Pendragon might try to protest, but she just scowled, rolling her eyes and staring me down as if she was daring me to start something.

Which I absolutely planned on doing, of course.

"We'll start with hand-to-hand sparring today," I continued, pacing slowly around the circle. I'd already decided supervising sharp weapons this first class was too dangerous. I wasn't going to risk Pendragon bleeding again and being mobbed by the younger, less-controlled students, especially while Sankara wasn't there to back me up. "But first, why don't we all acknowledge our guest of honor?" I started clapping my hands slowly as I turned towards Pendragon, watching in delight as a slow flush crept up her cheeks. "Miss Pendragon. How incredibly generous of you to grace us with your presence here today. I'm sure we're all eager to witness your prowess as Sangratha's newest dragon rider, aren't we, class?"

There was some scattered laughter and mocking applause.

I paused. "That is, if you're ready to show us what you've got. I mean, you did bring your dragon with you, didn't you, Pendragon?" I looked around the courtyard. "Damn, I don't see him anywhere. He seems to have disappeared. It's almost as if he doesn't like you very much."

Her cheeks turned redder, but she didn't rise to the bait.

"Took you for one ride and got bored and flew off, did he? Well, I think we all know how *that* goes. I mean, I certainly can't blame him," I said with a sly grin, loading my words with double meaning and giving the rest of the class a knowing look. "Anyhow, no dragons today. Sorry, everyone. But I'm sure we're still very eager to see what you can do, Pendragon."

I shrugged my shoulders, trying to loosen the tension that was building there just from being in her presence. "Let's have some volunteers. We'll watch our first pair spar. I'll observe and give some pointers. Who wants to go first?"

Hands immediately shot up. All good Drakharrow students. I was proud to see their enthusiasm. Unsurprisingly, Pendragon's hands stayed right where they were.

Theo and Visha were watching me suspiciously. After last year,

Visha had to know I was up to something. I grinned. I didn't give a shit if they knew. It wasn't as if they could stop me.

"Our first volunteer will be Pendragon," I said, pointing at her. "Step right up."

She frowned but did as I told her. "But I didn't volunteer."

I ignored her. I paused, as if still considering my other choices. "And let's have . . . Laurent." I pointed to the highblood student.

The First Year boy stepped forward with a sly grin, bouncing up and down as if only too eager to get going. His pale hair was slicked back, emphasizing his thin, ferrety features. Laurent was annoying, but I knew he could be useful if I let him. Plus, he was thin and wiry so he wasn't going to crush Pendragon to death with his weight, which was a bonus. I didn't want to kill her. I just wanted to toughen her up a bit. I'd already told Laurent not to hold back, but not to beat her to a pulp either. It was about humiliation. I didn't want her fucking maimed.

I walked over to one of the roped-off sparring rings and gestured for them to step inside. "Hand-to-hand," I repeated. "No weapons. You've had all summer to slack off. Show me what you've got."

Pendragon stepped into the ring reluctantly. The match began. Laurent circled her, his movements quick and calculated. He was taller than her and wasn't afraid to use his vampire speed to his advantage. He lunged forward, jabbing at her shoulder. But Pendragon was fast, too. Faster than she'd been last year with Visha. I wondered if she'd improved simply through practice. Had she been working out while trapped in that room day in, day out? Or maybe it had something to do with our bond. Were my powers still lingering within her? Or was this her rider blood finally showing up for her? Regardless, it didn't matter. She still couldn't possibly be faster than a vampire. She'd end up humiliated and on her back every class if I had my way this term.

Pendragon dodged, pivoting on her heel. She was moving cautiously but her fists were up. She didn't look as nervous as I'd hoped she'd be, even with the entire class watching. She should have been looking to me for guidance—or, better yet, mercy. Instead, she looked at Laurent as if she were assessing him. As if she planned to win.

"Sloppy," I called out, my voice sharp as a whip. "Laurent, are you holding back? Because right now it looks like you're fighting your kid sister."

There were some cackles of laughter from the watching students.

Scowling, Laurent lunged again, aiming a quick jab at her midsection. Pendragon sidestepped, moving lightly on her feet and countering with a sharp kick to Laurent's shin.

"Nice footwork, Pendragon," I called out, my voice sarcastic. "If we were practicing ballroom dancing, I'd give you top marks."

She didn't respond. But I saw her shoulders stiffen. A tiny crack in her armor. It was enough to motivate me to keep going.

Laurent moved towards her again, this time showering strikes. Pendragon blocked most of them, but one caught her on the shoulder, and she staggered back a step.

"Where's that fancy footwork now, Pendragon?" I called. "Loosen up or you'll be flat on your back in no time. We wouldn't want that, now, would we?" I grinned wickedly at the crowd of highblood students and a few of them laughed.

Pendragon shot me a glare. That fire in her showed no sign of dying down. It was maddening and magnetic all at once. Laurent pressed his advantage, coming at her again and forcing her to backpedal. A blow caught her in the ribs and she staggered slightly, but recovered quickly and landed a jab to Laurent's jaw. The highblood boy stumbled back with a look of surprise. I scowled as some of the watching students gasped.

"Not bad, is she?" Theo murmured. He'd come up beside me and I hadn't noticed. I glared at him. "Especially considering how you're taunting her."

"Lucky shot," I called loudly, my tone dismissive. "Laurent, don't let her bait you."

"Ironic, coming from you, Drakharrow," Pendragon called back.

Laurent came at her harder, his movements faster and more aggressive. She tried to duck but wasn't quick enough and his fist caught her in the eye. She let out a yelp and staggered back, clutching her face.

I leaned forward, my voice easily cutting across the ring. "Careful, Pendragon. You don't want to embarrass yourself. Or your dragon. Oh, wait . . . Too late."

I'd already looked her over. Her eye wasn't bleeding. Sure, it would probably be black and blue by tomorrow, but she'd recover. Still, she glared at me furiously. The exact reaction I'd been hoping for. In the meantime, she'd taken her eyes off her opponent and Laurent took advantage of the opportunity, kicking her in the side and sending her staggering, knocking the wind out of her. She doubled over, gasping. I winced, putting a hand instinctively to my own side. Then I caught Theo giving me a strange look and instantly dropped it.

"Focus, Pendragon," I barked. "Or are you done? Was that too much for you? Giving up already?"

Before she could reply, a sound split the air. A deep, rhythmic beating that grew louder with every moment. The class froze. Laurent paused mid-strike, his head snapping upwards. Above us, the courtyard went dark. My pulse spiked, no doubt in my mind who was making the shadow overhead.

Nyxaris circled the courtyard.

Oh, fuck.

"What the hell is that thing doing here?" someone whispered loudly, sounding as if they were about to piss their pants.

The dragon's massive wings flared as he descended and settled, his talons gripping the edge of the stone wall. I eyed the wall nervously. It was a wonder the thing could hold him. I imagined Sankara coming back to find his classroom in ruin. He would not be pleased.

The dragon's amber eyes scanned the training yard, lingering on Pendragon . . . before shifting to me. The weight of Nyxaris's gaze hit me like a slap of his wing. I felt dizzy, choked, as if I could hardly breathe. There was something in the dragon's expression that I recoiled from.

Disdain. Contempt.

It made my skin crawl. This creature saw right through me. And it was clear he didn't like what he saw. Pendragon hated me, I already knew that. But what I hadn't realized was that her dragon did, too. My hands clenched at my sides. I wanted to look away, break the connection, but I forced myself to stand tall. Heat began to bloom under my skin. My heart was hammering painfully in my chest. Sweat prickled my temples. And then, to my horror, I saw it.

A patch of scales shimmered on the inside of my forearm, just above my wrist.

I blinked, certain it was an illusion. Some sort of trick of my vision. I took a deep breath, trying to calm down. But the path of scales caught the sunlight, shimmering there like molten fire. They weren't going away. They weren't a figment of my imagination. Those fucking things were real.

I folded my arms over my chest, carefully hiding the scales from view. As my fingers brushed over them and I felt their rough texture, a chill went down my spine. What the fuck was happening to me? I clenched my jaw, forcing my attention back to the courtyard where the dragon still sat, perched on the wall. Students were whispering nervously. I was a little impressed that none had run away screaming yet.

The dragon was still looking my way, his gaze stripping me bare. I was suddenly terrified he'd noticed the scales on my arm. My chest tightened as the heat that had been building up under my skin suddenly flared again, my cheeks burning as if they'd been set on fire. The dragon roared. Students screamed.

And suddenly, I couldn't take it anymore. I snapped. "Class is dismissed," I shouted across the courtyard. Some of the students jumped, but others were already running for the door. They didn't need to be told twice. "We're done here. You can all leave early." I stalked out of the courtyard, not waiting to see if they'd listen. Sankara could deal with them when he showed up. I wondered if the dragon would still be there.

As soon as I was out of sight of the training yard, I darted into an empty classroom. I closed my eyes and let out a shaky breath. My chest still felt too tight. My pulse was erratic. The image of Nyxaris was still at the forefront of my mind. The dragon's eyes had been filled with what looked suspiciously like judgment. So Pendragon's dragon didn't like me. Hell, I didn't like myself half the time.

I rubbed a hand over my face, heart still pounding like a drum. What was I even doing? Torturing my consort to prove a point? Acting like a petty tyrant in front of my entire house? Was this who I really was now?

Unexpectedly, I found myself thinking of my older brother. If he were in my situation, Marcus would never have had a moment of self-doubt. He'd have laughed at me for even wondering if I might be wrong. He'd have encouraged me to take things further. But Marcus was a loathsome prick who had murdered one of his own consorts. Was he really the standard I wanted to aspire to?

Why had Nyxaris suddenly shown up? Why then? It meant something, it had to. Had he known what I was doing? Had she told him? More importantly, was Pendragon closer to bonding with the beast than she'd let on?

The thought made me feel stupidly, irrationally jealous. Now I wasn't just competing with Kage for her loyalty, I had to fight a fucking dragon for her attention. And the worst part was, I was pretty sure I'd already lost.

Nyxaris was clearly loyal to her. Protective. Had he come as a warning to me? To remind me I wasn't in control? Not of Pendragon, not of my house, not even of myself?

I blew out a hot breath and ran my hands through my hair. I wanted to be angry at Pendragon but the truth was I was impressed. A dragon wouldn't show loyalty to someone who didn't deserve it. The creatures were brutal. The Duskdrake had already shown that with Lord Mortis.

I couldn't deny that my consort had strength. She'd faced down Laurent without a complaint and she might even have won. She'd stood tall under my barbs. Maybe I was being an idiot, pushing her like this. Maybe there was another way to handle her, to get her on my side. I thought of how close we'd become last year. How good it had felt to think, just briefly, that she was on my side. The two of us against the world.

Now I was alone again.

Oh, I'd been alone before. Regan had never felt like a true partner. But this was somehow worse. Much worse. Now I knew what a real partnership could feel like. I'd had a taste of something real. And I'd destroyed it.

I glanced down at my arm. The fucking scales were still there. They were fading but still unmistakable. I thought of something: Had the dragon done this to me? Maybe it was just about proximity. Maybe I wasn't the only one it had happened to. I felt my body sag in relief. My stomach twisted as I stared at the scales, willing them to disappear. But was that really the explanation? After all, no one had reacted quite like I did. Nyxaris might have been Pendragon's problem. But now I had a new one of my own.

# CHAPTER 15

# MEDRA

My heart stuttered when I heard the beating of massive wings. Nyxaris.

The black dragon folded his wings by his side almost casually, as his sharp, luminous eyes scanned the training yard. Around me the highblood students had gone still. I glanced at Theo and Visha. Their eyes were wide, their nervousness palpable.

I grimaced. Nyxaris was like Blake in some ways. He didn't just enter a space, he dominated it.

*What are you doing here?* I demanded, reaching for the dragon's mind. *Why haven't you been answering me?*

Nyxaris snorted and a bunch of students yelped and backed farther away. *Why would I waste my time responding to your every petty whim?*

I ground my teeth. So, the dragon was not in a good mood, then. *I wasn't being petty. I've been trying to—*

*Were you skirmishing? What did this highblood do to provoke you?* Nyxaris interrupted.

I glanced over at Laurent. The tall highblood boy looked as if he might topple over. Evidently this was his first time seeing the dragon up close.

*Nothing. We were sparring. This is one of my combat classes.*

*And were you winning your match with the little highblood whelp?* Nyxaris asked with only mild interest.

*I was handling it*, I said, my irritation flaring. *I would probably have won if you hadn't arrived and distracted everyone with your dazzling beauty.*

Nyxaris's rumbling laugh filled my mind, dark and amused. *We could still win. Shall I dispatch your opponent for you? I have not yet eaten today.*

*That won't be necessary*, I responded hastily. *We're sparring, not trying to kill each other.* Laurent was an ass, but I wanted to beat him fair and square—not by cheating and having my dragon eat him.

Nyxaris tilted his head, the light catching on his onyx scales. His eyes moved to Blake, who was standing stiffly at the edge of the ring, looking back at the dragon. *And is this your instructor?*

*You know who he is*, I snapped grouchily. *He's my . . . archon.*

*Ah, yes. Your mate. He is unworthy of you.*

I wondered how exactly Nyxaris had come to that conclusion. I knew he didn't have a great opinion of highbloods in general, but he seemed to take personal offense at Blake. *He's not my mate*, I hissed, my cheeks burning. *We're bonded. That's all.*

*Mm*, Nyxaris said noncommittally. *I fail to see the difference. He is a highblood. He drinks from you, does he not? The highbloods could never resist rider blood.*

I bit the inside of my cheek. *Yes*, I admitted, feeling as if I were sharing something too personal. *He has to or else he'd die.* Was I actually defending Blake? No, that was an explanation. Nothing more.

Nyxaris let out a huff that sent pebbles skittering beneath him. *I already tire of him. He glares at me as if I've wronged him in some way. Is he jealous?* He snorted. *Now, that would amuse me.*

I glanced at Blake, who was still staring up at the dragon. He looked furious—yet there was something uneasy about his expression. *He's looking at you because you're looking at him*, I said, rolling my eyes. *It's not exactly commonplace to interact with a dragon these days, you know. He's not jealous.* Though, with Blake, who could really say? *Why are you here, anyways?*

*Perhaps I simply came to see how well you hold up under pressure*, the dragon replied, languidly stretching his wings.

There was something brooding about Nyxaris today. I almost had the impression he was depressed. Well, more depressed than the last time.

*Clearly, you have much to learn,* he continued. *Your stance was sloppy. Your focus wavered. And that boy landed a blow before I intervened.*

*You didn't intervene,* I replied hotly. *You landed. I was doing fine before you showed up.*

Nyxaris gave a low chuckle. *Stubborn child. So be it.*

I sighed. *I know you love scaring everyone, but why are you really here?*

He didn't respond right away. Instead, he flicked his tail as if irritated. *I grow impatient. Have you found something useful for me yet?*

My heart sank. *I'm working on it but it's only been a few days.*

*Working on it?* His tone was sharp, almost petulant. *You've had time. Perhaps I should find a rider with better initiative.*

*Yes, well, good luck with that,* I snapped. *Besides, I'm not your rider, remember? You've made that quite clear.*

That earned me a huff of amusement.

*You need to be patient if you want results,* I said, trying to find my own sense of patience. I thought about Professor Hassan. *The only news I have for you right now isn't good. I doubt you want to hear it.*

*Does it involve me having to come and save you again?* he said, sounding bored.

*Basically, yes,* I said reluctantly.

*Then, you are correct, I do not wish to hear it. Find me information before you ask for a favor. Do you know nothing of the ways of courtesy?* Nyxaris said primly.

Before I could retort, he reared back, tilting his head skywards and letting out a deafening roar. The sound shook the courtyard like a thunderclap.

I winced, my ears ringing. I knew he was doing it on purpose. The big show-off.

Students screamed, scattering like startled mice. I heard Blake yelling over the din, shouting that class was dismissed early.

*Nyxaris,* I said warningly, *I go to school here, remember? The nice highbloods decided not to execute me. Can we please try not to make them hate us both more than they already do?*

*Simply consider that a reminder,* he said coolly. *Dragons do not like to be kept waiting.*

Without another word, he spread his wings and launched into the air, his shadow momentarily casting the training yard into darkness before he soared away.

I found Theo waiting for me near the edge of the training yard. Visha had already vanished. "That was . . . interesting," he said, as I fell in step beside him and we started walking to our next class, Historical Strategy.

"That's one way to put it," I muttered.

"What do you think is really going on with Blake?" Theo asked, looking concerned. "It's not like him to storm off like that."

I hadn't even noticed Blake take off, but now I raised an eyebrow. "Are we talking about the same Blake Drakharrow?"

"Well, at least, not usually in front of such a big audience," Theo corrected. "Maybe he did it all the time with you." He glanced at me.

"He's probably just sulking," I said. "Because I wasn't as humiliated as he'd hoped for. Or maybe he wanted Laurent to beat me bloody but Nyxaris showed up and saved the day." I paused. "That probably threw him for a loop, too."

"Maybe," Theo conceded. "You think Nyxaris appeared because of Blake? What was he doing there, anyway?"

I shook my head. "I know for a fact he didn't. I think Nyxaris was mainly just bored."

Bored and impatient. The most powerful creature in the world was impatient with me. If that wasn't motivation to go to the library, I didn't know what was. Kind of ironic. Nyxaris and the tribunal had more in common than they realized. Both wanted results I couldn't just instantly give.

"Blake's been off lately," Theo said, his mind still on his cousin.

"Has he, though?" I asked cautiously. "Look, he's your cousin. Your friend. Maybe you should just try talking to him? I don't have any answers for you. But look at how he treated us all this morning. It wasn't right. You and Visha and Florence didn't deserve that."

"Neither did you," Theo said sadly, looking downwards.

I sighed. "Try telling Blake that. He's punishing all of you to try to get to me. But it isn't exactly out of character for him, is it?" I shook my head. "Listen to us. It's like our lives revolve around Blake. There are more important things to talk about."

"There are?" Theo said, perking up and giving me a little grin. "Like what?"

"Like *your* love life," I teased, nudging him with my elbow. "Who have you got your eye on this year? Come on, you know you can tell me."

He snorted with laughter and dodged. "I've decided to go celibate. I'm going to focus on my grades this year."

I nearly choked. "You? Celibate?" I tilted my head. "Well, I guess it would be even more of a shock if Visha had said that."

Theo laughed. "Visha doesn't give a shit about her grades, believe me. She's just here for the fun of it. But she gets decent marks somehow, despite all the partying she does."

"Visha." I shook my head. "She's a smart girl. Tough, too."

"I wonder how she's feeling about this morning," Theo said, a little reluctantly. "It has to sting. She told me Blake was considering her as his Second."

"What does that even mean?" I asked curiously.

Theo shrugged. "You know, just someone to back up the House Leader. Blake was Marcus's Second. You do what your House Leader says, help him hold things together. Fill in when needed. It has to be someone strong, supportive. Loyal above all."

"I would have thought you'd be Blake's Second," I remarked.

"He wanted me to. But I don't think I'd be a very good one," Theo said. "Besides, I doubt he wants me to do it now."

I slung my arm through his. "Blake is an idiot. I know you love him, but please try not to let him get to you. You're a good person and a good friend. Just look at what you did for Vaughn. You could have been, well, more selfish. Any other highblood would have chosen to keep him close. They wouldn't have even thought about what Vaughn wanted."

Theo laughed a little bitterly and I wondered if he was serious about being celibate this year. If so, had he made that choice because he wanted to or because he couldn't get Vaughn off his mind? "Yeah, I'm not a great highblood."

"That's right. Guess you're more blightborn than you think," I said jokingly.

But instead of laughing, Theo paled slightly. I wanted to ask him about it, but we'd reached the room where Historical Strategy was being held. We'd walked so slowly and talked for so long that the lecture hall was already half-full. I recognized most of the students—basically all of the ones who had just been in our Defensive Arts class with Blake were in this section, too.

"Let me guess," I muttered to Theo. "History with Hassan?"

He shuddered. "Probably. This is her specialty."

I sighed and found an empty spot for us in the middle of the room. "Well, there's nowhere to hide. Maybe she'll ignore me." I'd already given my friends an abbreviated version of what had happened in my private session with Hassan.

But when the door opened a few minutes later, it wasn't Professor Hassan who entered. Instead, Professor Rodriguez strode to the lectern. He set down a familiar-looking worn leather satchel and looked up at us. I realized Blake had come in at some point. He sat in the first row. To my surprise, Visha was beside him.

"Good afternoon," Rodriguez said, breezily. "Most of you know me already. If you don't, you should." There was some laughter.

"I'll be taking over Historical Strategy this term. Professor Hassan has been assigned to other duties."

The relief in the room was obvious. I saw some students let out sighs of relief. Evidently, I wasn't the only student Hassan was hard on.

As for me, I was thrilled. This meant I'd be seeing Rodriguez at least three times a week, but that was fine by me. More opportunities to try to get information for Nyxaris from the one person in the school who might actually know something about dragons—and be willing to share that knowledge, once persuaded.

Professor Rodriguez laughed at the class's reaction. "Make no mistake, I won't go easy on you. But hopefully you'll enjoy the material we'll be covering. Strategy can be fascinating. So can the history of warfare." His eyes swept over the tiers of seats and landed on me. He gave me a brief nod. "This class will focus on the historical applications of strategy in highblood warfare. We'll examine the tactical use of dragons in battle, as well as the role of blightborn infantry, scouts, and other auxiliary forces. Why? Because by understanding the past, we can better prepare for the future."

It was something all history teachers liked to say. But this time Rodriguez's eyes were hard as he looked at me, as if I should take more meaning than usual from the tired old phrase.

"We'll start the term by analyzing key battles from Sangratha's history, including the Siege of Skyreach and the Fall of Lutharion, two moments which helped to define our realm's military legacy. Your assignments will require both individual research as well as group collaboration."

Rodriguez started his lecture on the Siege of Skyreach and I began to busily write notes, firmly keeping my thoughts off both Blake and Nyxaris.

# CHAPTER 16

# BLAKE

By the time I got to Historical Strategy, I'd decided the dragon's proximity was what must have caused the bizarre appearance of the scales. Definitely once in a lifetime. Definitely nothing permanent. I was so relieved that it took me longer than it should have to realize Visha had sat down beside me.

"Thought I'd grace you with the honor of my presence since you didn't seem to be able to get enough at breakfast, House Leader." Her broad grin told me she hadn't been put off in the slightest by my attempt at intimidation that morning.

I glared at her and went to scoop my things back into my bag. She leaned over. "Don't do it."

"Do what?"

"If you leave now, it'll look like you're scared of me." She grinned, baring her fangs. "House Leader Blake Drakharrow scared of little old Visha Vaidya." She clucked her tongue. "Just think of the rumors."

"I'm not fucking afraid of you," I said in annoyance.

"Good to hear it," she snapped. "Then, why have you been acting like a fucking pussy? An expression I obviously hate using since my pussy is stronger than your dick any day of the week, but hey, if the expression fits." She shrugged.

I gaped at her, momentarily at a loss for words.

"Oh, please. Don't act like I've just insulted your mother," she said dismissively.

My lips twitched. I was trying not to laugh. "What do you want, Visha?"

"I want to know why the hell you're acting as if you're losing your mind these days, Blake." She'd lowered her voice again, thank the Bloodmaiden, but I still glanced around to make sure no one sitting nearby us had heard her.

"I'd say you're the one who's biting the hand that feeds you," I said angrily.

She had the nerve to scoff.

"I can't believe I was actually considering making you my Second," I complained, crossing my arms. "After the way you've been acting."

"And just how exactly have I been acting?" Her tone was deceptively calm, but I knew her well enough to know she was getting close to blowing her top.

I cleared my throat. "You've been behaving disloyally."

She raised her eyebrows. "By being friends with *your* consort? The same redhead you were so excited about last year that you cast off Regan? Funny, I'd have figured you'd have wanted us to be friends."

"I didn't . . . That was . . ." I blew out a breath. "Things have changed. Obviously."

"Obviously," she said pleasantly. "Who knows what the hell is really going on between you and Pendragon? It's not my business. And it sure as hell isn't Theo's. But you've made it everyone's. You've decided to include your entire house in your personal life. Now here you are, acting like the world has done you wrong." She leaned in a little closer. "You're being a big fucking baby, you know that?"

My face flushed. "You've got some nerve."

"I've got all the nerve." She glared back at me. "You know it's true."

"You sat at a House Avari table this morning," I said furiously. "Or have you forgotten?"

"Because you threw a temper tantrum and kicked us all out." She shook her head slowly. "Tell me this, Blake. Just where exactly do you think it's going to get you?"

"Get me?"

"Yes. Please enlighten me. Do you think Medra's going to come crawling back to you after you've embarrassed and humiliated and bullied her worse than you did last year?"

"She's the one who has me on her fucking leash," I hissed. "She's the one cavorting with the enemy. She turned her back on me first."

Visha snorted. "*Cavorting?* I don't think I've ever known anyone to cavort in my life. Next you'll be telling me she was *frolicking* with Kage. Let's be honest here. You've both stirred the pot. You fed from her when you know you shouldn't have. You had alternatives. You could have told her the truth about the situation. You had to have known how she'd react when you went all feral high-blood on her. You're not a damned idiot, Blake, even though you're certainly acting like one lately. So do me a favor and don't pretend like you're some innocent victim in all of this."

I bristled. "I did what any highblood would have. I took the blood I needed. *She's* the one who publicly announced she was through with me. That she'd break our bond if she could."

"Oh? And that makes it right?" She shook her head in disgust. "Since when do you hold with all that highblood nonsense, any-how? Since when does doing something just because it's tradition make it a good idea?"

I stared at her. "Excuse me, who am I talking to right now? The Visha I know is proud to be a highblood. Proud to feed. She takes what she needs when she needs it."

"I'm still proud," she said, tossing her head. "That doesn't mean I'm not allowed to question the system. And right now I'm questioning whether some of our traditions might be wrong and whether highbloods like you are really trained to all be entitled assholes."

"Takes one to know one," I muttered. "Next you'll be telling me you don't drink from the house thralls."

"I've switched to sellbloods. You made them sound so great, I couldn't help myself." She batted her eyes at me. I couldn't tell if she was being serious or not. "In any case," she went on, "I'd make a fucking fantastic Second and you'd be lucky to have me. That's if I even agreed to accept the position. Right now, with you constantly losing your shit . . ." She shrugged expressively.

"What?" I demanded.

"Well, let's see. You could pick a suck-up like Laurent who keeps following you around or you could pick someone who isn't afraid to tell it to you straight."

I didn't want to admit it, but she had a point.

"Like right now. I'm going to tell it to you straight, Blake. Are you ready? Oh, that's right, I don't fucking care." She leaned towards me. "You're losing her. Everything you do is making it worse, not better."

"Pendragon?" I tried to laugh. "I don't care if she hates me."

"But that's just it. You clearly do care. I don't know if you're falling for her—"

"That's absurd," I interrupted. "We're highbloods." Visha should know better. We didn't mate for love. That was the whole point of triads: stability and strength. My parents were the only exception I could think of, and look what had happened to them. Last year I may have come close to thinking of Pendragon as something more, but I'd been delusional. Just look at us now.

She shrugged. "Whatever you say. So maybe it's all about staking your claim and you just really, really want to get in her pants. Either way, what you're doing right now isn't going to get you there."

"Oh, no?" I snapped. "And just what would the genius Visha Vaidya do in my shoes?"

"You could start with apologizing for one. Because you and I both know you fucked up. And after that? Oh, I don't know. Maybe learn how to actually seduce someone instead of just acting like a cave bear and pounding on things hoping she'll swoon at your feet?" Visha suggested. Blunt as a brick, that was Visha.

"I've never had a problem getting a woman," I bragged.

"Right. You could have any highblood girl you wanted." She smirked. "Well, most of them. But that's the problem. You don't want them, you want *her*. So maybe you'd better stop doubling down and start trying to fix your shit."

I slouched in my seat. I knew Visha was right . . . even though I wasn't about to come right out and say it.

She glanced at the door. "Here comes Rodriguez. You're about to be saved. But think about what I said, asshole. And another thing," she added. "If you're going to keep treating everyone like pawns in your personal drama, could you at least pick a Second who won't let you spiral into self-destruction? Laurent would follow you off a cliff, but he wouldn't stop you from jumping."

I scowled. "Let me guess. You'd have my back, would you?"

"Without hesitation," she said. "That's assuming you managed to pull your head out of your own ass long enough to earn my respect again."

And with that she turned to her parchment, leaving me to stew in silence.

I leaned back in my seat as Rodriguez's lecture began, but my mind was far from historical strategy.

*You're losing her.* The words cut deeper than I wanted to admit. Pendragon shouldn't have mattered this much in the first place. She'd been assigned to me. I hadn't chosen her. We were both Viktor's pawns in a game of power I'd been trapped in my entire life. But it didn't feel that simple anymore. Not since she'd walked away, taking something with her, something that had left me with a burning ache in the vicinity of my chest.

Visha was scribbling notes, totally oblivious to the chaos she'd just unleashed in my head. I hated that I didn't know how to fix this. I'd started something and now, like a fire burning out of control, I wasn't sure I could stop it. Highbloods didn't apologize. Not to one another. Certainly not to blightborn. But maybe that was the problem. Pendragon wasn't like anyone else: not any other consort or any other blightborn or highblood, for that matter. She was like no one I'd ever met. And it terrified me.

I could feel the weight of our bond tugging at me. Always present, faint but persistent. I'd thought claiming her blood would bring things to a head, give me control over her—but also over myself. Instead, it had only turned me into a tangled mess of emotions.

*What if this bond isn't even real?* That's what Pendragon had said to me in the common room the other night. Which meant she believed it wasn't. I felt my heart harden. Visha was right: if I didn't stop spiraling, I'd lose everything. Pendragon, my house, my dignity. There had to be some middle way through this.

Because if Pendragon thought I was going to come crawling on my knees to beg her forgiveness, she had another think coming.

# CHAPTER 17

# MEDRA

I t was feeding time.

I made my way to Blake's room. I really didn't want to look at his face again that day. But I had no choice. We had a deal and tonight was our scheduled feeding session. But this evening I also had plans to head to the library. So I'd decided the sooner the better. I figured he wouldn't mind moving things up if it meant he got his blood meal a little earlier.

Now I stood in front of his door and raised my hand to knock. But as soon as my knuckles brushed the surface of the wood, the door creaked open slightly. The latch must not have caught all the way when he'd closed it.

I hesitated. Blake didn't make mistakes. He'd probably stepped out and hadn't bothered to close the door behind him properly because he knew he'd be back in a moment. And who would dare go into the House Leader's room without permission? The smart thing for me to do would have been to go sit in the common room and wait. Or leave. Definitely leave.

Instead, I pushed the door open slowly and stepped inside. The room was dark except for a single lamp burning on a wide oak desk in one corner. Blake's scent was everywhere, infusing the room. Both musky and masculine, light and fresh. I caught sight of a green apple on his bedside table and rolled my eyes. Maybe he rubbed them all over his body before he left for class every day. Whatever his secret, the smell wasn't exactly off-putting. Rather the opposite.

The room was neat, almost surprisingly so. Most boys' rooms I'd been in were a disgusting mess. But Blake's four-poster bed had been made perfectly, neater than mine, the deep crimson duvet cover smooth and unwrinkled. His papers and books were in orderly stacks on the desk over in the corner.

The only sign of disarray was a white linen shirt and pair of black trousers that had been tossed carelessly over the back of an armchair. That should have been my first hint.

"Blake?" I called softly. No answer.

I knew I should leave. This was his personal space and I doubted he'd take kindly to finding me there.

Then I heard it. The faint sound of running water. The bathroom. Blake hadn't stepped out, he was taking a bath. Common sense screamed at me to turn around and leave. But my traitorous feet carried me straight toward the sound.

I approached the bathroom door slowly. It was cracked just enough for me to peek inside if I wanted to. Before I could stop myself, I'd leaned forward.

And there he was. In all his glory.

Blake sat on the edge of a massive, tiled tub, his back against the wall. His head was tilted upwards just a little, giving him a swaggering, roguish appearance. My mouth went dry. He must have just stepped out of the bath. The fluffy white towel he'd used to partially dry himself lay discarded on the floor. His pale gold hair was wet and damp against his forehead, curling a little at the ends. Droplets of water still clung to his skin, catching the light and turning his torso into a living canvas of ivory and ink.

I couldn't take my eyes off him. Every line of his body was precisely crafted, maddening in its perfection. The faint sheen of water on his skin made him seem like some wild creature, caught in a vulnerable moment. His usually sharp features were unguarded in a way I'd rarely seen them. The tension that always bristled beneath his skin was temporarily gone.

Slowly my eyes dipped lower, fastening on the trail of light blond hair that led down his ribs and stomach and formed a slight triangle at hip level. My heart thudded in my chest. If he caught me . . . I couldn't even imagine what he'd say if he knew I'd seen him like this. I started to turn, my face burning.

Blake sighed. I froze. Then, slowly, I turned back.

He'd slipped a hand down his body and lazily curled it around his cock. His eyes were closed.

Oh, shit.

I couldn't look away.

He was long and hard. Bigger than I'd imagined—and yes, I'd imagined. I'd been with boys before but Blake put them all to shame. Were all highblood men like this? Or was he a special case?

My throat was tight as I watched as his hand wrap around himself. Slowly he started to stroke his cock up and down, almost absent-mindedly. The scene was incredibly intimate and I was very much an intruder. A wave of shame washed over me. But I was so turned-on I could hardly move. I felt trapped. Knowing I should run, knowing I should look away, but knowing I might never get another chance like this—to see this side of Blake again.

I watched his hand slip up and down his cock, the motion practiced, experienced. I wondered who he was thinking about. Was it Regan? Or that girl, Camilla? Had they . . . ? No, I didn't want to think about it. Not now.

My eyes were glued to the sight of his hand riding his cock harder and faster. There was something incredibly erotic about watching him touch himself. I couldn't take it anymore. With only a split-second's hesitation, I slipped a hand inside my pants. I closed my eyes, biting my lip. I was as wet as I'd known I'd be. My underwear was soaked through, my thighs damp.

I hadn't thought I'd missed that highblood asshole. But now, seeing him there, buck naked, pleasuring himself like that, it was too much to bear.

My eyes still on Blake, I slid my fingers over my clit and the contact was incredible. I let out a moan.

My eyes popped open. Shit. Had I moaned aloud or just in my head?

It didn't matter. Blake was still going at it. He hadn't noticed me. My hand stilled, I stood frozen in indecision. This was dangerous. I could run out of his room while I had the chance, or I could watch him bring himself to completion while I kept doing what I was doing. One of those things was a hell of a lot more tempting than the other.

I rubbed my clit again and bit my lip. Watching him touch himself was amazing. But it wasn't enough. I wanted more. My body felt tight. Pent-up and tense with longing.

Was he close? Was he going to come before I could?

I took a deep breath and sank a finger inside myself, imagining it was Blake's, remembering that horrible, wonderful, terrible night in the Sanctum when his hands had been all over my body, inside of me, filling me, taking me.

What would he do if he found me now? Would he punish me? Part of me almost wanted him to.

Blake let out a groan and my eyes popped back open, watching his hand skim over the head of his cock. He was close. I could tell. His beautiful lips were half-parted in a pant. "Fuck, Pendragon," he groaned, his voice low and rough as he stroked himself faster. "Yes . . . fuck."

*Well, fuck me.* I was so shocked to hear my name on his lips that it was almost enough to bring me over the edge myself—but not quite. And then I'd lost my chance. Blake's seed was spilling over the top of his hand, milky and white. He let out a low groan of frustration, as if jerking off still hadn't been enough to satisfy him.

Now was the time to get the hell out of here. I took a step backwards and the floor creaked.

I stood perfectly still.

A moment passed, then another. Blake hadn't rushed over with his vampire speed, so I figured I was all right. He was probably toweling off. Maybe he'd take another bath. I'd go back to my room, finish what I'd started, and wait for our usual meeting time. When he showed up, I'd act like nothing had happened. It wasn't as if he could read my mind.

I turned towards the door.

"Like what you see?"

Blake stood in front of me. Somehow he'd managed to get past me, moving from the bathroom to stand in front of the door leading out into the hall before I could even see him.

Fuck his vampire speed. Had he gotten even faster over the summer?

I bit my lip. "I don't know what you're talking about. I just got here. I was going to ask if—"

"Bullshit," he said, his voice clipped. "You've been here a while." He grinned lecherously. "I can smell you from here, Pendragon."

He looked down at my hand and I hastily shoved it behind my back. "No idea what you're talking about," I lied breezily. "I'll be going now."

"Take your clothes off," he commanded.

I froze. "What?"

"I said take your clothes off," he repeated. "All of them. I want a show, Pendragon. Just like you got."

"Are you insane? I'm not going to do that," I said, my face heating. I was still all too aware of the wetness between my thighs . . . and of the fact that he was still stark naked and apparently completely comfortable that way. He'd cleaned himself off but hadn't even wrapped a towel around his hips.

Then, before I could even process what was happening, the air shifted. I gasped as I found myself picked up by the waist in an iron grip. The next thing I knew I was landing unceremoniously on his bed on my back. The impact knocked the breath out of me.

Before I could scramble to my feet, Blake pounced on top of me, crouching over me like some wild animal. Damp hair clung to his temples. Water still glistened on his chest. His black tattoos rippled over taut muscles as he shifted, putting a hand on either side of my head and leaning down over me. He snarled and his fangs came into view.

"What the fuck are you doing?" I demanded, my heart pounding against my ribs.

"Fair is fair," he repeated. "So, what? You thought you'd just let yourself in?" He slowly smirked. "Trying to change the terms of our arrangement, are we? Well, if you wanted me naked, all you had to do was ask. I'm not shy."

I had to admit, the man had absolutely nothing to be shy about.

"I wanted us to meet earlier, you idiot," I snapped. "I didn't come here . . . looking for that."

"But you didn't leave either," he pointed out. "Why didn't you?"

I flushed. Just how long had he really been aware of me? From the moment I entered? From the time the moan slipped past my lips? I suddenly thought of something. Had he been jerking off because he'd *known* I was there watching? The bastard. I wouldn't put it past him.

"So what are we going to do to make this even, Pendragon?"

He shifted slightly and I couldn't help myself. I glanced down at his cock. He was hard again.

I closed my eyes. I shouldn't have been turned-on by that, but dammit if I wasn't. Knowing he was hard for me made the wetness between my legs only increase. I hoped he couldn't smell it. And this whole predatory cat thing he was doing was strangely working. But I had to get out of here. This couldn't go any further.

"You shouldn't have left your door open," I shot back. "It was careless. Anyone could have come in."

"Maybe I wanted them to. Did you ever think of that? Maybe I was waiting for someone." He looked down at me, his gray eyes burning with an intensity that made it impossible to look away.

I made myself think of all the girls who had probably lain just where I was now. But it didn't work. It just made things worse.

"I think you need to let me up," I said, my voice as firm as I could make it.

"And I think," he murmured, his voice a low, suggestive purr, "you owe me a little peek."

"I don't owe you anything," I snapped, raising my hands and shoving at his chest. "You're being ridiculous."

He didn't budge. "What's ridiculous, little dragon, is that you think you can walk into my space and walk out again without any consequences."

"What kind of consequences?"

His smirk vanished, replaced by something darker. "I think you're about to find out," he said softly.

Without warning, his hand was in my pants, slipping between my thighs. The touch of his fingers against my pussy was everything I'd been denying I wanted. I couldn't help it. I moaned, a low sound of frustration and pent-up desire.

Blake groaned. "You're so wet for me, little dragon. Let's get you out of these clothes."

"It's not for you," I lied between gritted teeth. "Not everything is about *you*. Now let me up, Blake."

He met my eyes. "Let's make a deal. All you have to do is scream once and I'll let you go."

His hand started to move inside me. He slipped a second finger in alongside the first, but it wasn't enough. I wanted more. His thumb slipped over my clit, gently rubbing back and forth. I gasped.

Notably, I didn't scream.

"What are you doing?" I managed to say.

"Exactly what you're too chickenshit to say you want," he said, lowering his head to my ear. "I told you what to do if you wanted me to let you go. I'm all about mutual satisfaction, Pendragon. And right now, it looks like you could use some satisfaction. Tell me I'm wrong."

But the problem was I couldn't. His hand moved against me again and I couldn't help myself. I lifted my hips to give him better access, biting my lip to contain another moan.

"I take it you're staying. Then, all this," he said, gesturing with his other hand, "has to go."

Before I could even formulate an answer, his hands moved. *Fast.* My shirt was ripped at the front, torn down the middle. My pants suddenly slid from my hips. Underwear and boots vanished, too. A split second later and I was as naked as Blake was.

He straddled me. I couldn't take my eyes off him. Maybe his arousal should have been off-putting, but all I could think about was how close his cock was to where I really wanted it.

He was looking back at me, his face a mix of shock and pure hunger. "By the Bloodmaiden, Pendragon. I thought I knew what you looked like before, but this . . ." His voice trailed off, his dark eyes raking over me with an intensity that made my stomach tighten. "So this is what you've been hiding."

Instantly, I felt my cheeks redden. He was laughing at me. The bastard was fucking laughing. I opened my mouth to say something angry, but he beat me to the punch.

"Magnificent. Utterly magnificent." And it was his tone of voice that caught me off guard this time. Reverent. No, worshipful. His eyes moved over my breasts, my hips, the downy red curls between my thighs and I felt every inch of my body heating up with desire.

"This can't happen," I whispered, the words almost a plea.

His face hardened. "Oh, it's happening."

And so help me, I couldn't muster the willpower to disagree.

# CHAPTER 18

# BLAKE

S he lay beneath me, her chest rising and falling with every uneven, ragged breath she took. Her fiery hair streamed out across
my bed like a halo of blood. Her wide green eyes stared up
at me, almost fearful as they met mine. I already knew what else
I'd find in her eyes if I looked hard enough. Hatred. Desire. Two
sides of the same coin. I knew because they were mirrored in my
own eyes.

Her bare skin glowed under the lamplight. She had freckles.
Not just on her face—those I'd known about. No, these were everywhere. Mapped out like constellations. I wanted to touch each
one, memorize them with my hands, worship every beautiful speck
with my mouth until she was moaning beneath me from the pleasure of it.

Fuck, but she was beautiful. Of course, I'd found her attractive
since that first day. But now I knew I'd really had no idea. She was
a work of art. Sculpted in a way that left no room for flaws. Pale,
smooth skin stretched over delicate curves. Every inch of her, a
perfect balance of strength and femininity.

My eyes lingered on the soft sweep of her shoulders, the curve of
her waist that dipped just enough to make my chest tighten. There
was something about her that felt untouchable. Like she was carved
from the same stuff as dragons and was just as otherworldly. Impossible to fully claim. But hell, if I didn't mean to try.

Though her gaze was still defiant, she couldn't hide the flush on her cheeks—or the perfect flush of red that swept across her breasts. I could smell the sweet wetness between her thighs. It was driving me wild. She might despise me—I already knew that much—but her body clearly didn't.

Pendragon had been hiding dark desires. Now I could see them lurking in her emerald green eyes. Sinful thoughts. Sinful lusts. I wanted to fulfill every single one she'd ever had about me.

I lazily trailed my hands over her breasts, brushing my fingers over the peaks of her nipples until she gasped.

"You're quiet for once, Pendragon," I murmured, my voice mocking. "What's the matter? Cat got your tongue?"

Her eyes flashed. "You're insufferable, even in bed."

I chuckled. "Yet you don't seem eager to leave." My gaze roamed her body, slow and deliberate, enjoying it as she flushed even more deeply. "You might hate me. But your body is telling a different story."

"I don't want you," she said, without any conviction. "You're detestable."

"And you're lying," I shot back. "You can hate me all you want. But part of you wants me, too. Just as much as I want you." I leaned down to whisper against her lips. "Admit it."

She shocked me then. She lifted her mouth and pressed it against mine. The moment our lips met the world ignited.

Her taste was intoxicating. Almost as good as her blood.

I moved my hands over her, gripping her hips, then cupping her breasts. I wanted to touch her everywhere. The heat of her skin burned beneath my hands. I wanted to consume her, devour every bitter retort and ounce of venom she'd ever dared throw my way. The fury in her kiss matched mine and fed whatever this was raging between us. Her lips parted beneath mine and I darted my tongue into her mouth hungrily, feeling her sharp intake of breath, hearing the faint, almost unwilling mew she made as her fingers curled against my chest.

Not enough. Not ever enough.

I intensified the kiss, my teeth raking her lower lip, demanding more, more, more. Her hands slipped into my hair, tugging me closer towards her. Our bodies moved against one another, and I let out a groan as our bare skin touched. Her breasts pressed against my chest and the sensation was incredible. Better than anything I'd ever felt in my life.

This. This was what I'd needed. What I'd wanted since last year from the very start. I didn't just need her blood, I needed *her*. All of her. I wanted her more than anyone I'd ever met.

I pulled back just enough to look her in the eyes, searching her gaze. Her cheeks were rosy, her lips already swollen from the force of the kiss.

"This is how it should be," I murmured. "Do you feel it?"

"What do you mean?" she whispered. Her hands twitched, like she couldn't decide whether to push me away or pull me closer.

"This is when I should be feeding from you. When you're like this—relaxed, turned-on. When your body's warm and pliant and your mind isn't screaming at me to stop. This is when it should happen."

She tensed beneath me, and I felt her pulse quicken. It wasn't just fear. I could sense her desire. She was tempted. I ran my thumb lightly over her jaw, the gentlest of touches that made her gasp and tilt her head, baring the smooth contours of her neck.

"We hate each other," she breathed.

"We don't have to like each other to fuck, little dragon." I laughed as her eyes widened. "It's true. Hell, it might even be better this way."

"Less complicated," she acknowledged.

I smiled. "Right. I could back off a little if you let me feed more easily." I felt her stiffen slightly. I'd made it sound too much like a bargain. "But it would be good for you, too," I added hastily. I'd definitely ensure that.

I skimmed my hand down her body and trailed a finger over her clit to remind her of just how good I could make her feel. Then I wrapped my hand around my cock and leaned back a little, letting her get a good look at me and all I had to offer. Her eyes widened even more.

"You're aching inside right now, aren't you, little dragon? Aching to have my cock in you. If just watching me jerk off turned you on this much, how much better would the real thing be?"

She bit her lip and my hand nearly slipped. She looked so damned beautiful there beneath me, her smooth freckled skin, her rosy full breasts. I knew she wasn't going to stop me now. She wasn't going to scream. If she'd wanted to, she could have sat up and punched me in the face. Hell, I would have let her.

But she didn't.

"Look at me, little dragon. Look at how hard I am for you. You've got my cock in a vise." My voice was a strangled growl. "And I'm not even inside you yet."

She gave a little gasp and I took it as a sign. I lowered myself over her, positioning myself against her entrance, nudging her open with my cock. At the contact, she moaned. I grasped her arms, pinning her wrists over her head and she gasped. She thought I was a monster? Then, in her darkest dreams, she must have imagined me as one in her bed. She wanted me to be a little rough. I could sense it.

"Let me show you how good this can be," I whispered, holding her down.

I started to push myself inside of her at the same moment I dipped my head to her throat. My lips brushed against the curve of her neck, a featherlight caress that made her shiver. Then, with deliberate slowness, I extended my fangs, giving her just enough time to feel the anticipation as they touched her skin, before I sank them in. At the same moment, with one powerful thrust of my hips I entered her fully.

She cried out as my length drove inside of her, her body tensing, her hips lifting up to meet me. I had no words. No words for how good she felt. I felt dizzy as I fed and fucked her simultaneously, holding her wrists above her head mercilessly as she squirmed against me. But she wasn't going anywhere. And in another moment, I let her go so I could grip her hips instead, bracing myself against her. Never letting my fangs leave her neck for a second, I drove inside her again.

Fuck, but she was tight. Her pussy clenched around me and for a second, I almost lost my hold of her neck. This would have been easier with her on top. But there was always next time.

Her blood was rushing over my tongue, trickling down my throat with an indescribable sensation. Like fire and silk, raw and powerful, filling me with a strength that made my very bones hum. I growled against her, unable to stop myself. Her blood was like nothing I'd had. She carried an essence in her that called to me, blood to blood.

As I moved against her, my cock thrusting into her again and again, my fangs drawing her blood, everything else faded away. There was no hate. No anger. No war between us. Only this powerful, primal connection that neither of us could deny. The question was whether she felt it, too—or if I were alone in imagining it was there at all.

My body wanted more and more from her. I slammed into her again, nudging her hips wider. She lifted herself against me in response, rocking her body against mine as if trying to take me deeper inside.

Her hands were all over me, her nails raking lines across my back, my neck, my shoulders. Regan had once done that to me. I'd told her to keep her hands to herself the next time. But with Pendragon, I'd wear the marks of her desire for me with pride. Maybe I'd even look at them in the mirror the next day as I imagined the look of sheer, beautiful anticipation on her lovely face just before I sank my teeth and my cock into her.

I could feel myself already teetering on the edge—the mix of her body and her blood pushing me more quickly towards another climax. But I wanted this to be good for her. I'd taken my fill. In the span of a few minutes, I'd drunk what would normally take me much longer feeding from her wrist so unwillingly as was our previous custom. A little reluctantly, I pulled back, savoring the last drop of her blood, running my tongue over my fangs. I looked at her neck nervously for a brief moment, then watched as the two small puncture marks quickly sealed and faded. She wouldn't need the scarf this time.

Then I looked at her face. She was flushed, her lashes lowered, her petal-soft lips parted as she looked up at me. I knew what she wanted, what she wasn't going to ask for.

I covered her mouth with mine, pushing my tongue into her mouth, fucking her with it as I thrust again and again inside her, taking her to the edge with me as my hand slipped between us, rubbing her clit. She tightened around my cock, hard, and a cry spasmed from my lips as I shuddered, our climaxes crashing around us like a wave of pleasure.

I felt the moment she came, the beauty of it. The way her body tensed, spasmed, relaxed. I lifted my mouth from hers and took in the look on her face—an expression beyond happiness, beyond contentment. And I'd brought it to her.

It felt good. So fucking good to know I could make her do more than hate me.

Dangerously good.

She looked up at me, her eyelashes fluttering softly.

"That," I said roughly, my voice hoarse and ragged from the rush of sensation. "That's how it should feel for you. Always."

Her eyes met mine, full of confusion.

"You can hate me all you want, little dragon," I murmured, gently brushing a strand of red hair off her face. "But part of you knows now. There's no going back."

I watched as she slowly came back to herself, her chest rising and falling gently with the remnants of exertion. The flush on her cheeks deepened as she glanced at me, as if realizing all over again where we were and what we'd just done.

I couldn't help but smirk. She looked incredible underneath me with her wild crimson hair. A red dragon, laid bare for me. I rolled off her and stood up, moving to the wardrobe to grab a plush black robe trimmed with red cord. Without a word, I handed it to her. She stared at it a moment before accepting it cautiously and slipping it on, pulling the soft fabric around herself.

The sight of her like that made something primal and possessive stir inside me. She was draped in my colors, my house insignia on her breast, her slender form swallowed up by the fabric that was marked with my scent. It was symbolic, whether she realized it or not.

"You can borrow that," I said smoothly, gesturing to the robe. "Can't have you walking back to your room in the nude." My gaze lingered on her bare legs, and she scowled, tugging the robe down.

"Very generous of you," she muttered. But I could see the faint flicker of surprise in her eyes.

I imagined walking into the refectory tomorrow with her by my side. Everyone would know. They'd see her and they'd understand. Medra Pendragon wasn't just some reluctant consort eager to break away from me anymore. She was mine in every way that mattered. Feeding from her wouldn't be a battle anymore, I'd make it a pleasure for us both. This was how it should always have been. I'd fucked up, but now I could make things right. Turn back the clock, so to speak.

"What are you smiling about?" she asked sharply, interrupting my thoughts. Her green eyes were narrowed in suspicion.

"Nothing," I said casually, leaning back against the headboard. "Just thinking about how good you look like that."

Her face flushed and she looked away, busying herself with tying the robe's belt. I was almost content to let the moment stretch, basking in the satisfaction of knowing I'd gotten what I wanted. Almost.

"You know," I said, my voice still conversational, "this doesn't have to be complicated. We can make things easier for both of us."

She froze, her hands stilling. "What do you mean?"

"I mean," I continued, "you don't have to keep pretending you hate me quite so much. If we're going to be doing this, we might as well enjoy it, right? You'll see. Things will be better if you stop fighting me all the time, Pendragon."

The sharp, incredulous laugh that burst out of her caught me off guard. "You really are unbelievable, Blake." She stood up and pulled the robe tighter as she looked down at me. "To think, I really thought for a second that you might actually have learned something."

"What the hell is that supposed to mean?" I snapped, sitting up straighter.

"It means you don't get it," she said, her voice dangerously low. "Nothing has changed between us. Like you said, we don't have to like one another to *fuck*."

I felt like I'd been slapped.

"I'm not yours. And I'm certainly not some prize you can parade around the school, if that's what you're thinking."

I felt my cheeks heat up. "That wasn't what I meant. But after everything . . ."

"Yes, after everything," she echoed. "After everything you've done to me and my friends, after that stunt you pulled today in class, I can't believe I'm actually sitting here, wearing this robe, still in your room. What the fuck is wrong with me?"

She said the words so bitterly. I stared at her. Was she really regretting this already?

My jaw tightened, anger flaring. "What is it you want from me, Pendragon? I've given you everything."

She slid off the bed and stood up. "You haven't given me shit. If anything, I'm the one always giving." She shook her head slowly. "Did you forget this morning so quickly?"

"I haven't forgotten you sitting beside Kage Tanaka, no," I snapped back.

"And I haven't forgotten you humiliating my friends. You made Florence cry," she burst out.

I winced. Florence. The dark-haired, quiet girl with glasses. I knew she was special to Pendragon. I'd tried to have her assigned to House Drakharrow so the girls could be together, but Kage had somehow overridden my selection. But Pendragon didn't even know that; I'd never told her.

Now I took a deep breath. She was already heading for the door. Without thinking, the words tumbled out, low and hoarse. "I'm . . . sorry. All right?"

She stopped, her hand on the doorframe, and turned to look back at me. For a long moment, she said nothing. Then, she nodded. "Fine. But you're still an asshole. And this? This doesn't mean you've won." Then she stalked out, leaving me sitting on the bed, staring at the door.

I leaned back against the headboard again, running my hands through my still-damp hair. I felt a strange mix of emotions brimming inside me. Anger, confusion, and something else. Sadness? No, that couldn't be it. I didn't do sad. Sadness, depression, anxiety—those were all blightborn traits. Highbloods didn't indulge in them.

I clenched my jaw. I should have been happy. I'd gotten what I wanted. The sex had been incredible. Better than anything I'd ever had before. Surely she must feel the same way. Soon she'd be back for more. That was enough. It had to be.

But it wasn't. I wanted more. But I didn't know what exactly.

I looked across the bed where she'd just been sitting. Her absence was a presence. She'd only been gone a moment. Already I missed her. If she'd stayed, what would we have done next? Talked? Cuddled? Fucked again? Fallen asleep in my bed? I imagined my body curled up around hers, protecting her. It wouldn't have been so bad.

But cuddling, talking, sleeping—those were all things you did with someone you actually liked. I'd been with girls before but when they stayed and talked, I usually wasn't listening and was just waiting for them to go. When they fell asleep, I stayed on my side of the bed. I didn't wrap myself around them like a spoon.

But with Pendragon? I wanted it all. I wanted to talk—and I wanted to hear her talk to me. I wanted to know everything about her—where she really came from, who her family was, her favorite book, her favorite class. I wanted to sleep beside her. Hold her in my arms. Above all, keep her safe. But I couldn't look forward to doing any of those things. Because she didn't trust me.

The only thing I could do was what I'd been doing all along: stay vigilant. Protect her, even if she didn't know it. She could hate me all she wanted, but I was her guardian, her soldier. That hadn't changed.

I closed my eyes and tried to relax. Tried not to think of how my older brother would call me pathetic if he knew half of what was running through my mind.

Tomorrow was another day. Maybe Pendragon would realize how good we were together. Maybe she'd show up at my door begging for more.

And if not? Well, I'd just have to remind her. Again and again.

# CHAPTER 19

# MEDRA

T he plush fabric of Blake's robe brushed against my bare legs as I slipped out into the hall. My room was only a few steps away. If I moved fast, no one would even see me.

I clutched the robe, tucking my chin into the softness. Then I realized what I was doing. Breathing him in. The robe was heavy with Blake's scent, rich and unmistakable. But there was something underlying his usual smells—sharp, almost metallic. Like blood. Or sex. The realization made my cheeks flame, even as I sped up my steps.

But luck wasn't on my side tonight.

"Well, well, well," came a silky voice. "What do we have here?"

I froze mid-step, stomach twisting as Regan stepped out from the shadows in the hallway ahead. She wasn't alone either. On either side of her stood Gretchen and Quinn, their identical silver-blond hair gleaming, their eyes shining with malicious delight.

"Did we interrupt your little walk of shame?" Quinn purred. She gestured to the robe I was wearing. "Is that Blake's robe, or did you bring your own to complete the whore-next-door look?"

"I guess Blake finally took pity on her, girls," Regan said, her voice oozing fake sympathy. I could tell she was furious. "After all, even a dog in heat gets thrown a bone eventually. Guess he finally gave her what she's been begging for since she got here. I mean, he's a man. Can we really blame him? She's been panting after him for months." She sniffed the air. "Ugh. I can smell her from here."

I could feel myself flushing with humiliation.

Gretchen snickered. "Did you plan on going down to the common room like that? Maybe putting on a little show?" She reached for the robe as if she'd like nothing better than to rip it off me and I stepped back, glaring at her.

"I don't recall asking for your commentary," I said coldly. "Now if you'll excuse me. You're standing in front of my door."

"Oh, but we're just trying to help you, Medra," Regan said, her tone dripping with false sweetness. "You don't want the whole school thinking you're Blake's little slut, do you?"

"No, I wouldn't want anyone to think I'd taken your position, Regan," I retorted.

She colored angrily. "Maybe that's exactly what you want. Riding Blake's coattails to keep your relevance since your dragon flew away?"

Gretchen giggled. "More like riding something else." She made a lewd gesture and the three of them dissolved into shrieking laughter.

"Do you want to know what I see when I look at you three?" I interrupted, my voice cold enough to make them pause.

Regan looked at me disdainfully. "What's that?"

I pointed at Gretchen. "I see you with a knife in your face, that gross piece of your cheek flapping in the breeze, because you were too slow and stupid to dodge your own blade. Remember that? Because I do." Gretchen paled and touched a hand to her face, which had healed remarkably in the meantime thanks to her highblood abilities.

"And you," I continued, looking at Quinn. "I see a little bitch who hid up in a tree because she was too scared to face me. But I got to you anyway, didn't I?" I made a ruthless motion as if I were driving that arrow into her side all over again and she stepped back quickly.

"And you, Regan." I smiled mirthlessly at the Queen Bitch of House Drakharrow. "I see a washed-out, desperate has-been lying flat on her back in the mud. Right where you belong. And that's what I'll always see every time I look at you: a pathetic wannabe, clinging to a man who isn't yours anymore, who doesn't *want* you anymore."

I took a step forward and hissed through my teeth. Regan flinched and jumped back as if she were afraid I was going to mess up her perfect makeup. The victory was almost sweet enough to mask the fury simmering in my chest.

"Now," I said, my voice low and lethal. "Get the fuck out of my way, *girls*, before you make me tempted to do it all over again."

I brushed past them without another word, slamming my door in their faces. The moment the door shut behind me, my bravado dissolved. I leaned back against it, my chest rising and falling as I tried to control my breathing. My hands were trembling. I'd let them get under my skin. It had been impossible not to. But it wasn't them I was really angry with. They were as miserable and despicable as they'd always been. That hadn't changed. It was myself I was furious with. I was the one who'd made the biggest mistake of my life.

I glanced down at the robe, then pushed it to the floor and stepped away from it. But Blake's scent still clung to me, wrapping around me like a second skin. I couldn't escape it. I couldn't escape him. He was on me. In me.

Feeling revolted with myself, I crossed the room in three quick strides, wrenching the bathroom door open. My reflection in the mirror caught me off guard. So this was what Regan and the others had seen: a wild-eyed girl with tangled hair, her lips swollen from kisses she should never have accepted.

The sight of myself, marked by Blake, made my stomach turn. What the hell was wrong with me?

I turned on the faucet, the sound of rushing water filling the silence. I held my hand under the water until it was hot enough, then poured in a flask of almond-and-cherry-scented bath foam, adding much more than I usually would have, and hoping it would be enough to wash Blake's scent away for good.

I stepped into the bath and sank down into the hot water. I closed my eyes, but instantly the memory of Blake's hands on my skin flooded back. With a groan, I pressed my palms to my face.

Since the end of first year, he'd acted like an asshole of the highest order. Not just to me—to Theo, Florence, and Visha. And instead of making him pay, what had I done? I'd gone to his room and given him exactly what he wanted. I'd been weak. Worse, I'd been selfish. I'd let myself conveniently forget about how he'd humiliated my friends.

I thought of Nyxaris. He was ignoring me again, but it wasn't too hard to imagine what he might say.

*A rider does not surrender her power for the sake of pleasure or indulgence.*

That sounded about right. Except I wasn't his rider.

I wonder if Nyxaris had been as hard on his former riders as he was on me. I supposed it didn't matter: they were all dead now. Did he mourn them as much as he mourned the loss of his fellow dragons?

I closed my eyes again and the memory of Blake's face rose right to the surface despite my efforts to banish it. I thought of him spread over me, our bodies pressed together, as if for a few brief moments they could be one and we could put all the hate behind us. I was wracked with guilt but the hard truth was it had also been the best sex I'd ever had. Everything had been easy. We'd fit together like a matching set.

He'd looked so beautiful as he stared down at me. For a moment, his skin had almost shimmered and I'd thought I'd seen his dragon tattoos spread out like real scales, dancing across his arms and chest.

When I opened my eyes, the bathwater had gone cold. I climbed out and wrapped myself in a towel, avoiding the mirror as I padded back into the room. The robe was still on the floor. I stared at it for a long moment, then kicked it under the bed.

Out of sight, out of mind.

The towering double doors of the Bloodwing Library creaked softly as I pushed them open and walked through. A familiar wave of awe swept over me as it always did. The sheer size of the place was overwhelming. Rows of tall dark wood bookshelves lined the main aisle, stretching far into the distance. Long wooden tables were scattered throughout, occupied by students hunched over books and stacks of parchment, their whispered voices blending with the rustling of pages. Above it all, the enchanted ceiling moved in its four quadrants. One caught my eye: a desert with rolling hills of reddish sand. The sun was just rising overhead, striking the sun with a golden light.

If every part of the mural showed some place in Sangratha, then Sangratha was huge. I'd only studied part of the realm's geography, but any hope I'd held out for some neighboring kingdom to save me from the highbloods was long since past. Sangratha was, for all intents and purposes, the entire world. If there were other realms, they were so far away as to not matter.

*A foreign world in every way*, my mother's voice said softly. I'd decided to bring the dagger she resided in with me that evening. She'd become too introspective, too solitary of late.

*Do you miss it?* I asked her. *Aercanum, I mean?* It had been her home much longer than it had been mine, after all.

*Not particularly*, she said thoughtfully. *I suppose that's strange. But I do miss my body. I miss riding a horse. I miss the wind in my hair. I miss the taste of wine. Not to mention the glorious feel of a lithe naked male pressed up against my—*

*All right*, I said hastily. *That's enough reminiscing.*

*Well*, she said smoothly, *you did ask. And you might have thanked me.*

*Thanked you? Was that supposed to be the start of some motherly lecture on the basics of reproduction? If so, I'm sorry to inform you but I learned about the birds and the bees quite some time ago.*

She laughed. She had a beautiful, melodic laugh. *I'm well aware, Daughter. I simply meant you might praise my forbearance in not remarking on your earlier . . . assignation.*

*You saw that?* I said hotly, my face instantly turning red. A girl carrying an armful of papers and books gave me a strange look as I walked past her.

*Not saw,* she said. *More like . . . received an overall impression when you picked me up earlier.*

*You can sense that much just from my touch?* I was both annoyed and impressed.

*Yes.* She yawned. *You see? I'm not even asking you questions. Like how good he was, how long he lasted, how well endowed—*

*Enough, enough,* I said firmly. *Let's find Florence.*

I tried to focus. I inhaled deeply, taking in the scents of parchment and leather, woodsmoke and candle wax. Slowly I walked down the main aisle, finally catching sight of Florence. She sat at a table surrounded by an ambitious-looking pile of books, her dark hair tucked behind her ears and her glasses sliding down her nose as she leaned over a tome, flipping quickly through the pages.

She looked up as I approached and broke into a smile. "Medra! You made it."

"Barely," I said, setting my satchel on the table and glancing at the books. "Impressive collection."

She colored slightly. "I'm getting a head start on some reading I wanted to do for The Alchemist's Garden."

"That's your favorite class this term, isn't it?" I asked with interest.

"How could it not be?" she exclaimed. "I adore Professor Allenvale and I already loved Professor Rodriguez . . ." She trailed off, blushing, as she caught my raised eyebrow. "Well, not *loved.* Oh, you know what I mean."

"I do indeed," I said, smirking. "You think he's handsome."

"He's a wonderful teacher and I admire his intellect greatly," she said primly.

"And his nice ass," I quipped.

"Medra!" Florence gasped. She looked around as if worried Professor Rodriguez would suddenly be standing behind her.

*Hypocrite,* my mother's voice teased.

*Shush,* I warned her. *Or I won't take you along next time.*

She sniffed but fell silent. I was bluffing, of course. But still, having her in my head was a distraction I could never seem to get used to. She couldn't stay in that dagger. Her earlier reminiscences about missing her physical form had filled me with guilt. There had to be a better solution than this.

I laughed at the look on Florence's face. "No one heard me, don't worry."

"Yes, well," Florence said. She pushed her glasses back up the bridge of her nose. "So, I take it Blake agreed to an earlier feeding?" She eyed me cautiously.

"Um, yes," I said quickly. "He did. He was . . . very accommodating. Surprisingly."

"Oh, I'm so relieved. After this morning, I was worried he'd make things hard for you," Florence said.

Orcades snickered inside my head. I tried to school my expression. "He was very civil about it."

"You aren't wearing your scarf," Florence said, looking at my wrist worriedly. "Did he bite you somewhere else? That bastard."

"No," I said quickly. I touched a hand to my neck, then yanked it away. "I mean, I didn't need it. It didn't hurt as much this time."

This was terrible. I hated lying to Florence. I was going to have to tell her the truth sometime. Why not get it over with now? Was it because it was Blake, or was it because of the subject matter? I realized I really did see Florence as rather innocent. I didn't want to, well, shock her.

"That's wonderful," she exclaimed. Her eyes widened as she looked at my arm and I resisted the urge to tug at my sleeve. "How fascinating that you're gaining some resistance to the pain. Or is it that you were more relaxed this evening? Did Blake put you at ease?"

*I won't dignify that with a remark because this is simply too easy,* Orcades complained. *It would be like shooting fish in a barrel. Please admire my restraint.*

I suppressed a groan. *You're exceedingly restrained, Mother.* To Florence, I said, "You might say that, yes."

"Well, the bite isn't supposed to be painful for most people," Florence said thoughtfully. "In fact, many blightborn seem to crave it after a while, which can be an entirely different problem all in itself."

I stared at her. "Crave it? I don't want to crave it."

"I know. But I suppose it makes sense. It's a symbiotic relationship, after all."

I took a deep breath and changed the subject. "Going back to your crush on Professor Rodriguez . . ."

Florence shrieked and picked up a book as if she were tempted to throw it at me.

"Girls, must I remind you that this is a library?"

Florence's blush deepened as a woman, slender and petite, appeared from behind a nearby stack. Jia Shen had dark eyes like her daughter, framed by wire-rimmed spectacles. She wore a dark blue cardigan with little white flowers embroidered along the hem, buttoned neatly over a crisp white blouse. Her long black hair was pulled back into a ponytail, stray wisps escaping around her face as if she'd had a tiring day.

Jia set down the books she was holding on the table with a soft thud and arched a brow at us. "I trust you weren't about to start throwing things at your friend, Florence. Library books, in particular."

"Of course not," Florence said, with a groan.

I laughed, enjoying her embarrassment. "Florence was just telling me about her enthusiasm for her classes this term. You know how excited she gets when she's speaking about academic pursuits."

"Academic pursuits, hm?" Jia looked back and forth between us, and I got the feeling I wasn't fooling her. "And what academic pursuits are you here for this evening, Medra?"

"Dragons, as usual," I said with a sigh.

"Ah, yes, the dragon project." Jia tapped a finger to her chin. "I must admit, I'm rarely stumped but this research project of yours has been more challenging than I'd expected."

I'd told Florence what I was searching for and why, but we'd decided Jia didn't need to know all the details—such as the fact that I didn't have a handle on Nyxaris and could be scorched to death at any time or executed by the tribunal for failure to perform.

"I've been through a good portion of our archives, and the results have been very frustrating," Jia continued.

"Still nothing useful?" I asked, trying to keep the disappointment out of my voice. If Jia couldn't find anything in the Bloodwing Library, what hope could I possibly have of turning up what Nyxaris needed?

But then, there was still Professor Rodriguez. Our first thrallguard session was coming up.

"We have plenty of books on dragons," Jia said. "Dragon physiology, dragon lore, a very few suspect treatises by blightborn scholars who clearly never encountered a dragon in their lives. Most of the authors writing about dragons were highbloods, however, and they often have very opposing views about dragons, usually contradictory ones. In any case, when it comes to the disappearance of dragons— such a monumental event in our history—there's almost nothing."

I frowned. "What about records from the dragon riders? Surely they—"

"So far, not a single firsthand account that I can find," Jia interrupted gently. "If they existed—and I think they must have—they seem to have been destroyed or hidden away long ago. It's infuriating. And fascinating."

"Fascinating?" Florence echoed, looking dubious.

Jia gave her daughter a wry smile. "Well, yes. You know I love a good mystery." She looked back at me. "In any case, I've taken drastic measures."

My eyes widened. "Drastic?"

"Yes, I've resorted to a letter-writing campaign. I've reached out to a number of librarians at schools and other academic institutes across Sangratha, asking if they can help."

"Interlibrary loans?" Florence said. "I thought you said they were a pain to process."

"Yes, well, when we lend books out to other libraries we seem to only receive two-thirds of them back again and half are damaged," Jia complained. "But in this case, that's a good thing. I'm owed many favors." She smiled down at me complacently. "I hope to hear back from some colleagues soon."

"Thank you for going to all this trouble for me, Jia," I said. "It's very kind of you. But I'm sorry to add to your workload."

She waved a hand. "Nonsense. You're a student here, after all. This is part of my job."

I glanced at Florence, slightly guilty that we'd told Jia this was all for another paper I was writing for Professor Rodriguez.

"Anyhow, I'll keep digging, Medra. There's always something. Even if it's buried deep. The truth never disappears entirely. Even when people would like it to."

Before I could respond, a blur of motion shot past us, knocking into a shelf of books.

"Neville!" Jia exclaimed, throwing her hands in the air as the fluffin turned around and zoomed beneath our table, his fluffy tail wagging furiously. "No, bad Neville," Jia said sternly, shaking a finger at him.

"Come here, Neville," Florence implored, pushing her chair back and holding her arms out to the fluffin. "Come to Florence. There's a good boy."

But Neville only paused long enough to give another yip before speeding off into the stacks again.

*That ridiculous little dog again,* my mother tsked. *What is that animal doing here? Don't tell me your friend believed she could teach him to read.*

*How many times must I tell you? He is not a dog, he's a fluffin. And no,* I added. *I doubt even Florence was that ambitious.*

*I've never seen such a silly creature in my life.* But there was an affectionate tone to her voice.

*I'm sure Neville would take that as high praise,* I said wryly.

"Not again," Florence groaned, burying her face in her hands. "He followed me in here and we've been trying to get him out ever since."

"If one of the other librarians notices him . . ." Jia wrung her hands.

"Don't worry," I said quickly. "If there's any trouble, tell them Blake brought him in. We'll blame him. Neville's half his problem, after all."

Jia blinked at me, then burst out laughing. "Oh, Medra, you're terrible."

"Well, he *is* a House Leader," I said innocently. "It's basically his job to take the fall for this sort of thing." And I certainly wasn't about to let Jia or Florence take the blame.

Neville zipped back around to us, leaping onto a nearby chair and then back onto the floor, his eyes glinting with crazed mischief.

Florence shook her head. "There's no stopping him when he's like this."

As if on cue, Neville skidded down the aisle only to halt in front of a new figure.

"What's going on here?" a voice said sternly.

Kage Tanaka. The House Leader stood at the end of the aisle, his tall frame casting a long shadow, his dark eyes glancing down at the fluffin before lifting to meet mine.

Something in the air shifted. I cleared my throat. "Neville," I said, gesturing towards the fluffin. "He's having a moment."

Kage raised one elegant eyebrow. "Neville?"

"The fluffin," I explained.

Neville chose that exact moment to shoot between Kage's legs, brushing against his boots as he darted away. Kage's hand shot out instinctively to steady himself against the edge of the nearest shelf. He didn't stumble, but a look of shock crossed his face. I bit my lip, trying to stifle a laugh, but it was no use. The sight of one of the most commanding highblood students at Bloodwing startled by a fluffin was too much for me and I burst out laughing. To my delight, Kage's mouth curved up in the faintest hint of a smile. Florence was laughing, too, but she was hiding behind her hands. Clearly she was too intimidated by her new House Leader to laugh at him openly.

"He's been terrorizing us all evening," I explained to Kage. "We're trying to catch him."

Kage's dark eyes lingered on me for a moment, then moved to the books on the table. "And what are you working on this evening?"

"Research." I shrugged. "Just a bit of light reading on dragons."

"Anything you need help with?"

For a moment, I was tempted. Kage was obviously sharp and methodical. I had no doubt he received excellent grades. If I were honest with myself, the highblood looked almost terrifyingly competent.

But the sight of the small black crescent-moon tattoo peeking over the collar of his shirt gave me pause. The symbol was a stark reminder of who he was. Who his family was.

I thought of Elaria Avari. If she found out I couldn't control my dragon, that I was desperately searching for answers on behalf of Nyxaris—answers the highbloods might not want either of us to have—what would she do? Still, Kage might have access to knowledge I could never hope to glean from all the books in the library. Who knew what secrets his family kept about dragons?

"I don't think so," I said, with not a little regret. "But thank you."

He cocked his head. "You don't think so?"

"It's . . . complicated," I said, hesitating.

He stepped closer and the subtle scent of pine reached me. I expected him to press the issue, but instead he nodded towards Florence and Jia, who were watching our interaction with interest. "Looks like you've already got a fine team on your side, anyways."

"Yes," I said softly. "I do."

Our eyes locked. Then Neville darted between us again.

"I've got this," Kage said firmly.

Before I could react, he moved. One moment he was facing me and the next he was crouched low, his hand gripping the little fluffin by the scruff. Neville squirmed in his grip for a moment, then froze, sniffing the air, as if sensing that Kage wasn't one to mess around with.

Kage held the fluffin out to Florence. "I believe this little troublemaker is yours?"

"Thank you." Florence took Neville and cradled him to her chest. "He's usually so well-behaved," she lied shamelessly. "I don't know what got into him tonight."

Kage's lips twitched. "Wild creatures can't help their nature." His dark eyes went to my face and something about the look he gave me sent a shiver down my spine.

*My, my*, my mother said admiringly. *Does anyone have a fan? I feel like the temperature in here just rose a few degrees.*

I tried to ignore her. "Perhaps the library was not the best place for Neville," I agreed. "We've learned our lesson."

Neville gave a half-hearted rebellious yip, but one look from Kage had him nuzzling into Florence's arms for safety.

"Walk with me?" Kage asked, his tone low.

I blinked. "Now?"

"Unless your friend still needs you," he said, his gaze moving to where Florence and Jia were arguing about what to do next with Neville.

I hid a smile. "All right. I'm sure they'll be fine."

As we walked, the cool air of the library surrounded us. Kage's pace was measured, his presence a steadying force. I felt calmer with him. Safe. We reached a quiet corner and he turned to face me.

"I know you've been working on controlling Nyxaris," he said, his voice low and even.

I tensed. "How did you—"

"You're the first dragon rider in generations. It's not exactly hard to guess. Especially when you're in here, scouring the library for answers." There was a glimmer of amusement in his eyes. "I pay attention."

I crossed my arms, trying to quell my nervousness. "So? What of it?"

He shrugged. "It's nothing to be ashamed of. Nyxaris is not just any dragon."

"No," I agreed. "He's not."

Kage leaned against the wall, crossing his arms over his chest. "Many dragons flew for House Avari. We bred and raised some of the strongest dragons Sangratha has ever seen." His tone was threaded with quiet pride. "And Nyxaris was one of the strongest."

My heart skipped a beat. Of course they'd have records about Nyxaris in their archives. "You've read about him? What do you know?"

Kage's gaze didn't waver. "There's a saying in my house: *A rider's strength comes from their dragon. But their wisdom comes from every dragon who ever lived.* We have records going back centuries. We recorded what each dragon was like, who their riders were, their medical histories. Countless details. I'm sure you'd find most of them quite dull."

I stared at him, my heart speeding up. I wasn't so sure about that. "And Nyxaris? What do you have recorded about him?"

Kage's expression turned thoughtful. "Nyxaris possessed a more tempestuous personality than most Duskdrakes. He had a mind of his own. He was loyal to his riders but that loyalty had to be earned first. He didn't give it freely."

That struck a chord. "Earned how?"

Kage held up his hands. "This is where I tell you I don't have any easy answers for you."

My heart sank.

"But reading between the lines, Nyxaris seemed to appreciate it when his riders showed him respect. When they listened to him. He wasn't just a beast of war. He was—" He smiled a little. "Sorry, he *is* a creature of immense intelligence. Not to mention pride. If someone training to be his rider ignored him, refused to take his advice—well, they didn't remain a rider for long. He wasn't easy to command."

I swallowed, thinking of how easily Nyxaris brushed off my pitiful attempts to control him. "What about his riders?" I asked curiously. "Who were they?"

Kage hesitated, then shrugged. "The records don't say much. Names, a few deeds in battles—if they ever had to fight any. But one thing is clear. Nyxaris was usually devoted to them. He didn't choose lightly or often. Dragons are much longer-lived, after all. But when he did, he'd fight to the death for his rider."

I stared at Kage. He was lying about something. But why lie to me about Nyxaris's riders? What was there to hide centuries later?

"Did House Avari . . ." I hesitated, but forced myself to continue. "Was House Avari responsible for what happened to Nyxaris and the other stone dragons? Did they do that to them?"

Kage's eyes darkened and he pushed off the wall to stand straight. "No," he said firmly. "My house had no hand in that. We'd never have given up a single dragon. Whatever happened to those dragons was not by Avari design. It was a tragedy for all of us."

Something was wrong. He doubted what he was saying, even

though I knew he'd never admit it. "But you know more about what happened, don't you?" I insisted.

He frowned. "I know enough to see that Nyxaris's awakening is a sign that power in Sangratha is shifting. Not everyone will welcome the changes the dragon heralds." He looked at me steadily. "Especially if Nyxaris's loyalty returns to House Avari."

I hadn't even thought of that possibility. Would Nyxaris really do that? Did he still care about his former house at all? I thought of something else. "Do you think I'm in danger? Is that what you're saying?"

"You're the only rider. You're always going to be in danger. But if you mean from Nyxaris, no. I doubt it. Earn his respect and he'll protect you if you let him."

I exhaled, trying to slow my racing thoughts. "If only it were that simple."

His gaze lingered on mine and for a moment I couldn't breathe. Kage's dark eyes seemed to see straight through me. What would it be like to have someone like him by my side? Someone steady, commanding, loyal. I flushed, horrified at the thought, a wave of guilt flooding through me. What was wrong with me? I'd just come from Blake's bed, and now . . .

I bit my lip. Still, I didn't owe Blake anything. What was it that I'd insisted earlier that night? That I wasn't his. That what we'd done together wasn't going to turn into a regular thing.

Kage tilted his head, a faint smile ghosting across his handsome face. "Distracted?"

"No," I lied quickly. Too quickly.

"Good," he said, stepping a little bit closer. The scent of pine mixed with something darker, something wilder, reached me and I felt rooted in place. For a fleeting moment, I imagined what it would be like to touch him, to trace the inked line of that crescent moon with the tip of a finger. "Because there's something else I want you to keep an eye on."

"What's that?" I asked.

"Blake," Kage said. I nearly jumped. "Have you noticed anything unusual about him lately?"

I couldn't help rolling my eyes. "You mean besides him acting like an egotistical, controlling maniac?"

Kage smiled slightly. "Besides that, yes. Just keep an eye on him. If he starts acting strangely, let me know."

"Strange how?" I said, frowning.

His expression didn't change, but there was something about the set of his jaw that told me he had deeper concerns. "You'll know if it happens, trust me."

My thoughts whirled. "Do you think he's dangerous? Would he hurt my friends?"

Kage hesitated, just for a fraction of a second. "No more dangerous than he usually is," he said lightly.

His cryptic tone set me on edge. "You're not telling me everything," I complained with frustration.

"I'm telling you what you need to know right now, Medra," he countered. He took a step back and I let out a breath. "By the way, about your request to move to House Avari—"

"Yes?" I said eagerly.

"I'm still working on it. These things take time," he added quickly, catching the look of disappointment on my face. "And there are . . . some complications."

"Complications? What kind of complications?"

"My mother," he said. "She doesn't trust outsiders easily. Especially when it comes to someone in your unique position."

I knew he didn't mean my being a rider.

"And you?" I asked. The question came out more challenging than I'd intended. "Do you trust me?"

The intensity in his eyes seemed to deepen. "I'd like to think we trust one another." He paused. "If you ever need help, you'll come to me."

It wasn't a request. I stared at him, my mind still whirling with unanswered questions. But before I could voice any of them, Neville darted past us with a delighted yip.

"Looks like your fluffin is on a rampage again," Kage remarked. "Good luck keeping him from tearing the library apart."

I laughed. "Hopefully it won't come to that." As Neville shot down another aisle, I sighed. "But I'd better go and find Florence."

Kage nodded. "Good night, Medra. And good luck."

I nodded, suddenly awkward. "Thank you."

I watched him as he stalked down a row of books, his back ramrod straight.

*Mmm*, my mother said appreciatively. *I like a masterful man. Especially one capable of taming wild beasts.*

*Neville is the size of a cat*, I pointed out. *Not exactly a ferocious monster.*

*Still, that Avari boy is capable. He has . . . finesse.*

She had a point. *He's very competent*, I agreed.

*Lacks Blake's fire, though*, she said. *How does the saying go? A prince in the keep, a dragon between the sheets?*

*There is no such saying*, I protested. *Besides, Blake is most certainly not princely in the keep. He's as hotheaded and explosive as he is . . .* I paused, suddenly aware of what I'd been about to confess.

*As he is . . . ?* My mother prodded, sounding as if she were trying to hold back laughter.

I refused to reply.

Back in my room, I placed the dagger on the desk by the window, kicked off my boots and flopped onto my bed.

Poor Neville had been carted back home to Florence's room in shame. We'd been forced to resort to trapping him in a basket, his little paws scrabbling at the sides while Florence muttered apologies and Jia shook her head in exasperation.

I couldn't help but grin as I remembered Florence marching

out of the library with him tucked under her arm like a contraband toy.

My amusement faded as my thoughts drifted back to Kage.

Sighing, I sat up and crossed my legs.

*Nyxaris? Are you there?*

For a moment, nothing. Then I sensed the dragon stir, almost as if he'd been sleeping.

*What do you want?* His voice was a huff of irritation. If I'd woken him up, that made sense. *I thought I made myself clear. I do not wish to speak with you until you have earned the conversation.*

I tried not to roll my eyes in case he could sense it. *I know. But I have something you might find interesting.*

A pause, then a skeptical growl. *Go on.*

I hesitated. I wondered if Kage knew I'd go straight to Nyxaris with everything he'd shared with me tonight. But then, it wasn't as if he'd sworn me to secrecy.

*I spoke with Kage Tanaka tonight. He's the school House Leader of Avari.*

I felt the weight of Nyxaris's attention shift fully to me. *And what did this Tanaka have to say?*

I repeated some of what Kage had told me—his assurances that House Avari hadn't been responsible for the enchantment that turned the dragons to stone. Nyxaris listened in silence.

When I finished, he let out an explosive snort that echoed through my mind like distant thunder. *You trust the word of this highblood? Scion of the very house that once enslaved me?*

I was shocked. *They didn't enslave you. I mean . . . Did they?* I could sense his rising anger. *Your riders came from House Avari. Didn't you choose to fight for them?*

*Choose?* Nyxaris's voice was sharp. *Does a child choose who their parents are? Do you really think dragons had a choice about who they would belong to?*

*You were the most powerful beings in the kingdom—* I started to say.

*We were bred by them.* He cut me off. *We were bound by blood magic* to serve their ambitions. *The Avaris used us, commanded us, manipulated us. Do not speak to me of choice.*

I swallowed hard. *I'm sorry. But Kage said you were loyal. That you didn't give your loyalty freely. So I just thought . . .*

Nyxaris fell silent for a moment. *Loyalty is a fragile thing. My loyalty to House Avari was once unbreakable. But time, betrayal, and that cursed state of stone eroded it to nothing.*

I hesitated. *So . . . do you feel nothing for them now? No loyalty to Avari at all?*

Another long silence. *Perhaps a faint ember remains. A shadow of the bond that once tied us. I can hardly remember.* His voice faded and for a moment, I thought he was gone.

Then he spoke again. *Do not let their honeyed words deceive you. Even those who may seem different.*

*I'll be careful,* I said quietly. *I'll find the truth for you like I promised. I have another class with Professor Hassan tomorrow. I'll try to get something out of her. I know she has answers for us.*

Though getting them would be another story.

*Good,* Nyxaris rumbled. *See that you make progress. Or you will be standing alone come time for your evaluation.*

With that friendly threat, his presence faded, leaving me alone in the silence of my dark room.

# CHAPTER 20

# MEDRA

Y ou must always remember your place," Professor Hassan said, pacing the front of the room as I sat on a stone bench, obediently scribbling messy notes on the parchment I held precariously on my lap.

The classroom with its open wall to the sea must have originally been used for dragon riders, but it wasn't particularly conducive to academic lectures. There were no desks to put my things on, for one. Not to mention when the wind picked up, we were both freezing. Not that Hassan would ever show it. She'd probably lecture through a snowstorm.

"Your allegiance belongs to the tribunal and to the highbloods who have allowed you the privilege of continuing to breathe Sangrathan air. A dragon is a weapon, a tool for power. It is your duty to wield it on behalf of those who govern the realm." Hassan was nothing if not repetitive. She tapped her cane on the stone floor, the sharp lines of her face set in a look of disapproval. Nothing new.

I studied her. The professor was dressed severely as always, her long hair streaked with silver pulled back into a tight bun, her ink-black gown devoid of embroidery or decorations. How had she gotten this way? Did she have any family of her own? How had she come to teach at Bloodwing? And more importantly, why the hell did she love highbloods so damned much? The coercion magic might have been wavering but Hassan's loyalty was unshakable. I doubted anything could change it.

Hassan's cane slammed down on the stone seat in front of me and I jumped. "Riders," she said, when she'd made sure she'd regained my full attention, "are not partners to dragons. Nor are they equals to the highbloods who command them. Riders are intermediaries."

I thought it was a little ridiculous that she kept referring to *riders* in the plural, as if I wasn't the only one. But I wasn't about to point this out.

"You are a bridge. A necessary tool to channel power from one point to another. That is all. Never forget it." I felt the weight of her eyes on me. "Highbloods, despite being the rightful rulers of Sangratha, may not speak directly to dragons. That is the role of the rider. The dragon may see you as its rider but never mistake its obedience for loyalty to *you*." Her lips thinned as she glared down at me. "The dragon's true loyalty, if a beast may be said to have any, belongs to the highblood house which commands it."

I wondered if Kage would disagree. After all, he'd told me Nyxaris had been loyal to his riders and not merely his house.

She leaned down, punctuating every word with a tap of her infernal cane. "You are an instrument. Your purpose is to convey the will of the highbloods and to ensure that your dragon performs its duty. Nothing more."

I forced myself to stay silent, swallowing all of the arguments that were threatening to burn a hole in my throat. I knew Nyxaris would hate Hassan.

There was a knock at the door and Hassan's head snapped towards it, annoyance crossing her face. She glanced at me, then moved to the door. She opened it, spoke to someone, then turned back to me. "Stay here," she ordered, before stepping out into the corridor.

The moment the door closed behind her, I sprang to my feet. Hassan was never going to give me the answers I needed. I'd be a fool if I thought I'd ever win her over.

I moved quickly to her desk, scanning the array of books and papers that covered it. Then I saw it. A thin leather dossier with a name emblazoned on the front: *Nyxaris, Avari Duskdrake*. My pulse racing, I grabbed it and began flipping through the pages.

The first sections were detailed and clinical. Descriptions of Nyxaris's physical capabilities: his wingspan, flight endurance, and firepower. I didn't know where the information had even come from or if it was accurate. Had someone from Avari put the dossier together based on their historical records? Or were these simply educated guesses based on what they'd seen of Nyxaris so far?

I flipped through the dossier and the content changed to something more harrowing.

> **Historically designated as an enforcer. Nyxaris exhibited unparalleled efficiency in subduing rogue dragons and riders.**

My heart flew into my mouth. Rogue dragons? Rogue riders?

> **Known for instilling terror among noncompliant factions. Deployment successful in 97% of cases.**

Someone from House Avari must have written this. That, or the information had been stolen from them somehow.

My stomach churned as I absorbed the details. Why hadn't Kage shared any of this with me? Nyxaris had been used as an enforcer. When other dragons or riders faltered or rebelled, he'd been sent to remind them of their place. The language was vague and militaristic, but the implications were horrifying. I read the term *punishment* more times than I could count.

Why hadn't Nyxaris told me this himself? Did he even remember the details of his brutal past?

The next page contained a dire summary of his capabilities,

alongside cryptic notes about *strategic utility* and *emergency measures.*
It was clear that the tribunal considered Nyxaris a weapon above
all else, but that was no surprise.

I flipped a few pages and saw a heading that made my blood
run cold. *Assessment of Rider Compatibility.* My name was scrawled
across the top and below it was a list of traits and observations,
clearly made by Hassan.

**Temperament: Stubborn. Questionable loyalty to
highbloods. Willful and lacking in discipline. Challenges
authority at every turn.**

**Connection to Nyxaris: Unknown. Rider is disrespectful
and evasive.**

**Psychological Resilience: Moderate. Displays reckless
tendencies.**

**Potential for Soul-Binding: Cannot be determined. More
sessions needed.**

I read the last line twice, my blood turning to ice.

**Potential for Soul-Binding.**

We learned about the ritual of soul-binding last year when I'd
attended one of Florence's Magical Foundations classes with Professor Wispwood. She'd told us about the practice in which highbloods would perform the ritual on blightborn. The blightborn was
supposed to willingly accept the vampire's soul, allowing them to
live on through them—but it hadn't always been done willingly.
And sometimes the blightborn had been riders. By binding their
soul to a rider, the highblood could control a dragon directly. That
is, if the ritual even worked. If it didn't, the highblood could die.

I wracked my mind, trying to remember what else Professor Wispwood had said about the ritual. But I couldn't remember everything. Still, the price was obviously steep. Who would want to risk their own death? And yet, the potential payout must have been worth it for some. A highblood could keep all of their vampire abilities, plus gain something incredibly elusive: the ability to control a dragon through their bond with their rider. Meanwhile, the rider lost everything. Their soul was either destroyed or overridden by the highblood. I wasn't sure what would be worse. Their body was invaded, taken from them.

My head was spinning. The checklist wasn't just about evaluating my performance in the class. It was about determining whether I could be sacrificed.

My eyes darted to the bottom of the page, searching for a name, for any clue as to who had ordered this. This couldn't be the tribunal's doing. Someone specific must have arranged for this class. Someone who wanted Nyxaris all to themselves. Someone willing to risk dying for the chance to fly a dragon.

Viktor Drakharrow was the obvious suspect. But I couldn't be sure. Hassan didn't belong to any house, did she? She was supposed to be neutral as an instructor, but some instructors clearly did have house affinities. I thought of Professor Allenvale who taught at a House Orphos school and wore their colors with pride. She was a highblood, though. Maybe that made a difference.

Who did Hassan really answer to? I had to find out.

The door creaked open. I slammed the dossier shut and darted out from behind the desk as quickly as I could, my heart pounding as Hassan stepped back into the room and her gaze swept over me.

"What are you doing?" she demanded suspiciously.

I forced myself to meet her eyes. "Waiting. You told me to stay, but I was bored and cold. So I was walking back and forth, getting some exercise." I faked a yawn. "Is that all right with you?"

"No, it's not," she snapped. "You should be contemplating what you've learned here today. Not wasting your time walking about like an empty-headed ninny."

"I was contemplating as I walked," I replied flippantly.

Her eyes narrowed. "Disrespect will not be tolerated."

"Would you like me to leave and come back another day?" I asked innocently. Now that I knew she was evaluating me for my death, I suddenly didn't give a shit if I failed her little course. What was the worst that could happen? They'd execute me sooner rather than try to steal my body later? "You seem a little distracted today. Is everything all right?"

Her face flushed with anger. "I am the instructor. You are the pupil. You will wait as long as is needed when I am required elsewhere. Is that understood?"

"Absolutely," I said, with false politeness. "Are we finished for today?"

She studied me in silence. "You may go."

It wasn't an answer. But I could tell she wanted me to get out. *Fine by me.* Right now, I never wanted to see the detestable woman again. I'd known she disliked me. I hadn't thought she'd be willing to actively plot my death. I'd been naïve not to expect it, though.

I knew I'd have to go back. I had to find out who was pulling her puppet strings. And how much time I had before they decided on my fate.

CHAPTER 21

# MEDRA

A fter my last class with Professor Hassan, I was on pins and nee-dles waiting for my thrallguard session a few days later. I ar-rived outside Professor Rodriguez's office early. I shifted from one foot to the other, my nerves coiling tighter with each passing minute as I waited for him to make an appearance. I was shaken. Desperate for answers or some semblance of reassurance from the only person who might be able to provide them.

By the time I finally spotted the dark-haired blightborn instruc-tor coming down the hall, I was a mess of anxiety.

Rodriguez raised an eyebrow as he saw me. "You're early."

"I really need to talk to you," I blurted, following him inside his office.

He set his leather bag down on his desk and gestured for me to sit. "That much is obvious. But after the skill you showed with thrallguard earlier this summer, I didn't think you'd have as much interest in continuing our lessons."

"I don't . . . I mean, I do. I definitely want to continue them. I'm not that much of an expert with thrallguard yet." I was a little surprised by his compliment. "We're talking about Viktor Drak-harrow here. Part of me is convinced my ability to block him out was simply a fluke."

"A fluke you were able to repeat," he reminded me. "I know he came to see you."

I didn't want to think about Viktor in my room and his awful threats. I still wasn't sure what had made him leave and not return.

"Still. I'm not going to turn down any help I can get," I said with determination.

Rodriguez frowned. "Is that why you're so on edge? Has Viktor been threatening you again?"

I took a deep breath. "You could say that. But I don't know if it's him or not."

Rodriguez cocked his head.

"I don't know who the real threat is. I mean, obviously Viktor is a jackass as usual, yes. But . . ." The words poured out of me and I told him everything I'd seen in the dossier. When I was finished, Rodriguez looked stunned. His face, normally so composed, had paled. The silence in the room was deafening.

"Well?" I prompted finally, gripping the arms of my chair. "Aren't you going to say something?"

Rodriguez ran a hand over his handsome brown face. "Soul-binding," he repeated, almost as if to himself. His voice was grave. "I didn't think . . . I hadn't considered they'd go that far."

His reaction only served to deepen the knot of fear in my chest. "But you thought something like this might happen?"

His gaze shot to me and there was suddenly fire in his eyes. "Dragons are dangerous," he practically snarled. "I knew that already, Miss Pendragon. I had hoped you had gleaned that from the many books I gave you last year. But instead of being cautious, you woke one up."

I gulped. "But I thought . . ." I tried to steady myself. "You said there was a time when riders and dragons might have ruled. Maybe this is a good thing."

"After what you've just informed me about Nyxaris's brutality? And the fact that at least one highblood, if not more, wants to attempt a soul-binding on you as soon as you've brought the dragon under your control and bonded with him?" Rodriguez shook his head. "If you were going to bring back a dragon, that Duskdrake is not the one I'd have hoped for."

"At least it wasn't the Infernus," I snapped.

He looked at me in surprise. "Vorago? No, that's true. That would have been even more disastrous." He ran his hands through his hair.

"Did you know this would happen?" I demanded. "That book . . ."

"That book was full of a great deal of knowledge, Miss Pendragon. Knowledge which you stole, I might add. And evidently, you read the wrong parts," Rodriguez barked at me.

I flinched. "Fine. I screwed up. As usual." I was curious, though. "Which dragon would you have wanted me to bring back? Not that I had any choice."

"Molindra," he said immediately. "The Luminthar."

"A House Orphos dragon?" I said, surprised. "Why?"

"She was renowned for her wisdom and courage," Rodriguez said. "Anyhow, it doesn't matter. What's done is done. What matters is what happens next. This problem . . . It has to be contained." He glanced at me in a way that suddenly made my blood run cold.

"Do you mean me?"

"No," he said hastily. He shook his head. "No," he said more firmly. "Although, I won't deny that thought didn't occur to me just now."

"Your face was an open book," I said hotly. "I suppose killing me here in your office would be inconvenient for you as a teacher, but it might save you a lot of trouble in the long run. Is that it, Rodriguez?"

His eyes flashed. "It would save the *world* a great deal of trouble, Miss Pendragon. The blightborn world which you, might I add, are a part of. In the wrong hands, a dragon is a source of pure destruction. Countless blightborn will suffer and die if the highbloods get hold of Nyxaris. Especially since the coercive forces highbloods depend upon to maintain order are slipping."

"You've noticed that, too?" I remembered the blightborn students I'd encountered.

He nodded grimly. "Rebellions will soon rise. How do you think the highbloods will expect them to be put down?"

"With an enforcer," I whispered.

His lips thinned. "Precisely. And if they could do it themselves, using your bond, your body, then so much the better."

"Everyone wants to use me," I said bitterly.

"Not everyone," he said softly. "It may come as a surprise, but I've come to admire and respect your spirit, Miss Pendragon. I do not wish for you to have to make the ultimate sacrifice unless it is the only way forward. Nor do I wish for you to suffer being possessed by a highblood. Not if we can find another way."

"What other way?" I demanded.

He frowned down at his desk. "You must leave that with me. In the meantime . . ."

He paused for so long I thought he'd forgotten about me. But I suppose I'd given him a lot to think about.

"Yes?" I finally prodded.

His head snapped up. "In the meantime, have you told anyone else about what you've discovered?"

I shook my head. "No. Not even Florence. Just you."

"Good. That's probably for the best. Miss Shen is a brilliant student. But telling her . . ." He gave me a sympathetic look.

"It could put her in danger," I finished. "Yes. I know."

"Good. Not to mention if Hassan finds out you're aware of their intentions, it'll put an even bigger target on your back."

I nodded, then added, "But Nyxaris . . . What do I do about him in the meantime? What I read scared me. In the dossier, they call what he did *punishment*. But . . ." I trailed off, my throat tightening ". . . it sounded more like slaughter."

Rodriguez leaned back in his chair, his expression dark. "I knew Nyxaris was one of the more powerful dragons. But I hadn't realized the full extent of his crimes."

"Crimes?" My voice rose in shock. "You're calling him a criminal? He's a *dragon*."

Rodriguez's gaze hardened. "What would you call it? Dragons are fiercely intelligent creatures. They're capable of choices, of knowing right from wrong. Nyxaris chose to carry out those orders. Whatever loyalty he felt towards his riders, it doesn't excuse the blood on his claws. Does it?"

My stomach churned. I knew Rodriguez was right. "He was a soldier in a highblood house. Are soldiers allowed to say *no* when they're given an order?"

"Always." Rodriguez narrowed his eyes. "Sometimes our choices are all we have, Miss Pendragon. They define us, for better or for worse. Obedience doesn't absolve anyone of guilt. Not dragons. Not riders. Not you or me."

My breath hitched at the bluntness of his words. But I couldn't deny they made sense. "So what am I supposed to do? Try to control a dragon who has a history of widespread murder, show the tribunal I can control him? But it's a contradiction, isn't it? I'm damned if I do and damned if I don't. If I can get Nyxaris to help me or even bond with me, I'm just making myself more valuable to whoever is planning to kill me."

Rodriguez studied me for a long moment, his face unreadable. I knew the wheels in his mind were churning. "You need to talk to him."

"To Nyxaris? I've tried. But I'm not sure how telling him what I've learned will help."

"You won't survive unless you understand him. Right now, you need his cooperation. But do not bond with him, Medra." He used my first name, startling me.

I nodded. "I know. He doesn't want me to, anyhow."

"Good. It would be too dangerous. For both of you. Once a bond is formed, Nyxaris will be as vulnerable to highblood control as you."

I clenched my hands into fists. "This is impossible," I muttered. "I feel so trapped."

Rodriguez leaned forward over the desk, his expression fierce.

"Stop thinking like a victim. We always have more power than we think. Now, use yours." He stood up. "If there's one thing I've learned in my reading about dragons, it's that they respect strength. Show Nyxaris you aren't just a rider in name, but in spirit."

I nodded.

"Now, enough of this. We have work to do."

I blinked, caught off guard by the sudden shift in topic. "Thrall-guard."

"Right," Rodriguez said firmly. "Like you said, you don't want your mind cracked open like an egg the next time Viktor or anyone else tries to delve inside."

I winced. That wasn't exactly the expression I'd used. But he was right in theory. As I prepared for his thrallweave attack, my mind was still a whirlwind of doubts and questions.

Then Rodriguez's voice snapped through all the clutter. "Focus, Miss Pendragon. Or you're already lost."

Our lesson began.

# CHAPTER 22

# MEDRA

A few nights later, the wind tore past, stinging my cheeks as I gripped the rough scales at the back of Nyxaris's neck. Below us the jagged peaks of mountains glinted under the moonlight, their snow-dusted crests bathed silver. I'd made contact with Nyxaris as soon as I'd left Rodriguez's office, but it had taken him this long to fly back to me from wherever he'd been hunting. I'd refused to tell him what I'd found until we were face-to-face—if one could call it that when you were riding on a dragon's back.

We'd met on the hill below the school, near the greenhouse. The rocky space was wide enough for him to land. And I didn't think either of us really wanted to spend more time in the Dragon Court.

I'd eyed him covertly before I'd started my ascent up his side. He looked healthy and well-fed. I had no doubt he was a skilled hunter, not that breathing fire necessarily required a lot of skill unless your target was small. Which then made me wonder what he'd been hunting. So far, I'd been too scared to ask. I decided he probably enjoyed a nice leg of lamb as much as most carnivores.

We sped over another mountain. But the beauty of the view was lost on me. I'd just told Nyxaris what I'd learned in the dossier, conveniently leaving out the part about highbloods wanting to make me into their rider thrall and steal my body. Not only did that sound like a ridiculous piece of fiction when I said it out loud, but it was also not going to happen. Rodriguez and I would stop them. Somehow.

I clutched Nyxaris's scales more tightly. I'd even call in the cavalry if I had to and go to Blake. He was an arrogant asshole, sure, but there was no doubt in my mind that he was courageous. He might not like me, but I knew he didn't want me dead. As for Kage and his offer to help me anytime? I was still on the fence about that. When it came down to it, maybe there was something to be said for the devil I already knew.

I shifted around a little. At least ten minutes had passed since I'd finished recounting details. Nyxaris's silence was ominous. But if he was going to flip me off his back and eat me, he would have done it already.

*Are you ever going to say something?*

*Ever? Most likely. Ever is a very long time. As for whether I shall speak to you, here, this evening . . .*

He was not happy. That much was clear. Because of what I'd learned? Had he wanted to hide who he was from me?

*This,* he said slowly, *was not what I asked you to find.*

His words made me bristle. *So you didn't want me to know the truth. Is that it?*

The dragon's neck snapped back towards me and I saw the molten fury in his eyes. *This was not the truth I needed.* The raw pain in his voice cut through my fear. Nyxaris turned his head back to the horizon, but a subtle tremor betrayed his confusion of emotions. *For years I slept in stone. I recall fire. Blood. Voices I no longer recognized. Now you come to me with this . . . this truth.*

His wings beat harder, forcing me to grab at a spine on his neck to stay steady. Still no saddle. At this rate, I doubted there ever would be one.

*What do you mean?* I asked, after waiting a few more moments. *Are you saying it's all lies?*

He growled. *If it is the truth, it's one I would rather have left forgotten.*

I swallowed, my grip tightening. His anguish rippled through him, as tangible as the icy wind biting at my skin. *I'm sorry. But I had to tell you.*

Yet even now I was keeping other truths from him. Ones which concerned my survival. I wasn't sure if Nyxaris was someone I could fully trust with my life yet or not. We'd already been forced to depend on each other more than either of us seemed to want to.

After a long time, Nyxaris's voice returned to my mind, quieter this time. *Does it frighten you?*

I blinked. *What?*

*What you've learned about me,* he clarified, his voice strained. *Do you fear me now?*

I almost laughed. I had good reason to fear him before, but I knew what he meant. Did I fear him? The image of him raining down fire on riders and dragons flashed through my mind. But he'd also shielded me from the tribunal's wrath. He'd never harmed me.

*I don't know what to think,* I admitted. *I made you a promise. I told you I'd help you find out what happened to you and the others. I still intend to do that.* My words lingered in the cool night air.

*A human who keeps a promise.* Nyxaris made a low rumbling sound. *It's more than I could have hoped for.*

My heart twisted at the melancholy I sensed behind the words. *I'll figure this out. For both our sakes. I won't let you down.*

In my heart, I knew it was true. I didn't know exactly what we were to each other. There was no bond between us. But at some point, I'd started to think of the dragon as less of an adversary and something closer to a friend. Sure, he might have been a mass murderer in his former life. But he had no memory of it. And after all, I didn't come from exactly a virtuous bloodline either. My father, Arthur Pendragon, had committed terrible crimes. But in the end, he'd done something right. So, was I really one to judge? Maybe Nyxaris deserved a second chance. Maybe he'd been punished enough.

Nyxaris flew on steadily, but his wings no longer cut through the air with an angry force.

*The tribunal evaluation approaches*, he remarked finally.

I grimaced. *Don't remind me.*

*You'll need to show them strength*, he continued. *Mastery over me. Enough to satisfy their blood lust.*

*Guess I'm going to fail, then*, I joked. *At least you won't have to put up with me anymore.*

Nyxaris snorted and a plume of steam rose overhead into the cold night. *You may count on my help.*

I blinked. *What? Really?*

*We have not been practicing. But I believe I recall enough to satisfy them. I will make them believe you control me.*

A lump rose in my throat. *Thank you*, I said softly.

*You've made a promise, little rider. The least I can do is ensure you survive to see it through.*

His wings shifted slightly, carrying us higher into the star-filled sky.

# CHAPTER 23

# MEDRA

T he Drakharrow Tower common room was quieter than usual after supper, though several students lingered, chatting or working on homework. Most were blightborn. To my surprise, no highbloods were around feeding from thralls. Maybe that explained the more relaxed atmosphere.

As for me, I'd decided I wouldn't hide in my room anymore. If I was stuck in House Drakharrow for now, I'd make use of the common room and refuse to let highbloods—or their feeding habits—intimidate me.

I'd taken over a large wooden table on the far side of the room away from the hearth where it was quieter. My books and notes were spread out in front of me in a chaotic mess as I worked on my essay for The Alchemist's Garden. It was due the next day. I knew Florence had finished hers a week ago. She'd even gone over the word count in her enthusiasm and now was worried Professor Allenvale might not accept the extra pages. She'd asked me if I needed help with my own essay but I'd breezily put her off, assuring her I was fine.

Now I sat there wondering whether my thesis statement was strong enough: *The dual properties of mirthleaf as an energy restorative and poison antidote highlight its importance in alchemical practices and its potential as a tool for survival.*

I wrinkled my nose. It still didn't sound right. What was the difference between a regular statement and a thesis statement? I was in my second year; surely I should have figured this out by now. I knew Florence would be more than happy to explain, but I didn't want to bother her when she seemed to finally have caught up with all of her own homework and extra reading and had a night off.

The soft scrape of a chair being pulled out beside me broke my concentration. I glanced up to see Blake sinking into the seat, a cocky grin on his handsome face. "Why so glum, Pendragon?"

"What do you want?" I snapped, not bothering to hide my annoyance at being interrupted.

Blake leaned back in his chair, stretching his long legs out in front of him. "Maybe I just want to spend some time with my favorite consort."

I glared at him, my face heating at his reminder of our so-called bond. "It's not feeding time yet, Blake."

I highly doubted he actually wanted to spend time with me for any reason besides taunting me, drinking me, or . . . Well, I wasn't even going to think about that. Not while he was sitting there looking so self-assured and gorgeous.

To my surprise, his grin faded slightly and his expression turned thoughtful. He didn't snap back with a mean retort. Instead he shifted forward and rested his forearms on the table. "That's not why I'm here," he said quietly. He glanced down at my paper. "Although, if you need a tutor . . ."

I blinked, caught off guard a little. "I don't. What do you want?"

"I wanted to talk to you about the tribunal evaluation."

I tensed up. I had one more week. But there wasn't much I could do to prepare. Nyxaris hadn't been interested in practicing. Even for a dragon, he was a huge know-it-all. "What about it?"

Blake glanced around. "Do you, you know, feel like you have a handle on what you'll need to do for the evaluation? How are things going with Nyxaris?"

I stared at him. "Spying on me? Really, Blake?"

Blake laughed. "If I were spying on you, would I really be asking?"

"Maybe you're just not a very good spy," I said grouchily, slouching forward over the desk. "Why do you care, anyhow?"

"Well, you're my meal ticket so I don't exactly want you to get executed." When I didn't reply, he leaned forward so he could look at my face. "That was a joke."

"Ha-ha," I said without breaking a smile. "You're hilarious."

He was quiet for a moment. "I don't want anything to happen to you, Pendragon."

"Of course you don't. You'd probably die without me. Literally."

He took a deep breath. "That's not it. Although, sure, probably."

"Right." I rolled my eyes. "You need me to survive. You have a pretty clear ulterior motive. But anyhow, let me put your mind at rest. Nyxaris has agreed to help me."

Blake looked relieved. "That's good. Really good." He looked around, as if making sure no one was listening. "I saw you with him the other night," he said, lowering his voice.

"So you *were* spying on me? Subtle," I said dryly.

"I keep an eye on you," he said quietly. "I know you won't like my saying that, but it's my job."

"Your job? As in, you spy on me for your family?" I said bitterly.

Blake's face tightened. "It's true that Viktor wants to know that . . . that I have things under control. With you and the dragon." He looked at me almost pleadingly. "You have to understand the pressure I'm under. I'm just trying to keep him at bay."

I studied his face. Was Blake Drakharrow actually confiding something to me? But he'd also confessed he was spying on me for Viktor. If it was progress, it was a tiny step. Ant-sized.

"I don't understand why you have to do whatever he tells you," I said softly, trying to keep my temper in check.

He met my eyes. "He controls my whole family, Pendragon. It's not just me."

"You mean . . . Aenia?" I guessed.

"Her, yes. Though, she's somewhere safe right now. Out of

the way. He doesn't care about Aenia as long as she's always out of sight." He sighed. "Then, there's my mother."

"Your mother?" I was curious despite myself. "I thought she was in the Sanctum. Like a priestess or something."

"It's complicated," he said shortly. "When my father died . . ." He shook his head. "Anyways, you don't want to hear about all my family drama."

I kind of did. But I didn't say anything. And in a moment, Blake changed the subject.

"Look, you might not believe this, but . . . I want to protect you. And not just because of your blood."

He met my eyes and I couldn't help it. I looked away. "The bond between us isn't real, Blake."

"Sure. And neither was what we both felt the other night," he said, his voice low. "But it was amazing. You can't deny that much."

"It was . . . pretty good," I admitted reluctantly. "But not good enough to make me forget who you really are."

His lips thinned. "You know what, believe what you want to about me, Pendragon. But I'm here right now. Trying to help you."

I was quiet. "Fine. So what's the tip?"

Blake's gaze locked onto mine. This time there was no sarcasm, no smirk. That alone was enough to make my heart speed up.

"What?" I demanded. "Tell me, Blake."

"They're going to have leverage," he said, almost reluctantly.

"Leverage? What kind of leverage?"

"They want to make sure you cooperate with the evaluation. That there's no repeat of what happened to Lord Mortis."

I stiffened. "I can't control everything Nyxaris does. He has his own mind, believe me."

Blake's expression turned cautionary. "Do not tell them that, Pendragon. Don't ever even speak it." He looked around and lowered his voice more. "They plan to push you. And if they think you or the dragon isn't giving them what they want, they plan to . . . use one of your friends."

My blood ran cold. "What are you saying?" I could hear the panic in my voice. "Are you saying they're going to hurt someone? Who?"

Blake tried to keep a neutral expression. But the awful thing was I could tell he was upset, too. "I don't know for sure, but if I had to guess . . ." He trailed off.

"No." The word burst out of me. Sharp and loud enough for heads to turn. I shook my head, clenched my jaw, trying not to let Blake see the tears welling up in my eyes. "No. Not Florence."

Not after Naveen. Not after what they'd done with Naveen. I couldn't bear it.

"Keep your voice down." But it was a plea. Not a command. "But yes, I think it'll be Florence."

"They can't. She has nothing to do with this. Nothing," I hissed.

"Try to stay calm," Blake said, looking at me with real concern. I resisted the urge to slap him for saying that. I knew he was trying to shield me from the other students in the room, but I didn't know if I could keep myself in check. "I don't think they're going to kill her."

I choked back a sob. "What a fucking relief." My quill snapped in half between my fingers. "But they *might*. That's what you're implying, right? That they might?" I swiped at my eyes. "So what will they do? Will they torture her?"

"Probably not. Not if you do what they want," Blake said, his jaw tightening. "Just complete the evaluation. Prove you can control Nyxaris. That's how you keep Florence safe. Play it smart. Do what they ask. Nothing more, nothing less. Make sure Nyxaris knows how serious this is."

"He's a dragon," I said bitterly. "He hardly cares about *me*. He's not going to care about one of my friends. Do you know how insignificant we all are to him? I—" I stopped before I could say too much.

Blake leaned closer to me. "Listen, I'll do everything I can to keep Florence safe. I swear it. I'll stay close to her. I'll hold her by the damned hand if they'll let me."

I nodded but the tears were still welling up in my eyes. I hated that I was crying—here in the fucking common room, with Blake, of all people. I blinked rapidly but I knew he'd noticed. Before I could respond to what he'd said, a new voice sliced through the air.

"By the Bloodmaiden, Blake. Did you make the poor girl *cry*?"

My head whipped up. Regan stood beside the table. She was alone this time, thank the gods. But her expression was unmistakable. Elation.

"I told you not to get too comfortable," she crowed. "Did you get your little heart broken, Medra? Let me guess—Blake finally told you the truth. That you were just a distraction? A phase?" She glanced at Blake, her eyes gleaming with satisfaction. "Honestly, I can't blame you."

I could hardly breathe. My fear and helplessness were on full display. And yet Regan was so stupid she'd gone straight to the wrong conclusion. I supposed I should be grateful she hadn't overheard what Blake had been warning me about.

"Regan," Blake said warningly.

But Regan ignored him, her gaze locked on me like a lion who'd spotted a wounded animal. "I mean, it must sting. Thinking you were special, only to find out you were the piece of trash I said you were all along." Her voice dripped with mock pity. "But don't take it too hard. Boys like Blake always come back to where they belong." She reached out a hand as if to touch my shoulder and I flinched.

"Don't you fucking touch her." Blake's voice was cool but strained. "That's enough, Regan."

Regan blinked, clearly surprised, but only for a moment. Then her lips curled into a sneer. "Really, Blake? Is this what you've sunk to? I thought you had standards. Maybe you've spent too much time with the blightborn. Maybe she's dragging you down with her mediocrity. Weak. Spineless. Pitiful."

I didn't have time for this shit. My throat was too tight to even try to respond to Regan's vitriol this time, even though she was completely off the mark.

"Just look at you," Regan said, shaking her head. "You're not even going to make it to the tribunal evaluation, are you?" She leaned down. "Tell me, Medra, are you going to cry like this when they chain you up? Honestly, I almost feel bad for—"

"I said that's enough." The sound of wood crashing against the floor silenced Regan mid-sentence. Blake's chair hit the ground as he shot to his feet, his face thunderous. "Get. Out." His voice was low and lethal.

The other students in the common room turned to stare, whispers rippling through the space. But Regan didn't seem ready to back down completely. She looked him up and down and for a fleeting moment I thought I saw something like actual regret in her eyes. Then her lips turned up in a malicious smile.

"You know," she said, her voice dripping with venomous honey, "I don't even need you, Blake. I've already moved on to someone with actual power. Someone who knows how to value a woman like me properly." Her voice dropped to a near whisper as she added, "The kind of man who can make or break someone like you."

Blake didn't react. "What did I just say, Regan?"

With a haughty toss of her silver hair, Regan stalked out of the common room.

When she was gone, Blake looked down at me. "Just ignore her."

I nodded. Without another word, I rose from my chair, grabbed my things, and shoved them into my bag, then walked past him towards the stairs. I had to get out of there, to escape. I had to find a place where the tears could fall without me having to hold them back.

# CHAPTER 24

# BLAKE

I watched Pendragon leave, her face hollow, her steps heavy and exhausted. She hadn't even made it to the tribunal evaluation, and already they'd nearly broken her. Not by attacking her directly. No, she would have triumphed in that case. But by threatening someone she cared about—someone special to her. It was an insidious way to get to her. Pendragon was the strongest person I knew, but when it came to her friends . . . Well, they were her one weakness.

I was livid. Furious with the entire world and everyone in it. But most of all furious at myself for what I'd done to her.

I'd made her cry.

The common room had fallen silent after my eruption. But I didn't sit back down, didn't walk out. I just stared up at the spiraling stairs, as if I could make Pendragon reappear just by looking. She had every right to hate me: I'd given her plenty of reasons. But watching her crumple, seeing her fight so hard to hold the tears back—something inside me snapped.

What had she said earlier? That the dragon wouldn't care about her or her friends because they were too insignificant to him? Was that how she saw herself—as insignificant, disposable?

My throat tightened. I wasn't blameless. I'd tried to make her feel that way. Weaker. Inferior. Now I wanted to grab her and shake her until she saw the truth. That she was fierce, stubborn,

and kinder than any of the self-serving highbloods around us with
their twisted politics and their willful cruelty. But what right did
I have? I'd helped bring her to the breaking point. My uncle was
probably the one who'd thought of using her friend at the evaluation. If Florence died, it would be my family that was to blame. *I*
would be to blame.

And yet . . . I couldn't just do nothing. Couldn't leave her alone.

I knew she'd gone upstairs to be alone, to wall herself off from
anyone who might glimpse her vulnerability. But to hell with that.

I crossed the room, ignoring the whispers that followed me as
I stalked towards the stairs. I climbed them two at a time, my re-
solve hardening with every step. I reached her door and knocked.
Loudly. No answer. I knocked again. Once. Twice.

"Open the door, Pendragon," I called, not caring who heard
me. "I'm not leaving."

Still nothing. I tried again, knocking harder.

And then, finally, "Please. Open the door, please."

The door swung open abruptly and there she stood. Tear-
streaked and blotchy. Her eyes red and puffy. She was beautiful in
a way that made my limbs weak and my heart hurt. For once, I had
no mocking grin, no teasing remark.

"What do you want, Blake?" Her voice was raw and tired.
"What could you possibly want right now?"

I opened my mouth. Closed it again. I didn't quite know what
I wanted. All I knew was that the sight of her like this was unbearable. "I don't know." My voice was low and rough. "I just . . .
don't think you should be alone right now."

Her breath hitched and she let out a choked sob. That sound. It
shattered something inside of me. Without thinking, I stepped forward. And then she was in my arms, melting against me, her fists
clutching my shirt like I was the only thing keeping her standing. I
kicked the door closed behind me, shutting out the rest of the world.

"I'm sorry," I murmured. I pressed my lips to her temple, her hair, every spot I could find, as she buried her face in my chest, her shoulders shaking. "I'm so damn sorry."

She didn't reply, but slowly she looked up at me. "I hate you," she whispered, her voice quavering. But her hands grabbed the fabric of my shirt even tighter, pulling me closer.

"I know," I whispered back, "you hate me." Deep down, I knew hatred was all I'd ever deserve from her.

I leaned down, kissing her eyelids, her cheeks, her lips. Every wet spot I could find, every tear. I kept kissing her, because if that was all I could give her at that moment, I'd give it all. I kissed her like she was the air I needed to breathe. Gently, reverently. As if I could somehow piece her back together with the touch of my lips. She trembled against me, her breathing coming faster. I wanted nothing more than to take away all of her hurt and replace it with something—anything—better.

My heart slammed against my chest as she pulled back and tilted her head to look up at me, her red-rimmed eyes searching mine. "Blake," she said, her voice somewhere between anger and despair.

I cupped her face with both hands, my thumbs brushing away fresh tears as they fell. "I'm here. I'm not going anywhere." My jaw tightened. "They can all go to fucking hell, Pendragon. Nothing is going to happen to your friend. I swear it."

She lifted her head, her lips colliding with mine, hesitantly at first, then more urgently, like the breaking of a dam. The kiss was fervent, desperate. Like she was trying to claw her way out of her own misery and find something solid. Her fingers slid over my chest, then lower. She tugged at the fabric of my shirt, her fingers curling in the waistband of my trousers.

"Off," she whispered.

"Are you sure?" I breathed, pulling back to search her face.

She nodded, her gaze steady, even as her lips quavered. I didn't have to be asked twice. I pulled my shirt over my head and tossed it aside. Her fingers trailed over my chest, over the snaking black dragon tattoos inscribed there, as if hesitant but curious. I shivered under her touch, every nerve in my body attuned to her.

"Why are you—" She stopped, swallowing hard.

"What?" I asked, gently brushing a damp curl off her face. "Why am I what?"

"Why are you being . . . like this?" Her eyes were filled with confusion. As if she couldn't reconcile the Blake she knew with the one standing in front of her now.

"Like what?"

"Kind," she whispered, her voice so soft I almost couldn't hear her.

My chest tightened. "Because you deserve it," I said roughly. "Because you've always deserved it."

She let out a shaky breath, her fingers tightening along the ridges of my back, pulling me towards her as her lips found mine again. This time the kiss was slower, deeper. The desperation was still there but it had been softened, replaced with something that made my chest ache with need. Her hands slid over my shoulders, and I held her tighter, feeling the delicate curve of her waist under my palms. I wanted to memorize every inch of her, every soft little sound she made. She was a storm of contradictions, all fragility and fire. If she let me, I'd be the one who'd hold her through every storm and tempest on the horizon. Our kiss deepened. Her body pressed more firmly against mine and I couldn't stop the low groan that escaped me. Her fingers tangled in my hair.

"Come here," I murmured against her lips, my voice a low growl as I tried to keep my need at bay. I didn't want to take from her, not today. Today I wanted to give her something. Everything. Anything she needed. Anything that would help the hurt, stem the tide of her tears. I held her by the waist and gently guided her backwards towards the bed in the center of the room until the backs of her knees hit the edge of the mattress.

She looked up at me, her eyes huge, unsure. I waited, giving her time to tell me to stop. She didn't.

I brought my hands to her shoulders, my touch gentle as I eased her back, lowering her onto the mattress, my weight hovering above her. My lips brushed hers, slow and patient, trailing down to the corner of her mouth, then down to her jaw. I kissed my way down to her neck, lingering there before forcing myself to move on. My fingers reached for the buttons of her blouse. I hesitated, looking down at her, silently asking for permission.

She nodded slowly, her breath catching as I undid the first button. Then the next. And the next. The blouse parted and I moved on to the little white chemise she wore underneath, the thin cotton fabric the only thing keeping me from her breasts. I could already see the tips of her nipples straining against the material. For a second, my fingers stumbled over the tiny pearl buttons, but then I continued steadily, as though I were unwrapping something infinitely precious. When the chemise finally fell away, my gaze swept over her.

"You're beautiful," I said, my eyes darkening. "So fucking beautiful, Pendragon." My hands moved to the waistband of her skirt. I paused, my eyes meeting hers. "Tell me if you want me to stop," I said, my voice a little hoarser now.

She shook her head. "Don't stop," she whispered.

I lifted her skirt slowly, taking in the sight of the white lace undergarment she wore. I slid my hand down her bare thigh, then between her legs, feeling the dampness. She gasped as I pushed the fabric aside, then moaned as I slipped a finger inside her. Her breaths came in urgent pants as I slid my fingers in and out of her. But it wasn't enough. I wanted to give her more.

I leaned over her, kissing the tips of her breasts, then moving my mouth down the plane of her stomach, across her hips. I lifted her skirt, sliding it up to her waist, and then lowered my tongue to her pussy. Her breathing quickened. She clutched the coverlet of the bed with her free hand as she tangled the other in my hair. I moved my thumb over her clit as I licked between her legs, the stubble along my jaw brushing her soft, sensitive skin. I went slowly, running my tongue up and down the length of her. Enjoying the sounds as her breathing sped up, becoming a ragged pant. Feeling the quivering of her thighs as I teased and tasted, savoring her scent.

Then, finally, the sweetest words. "Blake, please," she moaned. "I can't . . ."

"Fall apart for me, sweetheart," I breathed against her skin, then captured her clit between my lips, sucking hard enough to make her cry out my name so loudly it was almost a scream.

I felt her orgasm rip through her in a shockwave, her hand tightening in my hair as her hips arched against my mouth, her knees shaking. I slid my hands over her hips, her thighs, savoring the soft perfection of her skin. Memorizing the smell of her. The scent that had filled my dreams.

She reached down for me, pulling me up beside her and I complied, sliding up the bed and wrapping her in my arms. Her fingers skimmed over my chest restlessly. "Not enough," she whispered. "Still not enough."

I looked down at her in surprise. "Fuck, Pendragon," I teased. "You're shameless."

Her cheeks colored pink. But I didn't want to embarrass her. I wanted her comfortable, relaxed.

I kissed the tip of her nose, then her cheeks, then grazed her mouth with mine. "Maybe there's something we could do about that."

Her hand was already reaching for my crotch. She rubbed her palm over my cock and I groaned: I'd been hard for her since I stepped into the room and I was sure she knew it. "Maybe we can do something about this," she whispered teasingly. Her fingers were already fumbling with my buttons.

I let her push my trousers down over my hips, revealing the length of me. I hid a grin as her eyes widened slightly, taking me in. She'd seen it all before, but still, in some ways I seemed as new to her as she was to me. I didn't think I'd ever tire of her—or of seeing her body.

I slid my hand between her legs, stroking her up and down, as she panted with need, arching her hips to beg me for more. Finally, I moved over her, shifting myself between her legs and then thrusting inside her. She gasped, her hands clutching my back, pulling me against her and kissing me as I drew my hips back and thrust into her again and again.

"Fuck, Pendragon," I gasped, as I sank into her. "You sure we can't make a habit of this?" I bit my lip and looked down at her, scared I'd said too much, afraid I'd offended her.

But her eyes were closed. Instead of responding, she locked her legs around my hips and lifted her body to meet me. I watched in wonder as her lips parted, cheeks rosy and flushed, as the tide of pleasure raced over her. Her soft cry broke the silence, her body trembling against me as she reached her peak. And then my own pleasure cascaded through me like a burst of flame and I drove into her harder, finding my own release, as her name slipped from my lips over and over. The sensation was overwhelming. Like nothing I'd ever felt. Not just physical, but emotional. As if the walls between us had finally crumbled.

When I'd come down from the high, I rolled off her. But I didn't want to let her go. I shifted onto my side, lacing my fingers through hers and pulling her close. To my shock, she let me. She didn't pull away.

My heart was still pounding like a drum. I wondered if she could hear it. Our eyes met. I pressed my forehead gently against hers.

"Do you want me to go?" I asked, trying not to show how badly I wanted to stay.

The moment seemed to drag on forever.

Then slowly, she shook her head. "Bath? Then sleep?"

My heart sped up. "Sounds good." I felt a bone-deep relief. She wasn't pushing me away.

I stood up and reached for a blanket folded at the foot of the bed. Then I pulled her to a sitting position and wrapped it around her shoulders.

"Stay here. I'll run the bath." I moved to the adjoining room and turned on the taps. Water rushed forth. Soon steam was curling into the air. I looked around at the bottles on the edge of the tub, then picked one labeled *lavender.* The herb was supposed to calm and soothe. Pendragon needed that.

As I held the bottle in my hand, I froze. What the fuck was I doing? Since when did I stay in a girl's room after we'd finished fucking? Since when did I run a girl a bath? I'd practically been begging to stay and cuddle. Had Pendragon noticed? Did she think I was pathetic?

I went back into the other room. She was still sitting on the bed, the blanket draped loosely over her shoulders, her red hair tousled around her flushed, just-fucked face.

For a moment, I just stood there. Drinking in the sight of her. I wanted to tell her how beautiful she looked. How beautiful she always looked. But I didn't want to spook her, think I was demanding too much too soon.

"It's ready," I said, finally, holding out my hand. She hesitated a beat before taking it.

As the warmth of the water enveloped us, I pulled her close, her back resting against my chest as I wrapped my arms around her beneath the water. I could feel the leftover tension in her body gradually melting away, her breathing evening out as the soothing heat and soft scent worked their magic.

I rested my head on hers, trying to think of the right words to say. "I meant what I said. I'll keep Florence safe. I'll do whatever it takes."

She moved her head to look up at me, her expression tired but soft. "Thank you."

I pressed a kiss to her temple. "You should get some rest."

We climbed out, drying off in a silence that didn't feel tense or awkward for once. I helped her pull on a robe, then grabbed one for myself. It was a little small and I saw her eyes light up, as if she was trying not to laugh. But in the end, I think she was too tired to even bother. I followed her back to the bed, waiting for her to tell me to go. To say this had been another mistake.

But instead, she just climbed in, pulling the covers up to her chin.

After a moment's hesitation, I slid in beside her. For once, I didn't need to try to fill the silence. I just held her, our legs tangling beneath the blankets as the weight of the day slipped away.

"Sleep," I murmured against her hair, my fingers moving up and down her back. "I'm here."

And as her breathing slowed, I stared up at the canopy. She'd fallen asleep in my arms. It was such a simple thing. So why did it feel like a miracle I could barely process? I'd never been in this position before. Never felt this need to stay.

I tightened my arms around her, my chest filled with something too big to name. For once, I wasn't running, wasn't pretending. I didn't want to. The thought of leaving her side tonight—or any other—felt like sacrilege. Maybe I didn't deserve her. Hell, I knew I didn't. But that didn't mean I was going to let her go. Not when she was here, her breath warm against my skin, her trust fragile but real.

Her fingers twitched lightly against my chest, her body relaxing more fully into mine and I pressed a kiss against her hair and closed my eyes.

"Mine," I whispered, the word slipping out before I could stop it.

For the first time in a long time, I fell asleep believing that maybe, just maybe, I was capable of something better.

Because of her.

# CHAPTER 25

# MEDRA

The Bloodwing greenhouse was warm, the air heavy with the comforting and familiar scents of earth and herbs. I was getting rather attached to the classroom and getting used to being outdoors part of the week. Not to mention that Professor Allenvale was quickly becoming my favorite instructor after Rodriguez.

Professor Hassan could take a page from her book, I decided as I shifted on my wooden stool, trying to focus on Professor Allenvale's voice as she strode up and down between the long tables, handing back our essays. But my mind was a jumbled mess. Tangled with indecision over the things I'd been holding back from sharing with Florence. Everything that had been happening with Blake. The tribunal evaluation. Every glance in my friend's direction made the knot in my stomach tighten.

Florence sat beside me, completely oblivious to my turmoil, her notes lined up in neat rows in front of her. Her cheeks glowed pink as Professor Allenvale leafed through the essays. I knew she was excited to receive her mark.

I hadn't told her anything yet—about the tribunal's plan, about how her very life might be hanging in the balance because of me. She deserved to know, but how could I say it? How could I look into those trusting eyes and tell her that the highbloods she'd once worshiped were going to use her just to get me to do what they wanted?

Professor Allenvale's voice cut through the fog. "Miss Shen," she said, smiling brightly and holding up a sheaf of parchment, "an absolutely exceptional piece on shadowleaf. Thorough, insightful, and detailed. I was impressed that you even referenced an obscure text by Varison. How long did it take you to comb through the archives to find that one? Hmm?"

Beside me, Florence's face lit up in a grateful smile. "Thank you, Professor. I'm so glad you enjoyed it."

I grinned at her. "Good work, Florence."

I couldn't tell her, I decided. I'd go back to Blake and tell him he had to convince his uncle to use someone else. Anyone else. But who? What was I really going to do, lie and say I cared about Visha or Theo more than Florence? Or maybe sacrifice Vaughn Sabino again? No, I couldn't do that. Florence wouldn't want me to.

But . . .

A roll of parchment suddenly came into view. Professor Allenvale stood smiling down on me. "Miss Pendragon, a good attempt. A little room for improvement. Perhaps we might work on strengthening your thesis for next time, hmm?"

I grabbed my essay back and blushed. "I knew it needed work. Sorry, Professor."

"We learn through growing, Miss Pendragon. That's why we're all here after all, isn't it?"

*I thought we were all here because the highbloods wanted to use us for their own ends*, I was almost tempted to say. But when I looked at Professor Allenvale, I didn't see someone who seemed particularly evil or self-centered. So, I held my tongue.

"I told you I'd help you," Florence said accusingly. She eyed my parchment. "What's your mark?"

I unrolled the essay and sighed with relief. "C." Commendable. Professor Allenvale had been more than generous.

"I got an E," Florence whispered.

I nudged her. "I figured as much. Show-off."

She blushed but her face still glowed with pride.

There was a soft squeak at the greenhouse door, followed by a faint creak as it swung open. Everyone turned towards the sound. But the doorway was empty.

"That's odd," Professor Allenvale mused, stepping towards the door and pushing it shut again. "Must have been the wind."

It was a gusty day outside, with a wicked gale blowing in off the sea. We'd had a warm autumn last year, but this time, the seasons seemed to want to rush straight towards winter. Everyone thought we'd get snow soon.

Professor Allenvale began to turn back towards her desk, but before she could reach it, there was a high-pitched barking sound, followed by a blur of motion. Neville the fluffin bounded into view, his huge ears wiggling and his tail wagging as if he couldn't be more proud of himself. The little creature darted between the rows of tables, weaving between students' feet with a determined squeak. Gasps and giggles erupted around the greenhouse.

"Oh, no," Florence whispered, her cheeks flaming red. But it was too late. Before she could stop him, Neville leaped right onto her lap, nuzzling against her chest with a happy little yip.

"Florence," I whispered, torn between laughter and horror. "Why is he here?"

"I don't know!" she hissed. "I thought he'd run off to Blake's room this morning. He's been alternating between us all week. At least, I think that's where he's been going." She gently tried to lift the fluffin off her lap, but Neville wasn't having any of it. He squirmed and yipped more loudly, his large owllike eyes locked adoringly on her face.

"I see we have an unexpected guest," Professor Allenvale said from the front of the room. To my relief, she was smiling.

"I'm so, so sorry, Professor," Florence moaned. "Neville sneaks out. He must have followed me. But he's never snuck into one of my classes before."

"Just the library," I muttered under my breath. Florence shocked me by kicking me under the table. I covered my mouth with my hand to hide a snicker.

Professor Allenvale laughed. "Neville, is it? No need to apologize, Miss Shen. It seems your pet has excellent taste in company." She walked towards us, then reached into the pocket of the yellow apron she was wearing and pulled out a small sprig of mirthleaf. "Here, Neville. A reward for your boldness in running towards academic excellence wherever you may find it."

Around us, some of the highblood students looked a little shocked. Perhaps most highblood professors would have scolded Florence. I know Hassan would have.

"I had no idea a fluffin lived at the school," Professor Allenvale observed, still studying Neville. She looked delighted. "I haven't seen one of these little fellows in years."

I blinked down at Neville. In fact, the fluffin seemed to get around the school like a shadow. But how? He wasn't exactly subtle; it was amazing no one had complained about him before.

Florence was trying to gently place Neville on the ground again but he let out an indignant squeak and curled up in her lap, clearly intent on claiming his territory and staying put.

Professor Allenvale chuckled and reached down to pat the fluffin between his huge ears. "He's really quite charming. Not to mention resourceful."

"They're extremely rare now," Lunaya Orphos said, tilting her head thoughtfully. "I'm surprised to see one here."

Florence and I exchanged a look. I knew fluffins were unusual to see above ground.

"Rare?" Florence asked. "I didn't know that."

Professor Allenvale was nodding in agreement. "It's true. They're native to deep underground tunnels. They can often be found in dwarven communities. But even there, sightings have become more uncommon."

"Why?" I asked, my curiosity piqued. "What's happened to them?"

Lunaya shrugged, her silvery long hair catching the light. "Some say they were hunted. Their healing abilities are legendary. Others say they started to die off when the last of the dragons left our world."

I looked at Florence. She looked as surprised as I was to hear Neville had special healing abilities.

Professor Allenvale was nodding. "Lunaya is quite right. Fluffins were known for soothing injuries and even mending broken spirits. In fact, ancient texts say that fluffins were often companions to—" She broke off, pursing her lips as if she were debating whether or not to say more.

"Companions to who?" Florence asked, looking fascinated as she stroked Neville's soft fur.

Professor Allenvale hesitated for only a second, then smiled faintly at us. "To dragons and at times their riders."

My gaze snapped to Neville who was now rolling on his back in Florence's lap, shamelessly begging for belly pats and utterly unconcerned with the fuss his presence was causing.

"Dragons?" I repeated. "What does that mean?" Neville didn't look exactly like a dragon doctor to me.

"Fluffins were said to share innate sensitivity—especially to powerful energies," Professor said cautiously. "There are stories of them appearing in times of great upheaval."

Lunaya leaned forward, her blue eyes alight with interest. "When I was little, my mother once told me a story about fluffins. She said they could sense when a dragon was in pain. Even heal them."

I stared at Neville who had found another piece of mirthleaf on the table and now was batting it between his paws with gleeful abandon. Could it really be true?

Florence looked down at the little creature. "Well, he's always been special to me, but I had no idea he had any unusual abilities. How fascinating."

"Special indeed," Professor Allenvale said with a soft laugh. "Perhaps he chose you for a reason, Miss Shen. After all, healing is one of your primary interests at Bloodwing, is it not?"

Class ended with the distant chime of bells from the castle. As we stepped outside the greenhouse, I held Neville as Florence adjusted her book bag. A little ways across the rocky green lawn, Lunaya Orphos stood talking to someone. A tall man was leaning against the greenhouse with his back to us. I couldn't make out his face, but there was something about him that looked familiar. He shifted slightly, revealing his profile as he said something to Lunaya who gave a gentle laugh, and my blood chilled. It was Marcus Drakharrow.

What was Blake's older brother doing here?

Florence scooped Neville out of my arms and followed my gaze, her brow furrowing. "Who's that talking to Lunaya?"

"Marcus Drakharrow," I muttered. "Blake's brother."

"He's . . . quite burly, isn't he?" Florence remarked.

To put it mildly, Marcus was an intimidating-looking man. Violence seemed built into his very bones. I watched the pair together. Lunaya seemed completely at ease, her violet eyes almost sparkling as she listened to Marcus. I hoped she knew what she was doing: Marcus seemed like a creep. I wondered if Lysander knew who his sister was meeting. Marcus turned his head, as Lunaya began walking up the hill back towards the castle. His gaze landed on me. Instantly, the sweetness that had been in his smile as he looked down at Lunaya Orphos vanished, replaced by something cold and downright nasty. His eyes moved to Florence and he grinned slyly, as if in recognition.

My stomach churned and I stepped in front of my friend to shield her from view. "Come on," I said abruptly, tugging on Florence's arm. "Let's go."

"Oh, right," Florence hoisted her bag onto her shoulder. "I guess I'd better take Neville back to my room. Unless we come across Blake." She sounded hopeful. "Do you think he'd take Neville? I sometimes wonder if Neville respects me enough."

My lips twitched. "You mean, respects you as his mother?"

"Well, it's just that Neville doesn't seem to get into quite the same amount of mischief with Blake," Florence said consideringly.

"Blake is a little more intimidating than you are," I agreed. I sighed. Seeing Marcus had brought me straight to a conclusion. "I need to talk to you. Right away. Just the two of us."

Florence glanced at me, her expression puzzled. "About what?"

"Something important. Something you need to know."

As we walked up the hill, I couldn't help glancing back one last time. Marcus was still watching us, his gaze cool and calculating. I turned away.

The tribunal wanted to use Florence as a pawn. But my friend was the smartest, most capable person I knew. If anyone could handle the truth, it was her. Keeping her in the dark would be a disservice—and a betrayal. She deserved to know the truth.

# CHAPTER 26

# BLAKE

The winds tore across the cliffs, carrying the salt spray of the sea as waves crashed on the jagged rocks below. In the distance, I could make out the dark spires of the city of Veilmar. An open field had been adapted for the tribunal's evaluation. Now spectators gathered along the edge of the cliffs waiting for the event to begin—as if it were some sort of entertainment and not a day of judgment. Most of them were here for the spectacle; they didn't care what the stakes were. I hated them for that.

Pendragon and I had gone about our business separately the past week. I didn't think she was avoiding me, just distracted. We'd met the night before, just for a brief feeding. And by feeding, I meant we'd fucked and then she'd let me feed. I think it calmed her down. She'd fallen asleep in my bed before I'd even stopped drinking from her. I'd pulled out my fangs, tucked her in, even pulled a pair of my socks onto her feet because they felt too cold. When I woke up in the morning, she was already gone.

I looked around me at the highbloods who had come from all over the region. There seemed to be even more there today then had been at the tribunal hearing. Their rich clothing was a contrast to that of the simpler garb of the few blightborn who were scattered among them.

I stood at the edge of the crowd with my hands shoved into the pockets of the long black coat I wore. I'd ridden over here half an hour ago, tethering my horse far enough away that it wouldn't be spooked when Nyxaris arrived. Now I gazed around. An elevated platform had been erected in the center of the field. Rows of wooden chairs had been placed on it, along with tall banners that whipped in the wind and bore the sigils of the four great houses.

I scanned the gathering, finding some familiar faces. Professor Rodriguez stood to one side of the platform, his gray cloak billowing as he and Professor Sankara spoke to a petite blightborn woman who looked vaguely familiar. Then I realized who she must be: Jia Shen, Florence's mother. She had the same dark hair and dark eyes as her daughter. I knew Jia worked as a librarian at the school, but I'd never spoken to her that I could recall. Now I watched as Rodriguez leaned down, his expression calm as he spoke over the wind. I knew he must be offering words of encouragement—I'd told him privately what role Florence would be playing here today. But despite Rodriguez's and Sankara's solid presences, Jia still looked fucking terrified. And no wonder, the poor woman.

I heard footsteps and turned to see Theo and Visha approaching, their expressions grim. Visha was rubbing her arms. She'd only worn a light jacket and looked as if she were freezing.

"Where's Medra?" Theo asked, looking around. He seemed to have mostly forgiven me for the display I'd put on in the refectory that day. Though, I realized with a pang that I hadn't actually apologized. Maybe Pendragon had talked to him. I suddenly wondered if she'd told any of her friends—or our mutual ones—that we were screwing. Though, as the word crossed my mind, I suddenly realized it wasn't one I liked. *Screwing. Fucking.* Those words weren't enough to describe what was happening between us.

I shrugged, forcing myself to sound casual. "Probably already off with Nyxaris. Maybe the dragon wants to make a grand entrance."

Theo nodded, but still looked nervous. "Well, I'm sure she'll show up when they're ready."

I looked at my cousin, suddenly really seeing him for the first time in a long while. He looked thinner, paler. What had happened to the loud, jesting charmer I knew? He'd somehow vanished in the span of a year. Ever since our uncle had Vaughn Sabino beaten and nearly killed. I hadn't exactly been helping the situation. I'd made Theo feel even less secure in the place he should have felt most at home at Bloodwing: House Drakharrow.

As if on cue, the sound of wheels creaking made us turn. A row of black-and-silver-covered carriages were rolling to a halt along the rough, unpaved dirt road that ran alongside the field. I assumed the regents and the rest of the Tribunal Panel were inside. Liveried attendants hopped down and quickly marched forward to open the doors.

Catherine Mortis stepped out of the first carriage, her head topped with a crown of woven silver braids, her expression cold and imperious. She turned back to speak with someone still inside and a moment later, Florence Shen emerged, looking frightened but composed. My stomach twisted as I watched Catherine lead Florence over to the platform and direct her to a chair.

My gaze drifted back to Jia Shen. Florence's mother's face had paled. She was gripping the edges of her coat tightly. Rodriguez murmured something to her, while Sankara stood with his hand resting lightly on Jia's arm as if to steady her. The woman's fear was tangible and I couldn't blame her. Florence might be holding herself together well, but she was still a lamb in a den of wolves. I knew I should be over there, probably talking to her myself. But what would I say? *I'm sorry my family is so fucked up and evil and involved your daughter in this highblood mess?*

Lysander Orphos was helping Elaria Avari out of one of the other carriages. I thought about what Lysander had proposed that day in the tribunal hearing. I'd thought about it a lot since then, actually.

Then my breath caught in my throat. My uncle was emerging from another carriage. And there, stepping out after him, clutching onto his sleeve as if it was her lifeline, was Aenia. My vision tunneled as cold fury swept through me. My little sister shouldn't have been there: I'd made sure of it. Aenia was supposed to be guarded, kept away from the public, kept safe. Yet here she was, looking up at Viktor with wide, uncertain eyes, her tiny frame swamped by a too-large crimson cloak someone had draped around her. At first glance, she looked like any highblood child: delicate, pale, and strikingly pretty with her porcelain skin. But I knew better. Her mind was fractured. Her eyes darted nervously over the crowd. Bringing her here was sheer folly. Not only for her sake but for the sake of the blightborn around her. For now, she was lucid, thank the Bloodmaiden—but that could change in a heartbeat.

She didn't belong here. She didn't belong anywhere near my brother, who'd slaughtered her whole fucking family, or near my uncle, who clearly thought he could use her as his pawn.

I moved forward swiftly, stepping directly into Viktor's path. "We need to talk. Now."

My uncle raised a single brow. "I don't have time for your theatrics, Blake. Step aside."

"You think this is me being dramatic? You'll see real theatrics if you don't get Aenia back where she belongs right now."

Viktor narrowed his blood-colored eyes. "Funny, Blake, to me that sounded very much like a threat. Are you threatening me?"

I growled. "Do I have to? After everything I've done for you and our family, why would you bring her here?"

"Perhaps your little sister—" he stressed the last word and I stiffened "—simply wished to see a dragon in the flesh. Perhaps she asked for us to bring here today as a treat. She is a child, after all." He smiled slowly.

He knew Aenia was no real child. Her mind was fading in and out—because of me. Because of my pathetic attempt to "save" her. Some savior I'd turned out to be. Part of me knew she'd have been better off dead than what I'd turned her into.

"Is there a problem here, Uncle?" Marcus stood behind Viktor, his hand tight on Aenia's shoulder.

"Not at all. Take Aenia to her seat. I'll be right behind you."

My lips twisted as Marcus led Aenia away. The little girl glanced back at me once. But she showed no emotion. She reacted to me less and less.

I'd consulted a healer once, secretly. The woman confessed that she believed soon Aenia wouldn't even recognize me. She'd simply want to feed.

The moment they were out of earshot, I turned back to Viktor. "She's not a bargaining chip. You're putting her at risk. You know what she's capable of. Please, don't do this. I'm asking you as your family."

Viktor's smile was cold. "You should be asking yourself why I've brought her here."

My fists clenched. "Fine. Why?"

"To ensure your compliance," Viktor said smoothly.

"You think I'd rebel against you?" I said, barely controlling my rage. "I've done everything you asked."

"Ah, but it's not just you," Viktor replied, his tone as detached as if we were discussing the weather. "Your little consort. I can't risk the rider trying anything foolish today."

"She won't," I snarled. "And that's why the blightborn girl is here, isn't it? Why do you need them both?"

"I need all three of you," Viktor said.

So I was leverage here today, too. Strangely, I hadn't seen that coming. "Pendragon won't care if you kill me," I said flatly. "So leave Aenia out of it. She's a child. She's our blood."

Viktor's face twisted into a sneer. "Do not associate that foulblood animal with our family name. She is not of my blood and never will be. She is your great mistake."

"My mother accepted Aenia like her own daughter," I said tightly. "And my father—"

"Enough." Viktor shook his head in revulsion. "You say it as if it's a good thing. After all I've taught you, Blake. You should know better."

"I care about the girl," I said, my voice thick. "If she comes to harm, you'll have lost more than her life."

"You threaten to withdraw your loyalty? From me? You dare?" He started to walk away.

"Wait," I called, my voice sharp enough to make him pause. "If she's here, I'm staying with her. On the platform."

Viktor turned back slowly. "I don't recall that being part of the arrangement today, Blake. I'm afraid there aren't enough seats."

"I wasn't asking," I growled, stepping closer to the old man. My voice was unyielding. "Marcus can give me his. If Aenia's up there, if Florence is up there, then I'm up there. Or do you want to explain to the tribunal why your little piece of leverage suddenly went feral and attacked them all? Because I promise you, Viktor, she will if she feels unsafe. And you know damn well I'm the only one she really listens to."

Viktor scowled. "You're testing my patience, boy."

I held my ground, my pulse pounding my ears. I could see he wanted to hit me. If he wanted to, he could end me, here, now, in front of all these people. It would be a bit of a scandal, sure. But if anyone could get away with it Viktor Drakharrow could.

"And you're testing my limits," I said, my voice sharp as a shard of glass. "You can use me. You can push me to my breaking point. But I will not leave them unprotected. Not the blightborn girl. And not Aenia."

The wind whipped around us, stirring Viktor's long black cloak as he studied me. For a long moment, neither of us moved.

Then Viktor gave a dismissive wave of his hand. "Fine. If you're so determined to play the protector, go ahead. But remember, your presence there changes nothing. If you or the rider or that dragon step out of line today, someone will pay for it. And the tribunal will not be on your side if you challenge me."

I nodded, but didn't rise to the bait. I stalked past Viktor and marched towards the platform. I took in Aenia, her tiny frame perched on a wooden chair beside Marcus's hulking one. Her eyes met mine and for a fleeting moment I thought I saw gladness in them.

"Blake," she exclaimed, jumping up. "Sit with me."

My heart clenched. She could sound so much like a regular child still at times. I tried to smile at her. "Of course I will." I glared at my brother. "Uncle wants you. You're giving me your seat."

Marcus stared at me, then he shrugged and stood up. "Fine by me."

He stomped off the platform and I nudged Aenia over, taking a seat in between her and Florence.

"No one will touch either of you," I muttered to the blightborn girl, my voice low but steady.

Beside me Florence sat so still I didn't think she'd heard me. Then she nodded stiffly. "Thank you," she whispered. "Where's Medra?"

And then we both heard it. The sound of beating wings.

# CHAPTER 27

# MEDRA

N yxaris banked sharply over the cliffs. Below, the crowd on the field looked up, their heads craning like a startled flock of birds.

*They're all staring. I feel like a prize pig at a town fair,* the dragon complained.

*Oh, please. Part of you likes the attention, admit it.* I clutched the parchment that was folded in my sweaty hand. *We've gone over the list. You know what they want us to do . . .*

It was a little rich to use the word *us* when I mostly felt like a package Nyxaris was delivering. He'd be doing all of the real work. I had no words of advice. How could I even think of advising a creature this experienced and ancient? All I could do was hope not to fall off or make a complete fool of myself.

Well, that and hope that Nyxaris actually did as he was asked.

The dragon let out a rumbling snort that vibrated through my legs where they gripped his sides. *Maneuvers. Fireworks displays. A child's checklist of tricks. This is what passes for a rigorous exam? Hardly worth my time.*

*Yes, you have my sincere gratitude, O Great One,* I said hurriedly.

He sniffed. *Don't start with that again. Dragons can tell when you really mean it.*

*I do mean it,* I protested. *You are great. And you do have my gratitude.*

*Hmph.* But I could sense him preening a little. I felt a sudden impulse to rub his head just between his ears like I might do to Neville. I knew better, though. *So, I'll take that as a yes? You'll do what's on the list?*

*For your sake, little mortal, I shall endure the indignity. But if anyone dares to clap, I will not be held responsible for what happens next.*

I stifled a laugh. *Understood. Now, stop circling. We need to put on a show.*

Nyxaris tilted his wings suddenly and we plummeted into a dive. The air screamed past my ears. I held tight to the ridges of his neck as below us I saw the crowd react. With an abrupt pull, Nyxaris leveled out above the field, his huge shadow sweeping over the assembly.

A platform had been set up and as we flew over it I spotted the tribunal members, seated in their dark robes. Then I saw Florence, seated stiffly beside Catherine Mortis, her hands folded tightly in her lap. On her other side was Blake, just like he'd promised.

I stiffened. A small girl was sitting next to him. Aenia. My stomach dropped at the sight of the highblood child. What was it Blake had told me other highbloods called people like her? Foulbloods. I scowled as I remembered the horrid name.

Blake was looking up at me. For a brief moment, our gazes locked. He gave me a small nod, almost unnoticeable, and I felt a mix of reassurance and unease. I was grateful to him for staying close to Florence. But if he was up there with Aenia, it meant Viktor was pulling his strings again—and I hated that.

*Stop brooding. It's time.* Nyxaris's voice jolted me back to the present.

*Fine. Let's show them what you've got.*

He rose, his wings catching the wind with a crack. We soared higher and higher, until the crowd below us shrank to specks. Then Nyxaris twisted slightly, plummeting downwards in a spiraling dive that left me too breathless to even scream. He pulled up at the last moment, his claws skimming the tops of the cliffs as he executed a series of tight rolls and sharp turns.

Each maneuver was precise, fluid, and terrifyingly fast.

*Was that on the list?* I managed to get out, as I clung tightly.

*No. That was me warming up.* He didn't bother hiding his smugness.

"Show-off," I muttered out loud. *Are you sure we can't see about getting a saddle made? You might make it through today's evaluation but I'm not so sure about me.*

*Calm yourself, child. Do you think the riders of old required saddles and straps to stay atop their dragons?* Nyxaris chided.

I narrowed my eyes. *What do you mean? They used saddles. You said so yourself.*

*They used them but they were mostly for show. Or for poor riders who could not manage without them. Weaklings.* I could feel his contempt. *The saddles and straps were emblazoned with house colors. They marked the dragons as possessions more than they protected the riders.*

*So you're saying no one needs a saddle to ride a dragon?* I was incredulous.

*Not no one. But those with sufficiently strong rider blood should not require it. Your body was made for this.*

I looked down at what I could see of myself. My fingers and toes were slightly longer than the average human's. When I first arrived in Sangratha, the highbloods had spoken of doing experiments on me—to measure bone structure and density. I already knew I had quicker reflexes than blightborn did. That was why Sankara had let me continue taking combat classes alongside his highblood students.

*Your skin is heat-resistant, too,* Nyxaris added.

*I beg your pardon. Are you saying I can't be harmed by fire?*

*I said you are heat-resistant, not inflammable,* he corrected. *If I directed the full strength of my flames towards you, you would burn. But more slowly.*

I shuddered. *Delightful.*

*It is a useful trait when one is in combat,* he observed.

*In combat with another dragon, you mean?*

*Yes. Riders could sometimes make it through a blast that would kill a regular blightborn or highblood.*

I was suddenly grateful that there were no other dragons alive.

The first tasks on the list were methodical. The tribunal had set up a series of massive poles of varying heights. Nyxaris had to navigate around them in a specified pattern. I could see why he thought it was dull work, considering he had memories of real combat. In comparison, this really was child's play.

He moved through the obstacle course with ease, massive wings folding and snapping. At one point, he tilted just enough for me to see the spectators down below. Some of them were clapping—until Nyxaris let out a loud growl that sent them into an uncomfortable silence.

*Relax*, I said soothingly. *I'll tell them to hold their applause next time.*

Next came the fire demonstration. Targets had been arranged across the field—barrels painted red, straw figures, and even metal shields propped up on stakes. The tribunal wanted to see not just his firepower, but his ability to direct his flames accurately.

Nyxaris hovered high above the field for a moment, surveying his targets. Then, with a deep inhale, he unleashed a jet of flame. The fire streaked across the sky, hitting a barrel dead center and exploding it into flaming splinters. I could hear the crowd erupt into gasps and murmurs of appreciation.

He turned his head a little and aimed for one of the straw figures. This time, a narrow plume of fire shot out, igniting the figure's chest without touching the surrounding field.

*Satisfied?* Nyxaris asked, sounding bored, as the straw figure collapsed in a heap of ash.

*Well, I know I'm impressed*, I admitted. *But I think they expect you to keep going.*

Nyxaris growled in annoyance, but swept lower. His flames washed over the other targets in calculated bursts, alternating between wide sprays of flame and pinpoint blasts. After all of the targets had been destroyed, I could feel the heat rising up from the burning field below us even from my perch on his back.

I felt a sense of overwhelming relief. That was it. We'd gone through the tasks on the list.

Down below, I could see the Tribunal Panel members conferring on the platform. After a moment, Catherine Mortis and Viktor moved to one side, their heads bowed together like conspirators.

*What are they up to?* Nyxaris's voice rumbled. *Their scheming faces make me itch to melt them.*

I held on to him more tightly. *Nothing good.*

I watched Catherine and Viktor descend the platform steps, the other tribunal members trailing behind them. Kage's grandmother marched behind them. Elaria Avari looked distinctly annoyed. I decided that was not a good thing.

Viktor was gesturing to Nyxaris and me. He was shouting, too, but his words were lost in the wind. It was clear he wanted us to land.

Nyxaris snorted derisively. *Such authority. It's a wonder you don't tremble at their feet.*

*Just land*, I whispered urgently. *Please.*

Nyxaris gave a long-suffering sigh but complied, angling his wings and descending. His claws touched the ground, gouging deep into the dirt, and he lowered his head so I could slide off. My legs were shaky as I faced the tribunal. Blake, I noticed, had remained on the platform, keeping Aenia and Florence close to him. I glanced around and saw Rodriguez, Theo, and Visha standing to one side of the platform beside Jia, keeping her within their protective circle. That was a small comfort.

Catherine stepped forward. She was dressed in a tight suit of shining red leather, made to look as if it was formed from interlocking scales. I hoped Nyxaris wouldn't notice: it seemed in very poor taste to wear something like that around a dragon.

"Your dragon has demonstrated skill and precision," she said coolly, addressing me instead of Nyxaris. "But there is one more matter we wish to have addressed."

Viktor stepped up beside her. "Yes. Catherine and I have decided we must have an act of submission before the evaluation can be considered complete."

I felt like I'd been punched. My hand reached up instinctively to Nyxaris's side, feeling the ripple of his muscles beneath the black scales.

His voice growled in my mind and there was no mistaking his fury. *Submission? Do they mean to have me roll over? Or perhaps I should sit up and beg like a trained pup?*

*I think they want you to bow,* I murmured back to him.

I stared at Catherine and she looked back at me coldly. Gone was the girl I'd seen last year who'd passionately embraced her thralls in the middle of the refectory, as if daring anyone to pass judgment. Or maybe this was still her. Maybe she'd always been like this—completely controlled, utterly proud to the point of never caring what anyone else thought. Her father had been a hard man. How much of that hardness, I wondered, had he passed on to his daughter?

Nyxaris had gone dangerously silent. For a moment, the only sounds were the wind and the waves crashing on the rocks below the cliffs.

I couldn't wait any longer. *What should I tell them?* I asked, my voice trembling a little. *What are you going to do?*

*Walk toward them. Slowly. Do not say a single word.*

*What? Why?* I hissed. *What are you planning?*

*Go. Now.* His tone brooked no refusal.

Heart pounding, I did as he said, reluctantly walking towards the tribunal, my shoulders tight beneath the weight of their gaze. Viktor's eyes narrowed. Catherine's lips thinned.

"Rider!" Viktor barked. "What is the meaning of this? You will bring the dragon to heel at once."

I took a deep breath but said nothing. My gaze darted to Blake. He'd risen to his feet but still remained on the platform, his arms crossed over his chest, his feet spread wide, his stance unyielding—as if nothing would get past him. Aenia and Florence were safe, I told myself. For now.

I glanced at Florence. Her face was pale. She looked fucking terrified.

*That's far enough*, Nyxaris's voice snarled in my mind. *Run past them. Now.*

My heart leaped into my throat. *Nyxaris, no. Not like Lord Mortis. Please, don't—*

*I said run.*

I broke into a sprint, veering to the side to dart around the group of highbloods. The moment I'd passed the last one, a roar erupted from behind me.

I whirled around to see Nyxaris rearing up, his wings flaring wide as flames erupted from his jaws.

The crowd screamed, scattering like insects, but it was too late for the tribunal members. A ring of fire blazed to life around them, cutting the group off from the rest of the field. Viktor looked furious. Catherine, angry and terrified. Lady Avari and Lysander stood together. To my surprise, their hands were linked and they seemed calm in the face of the fire.

"Stand down!" Catherine's composure finally shattered as she screamed over the roar of the flames. "Stand down, dragon! You will obey your rightful masters!"

Viktor's crimson eyes glinted with fury as he spun to face Nyxaris. "You dare to—"

Nyxaris let out an earth-shaking roar that drowned out the rest of the highblood lord's words.

He breathed a second ring of fire, this time one which nearly touched the edge of Lady Avari's dress. I watched as she gasped and stepped back as Lysander quickly trampled out the flames closest to them. All of the tribunal members crowded together within the circle Nyxaris had created. I watched Lysander grasp the older highblood woman's arm to support her and realized I hadn't seen Kage or Lunaya in the crowd. Perhaps they had no interest in watching Nyxaris or myself be judged under these circumstances.

Regardless, Nyxaris had made his point. I ran back, placing myself between the ring of flames and the dragon. *Please, Nyxaris. Stop. You've terrified them. Isn't that enough?*

*They need to understand. They need to learn. I bow to no one,* Nyxaris growled.

But he did not add to the fire and within a few more moments, the flames dropped and the highbloods began to stamp them out until they were free of their confines.

*We are not through here.*

I froze as Nyxaris shifted on his clawed feet. I could feel his fury still radiating through our connection.

*You will speak for me.*

I swallowed hard, but raised my voice as the tribunal started to move away. "Nyxaris wishes to address the tribunal." I'd probably phrased it a lot more politely than he would have.

Viktor turned back slowly, his lips curling. "He does, does he?"

I ignored him. *What should I tell them?*

Nyxaris's voice rumbled in my mind, his words heavy with contempt. I paled as I listened, but hesitated only for a moment before speaking aloud.

"He says this has gone on for long enough. He wants you to leave me alone. I'm the only one with any measure of control over him, as you've all just seen. He says . . ." I hesitated just for a second. "He says if you attempt to harm me in any way, he'll know. And he'll act decisively."

I'd toned down his actual words and now he growled at the back of my mind, clearly not happy about it.

Viktor sneered. "Bold words, rider."

I wished he'd have kept his mouth shut.

Nyxaris roared, a sound that seemed to shake the very cliffs. I hoped the ground beneath us was more solid than it felt. The tribunal members froze, as Nyxaris reared up again, his chest expanding as fire swirled in his throat.

And then, with a deafening sound, he unleashed a new blast of flames towards the row of carriages that stood on the dirt road. The fire roared. Black smoke billowed into the sky as wood and metal melted. Some highbloods who had retreated to the carriages when Nyxaris had first trapped the tribunal now moved to escape but it was too late. Their screams were brief, drowned out by the crackling inferno.

I glanced at Blake, suddenly immensely grateful he hadn't attempted to take Florence and Aenia back to the carriages. His face was pale as he held his ground.

*Tell them that was their last warning,* Nyxaris's voice echoed in my mind.

I turned back to the stunned faces of the tribunal. "He says . . . this is your last warning. The next time, he'll burn down the Black Keep. Then find you each, one by one."

I could see the fear on their faces. I understood their confusion. I saw hatred there, too—on Viktor's face, on Catherine's. They weren't used to dragons not listening. Dragons who didn't remember their place in the old world order. They expected Nyxaris to behave, to fall in line, to be a weapon they could wield. The only thing they'd expected to have to fight about was who would get to wield him.

But everything had changed.

Behind me, Nyxaris's massive wings began to spread, stirring the smoky air around us.

*Wait,* I said to him softly. *One more thing.*

*Yet another favor?* But his fury seemed to be dissipating.

*Can you please tell them to leave my friends alone?* I begged him. *That girl over there, the one with black hair and glasses, standing beside Blake. They brought her here to use her against me. If you didn't do what they wanted, they were going to . . . hurt her.*

*She matters to you?*

My throat felt choked. *She does. The little girl beside Blake. That's his sister. They brought her here to use against him, too. In case he encouraged us not to comply.*

Nyxaris turned his head towards the platform with interest. *They fear the highblood boy possesses a rebel heart, do they?* He spoke of Blake with more respect than he ever had before.

*Viktor controls Blake.* I took a deep breath. *I think he hurts him to get him to do what he wants. And threatens his family.*

Nyxaris gave a rumbling laugh. *The highbloods are not kind masters. Not even to their own kin. Nothing about them will ever surprise me.*

I was worried I'd gone too far. *Yes. But Florence, my friend—*

*Very well,* he cut me off. *You have my word. They are included in my protection.*

"One last thing," I called out to the tribunal. "Nyxaris says my companions are under his protection, too. If any harm comes to my friends, he says his wrath will not be contained to your carriages. Your castles and keeps will crumble to ash and you will burn."

I was making enemies here today. Enemies of all the tribunal members. I glanced desperately at Lysander, praying he'd understand why I was doing this. He met my gaze calmly. I couldn't interpret the look in his eyes.

*That is enough. You will reach out to me if they do not obey,* Nyxaris said imperiously. I was sure he couldn't wait to get away from all of us.

*Yes,* I said quickly. *I will. Thank you, Nyxaris.*

He rose into the air and for once, I didn't watch him go. I was too busy sprinting across the field, through the scattered crowd, towards Florence where she sat frozen on the edge of the platform, with Blake and Aenia. Blake's arm was draped protectively around his sister, who clung to him, her small face pale.

"Florence!"

She practically launched herself into my arms.

"You're all right," she sobbed, gripping me tightly. "I was so scared, Medra."

Then Jia was there, her arms around her daughter, tears flowing freely down her face. I slipped out of Florence's embrace as mother and daughter turned to comfort each other. I looked over at Blake.

"Please," I begged, "let's get them out of here."

He nodded tightly. "There are still some carriages left."

We didn't ask first. Just strode towards a free one, Florence, Jia, and Aenia alongside us. Blake instructed the terrified-looking driver while I helped Florence and her mother inside.

"Is there room for us?"

I looked over to see Visha and Theo.

"Of course." It was Blake who answered before I could even form the words. "I tethered my horse nearby. I'll ride back with Aenia." He looked at me. "I'll follow alongside."

I nodded, suddenly too exhausted to do anything else. The inside of the carriage smelled like leather and lavender. The lavender was probably Florence. Her mother had no doubt drenched them both in calming herbs and scents. It was sweet, but also incredibly sad. I stared at my friend as she sat down beside Jia, across from Theo, Visha, and me. Her eyes closed as she rested her head on her mother's shoulder.

The carriage was bumpy as we traveled the uneven road back towards the bridge leading to Bloodwing, the only sounds the creak of the wheels and the occasional soft sniffle from Florence.

Theo was quiet, staring out the window. Visha's hands strummed on her lap as if she couldn't sit still. Outside, I glimpsed Blake riding alongside the carriage on a black steed. Aenia sat in front of him, her small frame nestled in his arms.

I was just beginning to relax and think about closing my eyes when a sharp crack split the air, followed by the terrified whinny of horses. The carriage lurched violently as horses screamed. Florence and her mother cried out as the carriage skidded to a sudden halt, then rocked back and forth, nearly tipping over.

"What's happening?" Florence exclaimed, clutching her mother tightly.

Jia Shen's hands trembled as she clasped her daughter. "Stay calm," she whispered, but her eyes were on me.

I was already leaning over Theo but before I could open the

door, it swung open, and Blake's face appeared. "Theo! Get Aenia inside the carriage. Now!"

Theo didn't have to be asked twice. He grabbed the little girl and pulled her onto his lap.

Visha was scrambling over us. She shoved past Blake without a word, her hand already on the sheath of the rapier she wore on her hip.

"Stay put," Blake growled at me, seeing the direction I was looking. "Stay inside the carriage."

I ignored him. "I'm armed and I'm coming. Don't try to stop me," I said, barreling over Aenia and Theo and moving to follow Visha. I pulled my dagger from my boot as I stepped out.

"Medra," Theo called from behind me, sounding anxious and frightened. "Maybe you'd better do what he says."

I turned back towards him. "Stay here and keep them safe." Then I slammed the carriage door in his face and looked around.

The horses that had been pulling the carriage lay crumpled in the road, arrows protruding from their bodies. The driver was hunched in his seat. Dead as well. A group of figures on horseback surrounded us, their faces obscured by black masks. I spotted at least two of them holding crossbows, while the others brandished swords.

"I told you to stay in the carriage," Blake hissed furiously as I moved to stand beside him.

"No chance. We're outnumbered. You really think you and Visha can take them? Especially if they're highbloods?"

"They *are* fucking highbloods. Which is exactly why you should have stayed in the carriage," he snapped, his voice low but furious. "We don't need you out here."

I tightened my grip on my dagger, feeling my mother's power reach out to me, ground me. She was alert and ready for blood. "Two against five? I think you need me."

*Sweet of him to wish to protect you darling, but unfortunately for you both, blood lust runs strong on both sides of your family,* she murmured.

I ignored her, suddenly too apprehensive to respond.

Blake swore under his breath, glancing at the attackers, who had begun to spread out. If they'd wanted us all dead, they'd have used their crossbows already, so it was clear they wanted something else. But what?

"This isn't a game," Blake snarled.

"You need every blade you can get," I shot back. "I'm not a child, Blake."

"Oh, shut up and let the girl help," Visha snapped, moving to stand beside me. "This isn't the time for one of your petty lovers' spats. Are we doing this or aren't we?"

Blake growled something under his breath but didn't argue. He turned to face our attackers, his sword raised. Next to me, Visha rolled her shoulders, her rapier poised in front of her, her grin wide and her fangs out with anticipation.

The highbloods on horseback spread out to encircle us. The two with crossbows kept their weapons trained on Blake and Visha, while the other three dismounted, blades glinting silver as they slowly advanced.

Blake didn't wait. He was the first to strike. He moved faster than I'd ever seen him, his sword clashing against the nearest attacker's. Crossbow bolts went flying, hitting the carriage, missing Blake by a mile. I prayed none of the bolts penetrated enough to hurt those inside. Visha had become a whirlwind, moving to the next attacker, her rapier darting.

For a moment, I stood in stunned awe. I'd seen both of them fight before in our classes, but never like this. It was as if being in true danger had unlocked a deeper well of their highblood skills. Their movements had never seemed more inhumanly fast.

I raised my dagger defensively as one of the highblood attackers, a tall figure with a jagged scar visible on his cheek above the mask, turned his focus on me. My heart hammered. His sword seemed nearly as long as I was tall.

He was bigger, stronger, and better armed but I wasn't about to back down. Not when my friends were trapped right behind me.

Our blades met. The impact sent a jolt of pain up my arm. My dagger was too small to block him effectively. I backed up, feeling the uneven surface of the road beneath my feet.

*What is it? What's wrong?* Nyxaris's voice was suddenly in my mind, sharp and almost panicked.

I barely managed to duck another swing of the sword. Still, my best defense was going to have to be my speed and my smaller size, I decided.

*Not a good time to talk. We're under attack,* I sent back to him.

There was a pause. Then to my shock, his voice came again. *I'm on my way. Hold on.*

I was frankly amazed he was turning around. He'd already saved my ass once that day. Still, I didn't know how long it would take him to get there. For now, we were on our own.

My attacker lunged and I twisted, avoiding the blow.

Suddenly, a blur of motion surged out of the tree line. A massive silver wolf sped across the road and launched itself at the highblood attacking me. The man screamed as the wolf's jaws closed around his arm, dragging him down to the ground.

Visha appeared beside me, panting and licking blood from her lips, as she stared open-mouthed at the wolf. "What the hell is that thing?" Then she shrugged as the wolf tore into the highblood attacker. "Fuck it. At least it has good taste." A manic grin spread across her face. In another instant, she was gone.

I glanced across the road where Blake was fighting two foes at once. All of the attackers were off their horses now. I saw one of their crossbows lying in the road where the man Blake was fighting must have dropped it. I darted forward, intending to pick it up. Before I could reach it, another attacker stepped in front of me. His sword was sheathed, his hands were up. He seemed more interested in grabbing me than harming me. But before he could even touch me, the silver wolf was there, knocking the man onto his back and pinning him beneath his huge paws. The beast didn't hesitate. It tore into the highblood with savage efficiency, crushing the man's skull like a grape.

I peeled my eyes from the gruesome sight and moved around the wolf, reaching the crossbow. I'd just picked it up when arms snaked around my waist, yanking me off my feet. I screamed, struggling, twisting and kicking, but he was too strong.

"Medra!" I heard Blake roar over the fray, but I knew he was too far away. Locked in combat.

Before I could raise my dagger to strike downwards, the man's blade pierced my side. I gasped at the burning pain and looked down to see a small knife sticking out of my side, the man's hand still wrapped tightly around it. Just as he pulled it out, a massive silver blur collided with us, knocking us both to the ground.

I rolled to the side, clutching at my gut, suddenly filled with terror at the thought of the wolf's huge jaws clamping down upon me. But it wasn't me the wolf wanted. He leaped onto my attacker, sinking his teeth deep into the man's shoulder. The highblood screamed and thrashed, swearing loudly as he fought to free himself. Blood spurted as the wolf's teeth penetrated flesh, but the man twisted violently, kicking at the beast's underbelly. They rolled across the dirt, a tangle of fur and limbs.

*Don't just stand there bleeding while you watch*, my mother's voice snapped. *Bandage it. Quickly.*

I forced myself to move, hands trembling as I yanked off my jacket, ignoring the sting of pain as I cinched it over the wound at my waist. My attacker was scrambling free of the wolf. I watched as he rolled onto his knees and spotted the crossbow lying just a few feet away. My stomach dropped.

*Ignore the pain*, Orcades ordered. *Move!*

I didn't have to be told twice. I staggered forward, reaching for the weapon. But the highblood was faster. He snatched it up, already loaded, as the wolf lunged at him again. The bolt flew true, striking the wolf in its flank. The creature let out a high-pitched yelp and staggered, rolling over and over again as it hit the dirt.

For a moment, I thought it was over, that the wolf was down for good. Then it pushed itself up, blood staining its silver fur, and growled low and menacing, its eyes locked on the man.

*Gods, the beast is tenacious*, Orcades murmured. *What on earth is it?*

*On our side*, I said. *That's all I need to know.*

The man didn't waste another moment. Still holding the crossbow, he turned and bolted, boots spraying dirt as he ran towards a nearby copse of trees.

The wolf turned its head towards me. It took a limping step forward, its ears flicking back, clearly in pain.

I raised my hand as if to touch it, then thought better of the gesture. "You did enough," I said softly. "I'll be all right. Go."

The animal hesitated a moment, then lowered its head.

"Medra!" Blake's voice thundered as he appeared at my side, a streak of blood on his cheek, his clothes torn, his eyes wild. As he saw my jacket wrapped around my midsection, he sank down to his knees in the dirt, hands hovering over me as if he didn't know where it was safe to touch. "What the hell happened?"

I opened my mouth to reply but a thunderous growl from above interrupted me.

*I sense blood*, Nyxaris snarled. *Your blood. What happened? Who did this?*

*It's over now*, I answered weakly. *Thank you for trying to help.*

*Clearly it is not over, if you are bleeding. Tell me who I may kill. The wolf, perhaps?*

The silver wolf was limping away.

"No," I exclaimed out loud. *No*, I answered more firmly in my mind. *You can't kill the wolf. It saved me.*

Blake didn't ask why I was talking to myself. He ignored me. His arms were like iron as he scooped me off the ground and began marching towards the carriage. Vaguely, I realized Visha was still alive. She was going from body to body, ripping each attacker's mask off. After looking them in the face to see if she recognized them, she plunged her rapier into each one—as if to make sure they were well and truly dead.

*You forbid me to eat the wolf? What am I to eat, then?* Nyxaris complained.

*Are you here to help or for supper?* I asked grouchily. The pain in my stomach was worse. I clenched my teeth. *I'm sorry to disappoint your appetite.* Then I thought of something. *The man who stabbed me. He ran off into the trees.* I lifted my arm shakily and pointed. Blake growled at me as if furious that I'd dared to move but I ignored him. *He went that way. Can you go after him?*

A deep rumble of satisfaction filled my mind. *I will enjoy grinding his bones into powder and savoring the taste of his blood.*

I winced. *I don't need the specifics. But . . . thank you for coming, Nyxaris. Truly.*

*Stay alive until I return, wingless one,* he replied, his voice softening. *I may not eat wolves but you are another matter.*

I wasn't sure if that was meant to be a threat or a compliment. But I managed a weak laugh as his shadow swept away.

Blake was muttering curse after curse as he carried me towards the carriage. When we reached it, he yanked it open with more force than was necessary. Then he froze.

Inside the carriage, Jia and Florence sat backed into a corner, their faces masks of terror.

Theo lay on the seat next to Jia and Florence as if he'd tried to shield them.

And Aenia . . . Oh, gods. The highblood child hunched over her cousin, paying no heed to Blake or me. Her fangs were sunk into Theo's neck. Blood dripped down her chin as she fed. Theo's face was slack, his eyes closed. He seemed past the point of being aware of what was happening.

Jia looked behind Blake and me, taking in the scene outside. Then she opened her mouth and began to scream.

# CHAPTER 28

# MEDRA

Warmth wrapped me in a cocoon as I blinked awake. The soft rustle of fabric and high narrow windows told me where I was: the infirmary in Drakharrow Tower back at Bloodwing. The faint scent of herbs and soap tinged the air, reassuring and familiar. This was my third time in the infirmary since coming to the academy. It was getting to be a regular little habit.

I flexed my hands, then shifted experimentally in the bed. To my surprise, I felt almost normal. No sharp pain. Just a faint, dull ache in my side where I'd been stabbed.

"So, you're awake," a female voice said. A short dark-skinned woman stepped into view, her brown curls pulled back into a loose bun. "I'm Healer Ailith. I've been following your progress. We weren't sure if you'd wake so soon. But you've been making a remarkable recovery."

"What day is it? What time is it?" I asked, wondering how much time I'd lost.

"It's nearly noon. You were brought in early yesterday evening."

I raised my eyebrows. I'd expected her to say it had been longer. "I feel good." Better than I had any right to, really. I felt almost ready to jump out of the bed, but wasn't sure the healer would let me. Still, I wasn't planning on spending another night in the infirmary if I could help it.

"That's thanks to the spellcraft we used," Ailith explained. "We were able to close your wound and accelerate your healing. Apparently dragon rider bodies are a little more resilient than blightborn ones."

"What do you mean?" I asked, surprised.

"Your blood seems to make you easier to heal," she repeated patiently. "Blightborn don't respond nearly as well to restorative spells as you did."

I turned my head and froze. Theo was lying in a bed not far from mine. His eyes were closed and his face was drawn and pale.

"Theo! How is he?" I struggled to sit up.

Ailith's smile faded. "He's stable for now, but his injuries are much more serious than yours. He was almost completely drained." She hesitated, then looked at me, her tone turning cautious. "How exactly did it happen?"

The scene in the carriage came rushing back. Aenia, hunched over Theo, her fangs sunk deep in his neck, his blood dripping from her chin.

"I . . ." I hesitated. "Who brought Theo here?"

"Blake Drakharrow and Visha Vaidya brought both of you in."

"And they didn't tell you anything?" Alarm bells were going off. I needed to be careful.

Ailith's expression sharpened. "Tell us what?"

I bit my lip. Blake hadn't explained. He'd left Theo without telling the healers that his sister had fed on another highblood.

Ailith was looking at me suspiciously. "We were told nothing. The House Leader left you both and couldn't seem to get away quickly enough. But he didn't have to tell us. The signs clearly indicate this young man was fed from. For a highblood to feed from another—" she shook her head "—it's a very serious crime. There will have to be a report. If the House Leader knows who did this to his cousin—"

"No." My voice came out sharper than I'd intended. "If he'd known who it was, don't you think he would have told you? Does Blake know you're planning to report it?"

The healer's brow furrowed. "We have no choice but to inform the headmaster. This isn't something that can be ignored, no matter who was involved."

This was bad. Worse than bad. If the tribunal caught word of this . . . If Viktor found out . . . I clenched my fists against the blanket, then made my decision.

"I wouldn't recommend that, Ailith," I said, making my voice purposely cool and throwing in a little of Blake's haughtiness. "I'd suggest you speak to the House Leader before you do anything. For everyone's sake. He is ultimately in charge, after all."

Ailith stared at me, then frowned. "Very well."

She was beginning to look as if she couldn't wait to get away from me. But I wasn't finished. "Will he recover?" I asked, my voice tight as I looked at Theo, his chest rising and falling faintly with each breath.

Ailith pursed her lips. "He has a chance, but he's very weak. Many of our techniques don't apply to highbloods. When injured, their greatest resource is themselves. They're usually quick to heal. The best way for him to recover would be to feed. But—" she shrugged "—he's unconscious. He can't take blood in this state. We'll have to hope he wakes up soon."

The implication was clear. Otherwise . . . I felt my heart tighten painfully in my chest. Blake was protecting Aenia, even though she'd done this to Theo—his own cousin. I wasn't sure what that said about him. Something good or something terrible. Was he taking family loyalty too far? Or not far enough?

All of this was stirring up my own memories. Back in Camelot, my aunt and uncle had been ready to sacrifice themselves to save me and our people. Other good people had lost their lives protecting me. For a while I'd been something of a feral child. A little like Aenia. I'd never really hurt anyone, though. At least, not intentionally. Still, the guilt of Odessa's death would stay with me all my life. I'd made a foolish, childish mistake. And she'd paid the price.

The door to the infirmary suddenly opened and a tall dark-skinned boy slipped inside. Vaughn Sabino. He wore a gold-and-purple armband that marked him as clearly belonging to House Orphos.

"I beg your pardon. What are you doing here?" Ailith snapped, marching straight towards him. "You seem to be lost, young man. I suggest you turn around and walk straight back to your own quarters—"

"Wait," I interrupted, my voice hoarse. I cleared my throat. "He's one of my friends. Vaughn is with me."

The healer turned to me with a frown. "He's not a member of House Drakharrow. You can't receive visits from—"

"Look, you know who I am," I said, forcing my voice to stay steady. "I'm Blake Drakharrow's consort. I'm saying Vaughn stays. If you have a problem with it, I suggest you take it up with Blake. But I can assure you, he'll side with me."

Ailith's mouth thinned, but after a moment, she nodded curtly and walked away, muttering something under her breath. Probably about how the dragon rider was as ungrateful and entitled as a highblood. I honestly wouldn't have blamed her.

I leaned back against my pillows with a sigh and watched as Vaughn moved hesitantly towards Theo's bedside, pulling out a chair and sitting down.

"What are you doing here?" I asked, my voice low. "How did you know Theo was even here?"

He looked over at me, his face troubled. "A note."

I blinked. A note? My first thought was that it must have been from Florence. Though, why wouldn't she have just gone to Vaughn directly? Perhaps she was too exhausted. Or too afraid.

"From Florence?"

"No." Vaughn shifted in his seat slightly. "From Blake."

"Blake?" My head spun. "He sent you a note?"

Vaughn nodded. "He said Theo had been hurt."

My heart sped up. "Did he tell you how?"

Vaughn shook his head. "Only that he'd been nearly drained and was in rough shape." He hesitated. "Blake mentioned the healers had discovered Theo hadn't been feeding himself properly."

My eyes widened. "What do you mean?"

Vaughn lowered his voice a little more. "Blake said Theo's been starving himself. Apparently he hasn't been using the house thralls unless it was absolutely necessary."

I stared at him, trying to process this. "But why? And why ask you to come here?"

Vaughn's face tightened. "I don't know why, Medra. Unlike most highbloods, Theo seems to actually possess a conscience. We already knew that, though, didn't we?" He looked sad. Was he feeling regret for not giving Theo another chance? "But as for why Blake asked me to come here . . . If I had to guess, he probably hoped I'd be willing to try to feed Theo."

The statement knocked the breath out of me. Blake had reached out to Vaughn. Blake Drakharrow, who hated to show any weakness or vulnerability. Blake had admitted he needed help. He'd not only admitted it, but it sounded as if he'd practically begged Vaughn to come. And yet the idea of asking Vaughn, of all people, who'd already been through so much, for a favor this immense . . . I swore under my breath.

Vaughn's gaze had returned to Theo. Now his voice was soft as he spoke again. "I thought Blake was exaggerating. That it couldn't be as bad as he'd made it sound. After all, I've never heard of something like this happening to a highblood."

The implication being that it happened to blightborn all the time. I thought of the begging children I'd seen in Veilmar and felt sick inside.

"I thought I'd misunderstood. But now, looking at him . . ." He shook his head. "I don't know if he's strong enough to even wake up on his own."

"What will you do if he does?" I asked quietly. "It's a big request, Vaughn. I'm not sure Theo would even want that."

"I know." The tall boy was quiet for a moment. "I'm not sure yet. I guess . . . talk to him? See if I can convince him to feed?" He frowned and looked over at me. "I won't let him die."

I nodded slowly. But before I could say anything in reply, the door opened again. Kage Tanaka walked in.

If Vaughn had seemed a little hesitant when he'd stepped into the infirmary, Kage looked the opposite. He appeared perfectly at home in his rival's tower, even though he was obviously an invader.

Ailith swept in from the wings as if she'd been waiting for another opportunity to defend her territory.

"By the Bloodmaiden," she exclaimed, shooting a pointed look in my direction. "I'm not sure what's going on here today. But out you go, Mr. Tanaka!"

The petite healer looked as if she were about to bodily try to heave Kage out of the infirmary. I eyed the Avari leader's tall frame up and down. I didn't think that would go well. Kage raised an eyebrow. He looked completely unbothered. As if he owned the place.

I hid a smile. "Kage. It's good to see you. But what are you doing here?"

"He's leaving," Ailith announced, moving to stand in his path. "That's what he's doing. Right now."

I sighed. Ailith was not going to think fondly of me after today—not when I was basically channeling Regan Pansera. Suppressing a groan of guilt, I raised my voice. "No, he's not."

My voice carried enough authority that the healer paused. She turned to look at me, shooting daggers with her eyes. "Miss Pendragon, you can't simply make unilateral decisions—"

"Look, I said Kage can stay, so he can stay." I hated playing the consort card, but if Kage was here, I knew it must be for a good reason. He wasn't the type to make a get-well-soon visit. "You know what, I'll make your life easier, Ailith. I'm checking myself out of this place. Kage will leave. But Vaughn can stay—for as long as he needs to. Do you understand?"

Ailith looked between Kage and Vaughn and me, clearly weighing her options. Finally, she threw up her hands, obviously fuming. "Fine. But I'll be including all of this in my notes."

I gritted my teeth, already swinging my legs over the edge of my bed and ignoring the dull flare of pain in my side. Kage was there in a heartbeat, taking my arm and gently helping me rise.

"Theo is the one who needs your attention," I said to Ailith. "Please watch over him carefully. I know Blake would want that." I glanced at Vaughn. "I'll be back soon. To check on Theo—and you."

Vaughn nodded. "Don't worry about me. I'll stay as long as I can. You can tell Blake that." He glanced between Kage and me as if slightly confused. "And you can tell Blake I'll make the offer."

I knew what he meant. I nodded gratefully. "Thank you, Vaughn. Truly." I turned to Kage. "Shall we?"

Once we were in the hall, Kage fell into step beside me, purposely keeping his pace unhurried as if concerned he might tire me out. "You're surprisingly spry for someone who just came from a sickbed."

"I wasn't sick. Just . . . injured."

"Yes, I understand there was an attack on your carriage while you were on your way back to Bloodwing," he said coolly. "What happened?"

I glanced at him, wondering if he'd already gotten the story from Florence. My throat tightened. Had she tried to visit me in the infirmary? Had Ailith turned her away while I'd been sleeping? Or had she even bothered? If Florence and her mother never wanted to see me again, I couldn't really blame them at this point.

"I don't really want to talk about it," I said finally, realizing Kage was waiting for me to reply.

He nodded politely. "In that case, I'll get straight to the point. I came to tell you I've received some news."

"News? What kind of news?" I asked warily.

"You've been granted permission to transfer to House Avari."

I stopped walking. "What?"

Kage paused, slipping his hands into the pockets of his trousers and turning to face me. "My family has decided they'll permit you to enter House Avari. Headmaster Kim received permission from Viktor Drakharrow this morning."

My head spun. "Viktor is *allowing* this? Why?"

Kage smiled slightly. "Isn't this what you wanted, Medra?"

"Yes," I said with confusion, looking into his dark eyes. "I mean, I think so."

I remembered what I'd announced to the entire tribunal that day—that I wanted to break my bond with Blake. If I moved into House Avari, I'd be one step closer to doing that. He'd still have to feed from me. But we'd be separate. The problem was . . . we'd muddied the waters. Something had changed between us. I'd let him get closer to me, closer than I'd ever thought I'd allow. I'd fucked up. Confused myself and him.

I thought of Florence—cowering in the corner of the carriage. My heart squeezed with remorse. Whatever was happening between Blake and me—it had to end.

"To answer your question," Kage was saying, "I have no idea why Lord Drakharrow approved the transfer. My grandmother didn't expect him to. Perhaps this is the first step towards him giving up his house's claim to Nyxaris." But the wry look on Kage's face told me he didn't think that was likely—and I didn't either.

No, Viktor didn't do anything without a self-centered reason behind it. And his reasons were never, ever good ones. If he was letting me go, it was because he thought he had something to gain—or something to hide.

The thought suddenly struck me. Was moving to House Avari the right move, or would I be trading one prison for another? What did I really know about Elaria Avari anyhow? She played the kindly matriarch well. But that could all be an act.

I glanced at Kage. Tall, dark, and handsome. More reserved, more contained than Blake ever was. He'd treated me with respect.

He deferred to my wishes. He was . . . almost courtly. Yet could that be an act, too?

I suddenly felt exhausted. Damn these highbloods and their intrigue and their lies and their games. Here I was, caught in the middle, trying to figure out who the hell I could trust. And it wasn't easy. There was only one person I knew for certain was good in all of this. And now I'd failed to protect her and her family.

I'd failed my friends once before. I couldn't do it again. Moving to House Avari would mean being closer to Florence. Could I really throw that opportunity away?

"The look on your face tells me this isn't the answer you were hoping for," Kage observed.

I tried to smile. "No, it is. I just . . ."

"Very well. You may have a day."

"A day?"

"One day to consider what you really want. No longer." He studied my face. "House Avari will not use compulsion on you, Medra. We want you only if you want us." I opened my mouth, but he cut me off again. "There's more."

"More?" I repeated.

He shot me a rueful grin. "But based on your reaction to my first piece of news, I'm not sure you'll like this one any better."

"What is it? Tell me." My voice was sharp. I tried to soften it. "Please. I really do appreciate everything you've tried to do for me, Kage. Really."

He nodded. "Very well. I've found a way—potentially—for you to break the bond between you and Blake."

My heart froze. "You've what?"

Kage's calm expression didn't waver. "But I don't think you're going to like what it entails. There's also absolutely no guarantee it would work."

"Tell me," I said quickly, stepping closer. "I need to know."

"There's an ancient ritual—"

Laughter broke from me. "Yes, isn't there always?"

He gave me a strange look and I remembered he didn't know about the first ritual I'd done. "I'm sorry," I said, clearing my throat and trying to be as calm as he was. "Go ahead. I'm ready."

He started speaking. This time I let him continue, uninterrupted.

# CHAPTER 29

# BLAKE

I paced outside the heavy oak door to my room. My shoulders were taut, my body exhausted. My sword was still strapped to my side. I'd cleaned it but that was about all I'd had a chance to do. I hadn't dared leave Aenia alone to bathe or even eat.

Each time a student dared to walk past, I'd glare at them or growl. They'd rush by with a squeak—or in some cases, a scream of terror.

Good. It kept the corridor clear.

When Pendragon rounded the corner, I felt relief cross my face. I strode towards her, stopping just short of touching her. She looked good. Better. Healed. But I'd already known she was going to recover quickly. The healers had told me they weren't worried about her. Not like they were about Theo.

"You're here. Good," I said, keeping my voice low. I glanced back at the door. "I was just about to go and find someone to help."

She frowned, glancing at the door behind me. "Find someone to help with what?"

"Aenia." I couldn't help it. I kept looking back at the door as if it might burst open. "She's in there, sleeping. For now."

"Aenia's *here*?" Pendragon's face turned horrified. "What were you thinking? What's going to happen when she wakes up?"

I didn't reply to her first question, just ran a hand through my hair. "That's the problem. I need to get her out of here. But I can't just . . ." I shook my head, trying to clear it. "Don't worry, she's safe for now. She's tied up. The door's locked."

I'd hated to take such drastic measures, but I knew they were necessary. When one of her feral periods came over her, she was difficult to control. She'd hurt me on more than one occasion.

"Safe? Safe for who?" Pendragon hissed.

I frowned. "I said I'd get her out of here. But I need to make arrangements. I just need someone to stay outside the room until I get back." I looked at her pleadingly.

Her eyes widened in disbelief. "You want me to stand guard? After what happened in the carriage? Blake, she nearly killed your own cousin."

I scowled, glancing around. But the hallway was still clear. "Keep your voice down, would you?"

When I looked back at her, she was shaking her head. "I don't understand you. I don't understand any of this."

"What the fuck do you expect me to do, Pendragon? Tell me." My voice rose, rough with exhaustion. "If it were your little sister, what would you do? Honestly, I'd love to know."

She crossed her arms, but her expression softened a little. "I don't know. But maybe you could start by letting Healer Ailith write her report. The one I know you're planning to tell her not to write. If the tribunal finds out, maybe that wouldn't be the worst thing for Aenia. Maybe they'd—"

"Do you have any idea what you're even saying?" I burst out. I could feel my temper spiking. I hadn't slept. Hadn't eaten. I'd just been with Aenia alone all this time, just waiting for help. Usually, I could have counted on Theo. "If they get that report, Aenia will be executed. I could be executed, too. Or had you forgotten that little detail?"

Pendragon paled. "Oh, shit. Blake, I'm sorry. I hadn't thought of that."

"Right," I said bitterly. "Well, believe me, I have. But it's not even about me, it's about Aenia. I won't let that happen to her.

Look, Visha went to make arrangements. But she's taking too long. I'll go find her. I'll smooth everything out, and then we'll get Aenia out of here."

"Florence and her mother were in that carriage, too," she said quietly. "They saw what happened."

"I already spoke to them," I snapped. "They aren't going to say anything."

The expression on her face told me she didn't approve, but she nodded. "Fine. I'll watch her. I'll stay here as long as you need me to."

I sagged with relief. "Thank you." I started to walk away, but she touched my shoulder. I looked down at her, suddenly wishing I could just sweep her into my arms. She'd been injured. She could have died. All I wanted was to keep her safe, comfort her. To lie down next to her, pull her close, and sleep. But I couldn't do any of that. Not until Aenia was out of harm's way.

"Blake," she murmured. "I know she's your sister . . ."

I flinched, knowing what was coming. Not wanting to hear it.

"But she's dangerous. You have to see that. She could have killed Theo." She took a deep breath. "Even now, he's not out of the woods. He could die." She looked into my eyes steadily. "You've tried to save her. Over and over again, you've tried to do the right thing. I admire you for it. But how long can this go on? She's out of control and you can't be responsible for her forever."

"Can't I?" I said sharply. My eyes stayed locked on hers, fierce and uncompromising. "She's a child. An innocent child. All of this is my fault. She never asked for this life, Pendragon. I brought this fate upon her. I've done everything I can to keep her alive. I won't just hand her over to people who'll butcher her like a rabid dog."

I watched her expression falter as she took in my desperation.

"Please," I said, my voice breaking a little. Fuck, I hated this. "I don't have anyone else to ask. Not someone I can trust."

She nodded slowly. "I'll be here. You can trust me." She hesitated, then added, "But you and I need to talk after this is all over."

My face hardened. "Just tell me now. What's wrong?"

"Kage came to see me," she said, not meeting my eyes.

I knew before she said the words.

"I've been given permission to transfer to House Avari."

Even so, I felt like I'd been dealt a blow to the stomach. For a moment, I couldn't speak. "You've got to be fucking kidding me."

She pushed a long red curl off her face. "I'm not."

My entire body felt raw. I'd never felt so betrayed. "What fucked-up game is my uncle playing at now?"

"Maybe he's doing us both a favor," she said quietly. "Maybe separation could be a good thing. Blake, you and I . . . Well, just look at us. We're like a fire."

"I know," I said softly, touching a finger to her chin and forcing her to meet my eyes. "I feel it, too."

"But not in a good way," she whispered—and I saw there were tears in her eyes. "We're burning out of control. If we stay together, more people will get hurt."

I stared at her, my face a mask of disbelief. "You can't seriously mean that. You'd really leave me to go to House Avari? To go to *him*?"

She didn't ask who I meant. She knew. "After all that's happened, can't you see, Blake? This bond—us—has to end," she said, her voice trembling. "Now more than ever. We put people at risk, just by being . . . us."

I shook my head. I had no words.

"I'm a danger to Florence already," she said, her voice wobbling. "But with you, I'm doubly dangerous. Because of Aenia, because of Viktor. He'll keep trying to use us against each other. Maybe he already is."

"And you don't think this isn't him trying to use us against each other?" I snapped. "Are you really that naïve?"

I watched her take a breath, as if to control herself.

"I shouldn't have said that," I admitted. "But stop and think. Aenia was just as much of a pawn at the tribunal evaluation as Florence was."

"I know," she said wearily. "But . . ."

"But what?" I held up my hands and shook my head. "You know what? Do it. If you're so determined to run, go ahead. Transfer houses, break the bond, whatever you need to do to make yourself feel better. Because I can't keep doing this."

I watched her breath hitch. "Doing what?"

"This." I gestured between us, my words coming out in a rush, blunt and unfiltered. "This goddamn exhausting mirroring of emotions. When you're sad, I'm sad. When you're happy, I'm happy. And when you're in danger . . ." My voice faltered.

"What?" she asked, her voice barely above a whisper.

I looked away from her, my jaw clenching. "When you're in danger, I feel like I'd gladly give up my life and everything in it to keep you safe."

The weight of my confession hung there between us, heavy and suffocating.

"Blake—"

"Don't bother," I interrupted, my eyes blazing as I looked at her. She was deep inside me now. Woven into my blood. Carved into my heart. But maybe these feelings were poison: sweet but deadly. Maybe she was right and I should have been fighting just as hard as she was to cut them out. "I have to go. When I get back . . . Well, if you're going to go, just go. But don't stand here and tell me we're better off apart like it's some noble sacrifice. Because it's not. It's just running away."

I held her gaze just a second too long, drinking her in as if I might never see her again. My chest was tight. My throat even tighter. Finally, I turned away and started walking down the hallway, the edges of my vision blurred.

The corridor leading towards my uncle's chamber in the Black Keep stretched out before me, a cold expanse of dead stone. I walked slowly. I'd chosen this meeting. That didn't mean I had to rush towards it. Seeing my uncle alone was never a good thing.

I'd gotten Aenia out of Bloodwing. She was safe—at least, for now. She'd been lucid when I'd handed her off. She'd begged me not to leave her, but what choice did I have? My mother wasn't around to protect either of us anymore. I'd asked Aenia about Theo, asked if she remembered attacking him. She'd looked at me blankly.

The madness wasn't her fault. I knew that. But it was a constant presence, a storm always waiting to break. And worst of all? Sometimes I thought she *could* remember the terrible things she'd done. She just didn't want to.

My mind churned, replaying the events from the carriage attack over and over, as if I could make more sense of them. I looked down at my fingers, flexing them gently. I'd been tempted to wear gloves, but I couldn't risk drawing even more attention to myself. My hands still felt . . . wrong. I'd scrubbed them raw as if cleaning them might help. But I could swear I still saw faint traces of scales when the light hit them just so. My palms burned a little even now—the same searing heat I'd felt when I'd ripped one of the attackers apart with my bare hands.

Fuck, I'd even dropped my sword in the middle of a battle—not because I'd been clumsy, because I hadn't *needed* it. My body had moved like something from a nightmare. I'd been fast, vicious. Transformed. I hadn't fought those men. I'd *slaughtered* them.

I shuddered. I'd never felt so strong before. So filled with reckless aggression. I could still see the look on Visha's face when she'd touched my arm, bringing me back down to earth. Her wide violet eyes had darted from my bloody hands to the mangled body on the ground. To her credit, she hadn't said anything. I knew she'd stay quiet about what she'd seen. But if anyone else had witnessed what I'd done . . .

My protective instincts had roared to life. Pendragon. Aenia. The others. No one was going to touch them. Not while I still breathed.

I'd fought like a man possessed. No, not a man. A beast. Like the silver wolf that had come out of the bush. Something primal. Something unrecognizable.

I stopped in my tracks, pressing my palms flat against the cool stone wall. Even now, my arms ached with a burning pain that hadn't subsided since the battle. The skin over my back felt tight, as though something was pressing, clawing, trying to break free. I rolled my shoulders, attempting to shake it off. But the sensation didn't dissipate.

What the hell was happening to me?

I'd been planning to talk to Pendragon about it, see if she had any insights. I'd been ready to take her into my confidence. I shook my head. How could I have been so stupid? I'd thought we'd have more time . . . after I took care of Aenia. I hadn't expected her to announce her departure.

Well, she'd made her choice.

The loneliness of that realization hit me harder than I expected. I tightened my jaw, refusing to show it, even to myself in this empty hall.

The door to my uncle's chamber rose ahead of me. Viktor Drakharrow, the man who'd managed to take a loving family, warp it, control it, twist it to serve his own purposes. But that was who I was. First and foremost. His nephew. His pawn. His tool. Except now, I was becoming something else. Something I didn't understand. Something that fucking terrified me. If anyone might know what was happening to me, it was Viktor. He'd lived long enough to have seen it all.

I hesitated, then shoved open the double doors and strode into the room, my fists clenched at my sides. Viktor's quarters weren't to my tastes. They were ostentatious and pretentious. Everything spoke of old wealth and old blood.

My uncle was seated behind his desk. He looked up as I approached. "You've got that petulant look on your face, Blake. The one that tells me this is going to be a tiresome conversation."

I ignored him. "Aenia shouldn't have been at the tribunal evaluation yesterday."

Viktor picked up a goblet filled with dark liquid in one hand. "You've come here to lecture me? To show me what a devoted brother you are? Look at that, I'm bored already."

I stepped forward. "You put her in danger. Not to mention all of the others." I couldn't tell him what had happened with Theo. And when Theo awoke—because I knew he would wake—he couldn't tell our uncle either. I knew he'd understand that. He cared for Aenia, too. He'd known her before she'd become what she was now. He'd forgive her. He had to. "You know what could have happened if she'd lost control."

"Yet she didn't," Viktor said, rising and rounding the desk. "You handled it, as I knew you would. That's what you're here for, isn't it, Nephew?" His hand shot out suddenly, grabbing me by the throat. "Or have you forgotten what your purpose is when it comes to this family?"

I didn't struggle. I didn't claw at his hand. I knew it would be useless. There would be a reckoning one day. Maybe even sooner than we both expected. But this was not that day.

Finally, he dropped me. I gasped for air. "She's not just some pawn for you to move around the board. She's my sister."

Viktor's hand lashed out again, faster than I could react. I staggered back a step, my jaw blazing with pain, but I refused to give him more of a reaction than that. I knew I'd have marks around my throat, another across my face. But I'd grown used to hiding all the bruises; the tattoos helped with that. So did using combat class as an excuse. What was another bruise or two, after all? I hardly felt them anymore.

"Aenia is whatever I decide she is," my uncle snarled. "She exists because I allow it. *You* exist because I allow it. You will remember your place."

I swallowed, everything in my body aching to attack him, to put him down like the old monster deserved. But I was fairly certain

Viktor was the most powerful highblood alive. How else had he managed to accrue all this power? So I forced myself to stay quiet. I'd done what I'd come here to do: show him he was jeopardizing my loyalty every time he treated Aenia like she was nothing. For now, he needed me. Though, most of the time, I wasn't quite sure why, exactly.

I straightened. "Pendragon's leaving House Drakharrow. But then, I suppose you already knew that."

Viktor raised a brow. "What of it?"

"What possible reason could you have for letting House Avari take her?" I snapped.

"What does it matter? Allowing her to transfer houses was a calculated decision. The girl is still yours. She's still bound to you, isn't she? Still yours to feed from. But placing her with the Avari calms certain tensions among the tribunal. Now we have more room to manipulate the situation while appearing cooperative to the other great houses." He eyed me coldly. "Not to mention it frees you up to focus on what truly matters. You've grown too attached to the rider. Allowing you to cast aside the Pansera girl was a mistake. I see that now."

"It was my mistake to make," I risked saying. "Regan and I weren't suited. I won't take her back, if that's what you're about to say."

Viktor waved a hand. "I've indulged you too much. She was perfect for you. Strong, loyal. Of excellent blood. A perfect highblood woman. The truth is, you've embarrassed yourself. This infatuation with the rider—it's weak, undignified. You've made a fool of yourself."

I felt my pulse quicken. "I'm not infatuated with her."

Viktor's lips curled. "Excellent. Don't grow too attached."

"What the fuck is that supposed to mean?" I demanded.

"As for Miss Pansera," he continued, ignoring me, "she has other options. I've initiated negotiations with her father. We need the Panseras to remain our allies. You offended them greatly with your dismissal. But all will work out in the end. I've been alone for far too long."

My jaw dropped. "Wait. What? You're . . . planning to take Regan as a consort?"

"I am," Viktor said, as smoothly as if we were discussing the weather. "She'll breed well. I've long admired the girl's tenacity. She'll be an asset to our house. Whether she's on your arm or mine." He glanced at me and narrowed his eyes. For a moment, I thought I glimpsed something I'd never seen there before: jealousy. But in an instant, it was gone.

"I . . . I hope you'll be happy," I forced myself to say.

The thought of my uncle breeding with Regan—or any woman, for that matter—made me want to vomit. I wondered what Regan thought of all of this. Then I remembered the powerful man she'd alluded to. She'd gain more power being with Viktor than she ever would have from being with me. In the end, that was probably all someone like Regan really wanted.

Abruptly, I realized Viktor was looking me over with unusual scrutiny.

"You look tense, Blake," Viktor said, his voice deceptively soft, like a snake about to strike. "Have you been feeling unwell? Any . . . changes I should be aware of? Sudden illnesses?"

"Illnesses?" I frowned. "I don't get ill. I'm fine."

Viktor studied me more closely, walking around me in a slow circle. I tried not to move, but secretly I was praying none of those damn scales would suddenly manifest.

"Are you? You've been off lately. Distracted."

"Who told you that?" I'd fucking pound them into the ground. I suddenly thought of Laurent. "Whoever it was, they were wrong. Things couldn't be better."

"Is it losing the rider girl from your bed that bothers you the most, Blake?" my uncle said, circling around to stand in front of me. He smirked. "Or is it the thought of losing her to Tanaka? If he wants her, I'm sure the girl will give herself to him. He's a powerful man. Try not to be offended. I'm sure she can warm two beds as well as one."

I opened and shut my mouth, then opened it again. "She can do whatever she damn well wants. It's her body."

"Good." He smiled. "I'm pleased to hear such rationality from your lips." He clapped me on the shoulder. "Don't doubt me, Blake. Never doubt me. There's always a plan behind what I do, though you may not know the details. Find another girl—a highblood one this time. Fuck her. Test her out. Then come to me if you want her. We'll arrange it. A triad is stronger, after all."

I couldn't picture forming a triad now, or another girl in my bed. Not after Pendragon. But I nodded tightly. "Sounds good."

There was no fucking way I was asking Viktor about what was happening to me now. Not after the way he'd just been looking at me. Whatever was happening to me, Viktor already knew. He'd expected it. He must have done something to me. But what?

I'd started moving towards the exit when my gaze landed on a door on the adjacent wall. I must have seen it a hundred times or more; it led to the Drakharrow archives. All of our historical records had been transferred here when my uncle took up residence in the Black Keep. I'd never had any reason to visit them before. They seemed to be used only by Viktor and a few scribes and secretaries who worked for our house. But now? If there were answers about what was happening to me—or about Pendragon, about her dragon—they might be in there. Viktor wasn't going to volunteer information that could help me.

It was time I stopped waiting for permission and took what was rightfully mine.

# CHAPTER 30

# MEDRA

T he House Avari tower was on the opposite side of Bloodwing. I hesitated at the threshold to the Avari common room, two canvas bags slung over my shoulder. My chest felt heavy as I stared at the door.

I'd made my decision. I wanted to see Florence.

But it wasn't as if leaving House Drakharrow had been easy. In fact, it was harder than I'd expected. Not only was there Blake, but I was also leaving Theo and Visha. How would they see my departure? Would they think I'd turned my back on them?

Before I could raise my hand to knock, the door opened and a smiling girl stepped out. I recognized her from the night of the ball last winter. "Evie?"

She smiled. Her hair was cropped short with points over her ears. Gold baubles hung from each ear and she had a ring in her nose. "That's me. Welcome to House Avari. I'm one of the wardens here. Kage asked me to show you to your room."

Even though I remembered her warmth at the ball last winter, I was still caught off guard by her friendliness. I hadn't known what to expect—or if I'd even be welcomed. I hadn't thought that far ahead.

"Thanks," I said, stepping inside and trying to smile back. The air was warmer inside the common room, with the faint scents of cinnamon and chocolate. I glanced around and saw some students sitting by the fire. One was pouring something from a kettle into a couple of mugs.

"Lucas is always hungry," Evie explained, watching where I was gazing. "You can almost always scrounge up snacks or tea or hot chocolate if you come down here at night. Amazing we don't have mice, now that I think about it. But I suppose the servants clean up after all of us when we don't notice."

The Avari common room was different from House Drakharrow's and reminded me more of the First Year's space. The large room was lined with windows and filled with dark wood furniture, softened by cozy throw blankets and soft pillows. The Avari colors—black and silver—were everywhere. Woven into intricate patterns on the blankets or striping some of the couches. I saw half-moon motifs carved into some of the wooden furniture. A large tapestry hung over the hearth depicting a pack of wolves chasing a stag through a moonlit forest.

"Your common room is lovely," I blurted out. I blushed. "House Drakharrow's is very nice, too."

"I'm sure it is," Evie said with interest. "I've never seen it."

"Yes, there's not much visiting between houses," I said lamely. "Which is too bad."

She shot me a look I couldn't interpret but didn't reply, just smiled pleasantly at me. I followed her up a winding staircase much like the one in Drakharrow Tower. Evie stopped in front of a door on the third landing.

"Well, here we are. If you need anything, just come and find me. I'll be in the common room all evening studying for a test." Her smile finally dropped and she rolled her eyes. "Professor Hassan."

"Ah," I said with sympathy. "In that case, good luck. You'll need it. And thank you, Evie. You've been so kind."

"Of course." She winked at me. "Kage wouldn't want it any other way. Welcome to Avari, Medra."

As she disappeared down the stairs again, I pushed open the door to the room, then blinked in surprise. "Florence!"

The room was about the same size as my room in Drakharrow Tower, but this one had two beds, neatly made up with black quilts covered with silver flowers. Florence was already sitting on one of the beds, her legs tucked underneath her.

Her glasses slipped down her nose as she looked up at me, startled. Then her face lit up. "Medra!"

Another figure stepped out from the shadow of one of the windows. Kage. "Welcome," he said, with a faint smile. "So you decided to come."

I nodded. "You said I had a day, but . . ." I took a deep breath ". . . I thought I'd better get it over with."

If he was insulted by the way I'd phrased things, he didn't show it. But his lips quirked slightly. "I thought you and Florence might appreciate some familiar company, so I asked her to move here. There aren't many double rooms in Avari."

I glanced at Florence. Her usual cheer seemed dimmed. I could see faint shadows under her eyes, as if she hadn't been sleeping properly. My chest tightened. "Thank you," I said softly.

Kage nodded. "Florence and I were just discussing her mother."

"Jia?" I said instantly. "What about her? Is she all right?"

Kage hesitated, then glanced at Florence before answering. "I've had the best healers visit her. Physically, they say she's fine. But she obviously went through something very traumatic . . ."

I saw Florence twist her hands in the bedcovers and wince. Jia wasn't the only one.

"And it's taking a toll," Kage finished. "She's taking some time away from her usual duties in the library to rest and recover."

"But . . ." Florence burst out, her face worried.

Kage looked over at her. "It's all right. I've spoken with your mother's supervisors, and she'll be given all the time she needs." He looked back at me. "I've arranged for healers to continue to check on her regularly. With time and care, they're hopeful she'll heal fully."

"I see." I studied his face, searching for any sign of an ulterior motive. But he looked sincere. "That's very kind of you."

He nodded. "Of course. Librarian Shen is a remarkable woman, as is her daughter. House Avari cares for its own."

I glanced at Florence. She wasn't blushing like she usually would have. She just seemed . . . despondent.

Kage was moving across the room towards the door. "I'll leave you to settle in. If you need anything, let me know." He paused. "Medra, one last thing. Your timetable hasn't changed. You'll be expected to attend the same classes. Perhaps in the new year . . ."

I nodded quickly. "I understand." Part of me was oddly relieved. When Kage left, I dumped my bags on the free bed and moved to sit next to Florence on hers. She was staring down at her hands.

"How are you holding up?" I asked gently.

She shrugged, but her lower lip trembled.

"Florence," I said softly, "it's going to be okay. You're not alone."

She looked up at me slowly, her eyes shining with tears. And then, all at once, she broke. Her face crumpled as she buried it in her hands.

I didn't hesitate. I slid forward, wrapping my arms around her. "I've got you. We'll get through this. Together." I paused, then added, "I'm so sorry. So, so terribly sorry. It's all my fault."

"It's not your fault," she sniffled.

"It certainly is my fault," I insisted. "They used you as a fucking hostage, Florence. Your mother must have been absolutely terrified. And then, in the carriage . . ." I shook my head mutely.

"I was so scared," she whispered. "I wanted to help Theo, but I didn't even know what to do. I just . . . froze."

"It's all right," I assured her. "You're still here, that's what matters. Theo is going to be okay." I hoped that was true.

"No," she said firmly. She pulled a handkerchief out of her skirt pocket and blew her nose. "No, Medra. You don't understand. It's not okay."

"What do you mean?" I asked softly. "Tell me, Florence."

She lifted her chin stubbornly. "I'm tired of being like this. I want you to teach me how to fight. How to defend myself. Next time, I need to be able to help." She clutched her skirt, gripping it with her hands. "I can't stand just sitting there again. Being so helpless. By the Bloodmaiden, I couldn't even protect my own mother."

I shook my head. "I should never have left you two. It's all my fault."

"You were trying to defend us, you didn't expect Aenia to overpower Theo. She was just so . . . so strong, Medra. Unnaturally strong. She's only a little girl, but . . ." She stared at me, then bit her lip.

"What is it?" But I already suspected what she was thinking. She was smart, my Florence.

"She was the one who hurt the blightborn child last winter, wasn't she? Blake's sister?"

I nodded slowly. I wasn't going to lie to her. "Yes. Blake loves her, despite everything. He's determined to protect her." The word sounded strange on my lips. Blake and the word *love* didn't seem to go together. Except when it came to Theo and Aenia.

"I understand. She's his family."

"She's gone now," I promised. "Blake's had her taken away. Somewhere she'll be safe and . . . won't have a chance to hurt anyone else." I sure hoped it was true.

"Good," Florence said. "But that doesn't change anything. I want you to show me how to be more like you. I want to learn, Medra. I need to be able to spill blood—when it's necessary."

I stared at her, my heart sinking. What was happening to my gentle, sweet friend?

*The little scholar,* a voice suddenly growled inside my head. *How does she fare?*

*Florence?* I didn't think Nyxaris would even remember who she was. *How did you know I was with her?*

*I can sense these things.* He gave a deep rumbling yawn. *Usually I do not bother. Your life is dull. No thrill of the hunt.*

I was rather relieved to hear him say I was too boring to spy on. *Yes, well, sorry about that.* I paused. *As for Florence . . . she wants me to teach her how to kill people.*

*Admirable,* Nyxaris declared immediately. *A brilliant mind paired with a brave heart.*

*She has the bravest heart of anyone I know,* I admitted. *She says she doesn't want to be helpless anymore. But . . .*

*But what? You would not leave a little bird without wings, would you?*

*I suppose not,* I said reluctantly. *But she's so gentle. Some people just don't seem made for fighting, Nyxaris. It seems wrong to teach her.*

*She's asked you to instruct her,* he pointed out with surprising softness. *You would do her a disservice not to respect her wishes. The scholar may be a soldier yet.*

*I don't want her to be a soldier,* I said wistfully. *I want her to stay exactly the way she is. She's perfect already.*

*Evidently she does not agree. Trust her. Teach her. She may lose interest, for all you know.*

*That's true,* I agreed, a little relieved. *I'll teach her the basics, at least. I suppose everyone should know how to defend themselves.*

I waited for Nyxaris to respond. But he was gone. Apparently I'd become too dull again.

Florence was looking at me.

"Nyxaris was speaking to me," I explained. "He wanted to know how you were."

Her eyes widened. "He wanted to know about *me*?" The words came out as a squeak.

I nodded, then looked around. "Do you mind sharing a room with me, by the way? I didn't expect Kage to make you move. If you were happier where you were—"

"No," she said quickly. "I think it'll be nice. I mean, if you think so?"

I smiled. "I like the idea." Maybe I could finally figure out what the hell a thesis statement was now. With Florence as my roommate, I'd have no excuse.

Bunking with Florence meant less opportunities for alone time with Blake. I supposed I'd have to go to him for feedings.

The thought of his mouth on my neck suddenly sent a tingle of anticipation running over my skin. I wasn't sure if I could go back to the way we'd done things in the past. Maybe we could find a middle ground where we'd both stay clothed, but he could feed more freely—and less painfully for me.

"Of course," Florence was saying with a doubtful expression, "Neville can be a handful as a roommate."

I laughed. "Neville. Of course. How could I have forgotten about that unruly little creature? Just tell me our third roommate won't wake us up every night."

"Well, he's with Blake almost half the time. But he does tend to get rambunctious some nights." She giggled. "He likes to jump on me in my sleep. I've screamed more than once. But then he snuggles in and usually falls asleep. Like an extra pillow made of fur."

I grinned and lay back against the headboard, thinking of my two new roommates. Florence . . . and a fluffin.

# Book 3

CHAPTER 31

# BLAKE

*Wintermark Term*

T he cold weather had arrived with a vengeance. The icy wind
whipped at the windows of the Black Keep, howling like a
tormented ghost. I pulled my black cloak more closely around
me, suddenly wondering whether I should have come. Every log-
ical part of me screamed to turn back. But logic had lost its grip
on me long ago.

Pendragon wasn't just slipping away. She was being pulled into
something that would destroy her, and I couldn't just stand by and
watch. I couldn't lose her. Not like this. Not to them. Maybe it
was insane. But insanity and resolve had started to feel like the
same thing. So, I had a plan. And this—breaking into the Black
Keep in the dead of the night and sneaking through my uncle's
office into the House Drakharrow archives—was all part of it.

It wasn't a good plan. Hell, it might not even have qualified as
a plan. But I'd see it through.

I'd been watching the keep for weeks, memorizing the guard
rotation, arriving unannounced for supposed visits so I could check
the times when the corridors were the least patrolled. I wasn't even
sure all the subterfuge was necessary. Maybe Viktor would have let
me take a peek into the archives if I'd simply asked. But I couldn't

risk it. Firstly, because he could say no. Secondly, because there was no way in hell I wanted to tell him what I was looking for.

And thirdly . . . because of Theo.

My jaw tightened. Theo was finally out of the infirmary. He'd agreed to feed from Vaughn, but it had taken hours of both myself and the blightborn boy working to convince him with everything we had. The healers said it could be weeks before he was back at full strength—if he didn't catch some other sickness first. Apparently, being drained to the brink of death had a way of leaving your body vulnerable to just about everything.

The guilt ate at me. Every time I thought of Theo and of what Aenia had done to him, I felt the edge of my control fraying. Aenia had been a part of my family longer than she'd been part of her own blightborn one. I wasn't just her older brother. In a terrible sense, I was her maker, too. The weight of responsibility that came with that knowledge was crushing. She was out of control, losing herself more and more every day. And the worst part was knowing there was a way to end her misery and make sure she never hurt anyone ever again—and knowing it was probably inevitable. I just couldn't bear to face it yet.

As for Theo, it wasn't his poor health that Viktor would care about, it was the fact he was once again associating with Vaughn Sabino. I knew it was only a matter of time before my uncle found out. And what then?

This couldn't go on forever. Rebellion was slowly taking hold of my heart. Viktor had led our family long enough. Maybe it was time for a change. I didn't know how I could overthrow him— just that at some point recently, the seed of the idea had become a sprout and now the sprout was becoming a tree taking root.

I would bring Viktor down. Marcus, too, if that was what it took. House Drakharrow didn't have to become what Viktor wanted it to be. We could rise again like a phoenix from the ash— led not by a man like Viktor but by someone else.

Me? I'd been raised to lead, yet in some ways that made me the least suitable candidate. What we needed was someone more like Theo. Someone who wouldn't be so easily consumed by power and greed.

Speaking of greed, here I was—creeping through the halls like a thief breaking into a dragon's den. I was playing with fire. Viktor probably wouldn't kill me for sneaking into the archives. But if he wanted to punish me, I could think of many possibilities that would be almost as bad.

Yet here I was. Did I have some kind of death wish? The answer, irritatingly, was *no*. I wanted to live. Needed to live. Not just for Aenia, but for Pendragon. She might have left my tower, but she was still my anchor. My reason for not burning this whole place to the damn ground. Because the more time that went on, the less I seemed to care about the things a typical highblood should care about. Status. Privilege. Wealth. Power. I'd been floating through my life, like an actor saying lines. Never really meaning them. Until she came along.

I reached the tall doors leading to Viktor's office and hesitated for a moment, pressing my ear against the wood. Silence. Guards weren't permitted inside. I knew my uncle was absent—he was off attending a gala hosted by some of his allies in a very posh inn somewhere in Veilmar. I'd snuck a look at his agenda the other day when I'd come to give him an update—leaving out everything that really mattered, of course.

I pushed open the doors. Viktor's desk sat like a throne at the far end of the room. I skirted the edge of the chamber, moving towards the smaller door hidden in shadows along the opposite wall. With a deep breath, I pulled out a thin knife and knelt down outside the door. My fingers were shaking as I worked the lock. The tool felt clumsy in my hand. Ask me to break some bones and I'd have no problem. But this was delicate work. My hands still felt wrong—too hot, too tight, as if my skin didn't belong to me anymore. It wasn't just physical pain. This was like an itch at the back of my mind, as if something or someone lurked there, waiting for my acknowledgment.

Eventually, however, there was a satisfying click. The door swung open. I was in.

A blast of cold air hit me from inside the archives, carrying the scent of old paper. Shelves stretched in every direction, crammed with scrolls and books that looked older than I was. I lit one of the lamps on the wall, then froze as I took it all in. So, I was here. Now what? It was quickly obvious someone could spend days in the room without turning up the information they were looking for. I wasn't an archivist or a librarian. What hope did I have?

The faintest scuffle broke the silence. I whirled around, my hand already on the sword sheathed at my hip. "Who's there?"

Nothing.

Then, from behind the shadows of a nearby shelf, a furry head emerged.

"Neville!" I let out the breath I'd been holding as the fluffin padded into the torchlight, his huge glowing eyes fixed on me with an expression that looked almost smug. "What the hell are you doing here? I thought you were with Florence."

Not to mention Pendragon. I'd heard Kage had put the two girls together. I felt a pang in my chest: Pendragon must have loved that. Kage had done something to make her truly happy. So why did that make me want to punch his lights out?

The fluffin hopped closer to me, his large tail flicking back and forth. He looked far too pleased with himself, as if sneaking into the Black Keep was all part of some grand adventure that he'd planned.

"You were following me the entire time, weren't you?" I muttered. "Some stealthy thief I am. Unbelievable."

Neville gave a soft little yip, his wide eyes still fixed on mine. I couldn't tell if he was here to mock me or to offer moral support.

I crouched down and rubbed his head. "You're lucky you're so fucking cute. Fine, stay quiet and don't touch anything. If Viktor finds us here, he'll probably eat you."

Neville cocked his head, clearly unimpressed by my threat.

I started working my way methodically through the shelves, running my fingers over the spines of volume after volume, scanning their titles in the feeble light. After an hour, I had a tall stack of books piled on a table. But when I flipped through them, none contained what I was looking for. I told myself it didn't matter. I'd come back. Again and again if I had to. The answers were here. I'd find them even if it killed me.

I went back to the stacks. The hours dragged on. Dust coated my hands and stuck to my palms. My head ached from reading snippets of ancient Drakharrow genealogies—endless records of deaths, marriages, births, and tedious disputes over bloodlines and borders.

Nothing on dragons. Nothing about what was happening to me.

I rubbed my temples, sighing with frustration, and reached for another dusty volume. The sound of small claws skittering on stone made me pause. I looked around and realized the fluffin was gone.

"Neville?"

I walked up and down the rows of shelves, scanning for any sign of the little creature. "Now is not the time for hide-and-seek, you little—"

A muffled yip cut through the silence.

I followed the noise towards a bookshelf that lined the far wall, a monolithic slab crammed full of stacks of ancient scrolls. Neville's yip came again. It was coming from behind the shelf.

I peered behind the bookshelf and saw it. A narrow opening, just wide enough for the fluffin to have slipped through. I grabbed the edge of the shelf and pulled. The opening grew wider.

Then I spotted it. I crouched down. "Clever little bastard." A tiny latch, hidden low to the ground and nearly invisible beneath a layer of dust. The fluffin must have brushed against it and accidentally opened up the panel. Neville appeared in the passage, giving a soft, triumphant bark.

I rolled my eyes. "Don't try to tell me you did that on purpose. You were stuck, weren't you?"

I ducked through the opening, making sure to leave the gap behind me wide enough for Neville to slip out when he wanted to, and stepped into a hidden room, only large enough for a desk and chair and a single floor-to-ceiling bookshelf along the opposite wall. I hurriedly lit the lamp that sat on the desk and the room burst into light. It looked as if someone had used the space fairly recently.

Two books lay on top of the desk. I reached for the first one, my heart pounding a little harder than I'd have liked to admit. *Bound in Blood and Flame* read the title. It seemed to have been written by a House Drakharrow historian. Suddenly grateful that my father had made us learn Classical Sangrathan, I scanned the first page. The faded ink and archaic script made for slow going, but the contents were immediately promising.

*The power of the dragon is not limited to flesh but rather is woven into the very—* The ink was smudged. I frowned, straining to make sense of the next word. *Bloodline? Spirit?* Both seemed plausible. I turned the page, only to find it jagged at the edges, the paper violently torn away. I flipped forward. Another page missing. Then another. My heart sank. Entire sections had been excised, leaving only uneven scars where the answers I sought should have been.

Neville was sniffing around a corner of the shelves. Now he let out a cheerful bark and wagged his fluffy tail as if to say *All good here!*

"Yeah, thanks, Nev," I said bitterly. "Glad at least one of us is having a good time."

The fluffin bounded up onto the desk and sat down. I gave him a half-hearted smile as I turned the page, finding little more than scattered words and fragmented phrases.

*. . . flesh and flame intertwined . . .*

*. . . the blood must remain unbroken . . .*

*. . . bond is the dragon's curse or its salvation . . .*

That was it. No context, no explanation. Just maddening little hints.

"This doesn't tell me anything," I muttered. "Nothing useful. Nothing I couldn't have guessed already."

I pulled out the wooden chair and sank into it, forcing myself to take slow, steady breaths. But it didn't help. My mind was a pounding hailstorm. Nothing I'd read had served to reassure me. There was no denying something was happening to me. But whether it was a curse or a gift, I had no way of knowing. I felt more terrified now than ever.

Neville nudged the book with his nose, his tail swishing across the desk. I gave him a wry smile. "You want me to read it to you? Do you understand Classical Sangrathan? Maybe you'll make more sense of it than I can." I looked down at the desk, my gaze drifting to the second book. I picked it up. The leather-bound tome seemed innocuous enough. Then I opened it. The handwriting was small, precise—and startlingly familiar.

I was holding one of Viktor Drakharrow's diaries.

I looked around the room, half expecting my uncle to materialize from the shadows. Neville had jumped down off the table and was patrolling the room again, as if resuming his guard.

I turned my attention back to the diary, forcing myself to focus. As I read, the familiar story of the Dragon Wars unraveled before me. Not as a blood conflict between the great houses—but as something far darker. The wars hadn't just been a civil conflict. They'd been a rebellion. A dragon uprising. Some dragons had wanted more power. Others had been pushed too far by the highbloods' brutality—towards blightborn, towards the dragons, towards each other.

My hands clenched around the edges of the book as I read about something called *soul-binding*—a process in which a highblood's soul could be forcibly merged with a dragon rider's. Highbloods had wielded this power mercilessly, using soul-bound riders as living chains, tying them to the dragons.

I felt sick. The more I read, the more horrified I felt. I could almost see it in my mind's eye: dragons roaring in fury as they turned upon their highblood masters, dragon fire sweeping through highblood fortresses, entire armies crumbling under the might of their rebellion.

My uncle's handwriting contemptuously detailed the fragile truce that finally ended the war. The rider bloodline had been systematically exterminated, hunted down by highbloods terrified of future rebellions—so terrified that they were willing to give up the dragons. The official story, of course—spread through more than a century of propaganda—was that the riders' race had simply withered away naturally because of the loss of dragons. Nothing could have been further from the truth.

The dragons' rebellion had been downplayed, rewritten into a story of noble houses clashing over petty disputes. The truth—the prevalence of soul-binding, the dragons' betrayal, the uprising—had been carefully erased.

My stomach churned as I read about how the highbloods had done it. Viktor wrote coldly about the meticulous destruction of historical records, then of how a council had agreed to plant a deep, instinctual aversion in their own future bloodlines, ensuring future generations wouldn't even *want* to dig into the history of dragons or riders. Any hint of curiosity had been suppressed before it could take root.

Until now. I'd stumbled upon this by accident. But I wasn't about to forget it.

"Of course," I muttered. "Why tell us the truth when you could just condition us into ignorance and then repeat history a second time?"

Neville hopped onto my lap, nudging at the diary with his nose as if he didn't want me to keep reading. I scratched behind his ears and he closed his eyes contentedly. "You don't even know how to read, Nev. Are you hungry or bored? Or just here to rub in how much smarter you are than I am for not getting involved in this colossal mess?"

My throat felt dry as I pieced it all together. Pendragon. Viktor's plan for her was crystal clear now. Soul-binding wasn't some ancient, forgotten cruelty. Viktor must know how to perform it. And it was the exact leverage he wanted to control Nyxaris.

Pendragon was in more danger than she realized.

And the dragon . . . The dragons had risen before. Did Nyxaris remember? Would he rebel again if Viktor tried to soul-bind Pendragon?

If Viktor forced her into such a fate, Nyxaris might try to destroy us all.

I closed the diary slowly and put it back on the desk, in the exact position I'd found it. Pendragon had to know. She deserved to know. And so did Nyxaris.

I gave the fluffin another quick pat on the head, then scooped him up and unceremoniously stuffed him into my satchel. "Good work. Now, let's get the hell out of here."

# CHAPTER 32

# MEDRA

T he library was quiet just before dark. Filled with the kind of hush that only seemed to come when heavy snow was falling. I sat at a table by the window, my legs tucked underneath me, the book I was supposed to be reading open but forgotten in my lap, and watched the huge fluffy flakes swirl in the fading light. My breath fogged the glass as I leaned a little closer.

Movement caught my eye. A wolf!

It was bounding through the snow along the rocky cliffs, its fur silvered in the dusk. My heart lifted as I watched it. I'd never seen a wolf here on the island before. Bloodwing Academy was so isolated, its grounds surrounded by icy sea waters. How had it gotten here? Wolves lived in packs, didn't they? It was hard to imagine a wolf pack managing to hide somewhere on the rocky little island.

The wolf made a leaping jump across a ridge of snow, looking graceful and powerful, then disappeared behind a mound of white. I smiled to myself: the wolf had seemed so carefree. In some ways it reminded me a little of Neville. I glanced around to see if anyone else had noticed the animal. But at the tables across the aisle, the few students working there all had their heads down.

My chest tightened as I thought of something. Could it have been the same animal who had helped us when the carriage was attacked? There had been something obviously uncanny about the creature. But after growing used to living in a world with vampires

and dragons, I hadn't given a whole lot of thought to the single silver wolf. Now I leaned my forehead against the cool glass, scanning
the cliffside. But there was nothing there except the falling snow.

"Enjoying the weather?"

I jumped at the sound of the deep voice and turned to see Kage
standing beside my table. He had a book tucked under one arm and
his pale hair was damp, as if he'd just come from a bath.

"I saw a wolf," I explained, "playing in the snow."

"A wolf?" The faint smile that tugged at the corner of his mouth
told me he was skeptical.

"I didn't imagine it, you know. I really did see it."

He held up a hand in mock defense. "I believe you. It's just a
little . . . unusual."

I rolled my eyes. "Sure. Says the vampire."

Kage frowned as if he hadn't understood the joke.

Hiding a grin, I stood up and crossed over to the nearby row
of shelves, running a finger along the spines and wishing Jia were
around to ask for help. Kage sat down at my table, taking a seat
across from mine. He stretched out his long legs and flipped open
the book he'd been carrying. The sight of him, so casual and unbothered, surprised me a little. I wasn't sure how it had happened,
but the House Avari leader seemed to have grown comfortable
around me. Or maybe he always had been and it had been me who'd
always been the one ill at ease. I studied Kage, trying to pin down
what I thought of him now.

A sudden, shrill voice broke through my reverie. "Miss Pendragon! Where is Miss Pendragon?"

I stiffened. It was Professor Hassan's voice. And she did not
sound pleased. I had no idea why she would be looking for me at
this hour. All I knew was that I didn't want to be found.

Kage had looked up, his dark eyes were dancing with amusement. "Sounds like trouble," he murmured.

"You can say that again," I muttered, glancing down the row
of shelves.

I could hear Hassan's voice growing louder as she drew closer. From the sounds of it, she seemed to be going up to every table and demanding to know if anyone had seen me in the library that evening. I slouched in my seat and covered my face with my hands.

"Quick," Kage said, suddenly standing. He grabbed my arm and pulled me to my feet, then tugged me into a shadowy alcove between two high bookshelves that I hadn't noticed before. "In here."

"Hide?" I whispered frantically. "This is ridiculous. I'm not a child."

"Yet here you are," he whispered back. "Better ridiculous than caught."

He grinned and I couldn't help smiling back. His amusement was infectious. We slipped into the alcove, stifling laughter. The space was narrow. My shoulder jammed against his chest. I tried to shift but my foot caught on something—a hanging curtain. I went to try to pull it shut around us and tripped, letting out a squeak of panic.

"Careful!" Kage said, catching me as I started to keel forward.

Then his balance gave way. Before I could reach out my arms to steady myself on the wall, on anything, down we both went. I landed hard against Kage, sprawled across his chest. The impact forced the breath from my lungs. For a moment, we both seemed too stunned to move. Then Kage laughed. The sound rumbled from deep inside his chest, warm and unguarded, as if it had broken free before he could stop it.

When I glanced down at him, his eyes were already on me. Dark eyes, framed by long, dusky lashes.

"Comfortable?" he asked, his voice deep, his grin lazy.

For a moment, that grin reminded me of Blake. I froze. I opened my mouth to reply, but the words twisted up on my tongue. I knew I should move. I should absolutely move. But I didn't. Instead, I noticed the way his hand had settled lightly on my hip, the way his touch suddenly seemed to be burning through the very fabric. The air seemed impossibly warm.

Then, from the shadows, came a growl. The sound was so primal, so reminiscent of Nyxaris, that my entire body went rigid. I whipped my head toward the noise, fully expecting to see the dragon standing there in the library.

Instead, Blake stepped into view, his expression thunderous.

This was bad. Very bad. And yet something went through me. Filling me from head to toe. Something that felt very much like . . . relief.

The moment Blake saw me sprawled on top of Kage, his composure seemed to snap. "Get your fucking hands off her," he snarled.

"Blake, wait—" I started, scrambling to get up, my face flaming. I felt a pang of guilt I couldn't fully explain. I hadn't done anything wrong and I knew it. But under Blake's gaze, I felt as if I had been caught tearing library books to shreds or stealing candy from a baby.

But Blake didn't wait. He lunged forward, grabbing Kage by the collar and hauling him to his feet.

Kage staggered but didn't retaliate. "Calm down, Drakharrow," he said, his voice even. "You're overreacting. As usual."

"Overreacting?" Blake's fist connected with the House Avari leader's jaw, sending him stumbling back. "You think I don't see exactly what you've been doing?"

Kage wiped the corner of his mouth, his calm facade cracking a little. "And what exactly do you think I'm doing?"

"Sticking your nose in where it doesn't belong. Trying to take what isn't yours," Blake spat, shoving him again.

"Enough!" I exclaimed, trying to step between them. But it was too late.

Kage's patience splintered. He surged forward, slamming Blake into one of the bookshelves. The impact rattled the shelves, sending a few books tumbling to the floor. The two men grappled. Blake fought like a tempest, all raw power and fury, while Kage's movements were more deliberate, strategic.

"Stop it! Both of you!" I cried, darting in again and trying to pull them apart.

Neither of them would listen. I glanced at the books on the table, suddenly tempted to whack both of them on the head with one. Then I thought of what Jia would say about a book being used as a weapon. Still, it was hard to resist.

A lone highblood student walked by, carrying a large knapsack. As he saw the two House Leaders fighting on the floor, he quickly picked up his pace. No other student would dare intervene. I was on my own.

Blake's fist collided with Kage's ribs. The sound of their scuffle echoed through the library, and my heart was pounding. They were going to get caught. We were all going to get in trouble. And then what? *Detentions, suspensions, expulsion*: the words danced through my mind. I couldn't afford to have even more attention drawn to myself right now.

"Enough!" I exclaimed again, a little louder this time. "Stop it! You're both being complete idiots!"

I grabbed Blake's arm, my hand gripping him tightly and the motion seemed to finally jolt him back to reality. He froze, his chest heaving, his eyes still locked on Kage.

Kage shoved Blake off him and scrambled to his feet, brushing himself off as if nothing had happened. "You need to get a grip, Drakharrow," he said coolly. "She's her own person. You can't control what she does."

Blake glowered at him, his fists still clenched.

"Kage, I think you should leave," I said firmly. I knew I was being unfair. He hadn't even started this. But I suspected I'd have better luck asking him to be reasonable than I would with Blake.

He hesitated, then he nodded. "I'll be seeing you, Medra." He kept his voice light but obviously was intent on reminding Blake where my new home was.

When he was gone, I turned to Blake, frustration flaring hot and fast. But it wasn't just frustration, and that was the problem. My heart twisted at the sight of him. He looked . . . wrecked. Exhausted. His entire body was tense, his face shadowed with stress.

Was this because of Kage? Or something more? I thought of Theo. I'd visited him in the infirmary since moving out of the Drakharrow Tower. I knew he was improving, but that didn't mean Blake wasn't still worried—or wracked with guilt.

I'd been keeping Blake at arm's length ever since moving into House Avari, trying to rebuild some measure of the distance we'd lost. Surprisingly, Blake had respected that—at least, until now. But here we were, standing so close, and suddenly I felt the heaviness of all the things we hadn't said. He'd accused me of running away. Now I wondered if he'd been right.

I crossed my arms, trying to mask the tangle of emotions I was feeling. "Do you want to explain what the hell that was?"

Blake's eyes were lingering on the spot where Kage and I had fallen. "Do *you*?" he asked, his tone cutting.

The guilt twisted tighter, but I shoved it down. "Nothing even happened."

"That's not what it looked like," he said.

Annoyance broke through the guilt. "You don't own me, Blake. We're not married." Not in the way I was used to where I came from. "We didn't make vows. There's nothing to say we have to be exclusive in . . ." I searched for the right word and failed ". . . in whatever the hell this even is."

This doesn't have to be *anything*, I reminded myself. But that wasn't true, was it? Not when I'd spent every spare moment turning over the possibility of breaking our bond. Not when I'd hesitated every time I'd come close to deciding. I thought of the ritual Kage had told me about—a severing spell. Dangerous, complicated, and completely forbidden. But it could free me from this bond—free us both. Blake had no idea the choice I held in my hands right now—and something about that seemed wrong.

Except just like with all blood magic, performing the ritual wouldn't be so simple. I no longer had my mother's soul inside me, providing me with magic to fuel the spell, so I had no idea if I'd even be able to successfully conduct it.

And severing a blood bond wasn't just a matter of cutting ties. It would demand a toll, something steep enough to match the power of the bond itself. The writings hadn't spelled it out exactly, but they didn't have to. There were phrases that lingered in my mind like ghosts: *the essence of life exchanged, the tether of existence undone.*

Why hadn't I acted? Because it turned out breaking a bond like ours meant dancing on the edge of life and death itself. And while I might want to be free, that didn't mean I wanted Blake Drakharrow to lose his life in the damned process. Was I really willing to live with his death on my conscience? Now, after all we'd been through together? Blake might not be a good person, but there were people in his life who he loved and who depended on him. He could be an asshole, a bully, even a tyrant. But he'd shown he could be kind as well as cruel. He'd held me, comforted me, cared for me. This . . . would be the ultimate betrayal.

There was another thing. What if I went through with the ritual and nothing changed? The feelings I had for him—the pull, the ache—what if they weren't just the bond's doing? That thought terrified me more than anything.

Now Blake turned to face me, his eyes burning. "No. But you know damn well it's not that simple. You don't see it, do you?"

"See what?" I demanded.

"How he looks at you," Blake said bitterly. "How he waits for me to slip up. To fuck up and lose you for good."

I opened my mouth to argue, but the words wouldn't come. The naked pain in his voice stopped me cold. However ridiculous it might sound to me, he believed what he was saying.

Blake moved over to the table where I'd been sitting and took Kage's chair. "Anyhow, I came to talk to you about something else. Not about . . . whatever that was."

"That was nothing," I repeated. I took a deep breath. "What do you need to talk to me about?"

# CHAPTER 33

# BLAKE

I wiped away a few drops of blood from the corner of my mouth, knuckles throbbing from where they'd connected with Tanaka's jaw. Part of me wished I'd just kept pummeling him. He was lucky Pendragon had intervened. Not just intervened. She'd sent him away. I'd wanted to crow aloud when she told him to leave, but I'd managed to keep the grin off my face.

Now I sat across from her, trying to remember the real reason I'd sought her out. Every moment in her presence was a distraction. I drank in the sight of her. She ran her hands over the books in front of her, absent-mindedly looking out the window at the falling snow. The light framed her hair, making the red strands glow like copper. I knew she was upset with me, but right now she looked almost peaceful. Out of place in a chaotic, brutal world like ours. My throat clenched as I thought of the news I had to tell her. None of it good.

"Blake?" She turned her head to look at me expectantly, her soft lips slightly parted. "What did you want to tell me?"

"I—" My voice caught in my throat. There was what I needed to tell her—and then there was what I wished I could say. The first book I'd picked up in the archives . . . What I'd read there had left me feeling more alone, more panicked than ever. But if I shared even a hint of what was happening to me with Pendragon, would she understand? Or would she see it as even more reason for us not to be together? I couldn't take that risk.

I glanced around. A few students had just sat down at a table across the aisle. A librarian walked past, pushing a cart of books to be reshelved.

This wouldn't work. I stood up. "Come with me."

She narrowed her eyes. "Where?"

"Somewhere else in the library where we won't be overheard. Not far, don't worry."

I led the way through the stacks towards a small study room hidden behind a row of shelves. I'd discovered it once when I was trying to escape Regan. She hadn't managed to find me and she'd been extremely pissed about it the next time I saw her.

The little room was lined with shelves that stretched higher than anyone could possibly reach without a ladder. The books were older here, dustier, and more obscure. Presumably few students needed access to them which was why they were tucked away. A single lantern hung from a chain in the center of the room, casting an flickering orange light.

I stepped aside and motioned Pendragon in. She sighed but reluctantly went inside. I glanced behind her. No one was around. No one had seen us come in.

She leaned back against one of the walls as I started pacing back and forth in front of her, suddenly anxious about what I had to say.

"I found something. Something you need to know. About the Dragon Wars."

She frowned. "I've been looking for information on dragons for ages. Where did you find it? Can I see the book?"

"No," I snapped. When she blinked in surprise, I softened my tone. "I mean, it wasn't a book in this library. I went searching . . . somewhere else."

"Your house has its own records," she guessed, and I nodded. "Kage mentioned something of the sort. So does House Avari."

I scowled. "So he already told you?"

"Told me what?"

"That the history we've been told is all bullshit," I burst out. "The wars weren't about the houses fighting each other. There was a rebellion—among the dragons."

Her wide eyes told me she hadn't known. "No, Kage didn't tell me any of that."

"Maybe he doesn't know about it himself," I said bitterly.

"What did you read, exactly?" she demanded. I could hear the excitement in her voice.

"Nyxaris hasn't shared any of this with you?" I asked, suddenly wondering how she could know so little when she was in contact with the dragon.

She shook her head. "He can't remember. Whatever was done to him to trap him in the stone caused him to lose most of his memories, too. He's desperate to find out the truth. He can't understand how he can be the last dragon."

Her last words made me freeze. The last dragon.

"What is it?" Pendragon was looking concerned.

I gave my head a shake. "Nothing. I was just thinking of how to explain everything," I lied.

"So why did they rebel? The dragons, I mean."

"Some wanted more power. I guess greed and ambition aren't solely highblood traits. But there was more." I paused. "High-bloods—my ancestors—found a way to merge their souls with dragon riders. They controlled the riders and used them to control the dragons. It was horrible. Exploitative. A violation. And the dragons—they felt it. They felt what their riders felt. It broke them."

Pendragon's face was pale but otherwise she didn't react.

"You knew," I said slowly. "You knew about this already."

"Not all of it," she whispered. "But the soul-binding ritual . . . Professor Wispwood mentioned it briefly in a class last year. It didn't seem like a big secret then. But that was before . . ."

"Before Nyxaris came back," I finished. I gave a wry laugh. "Well, you know what comes next."

"Next?"

"Of course. They want to use you, Pendragon. All the regents must know about this. I mean, Lysander probably doesn't give a shit. But Viktor? Catherine? Elaria?"

She paled. "You think Kage already knows that his family is plotting against me?"

"I wouldn't doubt it. You think the Avaris' hands are so clean? The Avaris were as bad as we were, Pendragon. Just because Kage plays the white knight doesn't mean he is one. Give your head a shake." Instantly I knew I'd gone too far. She was starting to look angry. I cleared my throat. "I mean—"

"I know exactly what you mean," she replied, her eyes blazing. "But if I had to place a bet, I'd bet on your uncle, Blake. If anyone means me harm, it's him."

"At least he doesn't bother to hide what he is," I shot back. "But sure, Viktor probably has something planned. I don't doubt it." I ran my hands through my hair. "There's more. I found out why there are no other riders. They were wiped out—intentionally." I explained what I'd read.

When I was finished, Pendragon was quiet. "Some of this I knew," she admitted. She told me about the dossier she'd discovered in Professor Hassan's classroom.

"You told Rodriguez about this but not me?" I exclaimed.

She looked caught off guard. "I thought . . ."

"You thought what?" I said furiously. "What do you think I'm here for, Pendragon? I want to protect you, for fuck's sake. So let me, dammit."

She laughed. "Protect me? You're intent on being my tormentor half the time, Blake. Do you even remember any of the fucked-up things you said to me at the start of the year?"

I flushed. "I was . . . upset. I felt . . . betrayed."

"Betrayed?" She shook her head, gazing over at the stacks, instead of meeting my eyes. "How do you think I felt when you fed from me that first night?"

"I was wrong, all right? I fucked up. I know that now." The words burst out of me like a dam breaking. But to my surprise, it felt good to say them. Might as well go all the way, I decided.

I sank down onto my knees dramatically. "I was wrong. I shouldn't have done that. There. I'm on my fucking knees. Begging you, Pendragon. Look at me. You wouldn't kick a man while he's down, would you?"

She shook her head but her lips were twitching. "Get up, Blake."

"Not until you've said you forgive me," I said stubbornly. "I'm an asshole. A bastard. A blackguard. Sure, I'll admit it. But I want to help you. You think our bond is bullshit? I respectfully disagree. But who gives a shit? The point is I *will* protect you. And . . . I won't torment you anymore." I cocked a grin. "I mean, I'll try not to. Unless you ask me to."

She rolled her eyes. "Sure. Whatever you say. Get up, Blake. You're being ridiculous."

I pressed my hands together in a mock prayer, unable to wipe the grin off my face as I looked up at the soft curves of her face. "C'mon, then, Pendragon. Just say you forgive me. We can jump ahead to the part where we defeat Viktor and save the whole damned world."

She crossed her arms and tossed her head, fiery curls falling in around her shoulders. "You think this is all some joke? That you can just kneel there and charm your way out of this?"

I shrugged. "Hey, it usually works."

She burst out laughing. "You know what? You're impossible." Then she surprised me and growled. "Seriously impossible, Drakharrow. I'm not Regan."

I cocked an eyebrow. "You think I'd have gotten on my hands and knees for Regan? Oh, no, Pendragon. This is just for you and you alone." I said the words slowly, putting a seductive edge on them and I saw her bite her lip. Success.

"Get up," she repeated, but it was a whisper this time. "Get up, you impossible, ridiculous fool. Fine. I guess I forgive you. Happy now?"

I *was* happy. Happier than I'd been in a long time. No, more than happy. I felt fucking ecstatic.

I rose to my feet and stepped towards her. She didn't back away. I noticed how her breath hitched the closer I got. "I may be a fool, but here we are. Together. Again. You're stuck with me, Pendragon. You know that, don't you?"

She sighed, stepping back slightly. "We need to figure out what we're going to do about Viktor, about all of this. I have to tell Nyxaris. I don't know what he'll say. But in the meantime, you can't just keep throwing yourself into fights with Kage or anyone else anytime you get jealous or think I need defending."

"Noted," I said, though my grin probably told her it wasn't a promise I could keep. I took another step towards her, then leaned down, letting my voice drop to a whisper. "But I mean it, little dragon. I'll protect you. From Viktor, from Kage. From anyone. Even myself, if I have to."

Her head snapped up, her green eyes flaring. "You think I need protecting? As if I'm some fragile, little—"

"No," I interrupted, my tone firm. "Not fragile. You're the strongest woman I know. But even strong people need someone in their corner. Let me be that for you. The world is against you, Pendragon. You think Kage is the man to stand by your side? So be it, if that's who you ultimately pick. But look at me. Really take a good fucking look. Because *I'm* the one standing right here, right now, begging you to let me be with you. Not Tanaka. Me."

Her lips parted, but whatever she was going to say disappeared as I reached for her. My hands slid to her waist, and before she could argue, I gently backed her up, guiding her towards the nearest shelf. The motion was so fluid, so natural, that when her back met the edge of the books, she didn't even protest. The glow of light from the hanging lantern overhead caught the details of her face—the stubborn look in her eyes, the faint flush on her freckled cheeks, the bloom of red on her parted lips. She stared up at me, her breathing shallow, hands by her sides, as if just waiting to see what I'd do next.

She wasn't mine, not really. Not until she truly said she was. But every part of me burned at the thought of anyone else touching her, holding her, kissing her.

Fuck self-control, I thought, as I leaned down and captured her mouth with mine.

For a heartbeat, she froze. Maybe she struggled with resolve just a second longer than I did. Then her hands came up, not to push me away, but to pull me closer. She kissed me back. Hard. The way her fingers gripped the front of my shirt, the way her lips moved against mine—it was as if all the tension between us these last few weeks had finally snapped, giving way to something we couldn't hold back any longer.

I kissed her fiercely. As if trying to erase every argument, every insult, every moment of doubt between us. And she let me, meeting my passion with her own. My hands slid up her side, skimming her rib cage. Her lips were soft, insistent, her body arching into mine as if she couldn't get close enough. She moaned softly and the sound sent a surge of heat through me. My hand moved to her jaw, gently tilting her head to deepen the kiss. Her fingers tangled in my hair, pulling me closer, her nails grazing the back of my neck.

The tingling sensation along my back suddenly returned with a vengeance, as if triggered by her touch. The itch of something foreign, something savage, clawing to break free. I closed my eyes, willing it to go away, hoping she wouldn't notice, and in another moment, the feeling subsided. But my heart was still hammering a warning beat inside my chest. I wasn't ready for this. Not yet. Not for her to see the monster that lay inside me.

I pulled back slightly, just enough to look down at her, my forehead resting against hers. Her eyes were wide, her lips swollen and parted. She looked damned perfect. I knew how I wanted her to look. Even more flushed, more disheveled, more freshly-fucked-looking than ever before.

"Blake," she breathed, her voice low.

"What?" I whispered, my mouth already moving to seek hers again. "Tell me, Pendragon. Do you want this to stop?"

"I just need to tell you something," she murmured.

"Yes?"

"I still hate you," she whispered against my mouth, her voice trembling not with anger but with barely contained laughter.

"You're a terrible liar," I shot back, my voice rough, before kissing her again, deeper than before, with a hunger I could hardly contain.

She made a sound low in her throat, almost like a snarl, and her hands slipped beneath the edge of my jacket, pushing it off my shoulders. I let it fall to the floor, not caring about anything but the way her touch felt. Her fingers traced the edges of my shirt, tugging it loose. When she pulled back to look at me, her eyes were green stars, alight with an internal fire.

"This is a bad idea," she murmured, but her words faltered as I pressed my lips to her forehead.

"Yeah," I said, my voice hoarse. "It is. So let's keep going."

I slid my hands to the hem of her tunic and tugged gently. She hesitated a moment, then let me pull it over her head. Her hair tumbled free, a cascade of fire and light, contrasting with the paleness of her soft skin. My breath caught as I looked at her, every freckle, every curve making me ache with how stunning she was.

"Damn, you're beautiful," I said softly, the words slipping out before I could second-guess myself.

Her lips quirked into a wry smile. "And you're trouble."

"Absolutely," I agreed, stepping closer, my hands settling against her bare waist. "And you love it."

Her laugh was soft, breathless, but it quickly turned into a gasp as I kissed her again, my hands roaming up her back and unfastening the black lace bodice that covered her breasts. She arched into me, her fingers curling into my hair.

"Blake," she murmured against my lips, her voice a mix of exasperation and longing, "you do know we're in a library?"

"Is that what this place is?" I nipped at her lower lip with my teeth. "All the books . . . I was starting to wonder."

"Don't—" She cut off with a sharp inhale as I rained a trail of kisses along her jaw, down the curve of her neck, then sank my fangs into the sensitive skin of her throat, giving her just a small taste of the pleasure my teeth could bring. She let out a moan of longing and I grinned, grinding myself against her so she could feel how hard I was for her.

"You were saying?" I murmured. I wanted to distract her before her hands moved to the buttons of my shirt. I leaned back, taking in the sight of her hair tumbling loose around her shoulders, of her bare breasts. The sight of her stole the air from my lungs.

"You're staring," she said, her voice quiet but teasing.

"And you're perfect," I murmured. I brushed a strand of hair from her face, letting my hand linger against her cheek. "I want . . ." I hesitated. Searching for the right words. "I want to worship you. Say you'll let me."

Her eyes widened slightly, but I leaned in and kissed her, my hands sliding down her arms, grazing her wrists. The heat of her lips on mine was everything. All-consuming. Her taste, her breath, her scent. The world around us was obliterated. I moved my hands down to her waist, gripping her hips as if I could anchor myself to her. Her fingers tangled in my hair, sending bursts of fire through my veins. I couldn't get enough. She arched closer and I lost all restraint.

Without thinking, I bent slightly, gripping her thighs and lifting her. She let out a soft gasp of surprise, but her legs immediately wrapped around my waist, her heels digging into my back as if they belonged there. Her arms looped around my neck as

I braced her against the bookshelf behind us. My mouth trailed down her body, drawing one delicate nipple between my lips. My tongue moved over her, fangs extending with the heat of desire, teeth scraping against her breasts in a gentle torment. I worked my hand between us, lifting her skirt and pushing aside the soft undergarment she wore so I could slide my fingers along her folds. I groaned as I found her ready for me. She gasped as I stroked her pussy and pushed my fingers inside her. I growled as she shifted her hips against me. Longing was coiling through my body, desperate for release.

"Pendragon." I pulled back just enough to meet her eyes. "You have no idea what you do to me, do you?"

"Then, show me," she whispered, practically shivering with need.

I undid my trousers, and her hands were suddenly there, freeing me, running her hands over my cock with a moan of desire that sent chills down my spine.

She tugged me against her and I didn't have to be asked twice. I pushed into her, thrusting my hips forward with a sharp inhale, filling her up, inch by inch.

Only one thing could make this better for us both. I lifted my head to her neck and sank my fangs into the soft white skin, sucking her greedily as I slowly thrust my cock into her again and again.

Her legs tightened around my waist as I pressed her harder against the bookshelf. Somewhere in the back of my mind, a voice whispered that we were still in the library, that someone could walk in at any moment. But that voice was drowned out by the sounds of her soft moans as I fed from her and fucked her and caressed her body with my hands as if I could imprint her, this, us into my memory forever.

Nothing mattered except the way she felt against me, the way her body responded to mine as if we'd been made for one another.

I shifted my angle, hitting the spot that had her biting her lip to stifle her cries. Knowing she was losing control drove me even more wild and I buried my face in her neck, sinking my fangs more deeply into her skin. She clung to me, her fingers pulling my hair, her thighs tightening around my waist. I could feel her trembling, teetering there on the edge and I wanted to push her over, wanted to watch her shatter right there in my arms. My hand moved down her body, pulling her closer, as if I could somehow fuse us together. I wanted to make her scream my name, make her tell me she was mine. I wanted to vow it would always be like this and wanted her to say the same. But I knew better than to push her that far. For now, this would suffice. It was more than enough. Because for now, the world outside didn't exist. There was only her. For the first time in a long time, I felt as if I wasn't lost. I wasn't broken.

I was exactly where I was meant to be.

I peeked out from behind the bookshelf. There was no one around. Now that night had truly fallen, the library had emptied out. It was eerily quiet.

Pendragon stood a few feet away, her fingers fastening the last few buttons on her shirt. I watched her, enjoying the lingering flush on her cheeks. I hated seeing her put the layers of her armor back on, cover herself away from me again. But I also knew we couldn't stay hidden here forever, as much as I might want to.

"Still staring?" she teased as she caught me.

I grinned. "Hard not to. What'll you do now?" I didn't want to let her out of my sight. But I knew where her home was . . . for now.

"I should go and talk to Nyxaris."

At the mention of the dragon, my stomach tightened. "What are you planning to tell him?"

Her hands paused. "I think I owe him the truth. About every-thing."

My contentment gave way to a fresh feeling of unease. "Are you sure that's a good idea? Rodriguez told you not to—"

"Rodriguez doesn't know Nyxaris like I do," she interrupted, her voice firm. I knew she was right. Hell, no one knew what was in that dragon's mind—except my consort. I was still in awe of her for that. "He deserves to know. I can't lie to him like everyone else in his life did. I won't be that person."

I hesitated. Part of me wanted to argue, to remind her of the risks, but the look in her eyes stopped me. This was her decision. Her choice.

I nodded. "Where? I'll walk with you."

She blinked in surprise. "You don't have to . . ."

"I know." I pushed off the shelf I'd been leaning against. "But I want to." I met her eyes. Her cheeks flushed again, but to my relief she didn't argue. "So, where are we going?" I asked, as I strolled along beside her. The few students who still remained in the library glanced at us as we walked past.

I noticed Larissa sitting at a table with some other House Drakharrow students and suddenly prayed she hadn't passed by while we were . . . busy. She glared at me but didn't say a word. Still, I had no doubt she'd be sneaking back to Regan with some sort of a nasty story to tell. I hissed at her, letting my fangs show, and she quickly glanced away. That was more like it.

Pendragon hadn't noticed. "That cliffside classroom where I've been meeting Professor Hassan," she was saying. "She won't be there at this time of night and it's the safest place to summon Nyxaris. There's a big stone perch where he can land outside. I think it used to be a landing spot for dragons a long time ago. Hopefully there'll be less of a chance of him being spotted that way when he comes in."

A colossal dragon the size of a battleship wasn't exactly unnoticeable, but I knew what she meant. Besides, Nyxaris was black and it was dark out.

"How are Hassan's lessons going, anyhow?" I asked curiously. "Learning a lot?"

"Oh, yes, the lessons are extremely advanced." I could hear the sarcasm dripping from her voice.

"Advanced, huh? Guess I'd better step up my game," I joked.

She rolled her eyes, but I caught the faint curve of her lips as she approached the library doors. I followed closely behind, my hand intentionally brushing against her as we left the library.

"You know," I began, my voice light. "We've been at Bloodwing together for almost a year and a half. But I still feel like we hardly know each other in some ways."

She glanced at me. "You know plenty. Probably more than you should," she said archly.

"Do I?" I countered, not giving up. "Because I don't know your favorite food. Or what your life was like before you came here. Or—" I shot her a crooked grin that had been known to melt a few hearts "—who your first kiss was."

The corridor we were walking through was chilly. Pendragon let out a breath, puffing out a cloud of frost. "Why would you care about any of those things?"

"Because I do," I said staunchly. "I want to know everything about you, Pendragon. The real you."

She hesitated, her steps slowing as we reached a turn in the hall. "Those aren't . . . easy questions to answer." She frowned. "Besides, you've already been inside my head. Didn't you see everything you wanted to then?"

I thought back to our disastrous thrallguard session, to the dark-haired man I'd seen looking at Pendragon as if his heart would break if anything befell her.

"I couldn't make a lot of sense of what I saw," I said slowly. "But I remember that there was a dark-haired man and a silver-haired woman." I glanced down at her. "Can you tell me who they were?"

"Can I?" She looked surprised. "You mean you aren't simply going to demand the information? I'm shocked."

I knew she was joking, but still. "I'm asking. Do I need to get on my knees again?"

She was quiet for a while. "I think you must have seen my aunt and uncle."

I felt a surge of relief. "Your uncle, huh?"

She whipped towards me. "You great oaf! Who did you think he was?"

"Your lover, of course," I said with a grin, getting a punch in the arm for telling the truth. "Ouch." She never failed to surprise me with how strong she was. "So that wasn't your first kiss, then? Who was he? A courtier? A prince? A farm boy?"

"*Farm boy* is closer to the truth," she muttered. "He was . . . a stablehand." She looked at me. "Who was yours?"

"My brother's consort," I answered immediately. "Well, one of them."

She stared at me. "You kissed your brother's . . . ?"

"Well, she wasn't his consort yet. And she didn't want to be. She and her family were visiting to see if she and her sister and my brother would suit each other."

Pendragon's eyes widened. "Her sister?"

I nodded. "Allesandra and Amaris. They were twins."

"Twins?" She wrinkled her nose. "Gross."

"I think that was what appealed to Marcus," I reflected. "No one ever said he had good taste."

Then my words seemed to sink in. "Wait. They *were*?"

I hesitated. "Marcus killed Allesandra after they were wed. Her sister is still alive."

"Well, what a fucking relief," she said disdainfully. "Gods, Blake. Your brother . . . He's a real piece of work."

"I'm well aware." I paused. "He wasn't always quite so . . ."

"Brutal? Savage? Sadistic?" she provided. "So how did he get that way?"

"My uncle," I said quietly. "He groomed Marcus. Brought out the worst in him intentionally. Undid all my parents' work."

"He's been hanging around Lunaya Orphos," she said. "Did you know that? If there's a girl less suited to your horrible brother, I can't imagine who it would be."

I nodded. "I saw them together at the tribunal. I didn't think it had gone very far."

"Well, he was here, at Bloodwing, picking her up from class a few weeks ago," she said, her voice grave. "Lunaya is a sweet girl."

"I'll speak with Lysander," I promised. "I doubt he wants Marcus anywhere near Lunaya."

She looked relieved. "Thank you."

"Of course." We walked in silence for a few minutes. Then, "Pomegranate seeds. With honey."

She looked over at me with a confused expression. "What?"

"My favorite food. My mother used to give them to me when I was little." I laughed. "For the longest time, I thought I was eating her jewels. I thought I was pretty special for her to feed me rubies."

"No wonder you grew up so self-assured," she said wryly.

"Don't you mean *cocky*? *Arrogant*?" I teased. "Aren't you going to throw a few insults my way?"

"I think you're more aware of your faults than you let on, so there's no need," she said calmly.

"What was your childhood like?" I asked, the words slipping out of my mouth. "Tell me something. Anything. Where did you grow up?"

She bit her lip, as if trying to decide something. "You wouldn't believe me if I told you."

I raised my eyebrows. "Try me."

She was quiet for so long, I added, "I swear I will. You could tell me you grew up on a cloud and I'd accept it, Pendragon."

"Not a cloud." She took a deep breath. "But what about another world?"

My footsteps paused briefly.

"See?" She shook her head. "I shouldn't have said anything."

"No," I said hastily. "So when I found you in the wreckage of that village . . . ?"

She met my eyes and there was no laughter there. She was serious as the grave. "I'd just arrived."

I nodded. "I see. That explains it."

"What?" she demanded.

"Well, you know." I blushed. "Your lack of clothes."

"Oh, that." She paused. "I'd almost forgotten."

I laughed. "Believe me, I haven't. I doubt I'll ever get the picture out of my head."

"Yes, I seem to recall you looking far longer than you should have," she said, eyes narrowing. "But then, I forgot, you aren't exactly a gentleman."

I snorted. "A gentleman? Were there a lot of those in your world?"

"I wasn't there long enough to really find out." She glanced at me as if trying to decide what to say next. "You really believe me? I know it must sound mad."

"I believe you," I assured her. "It does sound mad. But when you first got here, you were so shocked. Everything seemed new to you." I studied her curiously. "There were really no dragons where you came from? No vampires?"

She shook her head. "Nothing like that. Only fae."

"Fae?"

"People like me." She lifted her hair to expose her pointed ears. "The things you see as marking me as a rider? Those are just normal fae traits in my world."

"Does everyone have red hair there, too?" I asked.

She laughed. "No! Of course not. And not everyone is fae either. There are mortals. You call them blightborn."

"And do the fae rule over the mortals?"

"No! Well, in some places. But there are mortal kingdoms, too." She sighed. "There are places where people dislike the fae and places where fae look down on mortals. But there are also places where everyone gets along. Well, tries to."

"It didn't look exactly peaceful when I was there in your memory," I recalled.

"What did you see, exactly?" she asked curiously.

I described the scene. The tension and fear had been palpable.

"Oh. I know what you saw." She was quiet for a second. "That was when I died."

I choked. "You . . . died?"

She nodded. "Now you really will think I'm mad."

"I don't think you're mad," I said quickly. "You're different. But I already knew that." I grinned down at her. "I like it."

She quirked her lips. "If you say so."

"Tell me about how you died," I said. "How is that even possible?"

She shrugged. "Magic, I guess. You have things here in your world that don't make sense either. I thought I'd died. I woke up here instead. Believe me, I was confused by it, too."

"You must have been homesick." I tried to imagine what it had been like. "You were ripped away from your family."

She stopped walking. "Yes."

"And all of your friends." I thought of something. I tried to keep my voice casual as I asked, "Did you leave anyone special behind?"

She gave me a sardonic look. "You mean besides my aunt and uncle and everyone I'd ever known?" She shook her head. "No. No one special. There wasn't anyone like that. Not yet. And I was too young to wed."

"Your aunt and uncle looked like warriors," I said softly. "They seemed to be trying to protect you. They must miss you very much."

She nodded stiffly. "I think about them all the time. They have no idea I'm still alive. If only there were some way to tell them."

We walked in silence for a few minutes.

"So," she said suddenly, "first kiss. His name was William. He kissed me at a fair, then ran off like his feet were on fire."

I laughed, imagining it. "He was probably half in love with you."

"In love?" She sounded shocked, as if the idea hadn't even occurred to her. "He wouldn't have dared. Not when I was—" She broke off.

"What?" I asked. "Tell me."

She took a slow breath, then looked up at me. "The Pendragons. My family name."

"Yes?" I said expectantly.

"It's the name of the royal family of Pendrath. I lived in Camelot. In the Rose Court."

I stared at her. "You were a princess?"

She blushed. "Sort of. Well, yes."

"Damn, Pendragon. Not a farm girl, after all." I shook my head.

"Would you have cared if I was?"

"I wouldn't care if you grew up in a swamp." So, my girl was a princess. It wasn't that much of a surprise, really. She'd always looked like a queen to me. I looked down at her and suddenly felt that fire again. I wanted to grab her by the waist, press my lips against hers, push her up against the nearest wall and . . .

"No," she said warningly. "I mean it, Blake."

"What?"

"You've got that look in your eyes." She blushed slightly. "We can't. I must go to Nyxaris. He's nearly here."

"Right." We'd almost reached the classroom.

"Well, what about your first kiss?" she asked, almost shyly.

I smirked. "Regan. She kissed me on a dare. I think she thought I'd kiss her back."

"And did you?"

"No," I said, my grin widening. "I tried to push her away. She fell in a puddle and started to cry."

Pendragon chuckled. "A little bully even then, hmm?"

"No, but we were never suited," I said softly, "Regan and I. I just want you to know that. It was an arrangement. Nothing more. For a while, I gave it a shot, but . . ."

She nodded. "You don't have to explain."

Right. We didn't own each other. I didn't owe her an explanation. She didn't want what I wanted from her. Possession. Exclusivity. My heart tightened, but I tried to ignore it. Except for that, the moment was perfect. I could have walked beside her like that forever.

But the classroom lay just ahead. The significance of what Pendragon was about to do suddenly dawned on me a second time.

"You're sure about this?" I asked as we entered the room. The sea stretched out below us, dark and restless. The wind snapped at her hair, sending the flaming strands flying around her face. I couldn't see the dragon yet, but doubted he'd want me around when he arrived.

"I have to do this," she said, her voice steady.

I nodded and then leaned down, brushing my lips against hers. "I'm glad I got to know you a little better tonight."

She seemed surprised, then nodded. I watched her turn and walk towards the perch to wait for her dragon.

# CHAPTER 34

# MEDRA

T he night air was frigid as I clung to Nyxaris. We soared over
the dark sea, the only sounds the powerful beating of wings
and the wind screaming past my ears. I should have been a
block of ice. Yet, while the chill was uncomfortable, two things
seemed to be keeping me warm—my proximity to Nyxaris and, I
suspected, my rider blood. In some ways, I'd been made for flying.

When we'd flown some distance from Bloodwing, Nyxaris's
voice rumbled to life in my mind. *You spoke of truths. Now, tell me.*
*What have you learned?*

I could hear the impatience in his voice. I closed my eyes for
a moment, bracing myself. Then I spoke, telling him everything.
The soul-binding, the rebellion, the slaughter of dragons and riders
alike. I spun a story of betrayal and control, the lies that had been
spread to cover up the great evils.

Nyxaris didn't interrupt. He said nothing as I spoke, his massive wings carrying us farther and farther away from the place I'd
come to consider my home. But I could feel the dragon's growing
tension, the faint tremor in his powerful muscles.

When I finished, there was silence. For a while, I wondered if
he might not respond at all, simply turn around and drop me back
at the school.

Then his roar split the night.

It was a sound of pure anguish, shaking me to my core. The very air vibrated. I clung tighter to his back, my heart pounding.

*Lies*, Nyxaris growled. *All of it. Lies. You must have read wrong. Go back and read again. They would do this to us? To our riders?* But I knew he knew it was the truth.

*Nyxaris*, I said softly, trying to reach him through the storm of emotions. *I think—*

*Silence!* His roar left me trembling. *Do you understand? Do you truly? You are no dragon. You cannot. The horrors we unleashed at their commands.*

So, he *was* remembering. He banked and turned back towards Bloodwing. He landed on a rocky outcrop, not far from the school, and crouched low, his tail lashing violently against the rocks as I dismounted.

*I didn't mean to cause you pain*, I said, sliding from his back. *You know I would never want that. But you deserved to know the truth.*

His glowing eyes fixed on me, full of pain and fury. *The truth? The truth is a sword, cutting deep and filled with poison. You have poisoned me.*

My heart was breaking for him. *You weren't to blame for what happened. None of it was your fault. You were as much a victim as—*

*Stop!* he thundered. *Do not speak to me of blame. Do not speak to me of what was forced upon me, of what I did in their name. The fire I unleashed, the lives I extinguished.* His voice cracked and his wings flared wide. *My brethren—slaughtered. My riders—used as puppets. And I . . . I allowed it. I obeyed.*

*You didn't know*, I defended him. *You couldn't have known.* And yet part of me wondered just what he was remembering, just what he had done.

He bared his teeth at me and for a moment I thought it was the end. *I remember. I remember all of it. I was their weapon. I was their slave. And when my brethren rebelled, I did not stand with them. Not at first. I fought against them.*

The torment in his voice was palpable. I took a step towards him, my hand instinctively reaching up. *Nyxaris, please . . .*

*Enough,* he snarled. *You have said enough. Take your truths and go.*

My chest ached as I watched him shudder under the burden of his memories. *I'm sorry. Are you angry with me?* It was a stupid question and I knew it. Of course he was. He was furious. Yet still, I asked.

*I am angry with the whole world, Medra Pendragon,* he said, turning his gaze fully upon me, the fire in his eyes tinged with sorrow. *Were it within my power, I would raze it all to ash.*

If he started now, perhaps the goal wasn't so impossible. My throat tightened. *Should I not have told you?*

There was a long pause. When he answered, his voice was weary. *No. You did what was right. You were honorable. But understand this. If the highbloods think to use me again, they will be disappointed. I will not allow it. Never again. I will die first.*

I nodded. *I understand.*

*Do you?* His gaze bore down on me. *You will not summon me again unless it is with truths even more significant than these. I will not risk myself—or you—by returning here.*

There were tears in my eyes. I wasn't sure when they'd gotten there. *I understand,* I repeated. Nyxaris had already done far more for me than he had to. Far more than I deserved.

*Do not let them crush you,* he said roughly. *This world will try to break you, as it has broken so many others.*

Nyxaris tilted his head up to the dark sky and roared. Then he spread his wings and leaped into the sky.

# CHAPTER 35

# BLAKE

T he classroom used for Sanguine Rites was a foreboding space,
reserved for the more advanced students of House Drakharrow. Located in the lower levels of the academy, the walls of
the room were black stone veined with crimson. Sanguine Rites
was my least favorite class and I'd have dropped it if I could. I was
an excellent student, one of the professor's favorites. But using
blood to force compliance or binding individuals or creatures to a
caster was low-down on my list of goals to accomplish outside of a
classroom. Blood magic was too close to thrallweave for my liking.
That said, crafting sigils and glyphs from blood to protect ourselves
against other kinds of magical threats was potentially useful. Next
year, I knew we'd be using blood magic in duels against one another and practicing offensive and defensive techniques. Now, that
I might be able to get behind.

I walked in with Theo by my side. Students from the previous
class were still trickling out. We'd arrived early. Standing at the
front of the room was our professor, Alastor Vane. He was a tall thin
highblood man with hair so pale it almost seemed white. He wore
it tied back in a long greasy-looking tail. Vane's face was angular
and almost skeletal, perfect for a professor of blood magic. Professor Vane was brilliant but I'd never warmed up to him.

Now I narrowed my eyes as I saw who he was conversing with.
Standing next to the professor's desk was my brother, Marcus.

"What's Marcus doing here?" Theo muttered.

"I don't know. But if he's here, then it can't be for any good reason."

"You mean because he's a bloodthirsty psychopath?" Theo supplied helpfully.

I shot him a look. "I would have just said *asshole*, but sure, that works."

Marcus was leaning against Vane's desk with the casual arrogance of someone who thought himself untouchable. With a pang, I realized the pose was easy to recognize—since Marcus had taught me how to come off that way myself. I'd learned from the worst. From this angle, Vane's face was unreadable. But Marcus's face was stretched out in an easy smile. Whatever Vane was telling him, it was making Marcus happy. And we didn't want Marcus happy. No, we did not.

Before I could approach them, Marcus glanced in my direction. Our eyes met briefly, then he said something to Vane and strode out of the room.

I dropped into a seat next to Theo, my shoulders suddenly tense. "What the hell do you think that was about?"

"Maybe he wants to audit a class," Theo suggested, as he set his books down. "Some older highbloods come back to do that from time to time, you know. Keeps their minds from becoming stale."

I glared at my cousin. "Right. Because Marcus is the type to worry about his mind." I slouched forward, draping my arms out over the table and wondering about why Marcus was at Bloodwing.

At least he hadn't been hanging around Lunaya. I'd talked to Lysander about his sister and my brother that morning. The Orphos leader had told me he was as concerned as I was and that he'd be keeping a tighter watch on Lunaya, as well as speaking to her about the danger my brother might pose to her. Honestly, I wasn't offended when he'd said that. I was just relieved to hear my uncle hadn't gotten to Lysander and made him some kind of an offer to have Lunaya become Marcus's next consort.

I realized Theo had become unusually quiet. When I glanced at him, he was staring at me with wide, alarmed eyes.

"What?" I asked, irritation creeping into my voice.

Theo didn't respond. His gaze moved downwards. I followed his line of sight—then felt my stomach drop.

Scales. All over my hands and wrists. Red, iridescent scales, bright as flames.

"Shit," I hissed, yanking my arms off the table and scrambling for my jacket. I pulled it on with phenomenal speed, fumbling to pull the sleeves down as low as they'd go, then crossed my arms over my chest.

"Blake," my cousin whispered, "what the hell was that?"

"Nothing," I said defensively. I pretended to adjust my cuffs.

"Nothing?" Theo's voice rose slightly. I shot him a warning glare—which he proceeded to ignore. "Blake, those were scales. Why the hell do you have scales?"

"Keep your voice down," I growled. But my heart was pounding. I lowered my voice to a harsh whisper. "Look, it's complicated. But everything is fine. I have it under control." This was an exaggeration at best. A great big blatant lie at worst.

"I don't believe you," my cousin said, shaking his head. "How long has it been happening?"

I hesitated. I could see the worry etched on Theo's face and for a moment I considered telling him the truth. "It's not a big deal," I said finally. "I've been . . . sick."

"And one of the symptoms is growing scales?" Theo said in disbelief. "Maybe you should see a healer."

"I've seen a healer," I lied. "They said it's nothing to worry about."

Theo shook his head stubbornly. "Lying again."

I sighed and stole a peek at one of my arms. The scales had vanished. "Look," I said, holding out my hand. "See? Nothing to worry about. I told you."

"What if they come back?" Theo insisted. "What if they get

worse? What if someone else sees? Wouldn't you rather talk to me about it?"

"No," I said, setting my jaw tightly. Theo had enough on his plate. He'd finally recovered from his ordeal with Aenia, though he needed to regain some of the weight he'd lost. He was still looking too peakish for my liking. "And you can't tell anyone about this. Not Vaughn, not Visha, not anyone. Do you understand?"

Theo hesitated, then nodded. "Fine. But I'm here, Blake. If you want to talk, you can trust me. You know that."

He looked so hurt that I felt like a total bastard. I clapped him on the shoulder. "I know, coz."

"You've been there for me," he said quietly. "Every step of the way."

I cringed. "You mean when I almost let Aenia kill you? I wouldn't be so quick to give me any credit."

"You didn't *let* her do anything," he insisted. "You couldn't stop her. Neither could I. She's incredibly strong for a child when she gets like that."

"I should never have left you alone," I said morosely.

"I'm fine now," Theo assured me. He smirked slightly. "Maybe better than ever."

I looked at him, then felt a smile tug at my lips. "You mean . . . ?"

"Vaughn might be in House Orphos, but it's my bed he sneaks into most nights," Theo said with a wink. "He knows my House Leader won't kick him out if he sees him."

I felt a twinge of guilt. "I certainly won't, but . . ." I hesitated. "Maybe you'd better use his room sometimes. Most of the time, Theo." He looked so crestfallen, I quickly added, "We have spies."

"Spies?"

I nodded. "Viktor is watching us—this year more than ever. Please, Theo. You and Vaughn have to be careful."

"You don't have to tell me twice," Theo said, sitting up straighter and scowling. "But if that fucking monster dares to hurt Vaughn again—"

"He'll have both of us to deal with. We're stronger together," I said firmly. "And that's what I wanted to talk to you about, actually. You and Visha."

"Visha? What did you want to talk to Visha about?" Visha sauntered up to us looking far too perky for a blood magic class. "Miss me, boys?"

I looked her up and down. "Someone looks pleased with herself."

She sank onto the bench beside us. "You have no idea how pleased I am," she practically purred. "Did you know dwarven women have incredible stamina?"

"No," I said, eyeing her with amusement. "But I have no doubt you're about to tell us as you regale us with your most recent exploits."

"You couldn't stop me if you tried," she said, batting her long lashes. "Lace Ironstride. Scout. Third Year. Fucking goddess in the sack." She paused. "You know, I may just have to go exclusive."

Theo leaned forward. "I beg your pardon. Did she just say what I think she said?"

"Good luck telling that to Lucian and Evander," I said wryly. "Don't they, um, appreciate a third from time to time?"

"They'll live," Visha said placidly. "But I won't. Not without Lace."

Theo hooted. "Who is this girl, exactly?"

"Some dwarven scout who has excellent stamina," I summarized. "I assume it's with her tongue."

"And fingers," Visha added. "And toes."

Theo gaped. "Toes? You let her . . . stick her toes . . . ?"

"I'd let her stick anything anywhere," Visha drawled.

I shook my head admiringly. There was no one like Visha. "Well, in that case, I doubt you want to hear about how I've chosen my Second."

"About damned time," Visha said, eyeing me with a little bit of interest. "Who is it?"

"You," I said. I turned to Theo. "And you."

"Both of us?" Theo exclaimed.

"Interesting." Visha looked me over. "Because you love us so much you just can't choose? Or because all hell is about to break loose and you want us to clean up your mess?"

I thought for a second. "Probably both. We're at Bloodwing, after all."

Visha cackled. "Right."

"Besides," I said with mock seriousness, "I can't count on you alone. You might be off with your little dwarf girlfriend when I need you to deal with something."

"I might be off with Vaughn." Theo pretended to pout.

I grinned at him. "In that case, I'd deal with it myself. Wouldn't want to upset your boyfriend."

Theo smiled, pleased. "Very considerate." He glanced at Visha and his eyes widened. "He's being *nice*. You know what this means, Vish."

She nodded.

"What?" I asked, narrowing my eyes.

Visha smiled slowly. "You got some."

"Some what?" Then I groaned, realizing what was coming. "Stop it."

"He did," Theo crowed.

"Some of that rider ass," Visha said, not pulling any punches.

"She's not a piece of ass," I grunted. "Though, she does have a fucking amazing one."

They both laughed and as the lecture started all thoughts of scales and my brother were far from my mind.

# CHAPTER 36

# BLAKE

I always enjoyed my thrallguard sessions with Rodriguez. But when I pushed the door to his office open a few days later, my mood immediately soured. Kage Tanaka was flipping through a book as he leaned against one of the tall shelves that lined the room.

"What the hell is he doing here?" I barked as I strode in.

Rodriguez sighed and turned towards me. "Good to see you, too, Blake. Come in and shut the door."

I slammed the door, glaring at Tanaka. "I didn't come here to play nice with an Avari. This is a private lesson."

One which I paid handsomely for. Though, over the last few years, my relationship with Rodriguez had developed into something more than that of teacher–student. He was a man I respected. A good man. A mentor. Hell, some days I secretly thought of him as the father I no longer had.

"I invited Kage here," Rodriguez said, calmly but firmly. "Both of you need to hear what I have to say."

Kage raised one thick, perfectly arched eyebrow. The bastard was handsome, I'd give him that much. Too buttoned-up for my taste, though. Probably the kind of guy who kissed with his eyes open and apologized afterward. But maybe Pendragon was into that whole *stoic restraint* thing. The thought made my blood boil all over again.

"Try not to pass out, Drakharrow," Tanaka drawled. "I know this may come as a shock to you, but not everything is about your fragile ego."

I growled. "Say that again, Tanaka. I dare you. Sounds like you want to go a second round."

Tanaka just smiled.

"Enough," Rodriguez snapped. "If you two can't handle being in the same room as one another, then I suppose you can't handle what I'm about to tell you." He looked back and forth between us. "So, what's it going to be? Make up your mind. Are you just little boys fighting over a girl in the schoolyard? Or are you men I can count on to lead the way?"

I kept my mouth shut. So did Kage.

"Good," Rodriguez said with satisfaction. He walked behind his desk and sat down. "Before I begin, let me make one thing clear. What I'm about to tell you here today is tantamount to treason." He pointed to the door. "There's your out if you need it."

I glanced at Tanaka and saw he was looking at me, too. I didn't particularly have a hankering to be executed. But hell, the ax was already hanging over my head thanks to Aenia. *Fuck it.* I shrugged. "I trust you, Rodriguez," I said loyally. I looked over at Tanaka and waggled my fingers. "See you around, Avari."

Kage stayed put. He walked slowly over to one of the two chairs that faced Rodriguez's desk and planted his hands on the back. "I'll need to know a little more than that."

Rodriguez hesitated. "You don't know me as well as Blake does, so I can understand that. But once I begin talking, what I say doesn't leave this room regardless of what you decide."

"Fine," Kage said. "But what's this about?"

"It's about protecting blightborn lives," Rodriguez said simply. "If I've read you correctly, that's something you care more about than most highbloods do."

I glanced at the other House Leader. Was Rodriguez right? I'd never given Tanaka's personal moral code much thought.

Tanaka gave a brief nod. "So what? What about that is treasonous?"

Rodriguez laughed. "Everything, Tanaka. Protecting blightborn *is* an act of treason and always has been. Most highbloods just don't like to admit that."

Memories of last year flitted through my mind. Walking through the slums of Veilmar with Rodriguez, delivering food and medicine to the blightborn families of those who'd been slaughtered by a nameless highblood killer who still roamed free. I recalled the desperate poverty, the grief, the hollow-eyed children. And that was only when we could find the survivors. Some children had already vanished by the time we went searching, both their parents murdered. It had been a vision of hell. The killings had stopped for now, but Rodriguez and I had always suspected Marcus was behind it all.

"I could get killed for what I'm about to tell you," Rodriguez said, the easy smile on his lips belying the seriousness of his tone. "And if I hear you speaking of it to anyone else, I may have to kill you myself."

My eyes widened slightly. Rodriguez had never threatened me before. I couldn't help it: my eyes went to Tanaka again. His expression was neutral.

"Unless you're asking us to incite a civil war," Tanaka said coolly, "I don't see how anything you have to say today could be construed as treason. So please, proceed. I'm all ears."

"Civil war?" Rodriguez shook his salt-and-peppered head. He must have been at least thirty-five, by my estimate. For an older professor, he was still fairly handsome. I wondered if the rumors about him and Sankara bunking up sometimes were actually true. "No. Not yet. Though, I have no doubt one could arise. But what about dragons?"

"Dragons?" I echoed.

Rodriguez nodded. "That's what this is about. Dragons. Last chance, boys." He gestured to the door again. Neither of us moved.

"All right, then." He leaned forward over his desk. "I'm part of a secret order. One with an exceedingly long legacy. The Emberwatch."

"I've never heard of it," Kage said immediately.

Rodriguez smiled ruefully. "Well, I'm currently the only member."

"What does this order do, exactly?" I asked slowly. Rodriguez was acting a little strange, sure, but I was prepared to indulge him. Obviously this was important to him.

"The Emberwatch was created to safeguard blightborn lives. I may be the only surviving member, but at one point there were many of us. My family has guarded the Emberwatch's memory for generations. Many of my family were members themselves." He picked up a quill from his desk and began tossing it in one hand. "I want you to think back to the age of dragons. During highblood wars and feuds and squabbles, blightborn casualties weren't just common, they were accepted and expected. Entire villages burned, cities razed—all to fuel highblood rivalries and power grabs. The Emberwatch believed in protecting the innocent however we could." He took a deep breath. "Even if it meant standing against the dragons."

The room seemed to grow colder.

"You're talking about sabotage. Fighting those who rule Sangratha," Kage observed with a frown. "Is that the treason you meant?"

"The Emberwatch did whatever they needed to do to thwart dragons from harming blightborn civilians. Even if that meant sabotaging the dragons themselves," Rodriguez said coolly.

"You killed dragons?" I asked in disbelief. I frowned. "What about riders?"

Rodriguez looked away. "Yes. Sometimes both."

The burden of his words settled over the room like a mist of blood.

"If this is about harming Pendragon in any way, I'm out," I said, moving towards the door. "I'll see you dead before I let you hurt her, Rodriguez—and you're a fool if you didn't already know that. You should never have invited me to this . . . this little conspiracy club."

"Blake, stop. It's not about that." My teacher sounded weary.

I paused. "It had better not be."

Rodriguez shook his head. "It's not. I swear it. You know, when Medra appeared, I thought she could be different. I believed she represented hope."

I scowled at the implication. Pendragon did represent hope—at least, she did to me. "Different? She's not exactly commonplace."

"No, she's one of a kind," Rodriguez agreed. "I believe her heart is in the right place. She's brave. I hoped she could bring balance, be more than a tool for highblood domination. But now . . ." He paused, his face turning gloomy. "Now we know there's a plan in place to soul-bind her. And that changes everything."

I glanced back and forth between Rodriguez and Kage, grasping the context. "Wait a minute. You *knew*? You already knew and you didn't fucking tell her yourself?" I spat at Tanaka. It took everything I had to resist grabbing him by the collar and throwing him across the room.

"Keep it together, Blake," Rodriguez commanded. "Kage brought his concerns to me. Which is why I decided I could trust him now."

"He should have brought his concerns to Pendragon," I snarled. "Or better yet, her archon."

"Archon in name only," Kage said coolly.

*Oh, it's more than in name, believe me,* I wanted to say. But Pendragon would punch me in the face if she heard me say something asshole-ish like that. And then I'd never get her alone in a library—or any other place for that matter—ever again.

"Are you two done comparing whose is bigger?" Rodriguez snapped. "We're talking about damned dragons here."

"One dragon. One dragon who Pendragon has under her control," I retorted.

"Under her control?" Rodriguez shook his head. "No. I highly doubt that will ever be the case."

"What do you mean?" I demanded.

"So long as Nyxaris remains free, Medra will constantly be in danger. And if she's successfully soul-bound, we'll have lost her completely—along with any hope of controlling Nyxaris. With only one dragon under the control of a single highblood family, the blightborn will suffer more than they ever have. A war between the houses will be inevitable." He grimaced. "Even more than it is now."

"We don't even know which highblood family is trying to soul-bind Pendragon," I pointed out.

Tanaka laughed. "Oh, I think it's fairly obvious."

"Elaria Avari is many things, Blake. But Kage assures me his grandmother has no interest in risking her own life in an attempt to control the dragon. She values her life and her family too greatly for that," Rodriguez said.

I rolled my eyes. "As if I'm going to just take the word of Kage's grandmother. Apparently highbloods used to do this all the time. Why wouldn't she want the power now?"

"Because she's not your fucking uncle," Tanaka snapped. "She's ambitious, yes. But not a monster."

For a second I bristled. Then I shrugged. "Fair enough. I'm not going to defend good old Uncle Viktor." I looked at Rodriguez. "So we know it's him?"

"I have every reason to believe so, yes," Rodriguez said.

"Well, he'll fail. He won't get within a foot of Pendragon." I glanced at Tanaka. "I'll make sure of that."

"*We* will make sure of it," Tanaka had the nerve to say.

"I can protect her on my own," I growled. "Back the fuck off."

"Stop it," Rodriguez roared, slamming his hands down on the desk. "Both of you. The girl is too difficult to protect. It would be all too easy for your uncle to take her prisoner, Blake, you know this. And what could you do to stop him? Take a stand against the most powerful highblood in the land? You're useful to him right now, but if Viktor were pushed, I have no doubt he'd kill you."

I was quiet. I had no doubt about that either. "Fine. So what's your grand plan?"

"Dragon's blood is key to forging the bond. Without it, Pendragon is useless to them. We need to return Nyxaris to stone."

I stared at him. "Are you out of your damned mind? We don't even know how the dragons became stone in the first place."

"Yes, we do," Rodriguez said, looking completely unfazed. "The Emberwatch performed the ritual."

Tanaka moved around the chair he'd been standing in front of and sat down, looking for once in his life a little shaky. "You're saying your order turned four living dragons into stone? When no one in Sangratha could figure out what had been done and still hasn't figured out how to bring the others back?"

"Me, personally? No." Rodriguez shook his head. "But the order, yes. We had that power."

"Do you know how to bring the other three dragons back?" I demanded, striding over to the desk.

Rodriguez hesitated. "I have some idea. But if you're asking if I'll do it, the answer is *no*. And it would take more than me, in any case."

"Pendragon," I guessed.

He nodded. "She woke up Nyxaris by mistake. I think she was trying to do something else, work some kind of a ritual. I'm still not exactly sure what."

I froze. Had Pendragon been trying to break our bond last year? Was *that* why she'd been in the Dragon Court?

"Whatever she was trying to do, I don't believe it succeeded," Rodriguez continued. "Nyxaris's awakening was simply an unexpected by-product of that failed ritual."

"So you didn't tell her to bring the dragon back?" Tanaka asked, looking a little surprised.

"No. I was . . . tempted," Rodriguez admitted. "Until I recalled the matter of soul-binding. I also wanted to get to know Miss Pendragon better before even considering something as extreme as awakening a dragon."

"So you didn't get her to bring Nyxaris back, but you know how to put him back to sleep?" I said skeptically.

Rodriguez hesitated. "Basically, yes. We would require Miss Pendragon's help to do it, though."

I laughed. "You think she'd help you? If she could hear us talking now, about returning Nyxaris to stone, she'd probably try to kill us all."

"I have no doubt she'll be furious if we succeed. But if we don't act, Medra could become the ultimate weapon," Rodriguez said quietly. "Her soul lost. Her body either destroyed or inhabited by your uncle."

I shuddered.

"I'm asking you to protect her. But more than that, I'm asking you to think beyond yourself and to do something which will protect all blightborn. Perhaps even prevent another war."

"No, you're asking me to betray her," I said, my voice tight but controlled. "Because make no mistake about it—what you're proposing is a complete betrayal. You know she'd never accept this, Rodriguez."

I didn't know how much Pendragon cared about Nyxaris, but I had no doubt she did. Even though she'd never said so, everything led me to believe that. I doubted the dragon returned much of her affection. Still, Nyxaris had stood by her. He'd protected my consort when she'd needed him to. How could I betray him, knowing that?

"You think this is all about you, Blake?" Rodriguez exclaimed, looking disgusted. "Your relationship? Your feelings? Or even Pendragon's? Grow the fuck up. This is bigger than any of that."

Kage was watching me in silence, his expression unreadable. For once, he didn't seem eager to insert himself into the conversation. He must have been weighing the decision just as I was. I ran a hand through my hair and started pacing the room. I wanted to protect the blightborn. Of course I did. But this was different—this was about Pendragon. And a beast I'd believed I'd only ever see in the pages of storybooks. But this dragon had lived for who knew how long before Pendragon had awoken him. Nyxaris had already had a full life. She hadn't. So, maybe the dragon would understand why I had to do this now.

"You're asking too much," I said, my voice strained. "There has to be another way."

"If there is, we don't have the time to find it," Rodriguez said grimly. "Based on everything I've heard, your uncle is losing patience. Do you understand that he'll torture her? Force her to bring the dragon to him? He'll make her lift the knife herself, take the blood, complete the ritual that will destroy everything about her that you care about."

I glanced at Kage. His face was stony. If he was feeling the same turmoil I was, he was doing a damned good job of not showing it. "What happens if she finds out?" he asked, finally.

Rodriguez's face hardened. "Neither of you will tell her. And that's a risk we'll just have to take. If we follow my plan, by the time she realizes what we're doing, it'll be too late to stop us."

I clenched my fists and paused my pacing. Pendragon would hate me for this. There was a good chance she would never forgive me. I gave a bitter laugh. If I'd thought she'd hated me before? This would change everything. I doubted she'd ever understand why I'd done what I'd done. But could I really stand to live in a world without her? Having her hate me was better than her not being alive to feel anything for me at all.

I looked at Rodriguez. "I need to think this over."

He nodded. "Fine. But don't take too long. Time isn't on our side."

"If we do this," Tanaka said, his voice quiet but steady, "it has to be done carefully. No mistakes. No risks to her."

Rodriguez nodded. "Agreed." He glanced at me. "We'd need you to convince her to get Nyxaris to the Dragon Court. That's if you agree to help."

"When?" I said simply.

"The night of the solstice. It's a night of great power. High-bloods already know this," Rodriguez replied.

I nodded. The Bloodmaiden Rite had been canceled this year. I wasn't surprised. There was no point trying to reinforce the coercive magic that kept the blightborn in check when the dragon's very existence was working against it. I knew other measures had been suggested instead, including martial law.

I turned to leave. As I reached the door, Rodriguez called after me. "Think hard, Blake. The cost of doing nothing could be worse than the one you're worried about."

As I stepped into the hall, I realized Tanaka was on my heels. He'd followed me outside. I stopped and turned to glare at him.

He held up his hands. "Sorry. Just wanted a quick word."

I narrowed my eyes. "About what?" I thought of something. "You're not going to rat Rodriguez out, now that you've heard all that, are you?"

He shook his head. "No. Although, I'm not sure my family would want me to support him in this."

"Fuck your family," I said bitterly. "Fuck all our families."

He looked at me with something approaching sympathy. "Viktor's pretty rough on you, isn't he? I can't imagine having him for an uncle."

"Don't pretend to care, Tanaka," I snapped. "Say whatever it is you have to say and then fuck off."

He chuckled under his breath and fell into step beside me as I started walking. The hall was empty at this time of the day. "Always so charming, Drakharrow. Is that what she sees in you? But fine. I'll get to the point. How long have you been showing symptoms?"

I froze mid-step. "Just what the hell is that supposed to mean?" I said, trying to make my voice light. But I could feel the tightness in my jaw, the unease in my eyes—and I knew Kage was watching every move I made.

Tanaka's eyes glinted. "You know exactly what I mean. I'm sure I'm not the only one who's noticed either."

I didn't hesitate. I grabbed him by the collar and slammed him up against the wall. "What did you see?"

"Easy, Drakharrow," he murmured. He wasn't even trying to fight me back. Maybe that's what disarmed me the most. I released him and he smoothed down his jacket. "You're not exactly subtle, are you?"

"Fuck off," I snarled.

But instead he stepped in front of me, blocking my path. He'd moved so quickly—faster than any highblood I'd seen. My heart started to pound. It reminded me of how I'd moved that day after the tribunal evaluation.

"What the hell was that?" I demanded. "How did you do that?"

"Patience," he said smoothly. "That might be hard as I can see you don't have any. But I'm being serious with you now. If you can't control *this*, that's going to be a big problem, Drakharrow."

"Control this? What even is this?" I demanded, breathing harder. "What the hell is happening to me? What do you know about it?"

He shook his head.

"Fine," I said, my voice cold. "Maybe my being a threat will be a good thing. It'll make it even easier to dominate you."

Kage gave a snort of derision and folded his arms over his chest. "Don't be so sure about that."

"Care to test me?" I stepped closer, pushing my chest up against his. My anger was spiking and I wasn't even bothering to rein it in.

"Careful, now," he said quietly. "You don't want to shift right here in the hall, now, do you?"

"Shift?" I ran my hands over my face. "What the fuck does that mean? Shift into what?" I couldn't help it. I knew it was pathetic but I was practically begging. "Come on, Tanaka. If you know something you have to tell me."

"I think there's someone better suited for that job," Kage replied softly.

I scowled. "Who?"

"Ask your dear uncle," Kage said, his voice dripping with disdain. "Ask Viktor Drakharrow what he knows. Ask him about your father. About his death."

The words stabbed into me like a sword. I stared at him. "What? What are you talking about?" I shook my head. "I should have guessed. You're so full of shit."

"Am I?" Kage's dark eyes narrowed. "You think your house is the only one with secrets? We all have them, every one of the four houses, every bloodline."

I stared at him, trying to make out the meaning in his words. "You're saying . . . the other houses . . . they can—"

"Don't," he interrupted. "Don't even finish that sentence."

"What the hell does that mean? You've been through this, too, haven't you?"

Something passed over his face but I couldn't pin down what it was. Fear? Regret? Sympathy? All three?

"No," he said firmly, shutting me down. "What you're going through . . . It's different."

"Different? Different how?" So, I was alone in this? Great. Just fucking great.

He didn't answer me directly. "Look, I want to help you, Drakharrow. Believe it or not, I do. But all I can say is, you need to be careful right now. What's happening to you, it's not just going to affect you. It'll impact everyone around you. People could get hurt. I don't want that to happen. Especially if it's Medra."

"Keep her name off your lips," I growled. "Stay the hell away from her."

Kage rolled his eyes. "Think about what I said. If you can't learn to control yourself, you'll be a danger to her, too. Do you really want that? She's vulnerable enough already."

"I don't see you exactly stepping up with words of wisdom," I spat. "Only cryptic bullshit."

"Look, when the time comes, you'll know it. You'll learn. Just like I did." It was the closest thing to an acknowledgment that he'd gone through something similar. But what, exactly? The Avari bastard. He'd rather keep his secrets than actually help me. "If you survive . . ."

I stared at him. "Survive? What the fuck does that mean?"

"If you survive," he repeated, "you'll have to start working on control. If you can't figure it out . . ." He sighed. "Well, come see me then. Maybe we can talk more."

"I'd never hurt Pendragon," I said, my voice low.

"Let's hope you're right," he said lightly, then turned to go. "For her sake and yours."

# CHAPTER 37

# FLORENCE

I smoothed down the lavender tunic for the tenth time. It was simple and practical, long enough to cover my thighs, paired with dark blue leggings that were stretchy and comfortable, and more importantly, wouldn't get in the way like the long skirts I normally favored might.

But did the outfit say. *Ready to fight?* Or *Ready to read?*

I looked across the room to where Neville sat, perched on the edge of my bed, watching everything. "Do I look ridiculous, Neville?" I asked out loud.

The fluffin's oversized ears swiveled at the sound of my voice. He let out a melodic chirp and bounded across the covers towards me, his tail wagging like mad.

"No, no," I said warningly, wagging a finger and backing away. "This is serious. I can't show up covered in fluffin fur. You can't distract me right now."

His tufted ears dropped dramatically.

I sighed. "I'm learning to defend myself, Neville. That means I have to be focused. Disciplined. Tough as nails." I straightened my back, then adjusted the silver House Avari brooch pinned to my chest. "No fluffin nonsense."

Neville tilted his head as if he were unconvinced, then plopped onto one of my pillows with a sigh.

"Stay here and be good," I told him, grabbing my satchel and slinging it over my shoulder. I gave myself a final once-over in the mirror. Tunic, cinched belt, leather boots: simple, practical, and hopefully good enough for my first fighting practice. "Wish me luck," I told Neville, who perked up again as I made my way to the door. I shook a finger at him. "Don't you even think of following me."

I slipped out into the corridor, carefully pulling the door shut behind me and checking it twice to make sure it was firmly latched. Satisfied, I set off down the hall.

I hadn't told my mother I was doing this: I wanted it to be a surprise. Once I had something to show her, maybe I'd tell her. But right now, I knew telling her would only make her worry more. She hated violence. And what we'd witnessed in the carriage with Theo . . . Well, *violence* didn't even seem like a strong enough word to describe it. What Aenia had done had been carnage. And she was only a little highblood girl. How was I supposed to protect myself or my mother from something more? Something bigger?

I was a bundle of nerves, butterflies flapping in my chest. What if I tripped over my own feet? What if I was just wasting Medra's time? What if she thought this whole thing was ridiculous but just wasn't telling me?

I squared my shoulders and sped up my pace. Medra wouldn't laugh. She was brave, kind, and confident. The sort of person I'd always admired but never thought I'd be lucky enough to call my best friend.

A few minutes later I was standing outside the training room used for scouting classes. The heavy wooden door stood ajar. I pushed it open nervously and stepped inside. The faint smells of sweat and old leather greeted me. Racks of wooden practice weapons lined the walls, while padded mats were scattered across the floor.

"Florence!" Medra's voice rang out from across the room.

My heart lifted as I spotted my friend sitting on one of the mats, going through some stretches. As I walked towards her, she jumped to her feet. Her fiery hair was tied back in a braid. Paired with the black fitted leather pants that covered her legs like a second skin, she wore a sleeveless black tunic cropped over her midriff, exposing a bare stretch of toned muscle. Her arms and hands were covered with some sort of leather guards. She looked like she'd just stepped out of a warrior's tale.

"You made it!" Medra stretched her arms out over her head and smiled. "You ready?"

"I hope so." I suddenly remembered all the physical education classes I had missed over the course of my childhood—preferring to read in the library or pretending to be sick so I wouldn't have to run and break out in a sweat. My stomach sank. This had been a terrible idea. "I think I forgot to mention that I'm not exactly coordinated," I said miserably.

Medra laughed. "That's okay. That's what practice is for. Everyone starts somewhere, right?" Then her eyes moved downwards. "Um, but Florence . . ."

I followed her gaze and gasped. There, sitting proudly at my heels, was Neville. He looked up at me with his tongue lolling out in a way that could only be described as a grin and thumped the mat with his fluffy tail.

"Neville!" I groaned. "You were supposed to stay in the room."

Neville tilted his head.

"Now you pretend you can't understand me?" I complained. "I know you understand every word, you little rascal."

"Get back to work or get out of my classroom, ladies!" a loud voice boomed out.

I jumped.

"Don't worry," Medra assured me. "She's not talking about us."

She gestured across the room where I saw two other students. Visha Vaidya was one of them. I was surprised to see a House Drakharrow student visiting a blightborn classroom. Then I saw the pretty tough-looking dwarven girl she had her arms around. The pair were very much occupied, leaning up against the wall and . . . well, decidedly not sparring.

"That's it!" A stout dwarven woman strode up between Medra

and me. "Out, ladies!" she roared at Visha and the other girl. "I expected better from you, Lace."

The dwarven girl Visha had been kissing glanced over guiltily, licking her lips. "I'm so sorry, Professor. I swear it won't happen again."

I watched as the girl glared at Visha, then jabbed her sharply in the stomach with a fist. Visha grabbed her midsection and pretended to fall over.

The professor narrowed her eyes. "I want to see real competition happening over there, Vaidya. You promised me you'd make Ironstride work for it—" I assumed that was Lace's last name. "I want to see her break a sweat. And not just from your damned lips," the professor barked.

Visha smirked but nodded. "Yes, ma'am!"

"Now, who's this?" I realized the dwarven professor was staring up at me.

I gulped.

"Professor Stonefist," Medra said quickly, "you remember I asked if I could invite my friend, Florence Shen, to one of our practice sessions? Florence wants to learn how to defend herself."

The scouting instructor's dark blue eyes scanned me, narrowing slightly. "Defend herself, eh? She's a wee bit scrawny for this sort of thing. Not one for roughhousing are you, Miss Shen?"

"No, ma'am," I blurted. "I like books."

"Books, eh? All good and well in their place. What are you? A strategist? A healer?"

"Both," I squeaked. "I mean, maybe. I also like plants." Shut up, Florence, shut up, I silently told myself.

"And what about pets? Do you like those, too? I see you brought a little friend to class with you." Professor Stonefist gestured pointedly to Neville.

"Oh, Bloodmaiden," I moaned. "That was an accident."

"You accidentally brought a pet?" Professor Stonefist rubbed her nose. "I didn't even know students were allowed to keep animals."

Technically, we weren't, but somehow, no one had ever commented on Neville. The little fluffin could be surprisingly stealthy when he wanted to be. Practically invisible. The instructor squatted down, her muscular form folding neatly despite the layers of well-worn studded leather armor she was wearing. As she studied Neville, I saw her face soften slightly.

"Well, well," she murmured. "Haven't seen one of these little beasties in a long time. You know much about these creatures, lass?" She glanced up at me.

"A little," I said hesitantly. "They usually live underground."

Stonefist nodded. "Used to be every dwarven family had one. Kept our homes free from pests. Protective, loyal little things, too. But now . . ." She sighed, her fingers brushing gently over Neville's ears. "Now it's a rarity to see one."

Neville was leaning against her hand like a cat basking in sunlight.

"Medra found him, actually," I said. "She rescued him."

The professor looked up at my friend with interest. "Did you, now?"

Medra nodded. "I found him injured on the beach. We think he must have come up from underground. He was only a little pup then."

Professor Stonefist nodded. "There are dwarven ruins beneath the school. Impossible to get to now, of course. But for a creature small enough, I suppose it might be possible." She looked at Neville fondly. "My family had one when I was a child. Named him Tumbles. Used to follow me everywhere. My dad said Tumbles liked me best because I always shared my supper with him. They're smart creatures. Never forget a kindness."

I glanced at Medra, thinking of Blake. I knew my friend had mixed feelings about the House Drakharrow leader. So did I. But Neville wouldn't be here without him.

I tried to picture Professor Stonefist as a child, but the image refused to take shape. It was easier to imagine her wrestling a band of pirates than sneaking table scraps to a fluffin. Neville chirped happily, clearly delighted with all of the attention. The professor chuckled, then glanced up at me, catching me staring.

"The beard, is it?"

"What?" I blurted. "Oh! Goodness! By the Bloodmaiden, no, I hadn't even noticed." But my eyes betrayed me as they skipped straight to her beard. It was impossible *not* to notice. Silvery-gray streaks wove through the neatly groomed hair, which curled gently at the ends. The whole thing seemed to have a life of its own, as though it had been sculpted into its artful twists with care. I'd always known some female dwarves grew beards. Many took pride in them, especially the older generations.

"I—" My cheeks flamed. "It's . . . just lovely." The words tumbled out. "Your beard, I mean. Very impressive. So . . . twirly."

The professor's eyes twinkled with amusement. "*Twirly*, eh? I can't say I've heard that before. I suppose it has grown out quite a bit. Should give it a trim. A dwarf's beard is a matter of pride, Shen. A beard tells a story. And mine could tell you plenty."

"I'm sure it could," I gasped, trying not to shrink back in embarrassment.

"Florence," Medra muttered under her breath. I could see her lips twitching with suppressed laughter.

"Well, that's just about enough chatter." Professor Stonefist clapped me on the back so abruptly I nearly fell over. I started coughing into my arm, hoping she wouldn't notice. "We're here to toughen your friend up, not talk about my beard all day. Though, your beard could use some work, too, Shen." She smirked as I squeaked and touched my chin self-consciously, as if expecting to find hair had suddenly sprouted. "Let's start her off with some basic work, Pendragon. Teach her how to take a hit without toppling over like a spindly sapling."

"Yes, Professor," Medra said, grinning as she motioned for me to follow her to a mat.

Professor Stonefist was eyeing Neville. "I suppose we'll say he's here for moral support. Keep him out of the way, Shen. No fluff-ins on the mats."

"Yes, Professor." I quickly scooped Neville up and he immediately started to snuffle his head towards my satchel. I let him climb into it gratefully.

I turned to Medra. "This is already the most embarrassing day of my life."

She laughed, pulling me towards the mat. "Relax. You're doing great. She likes you, I can tell. Besides, there's hardly anyone around."

"Really?" I pointed across the room where Vaughn Sabino was bouncing up and down as he hit a punching bag. "I see Vaughn." The tall boy waved as he saw me staring and I waved back. "And oh, look, over there is Visha."

"Visha'd better get her tongue out of Lace's throat or Professor Stonefist might wind up being the first instructor to ever physically launch a highblood into the sky with her foot," Medra muttered, as she eyed the two girls who were wrapped around each other again, this time as they lay on top of the mat.

"I think they started off fighting," I said dubiously as I watched them. "But they got distracted. Again."

"Yeah, that happens with Visha. A lot. She spars with her tongue." Medra rolled her shoulders. "Okay, let's start with some warm-ups. We don't want you pulling a muscle on your very first day."

"Warm-ups?" I asked nervously. "That doesn't involve running laps, does it? Please tell me it doesn't involve running laps."

She laughed. "No laps, I promise. Though Professor Stonefist will make you run them if she hears you talking like that. We'll just do some stretches. Don't worry, you'll be fine." She lowered her voice. "And don't worry about the beard. She didn't have one last year. She's been growing this one since Autumntide. She's very proud of it. I think she appreciated that you noticed it so quickly, actually."

I was pretty sure Medra was lying to spare my feelings, but I decided I'd take it. I sat down on the mat with her as she started guiding us through some basic poses. Touching my toes and lunging felt harmless enough, though I couldn't help but notice how much more gracefully Medra moved compared to me. I felt like a baby deer attempting to walk for the first time.

"So," I said conversationally, "late night at the library the other day. Did you find what you were looking for?" I hadn't meant anything by it, but to my surprise Medra blushed. "Medra!" I exclaimed. "What happened at the library?"

"Nothing," she said defensively. Then she sighed. "I've been meaning to talk to you about it for a while. I guess now's as good a time as any."

"Talk to me about what?" I asked curiously. "What happened?"

"I was researching for my essay and Kage came in—"

"Kage!" I practically shrieked.

"Keep your voice down," she hissed. "Nothing happened with Kage."

"But something did happen? With someone else?"

She hesitated. "Well, then Blake came in and . . . well."

I clapped a hand over my mouth. "Kage and Blake? *Together?*"

"By the gods, Florence! Not like that. Visha is rubbing off on you too much," she said, shaking her head.

But I refused to be put off. "Did something happen?" I whispered. "Did they fight?"

I wasn't actually expecting her to say yes but to my surprise, she blushed harder.

"They did!" I exclaimed. "They fought! Over you? Oh, Medra!"

"It's not like it sounds," she protested.

"Two House Leaders, fighting over you? No, it's exactly what it sounds like," I said knowingly. This reminded me of the book I'd been reading the night before. It was full of handsome men and duels and true love. Medra always laughed when she saw me reading one of my romance books, but I didn't care. They helped me relax. Still, I should have known my best friend's life would be just like a piece of fiction, full of passion and romance. Whereas mine was flat and dull . . . and part of me didn't mind if it stayed that way forever. Books were a lot safer than people. "And then what happened?"

She nibbled her lip. "I'm not sure I should get into the details."

My eyes widened. "Was it Blake?"

She nodded slowly. "We've been . . . getting closer. I've been meaning to tell you." She looked guilty. "Since before the tribunal evaluation."

"The tribunal evaluation?" I gasped. "But that was weeks ago." I shook my head. "I knew you two seemed nicer to one another that day. I should have known." My curiosity was still bubbling. "So, you do care for him?"

"I don't know what I feel," she said immediately, in a way that told me she might know but didn't want to talk about it.

"Well," I said after a moment, "I'm glad you told me. Blake has a lot to prove. But if anyone can handle someone like him, it's you. You know I won't judge you, Medra. If he's worth caring about, I'll support you."

She blinked. "You will?"

"Of course I will," I exclaimed. "But if he steps out of line, I'll unleash the wrath of Neville on him."

Medra laughed aloud. "I've never known Neville to be especially wrathful. Especially not towards Blake."

"Neville is loyal to you, too," I said stubbornly. "He'd want Blake to treat you nicely."

"I'm not sure the word *nice* is in Blake's vocabulary," she said a little doubtfully. "But don't get me wrong," she added hastily. "He's not terrible to me. In fact, he's improved quite a bit."

"He sure as hell better not be," I said loyally, shocking myself with my language. I lowered my voice. "What about the . . . feedings?"

Medra's face turned even redder. "Oh, they're not so bad lately."

"Oh, no?" I said knowingly. "I understand the bite of a high-blood can be exceedingly pleasurable if matched with—"

"Don't you dare even finish that sentence, Florence Shen," she moaned, covering her face. Then she looked up. "He's asked me to go to the ball with him."

I thought of Naveen and felt myself pale a little. I wasn't particularly looking forward to the Dance of the Longest Night this year. From the look on her face, I could tell Medra was thinking of Naveen, too. "What did you say?"

"I told him I'd already made plans to go with you, of course," she said promptly. "We already discussed it, remember?"

I shook my head. "We did, but that was before Blake invited you to go with him. If you want to accept, I'll understand. You know that. I doubt I'll be very much fun to go with."

"I don't want to go with him. I want to go with you," she said stubbornly. "Besides, I already refused. I explained why. Don't worry, Florence, he understands. He knows how important you are to me." She stood up and offered me her hand. "Enough talking. Back to business. Let's see if you can survive learning how to throw a punch."

I took her hand, suddenly nervous again. "All right."

"Don't worry," she whispered, a twinkle in her eye. "I'll go easy on you."

I suddenly remembered why I was there, how it had been my idea in the first place. I forced myself to recall the worst moment of my life: when my mother and I had been trapped in that carriage, helpless, weak, unable to do anything but cower as Theo was injured. I didn't want to be that person anymore. I needed to be more like Medra: strong, practically invincible. Or at least, it sometimes seemed that way.

"I'm ready," I said, giving her hand a squeeze. "Show me how it's done."

# CHAPTER 38

# BLAKE

A blizzard was brewing outside the House Drakharrow tower, but a warm fire crackled in the hearth inside my room. I barely noticed the weather or the fire. My focus was on the mirror. I adjusted the red velvet waistcoat I wore beneath a black jacket, wondering if it was too flashy. I didn't want to look like a total jackass.

What would *she* be wearing? Hopefully not Kage Tanaka's damn moon pendant again.

But it didn't matter, even if she were. Tonight would be different. It wouldn't be like last year.

We weren't going together. Not exactly. Pendragon had wanted to go with her friend, Florence. I understood the gesture. Florence had attended the ball with their friend Naveen last year. Later on that same year, Pendragon had been forced to kill Naveen in the Consort Games. The night was probably full of unpleasant memories for her and Florence.

But I still had a plan. A way to make the night special—at least, in the few hours we had left before it would all go straight to hell. Because tonight was the night. The night that Tanaka and I would be helping Rodriguez with his insane plan: to turn a dragon back to stone. As far as I was concerned, my role was the worst one: I had to convince Pendragon to bring Nyxaris to the Dragon Court. Then I'd have to deal with the aftermath as she realized what we'd done. But for now, I was trying not to look that far ahead. This might be our last good night together for a while.

I reached for the small black-and-red box that sat on my desk and sensation struck—sharp and sudden like a blade to the ribs. "Fuck," I gasped, clutching at my side. The pain spread quickly, searing through my chest and down my arms. My knees buckled. I staggered, clutching onto the desk for support. Heat radiated from beneath my skin.

I looked down at my hands and groaned. Red scales covered them. And my fingers—something was happening to them, too. The nails were elongating, shifting into sharp, curved claws.

"No, no, no," I muttered through clenched teeth. "Fuck no. Not now. Not tonight."

But the changes racing through me were like a fire I couldn't outrun. My back arched as searing pain tore through my shoulder blades. I let out a hoarse cry as the sound of fabric filled the air, waistcoat and jacket both splitting into shreds as if they were paper. A new pressure was building in my back. I screamed as my skin tore and the feeling of something pushing outwards overwhelmed me.

Through the pain, I realized what it was.

Wings.

In the mirror, I could see they were only half-formed, grotesque and skeletal. But I could feel the raw power in them, the promise of what they might someday become.

Sweat dripped from my face as I crumpled to the floor, my breathing ragged. Firelight spilled over my body. I shone crimson. Scales covered my arms, my chest, my collarbone, hiding my tattoos. I touched a hand to my face, then looked up at the mirror again . . . and instantly wished I hadn't.

I was unrecognizable. Red. Monstrous. Neither highblood or blightborn.

Dragon.

Then the rage crashed through my mind. Wiping aside every other thought.

Blood. Death. Destruction. The room was too small, too confining. Every sound was too grating, too loud for my senses. I wanted to destroy, to break, to rend anything in my path.

"Stop." My voice came out as a hiss. I dug my hands into the floorboards, and my claws left deep gouges in the wood. "Get a . . . fucking grip . . . Drakharrow."

Pendragon. The ball. My gift.

I tried to latch on to those thoughts. Picturing Pendragon's face as if she was a lifeline and could bring me back, undo what was happening to me. Slowly, the heat started to subside. But my body still ached. I lay on the floor, the remnants of my shredded clothes sticking to my sweat-soaked skin. The wings gradually retracted, leaving my back aching and raw. The scales on my hand were disappearing, but a few were still visible.

There was a knock at the door. "Blake?" Theo's voice.

Swearing under my breath, I pushed myself up, then grabbed a towel from the back of a chair and draped it around my waist. Every inch of my body throbbed.

"Blake? Hurry it up. We know you're in there."

*Shit.* Visha was there, too.

I staggered to the door, leaning heavily on the frame for support as I opened it.

Theo's eyes went wide the moment he saw me. "Blake! What the hell happened?"

"I'm fine," I croaked. "Feeling a little under the weather. I'll catch up with you later. You two have fun without me."

Visha whistled as she looked me up and down, then swept into the room. "Under the weather? Hungover more like it. What the hell did you drink? You look like you've been through the wars."

"Nothing," I muttered, staggering towards her and trying to block her path. "Visha, seriously, just go—"

But she wasn't listening. She was heading straight across the room. Straight towards . . .

I suppressed a groan as her gaze landed on the pile of shredded fabric that had once been my clothes. She froze. Slowly, she bent down, picking up one of the pieces.

"What the . . ." She straightened up. "Did you get mauled by a bear?" She looked over at me and grinned. "Naughty, naughty. Did the rider do this to you?" She looked me over. "I didn't know you liked it rough. But this . . . This is even rougher than my tastes." She whistled again.

Theo had stepped cautiously into the room. Now his eyes widened as he caught sight of the pile of shredded clothes. "Blake . . ."

I growled, shooting him a warning glance.

Visha was looking back and forth between us with a raised eyebrow. "What's going on? You two are acting weird. Weirder than usual."

"It's nothing," I said.

"Bullshit." She shrugged. "But fine, keep your secrets. Let's get you cleaned up and dressed. Don't you have a girl waiting for you?"

She marched over to my wardrobe and began yanking clothes out. "Get your ass into the bathroom. I can smell you from here."

I sniffed myself. She was right. Dammit, I'd just bathed, too. And used up the last of the scent I liked. With a sigh, I headed to the bathtub. This was happening. I just hoped I could stand on my own two feet the entire night. Because I planned on asking a dragon rider to dance.

# CHAPTER 39

# MEDRA

I adjusted the gold sash draped across the waist of my strapless black gown, fidgeting with it for at least the fourth time since I'd put it on. I always felt unnatural when I tried to look elegant, since I never felt anything of the sort. I caught sight of my reflection—the sleek, fitted bodice of my satin dress shimmered with gold embroidered flowers. I'd braided my hair into a crown, weaving a gold ribbon through it, and leaving just a few loose pieces to frame my face.

Beside me, Florence's delicate blue dress caught the lamplight as she bent over to fasten a pair of silver earrings. The skirt of her gown was made of many layers of tulle and looked as if it had been spun from frost itself—perfect for Winter Solstice night.

"You look so pretty, Florence. That dress was definitely the right choice." My eyes wandered to the ledge by the window where she'd carefully placed a book last night. It had been one of Naveen's favorites, a fairy-tale collection he'd grown up reading. She planned to read it before the school break was over and we went back to class. The sight of it reminded me how much he must be on her mind.

"I've been thinking about him, too," I said softly, gesturing to the book.

Florence had been brushing out her long black hair; she was leaving it down this evening. The silky tresses gleamed as they fell straight down around her shoulders like a midnight waterfall. Now she paused and looked at me. "He was my friend for so long. I still can't believe he won't show up at the door in a moment."

"I know," I whispered.

"I miss him, Medra. I miss his laugh, his silly sense of humor." She put a hand to her mouth. "I don't know if I'll ever be able to stop."

I saw the tears in her eyes and quickly moved over to put my arms around her shoulders. "Tonight would have been a lot more fun with him here," I said softly. "I wish he could see you in that dress. His eyes would pop right out of his head."

Florence gave me a watery smile. I knew she'd been torn about what she felt for Naveen. He'd wanted to move from friends to something more. Would he have been the right person for Florence? The one to make her happy? I tried to picture Florence with a partner, but it was no use. The problem was, in my mind, no one was good enough for her. She was a shining star. Brilliant, beautiful, and the sweetest person I knew.

"Do you still want to go tonight?" I asked. "Or should we stay in our room and make hot chocolate and read books? And by *read books*, I mean *talk*, of course."

But I never did find out how she'd have answered. There was a knock at the door. I glanced at Florence, then crossed the room to open it. Blake stood on the other side. He was dressed sharply, all in black, his waistcoat embroidered with red silk dragons. He looked handsome and regal as always, but there was something different about his posture. His usual cocky grin had been replaced with a sheepish smile. Behind him stood Visha and Theo, both equally well-dressed.

"I know you wanted to go with Florence tonight," Blake said quickly. "But we were thinking, maybe we could all go together? As friends."

"Vaughn and Lace are meeting us there," Theo said, speaking up from behind his cousin.

I raised my eyebrow. "Students from different houses attending a ball together? I don't know. Sounds scandalous if you ask me." I turned to Florence, who giggled. "Florence?"

She stepped forward, tucking a lock of hair behind her ear, and smiled warmly at the trio. "I think that sounds very nice."

"Good. It's settled, then," Visha declared. "Let's go and get this party started."

Theo rolled his eyes. "As if you and Lace will even be at the party for long."

"We might be," she said innocently. "I told Evander I'd save him a dance."

"What does he think of Lace?" I asked curiously.

"I don't know," Visha said nonchalantly. "Haven't asked. Don't plan to."

I met Blake's eyes and he grinned as if to say *Typical Visha.*

Florence moved back into the room to fetch a soft white shawl she'd left draped over the back of a chair. As she wrapped it around herself, I noticed Blake's eyes lingering on me.

"I have something for you." He held a small black box out to me. "A gift."

I took the box with some trepidation. "Blake, you didn't have to get me anything."

"Please," he interrupted, his voice unusually hesitant. "Just . . . open it."

I bit my lip, but lifted the lid. Inside was a pendant—a dragon carved in onyx, wings flared as if in mid-flight. "Nyxaris," I breathed, immediately seeing the likeness.

"Do you like it?" Blake asked. "No house colors. No insignia. Just . . . your dragon."

I understood what he was trying to say. That wearing the pendant wasn't a claim. He wasn't trying to mark me or label me. I knew he and Nyxaris didn't even like each other, to put it mildly.

"It's beautiful," I murmured. "Thank you."

"May I?" he asked, gesturing to the box.

I hesitated, suddenly aware of the intimacy of the moment, of the others watching us. But slowly, I nodded and turned around, lifting some strands of hair off my neck. Blake stepped closer, his breath brushing against my skin. His fingers were warm and steady as he fastened the necklace around my throat. Even the brief touch of his skin against mine was enough to send a shiver down my spine. I closed my eyes for a moment.

"There," he murmured.

I turned back to face him and his gaze held mine, the tension between us crackling.

"Perfect," he said softly. "Black for Nyxaris, but you bring the fire. You make even the darkness shine. Even dragon fire can't compete with the way you burn, Pendragon."

"Ahem. Time is ticking." Visha's voice broke the moment, as she leaned against the doorway, a wicked grin on her face.

"Do you need a moment? Should we go on without you two?" Florence asked innocently.

"Not if we ever want to see them again," Theo said jokingly.

I felt my face heat up. "No, we're ready," I said hastily.

"Actually, just one more thing." Blake reached into his pocket and pulled out another small black box. But this time, he handed it to Florence. "For you, Florence. You already look lovely. But if you wanted another accessory, I thought . . ."

Florence opened the box and gasped in delight. A small silver pendant in the shape of a fluffin sitting on a stack of books rested there.

"It's beautiful. Thank you, Blake," she said, with a happy smile. She flung her arms around his shoulders, surprising everyone—but Blake most of all, I thought. "I love it."

Blake looked a little nervous, but he patted her awkwardly on the back and smiled. "Of course."

I helped Florence fasten the pendant around her neck, suddenly feeling choked up.

As we left the room, I felt the press of the necklace resting against my collarbone, but I didn't feel claimed or chained or possessed. Instead, its presence was reassuring, oddly grounding. Blake walked at my side, his usual arrogant swagger tempered tonight. He was quieter, as if he were thinking about something. I wondered what it was, if we were both thinking the same thing. Because for the first time in a long time, I was seeing possibilities spinning out before me that I'd never let myself consider before.

I'd hated Blake Drakharrow. Truly hated him. He'd been arrogant, cruel, and entirely too eager to exert power over me when he thought he could. That hadn't disappeared entirely. I'd seen flashes of his petty, vindictive streak earlier that year, his need to dominate. But tonight, he was here. Giving me gifts, being kind to my friend, trying to get to know me. I glanced up at him, his sharp profile outlined by the lanterns as we moved down the hall. There was a shyness to his expression that I'd never seen before, as though he were waiting for something, hoping for it, but too afraid to ask.

Before I could stop myself, I slipped my hand into his. The moment I made contact, he turned to look at me and his expression made my heart wrench. His gray eyes had gone wide, almost disbelieving, as if the world had shifted beneath his feet and he hadn't quite caught up yet.

That look. It took my breath away.

At that moment, all I could think about was how close he was—and how much closer I wanted him to be.

# CHAPTER 40

# BLAKE

T he ballroom was a sparkling spectacle of brilliance—no ex-
pense spared, no surface left undecorated. The air was heavy
with the mingled scents of blood wine and expensive per-
fumes.

It was torture.

I moved through a slow waltz with Pendragon in my arms, her
body close enough to drive me mad. All I could think about was
getting her alone. Away from our friends, from the crowd, from
the music. Away from the infernal layers of satin and silk that stood
between us. I wanted to peel her gown away and trace every inch
of her body with my lips, hear her gasp my name in that breathless, unguarded way I craved.

But I knew it was hopeless. She wasn't going to leave Florence.
Not tonight.

The worst part was I understood. I fucking got it. The old Blake
might not have. But I did.

I knew Pendragon had to stay with her friend and maybe the
weirdest thing of all was that I didn't really want to abandon Florence either. She'd kind of grown on me. There was something
about the dark-haired bookish girl that reminded me of Aenia a
little. Something that filled me with that urge to protect.

So, we waltzed. I kept my hands steady on Pendragon's satin-
draped waist—even as every fiber of me burned to rip the stuff off

her. The soft sway of the dance made the loose strands of her hair catch the light, shifting between fire and gold with every turn. It was wild in a way nothing else in this meticulously perfect room could ever be, rebellious in its very beauty.

Red was never a color I'd given much thought to before. It was one of the colors of my house. It was anger, danger, blood. Then I saw Pendragon—her hair wild, untamed, burning like dragon fire. And suddenly red wasn't any of those things. It was the scent of jasmine and vanilla, autumn leaves swirling in the wind, the crackle of a fire on a chilly night, the first light of dawn rising golden and rosy. All the things that made life sweet. All the things that made it worth living.

So, yeah, red was officially my favorite color now.

I thought of the red scales that had covered me just a few hours before. In some small way, Pendragon and I matched now. I wondered if I'd ever be able to tell her that.

As we pivoted slowly on the floor, I caught sight of Regan across the room. She stood alone near one of the refreshment tables, her blond hair pulled into an elaborate twist, her white gown covered in tiny jewels that made it sparkle under the chandeliers. Objectively, I knew she looked very pretty. But she couldn't hold a candle to the woman in my arms. Our eyes met. I inclined my head. I meant it as a small gesture of acknowledgment, maybe even respect. But as I watched, her lips curved up into a cruel smile, her eyes glinting with that familiar malice, before she turned away. *So much for that.* Regan wasn't one to forgive or forget. I doubted she'd ever forgive me for rejecting her. Still, it had been worth a shot.

I glanced at her retreating figure, wondering what awaited her next. Was she really about to be betrothed to my uncle? Was that what she really wanted or had her father convinced her she had no other choice?

The music began to fade and I finally snapped.

"Come with me," I murmured, looking down at Pendragon.

She looked up at me, her green eyes searching mine. "Where?"

"Just outside. Only for a moment," I added quickly, already seeing her eyes dart to her friend.

But Florence seemed fine. The dark-haired girl was sitting at a table with Visha, Theo, Lace, and Vaughn and laughing at something Visha had just said.

Pendragon nodded and I led her across the room, my hand holding hers. We passed by the House Orphos tables. Briefly I saw Lysander. He was leaning across to speak to his sister. Lunaya's head was down and she looked sullen as her brother tried to talk to her. But I didn't have time to wonder about any of that. The moment we stepped out onto the terrace, the cold hit us like a slap in the face. The winter air was sharp and biting. Above us, the sky stretched out, black and endless.

Pendragon shivered and I quickly shrugged out of my jacket, draping it over her shoulders.

Her lips parted in surprise but she pulled it around herself. "Blake, you'll freeze. Let's just go back inside."

"No," I said stubbornly. "I needed to get you alone."

I stepped towards her, my hand sliding up to cup her cheek. Her skin was soft and as my thumb brushed against her jawline, her eyelashes fluttered. I leaned in, my lips finding hers in a kiss that was anything but gentle: it was heat and desperation. A clash of want and need that I couldn't hold back. She responded instantly, her hands sliding over my chest, her mouth deepening the kiss.

And then it hit me.

A prickle along my back and neck. The telltale itch of scales threatening to erupt. I pulled back, my chest heaving.

"Blake?" She reached out her hand, cupping my jaw. "What's wrong?"

I forced a smile. "It's nothing. Just . . ." I hesitated, the burden of Rodriguez's plan hanging over me like a shroud. I hated what I was about to do, but I had no choice. Not if I wanted to keep her safe. I'd put this off too long as it was. I took a deep breath and took the plunge. "Look, I've been meaning to ask you all evening. Are you in contact with Nyxaris?"

She grimaced. "If you can call it that. He doesn't really want to talk much lately. But I know where he is, roughly. I know he's safe."

"Great. Good. Can you get him to come back to Bloodwing tonight? At midnight?" I blurted out. "To the Dragon Court."

She frowned. "Why would I get him to do that?"

I'd rehearsed this in my mind. Thought of what I was going to say. But now that the moment was here, I felt myself scrambling for the right words.

"I want to apologize to him," I said, stumbling a little. "For not treating him with the respect he deserved when we first met. Or his rider." I met her gaze, willing her to believe me. To trust me. Feeling like a total asshole for what I was doing. But knowing it was the only thing I could possibly do if I wanted to keep her alive. "But also, because I have something important to tell you both. Something he needs to hear."

She studied me for a long moment. "This feels . . . strange. Why can't you just tell me instead? I'll pass it on."

I forced a smile, trying to reassure her. "Look, just trust me on this. Please. You know I wouldn't ask if it weren't important."

I was giving her the ultimate guilt trip. I cringed internally, waiting for her to see through my bullshit and say no. This was awful; I hated lying to her like this. Hiding what I was going through from her was one thing. But getting her to lure her dragon back . . . It felt wrong. I felt utterly disgusted with myself for doing it.

But she was nodding reluctantly. "Fine. I'll talk to him. If you have information for him, I know he'll want to hear it."

Relief and guilt warred inside me. "Thank you."

The terrace door opened behind us. Theo stepped out, his expression grim. "Blake," he said, glancing between us, "Viktor wants to see you. Now."

A chill that had nothing to do with the winter's night settled over me. Of course Viktor had to choose this exact moment. But there was no avoiding it. Not if he'd sent word for me.

"Fine." I looked back at Pendragon, already stepping towards the door. "I'll be back for our meeting at midnight, I promise. Wait for me, all right?"

She nodded, her face so open and trusting for once that it made my heart hurt. I wondered if it was the last time I'd ever see it that way.

I pushed open the doors to Viktor's chambers. He was already seated behind his desk. Even though he'd been the one to summon me, he didn't look up immediately, just kept scribbling something on parchment, the scratch of the quill setting my teeth on edge as I waited for him to give me his full attention.

"Blake," he said, finally, setting the quill down and leaning back in his chair. "I trust you're enjoying the ball."

I stared down at him. Right. The ball he'd purposely yanked me away from. "Why am I here?"

Viktor raised a brow. "Such impatience. I thought I taught you better manners."

My parents had taught me everything good that I knew. Viktor had been the one to try to strip it all away. But I kept my temper and didn't reply. He was goading me but that was nothing new.

"Aenia is missing," he said abruptly.

I stared at him, hoping I'd misheard. "What?"

"The foulblood girl," he said, each word clipped. "She's on the loose."

"How?" I demanded, stepping towards the desk. "She was under guard, restricted to one suite in the castle. A healer was supposed to be supervising her at all times. I'd arranged everything. I—"

"Yes, yes," Viktor interrupted. "You were very conscientious. I'm well aware. Don't expect a pat on the back for it. She was being moved to a different location when the incident occurred. My men are searching for her now."

"Moved?" Fury was bubbling in my chest. "Who ordered her to be moved?"

"Who do you think?" Viktor asked lazily. "The castle you were using was no longer available."

"What?" I stared. "Why? What happened to it?"

I half expected him to say Aenia had burned it down. But instead he replied, "It's been given away. To the Pansera family as part of Regan's dowry. A suitable gift for a bride, wouldn't you agree?"

"You moved my sister so you could give Regan a fucking wedding present?" My voice shook with rage. "And now Aenia's gone? If you'd told me, I could have dealt with Aenia myself. I knew you were insane, but are you such a fucking idiot as that, Uncle?"

I'd crossed a line and I knew it. The trouble was I couldn't seem to make myself care.

Viktor's expression hardened. "Watch yourself, Nephew. You forget who you're speaking to."

"Oh, I know exactly who I'm speaking to," I shot back. "A man too concerned about his cock for the first time in a century to care when he's fucked his family over."

Viktor stood, the movement slow and deliberate. "You dare to speak to me in such a way? After everything I've done for you? For your mother?"

"Don't," I growled, stepping a little closer. "Don't you dare bring Desdemona into this. You won't like how that goes."

"Oh, really? And you'll do what?" Viktor snapped. "Kill me? Impossible. Overstep just once and I'll make sure your mother dies screaming. As for Aenia, if she's found, I'll have her dealt with accordingly."

"You wouldn't." But even as I spoke, I knew better. His men were already looking for my sister. I thought of Rodriguez and the plan for tonight. *Fuck. Double fuck.* I was trapped. I had to get back to Bloodwing—and soon.

I turned away. Tomorrow, I'd go searching for Aenia myself. I had my own people. I'd set them all looking. We'd find her before my uncle could. And this time, I'd learn my damned lesson and keep her somewhere Viktor would never think to look for her. She'd be out of his control completely. I'd never have to worry about this again.

"Where do you think you're going?"

I stopped in my tracks. "Aenia. I thought—"

"You thought I made you come out here simply to discuss your foulblood creation?"

"Don't fucking call her that," I snarled turning back to face him. "Well? What do you want? Why did you summon me?"

His lips curved. "The rider. I want her to be brought to me later tonight. When the ball ends, you will escort her to the Black Keep. She'll be kept here for the foreseeable future. She and I need to have a conversation about her progress with Nyxaris."

I stared. He wasn't talking about progress. He was planning to do the soul-binding ritual. This couldn't be happening. Not tonight.

"Tonight's the ball. Or had you forgotten? She's occupied. I'll tell her but I doubt she'll be able to meet tonight." I started turning away again. "And have you forgotten? She's in House Avari now."

"You'll bring her here tonight and that's an order," my uncle snapped, his tone laced with finality. "How many times do I need to remind you of the consequences of disobedience? Does your mother really mean so little to you?"

The second mention of my mother sent a spear of white-hot rage piercing through me. I was trying to hold it together, but my body was intent on rebelling. My breath caught as I felt the familiar prickle, the warning signs of something I couldn't yet control taking shape inside. My skin itched. The heat in my veins began to build.

"Well, well," my uncle murmured. "What's this, now?"

His eyes were on my hands. I yanked them behind my back, but it was too late. I'd already seen the crimson scales. I could feel them, spreading up my wrists like wildfire.

"Step forward," Viktor commanded.

I stayed put.

"I said step forward." His voice was like steel.

Before I could fully process the command, my legs moved of their own accord, dragging me closer. He was using thrallweave on me. I hadn't even had a chance to try to block him out. But fortunately or unfortunately for me, Viktor wasn't interested in searching my mind. He was more interested in my body. His presence was suffocating. His will was a cage I couldn't seem to escape. My instincts were screaming at me to fight back, but the pressure he exuded was overwhelming.

As I moved closer, Viktor reached out with preternatural speed, seizing my wrist in an iron grip. I winced as his fingers tightened, nearly crushing the bones beneath the spreading scales. He yanked my hand up into the light. "How long has this been happening?"

"Not long. It's nothing," I said, gritting my teeth and willing the scales to disappear. "Just a rash."

There was no way I was bringing Pendragon to him. Not tonight. Not any night. We'd have to leave Bloodwing. Get away somewhere he couldn't find us. But she'd never agree to leave Florence. And the thought of leaving Theo to Viktor's evils filled me with trepidation.

"Don't lie to me, boy," he hissed, his grip still tightening like a vise. "How long?" His eyes glinted with something dark and hungry.

I suddenly understood. I jerked my hand free. "Why don't you tell me?"

Viktor's red eyes narrowed as his lips formed an infuriating smirk. "If you don't understand by now, you never will."

I stared at him, not wanting to ask the question, but knowing I had to. "How did my father die?"

He waved a hand. "You know the sad tale just as well as everyone else in this family."

"Suicide," I said coldly. "Only that was a lie."

Viktor gave a sharp laugh. "Oh, Blake. So quick to jump to

conclusions. If only your father had been so spirited. Perhaps he'd still be alive."

For years I'd lived with the knowledge my father had intentionally left us. The truth had been covered over to protect our family name. No one could know that the great Peacebringer, as some had called him, had despised his highblood life so much that he'd chosen to end it.

"He didn't kill himself, did he? That's not what happened."

Viktor's smirk widened. "And what exactly do you think happened, boy?"

I leaned forward, resting my hands on the desk, not bothering to hide the scales. "He was like me, wasn't he? He started to . . . change." More and more pieces fell into place as the words tumbled from my mouth.

"He killed himself because the strain of his monstrousness was too much for him to bear. Weakness runs in bloodlines, it seems," my uncle drawled.

Weakness? No. If I knew one thing, it was that whatever was happening to me was strength. If I could only learn how to control it.

"No," I growled. "That's not what happened. My father was strong. Strong enough to try to fight you. He didn't want to become your weapon. Did he kill himself to escape you, you evil old bastard? Or did you kill him?"

Viktor's smile faltered for the briefest moment.

I clenched my fists, the itching in my skin intensifying as if the scales longed to burst free in response to my rage. "How did this happen to him? Why the hell is it happening to me *now*?"

He leaned back, his expression becoming remote. "You're so clever. You tell me."

I thought back, combing my mind over every detail, every possibility. Then it hit me. My throat went dry. "Rider blood."

Viktor gave a barking laugh. "Don't be ridiculous. Your mother wasn't a dragon rider."

"She's a halfborn," I said slowly, piecing it together. Which was why my father's family had been against the union in the first place. I could remember overhearing my parents talking about it when I was a child. "Rider blood seeped into blightborn bloodlines. You couldn't extinguish it altogether, could you?" I didn't even bother to hide the fact that I'd been in the archives. I watched his gaze sharpen. "My father must have fed from her. That's what triggered his transformation."

What Aenia had done—taking blood from another highblood without consent—was a crime. But highbloods feeding from one another was not strictly against the law. What happened in private generally stayed in private. No one wanted to think about what their parents did in the bedroom. But feeding between highblood mates was said to be the height of, well, pleasure.

My chest heaved. "You wanted this. You gave me the rider because you hoped this would happen. You wanted to awaken this . . . this *thing* inside me."

Viktor's laugh was genuine. The warmest I'd ever heard it. "There's a reason I didn't feed from the girl myself when I had the chance. Though, believe me, I was tempted. Very tempted."

He moved around the desk towards me, shaking his head. "Look at you. You're becoming something extraordinary." For a moment, he seemed truly admiring. Then he lifted his shoulders and let them fall. "Or perhaps not. Perhaps you'll die like your father did. Weak and pathetic. Writhing and screaming until the power consumes you. Experimentation has its price. But you already knew I'd be willing to pay any price for the sake of the greatness of our house, Nephew."

My hands trembled. I could feel the scales creeping up the back of my neck, along the edge of my jaw, across my cheeks.

"There's no escaping what's in your blood," my uncle murmured. "If you're changing, then you're becoming exactly what you're meant to be. And if you survive the transformation, you'll be the greatest weapon our house has ever possessed."

The fire in my blood erupted. Like nothing I'd ever felt before. And as the pain and rage started to spread, all I could think of was that I was going to make my uncle regret every moment he'd spent on this earth if it was the last thing I ever did.

I staggered back, clutching at my chest as if I could hold my body together through sheer force of will. But there was no stopping it. Whatever was happening, it was bigger than me.

And it was ripping me apart.

I fell to my knees, my hands clawing at the stone. Scales surged, spreading up my arms, curling around my neck. My skin burned, as if molten metal had replaced my blood. My muscles twisted and stretched, bones grinding with sickening cracks.

"Fascinating," my uncle murmured, "to witness it firsthand . . ."

I could hardly hear him. The pain. It was too much. It felt as if I were being torn apart from the inside out. I writhed and screamed on the ground, just like he'd predicted. My vision blurred, everything fracturing into disjointed shapes, shards of light and shadow. As if from a distance, I heard guards rush in. Heard the sound of steel swords drawn.

A guard rushed towards me, his face tight with fear. "A monster," he shouted, his voice cracking. "My lord, we must get you out of here. We must destroy it—"

"No," Viktor screamed, but the guard was too far gone, driven by his panic.

I saw the blade glint overhead, saw the arc it made as it swung down toward me. My reflexes were slowed, my body overwhelmed by the chaos erupting inside me. I turned my head just as the blade struck. Blinding, searing agony exploded across my face. I roared as the blood rushed down my face, warm and sticky, my vision blurring.

"You fool!" Viktor's voice thundered through the haze of pain.

I looked through a blur of red just in time to see my uncle reach the guard and rip his throat out with his fangs. The man gurgled, dropping to his knees before collapsing in a heap.

It had taken my becoming a fucking dragon but for once in my life, my uncle was standing up for me.

The other guards backed up.

"Let him be," my uncle commanded, wiping the blood from his mouth. "I order you to remain where you are."

"But my lord," one guard foolishly tried to protest. "Surely, you—"

"Do as I say!" Viktor barked.

I wanted to scream, wanted to make it all stop. I opened my mouth to beg for help, but all that came out was a strangled roar. My vision swam, tinted red. Dimly, I saw the guards stepping away, their backs to the walls. My back arched violently. I felt a horrifying, wet tear, as something burst free. I collapsed forward, panting, trembling. I glanced back. Wings. Dark, crimson, slick with blood, unfolding from my back like some misshapen flower.

I caught Viktor's expression: triumph and awe. He was basking in this. My agony was his victory. Was this how it had been for my father? At what point had he ended it? Had the transformation really killed him? Or had he attacked Viktor and failed? Been put down like a monster, an animal?

"Larger," Viktor murmured, almost reverently. "Stronger. Perhaps this one will survive."

I slammed my fists down against the ground, hearing the stone crack beneath them. My body convulsed again. I felt my jaw elongate, teeth sharpening, hands twisting into claws.

Suddenly, the room felt impossibly small. The air pressed against my chest. Between spasm after spasm of pain, I felt panic. The walls closed in as my body twisted and stretched. My bones cracked like thunder, shifting and reshaping themselves. The fire in my blood burned hotter.

But then . . . the agony began to shift. The pain receded. Replaced by something else—strength. Power. Possibility. I grew. Bigger and bigger. My wings unfurling with a loud leathery snap.

Something was happening to Viktor's face as he watched. It was transforming, too. Eager anticipation was bleeding away to something I'd never seen from him before.

Dread. Fear.

He stumbled back against his desk, his bravado faltering. "Guards!" He raised his arm, pointing at me, at whatever I was. "We've waited long enough. Bring this creature down. Now!"

The guards didn't have to be asked twice. They lunged towards me. The first guard's blade gleamed as he raised it. I swiped a massive claw. The man flew across the room, slamming into the far wall with a hideous crunch.

Another came at me from the side. My tail lashed out, sending him sprawling to the ground like a broken toy.

They kept coming and coming and I reacted as quickly as they came. I was no longer human. No longer highblood. No longer breakable.

Their weapons glanced off my scales. One by one, I tore through them, ripping and shredding. The carnage was effortless. What was more, I craved it. I enjoyed it. The blood was beautiful to see, splattering across walls, pooling along the floor. The fire within me surged and I let it, roaring so loudly the Black Keep seemed to tremble.

"Stop!" Viktor shouted. He looked so small standing down below me. How had I ever been afraid of him? "Blake, listen to me!"

I turned slowly, my massive frame towering over him. The heat of my breath steaming the air between us.

"Think about what you're doing! Remember who you are!" Viktor's voice was weak, cracked with panic. I'd never seen him like this before. And yet I'd always known this was who he really was. "Control yourself. Control your fears. You don't have to do this. I can give you anything. Anything you want. Riches, power, women. Anyone you desire. The rider? You want her? She's yours. Forever."

She was already mine. Forever. Nothing would take her from me. Even through the haze of flames and blood, I knew that. Our blood was bound. But once she saw what her blood had done to me? What would she do then?

I shuddered, roaring again. I watched my uncle back up against the wall.

"Blake, you're better than this. You're the better man. I've always known it. I'll make you my heir," my uncle babbled. "All that I've built will be yours someday. Marcus—your brother will bow at your feet. Just think of it!"

All I could think of was how much he looked like prey. And of how his bones would crunch and shatter as his blood filled my mouth.

But something in me held back. I didn't want the taste of Viktor Drakharrow in my throat, sticking to my tongue like poison. My vision was tinted red. Was this how my uncle saw the world, through rims of blood? He looked so fragile now; he was just a man. A man who had controlled my life. Destroyed me, bent me, broken me in ways I hadn't even realized until now.

Now? There was nothing left but what he'd made.

The fire in my blood demanded release. A strange sensation was welling up in my chest. Coiling and burning. A living inferno. My throat ached. I gagged as the heat spiraled upward. I thought of Nyxaris. Of the devastating beauty his flames unleashed.

My mouth opened. Viktor's face changed. His calm veneer cracked, giving way to sheer panic. He shielded his face with his arms, his voice desperate now and thick with thrallweave. But thrallweave didn't work on dragons. "Blake! Stop! You need me. Think about what you're doing. You're better than this. Don't let the beast control you."

But I wasn't better. Not anymore. Wasn't this exactly what he'd wanted me to be?

I advanced, embers spewing from my maw with every exhale. For once, Viktor Drakharrow looked exactly as he should have all along: small, weak, and utterly terrified. He had ruled me through fear. Now that fear was gone.

The fire rose. And I let it.

# CHAPTER 41

# MEDRA

I stepped into the Dragon Court, tugging my cloak around my shoulders, its edges brushing up against the hem of the black-and-gold gown beneath. Blake's pendant rested against my collarbone. I touched it gently with one finger. It suddenly felt heavier.

All he wanted was to talk to Nyxaris. So why did I have such a bad feeling about this?

The ground was icy underfoot. Frost glittered across the stones, shining like a field of stars.

I had avoided the courtyard since Nyxaris's awakening last year. Most of the rubble from his dramatic rebirth had been cleared away. Nothing had been erected to take the place where he had once stood for more than a century as a statue of stone. Instead, his brethren remained without him. Three massive stone dragons, frozen in time.

I'd once looked at them as beautiful works of art, in awe of the craftsmanship that had gone into creating them. Now I knew the truth: not art, but some kind of dark magic had worked to defile the dragons, keeping them in a horrible captivity that seeped away at their memories, if not their very souls.

My gaze rested on the first dragon I saw—Vorago, the red Infernus of House Drakharrow. Carved from red sandstone, the dragon's surface was rough and raw. Vorago's eyes seemed to burn even now, flared nostrils capturing a timeless expression of passion and rage.

I turned my attention to the gold dragon, Molindra, the Luminthar of House Orphos. Rodriguez had said this was the dragon he'd have awakened, if he'd had the choice. The veins of golden marble running through Molindra's stone surface seemed to make her shimmer. Her regal face looked down on me, nostrils flaring delicately, mouth curved in what some might call a smile.

Finally, my eyes fell on Alabryss, the Silvrayne dragon of House Mortis. The white dragon's expression was serene and tranquil. Yet something about that peace was unsettling. A dragon with ice in its breath and battle in its blood had no place looking so calm.

I glanced up as a reverberating rumble rolled across the night's sky.

Nyxaris. He appeared against the starry backdrop, his dark wings spread wide. Sweeping downwards, he landed with a thunderous boom, his claws scraping against the frost-slick stones.

*Here I am.* The resentment in his voice was palpable. *Why have you called me here?*

*I told you. It wasn't me, it was Blake. He has something to tell you. He said it was important.*

Nyxaris looked back at me, his gold eyes narrowed. *I do not trust this. The air reeks of deceit.*

*Well, I do,* I said firmly. *Trust him, I mean.*

I thought of what Blake had said about wanting to apologize to Nyxaris. Was it completely naïve to think they might start afresh? Not that Nyxaris had plans to be in my life for long, let alone Blake's.

The sounds of approaching footsteps sent both our heads swiveling towards the far entrance by the cloisters.

Nyxaris bristled. *If this is a trap, know that I will not fall easily.*

*It's not,* I said hotly. *I would never do such a thing to you. Surely you know me better than—*

I came to an abrupt stop. Because it wasn't Blake who stepped out of the shadows. Instead, Professor Rodriguez came forward, followed by Kage Tanaka. Both men carried crossbows.

My stomach dropped. "Rodriguez? Kage? What the hell are you doing here?"

"Medra," Rodriguez said, his voice hard, "step away from the dragon."

I stayed exactly where I was. "What are you doing here?" I demanded again. "Why are you holding those?"

Nyxaris growled, the sound vibrating through the air. But Rodriguez didn't even flinch.

*If they think to harm me with those piddly instruments, they will be disappointed,* Nyxaris said, sounding almost bored. *Their bolts will shatter against my scales.*

That made me feel a little better. But not much. *Are you sure?*

*I am no hatchling, wingless one. My hide has withstood greater threats than those.*

"Medra." Kage spoke up. "Move. You don't understand. What we're doing is necessary. We're not here to hurt you, we're protecting you."

*Necessary? A word I have heard before. Usually preceding betrayal,* Nyxaris murmured.

"I don't need your protection. And I think I understand plenty," I snapped. "You're threatening Nyxaris."

*I will destroy them both now,* Nyxaris said, almost idly. *You must move out of the path of the flames.*

This was getting out of hand fast.

"We're saving you," Rodriguez said firmly, raising his crossbow. "Saving all of us."

Nyxaris shifted behind me. His wings unfurling. *If you do not wish them destroyed, then I will depart.*

That seemed like a vastly better idea. I couldn't believe he was giving me a choice. Then I thought of the statues. Perhaps he didn't wish to risk destroying them.

*Yes, please, go. They're idiots. I'll deal with them,* I said with relief.
*The only reason I do not destroy them now is out of respect to you. If I see either of them again, they will be meals, not men.*

*I understand. That's incredibly gracious and more than they deserve,* I replied hastily.

"Kage," Rodriguez barked. "Now."

Kage lunged—not towards Nyxaris as I'd expected, but towards me. I was so shocked that I spun too late. My fists went flying but he caught my wrist mid-strike. I twisted, cloak tangling as I tried to kick out, but Kage's grip was unyielding. He caught my other arm, pinning it behind my back.

"Let me go," I screamed, thrashing against him. "You bastard. Let me go!"

Nyxaris roared, his massive body shifting forward. *I have changed my mind.*

"Nyxaris," I screamed. "No! Get out of here!"

Rodriguez lifted his crossbow.

*Let their pitiful bolts fly,* Nyxaris rumbled in my mind. *I will crush—*

The twang of the bow cut him off. The bolt flew true. I waited for it to glance off the black dragon's scales and fall to the ground.

But instead, the bolt struck Nyxaris just below his shoulder, piercing through his scales with horrifying ease. His roar of anger suddenly shifted into a cry of pain.

"No!" I shouted, struggling harder against Kage.

Nyxaris staggered forward slightly and I let out a roar of fury at the sight of him like that, dazed and in pain, his golden eyes full of shock.

Then the second bolt hit him. Embedding lower down, deep into his flank.

*How?* His voice trembled in my mind. *Their weapons should not . . .*

Tears were streaming down my face. "What are you doing?"

I screamed. "What the fuck are you doing, Rodriguez? Why are you doing this? I will never forgive you. *Never.*"

Rodriguez stepped forward, looking at me with sympathy in his eyes. I hated him for that. He gestured to the crossbow. "This isn't just any weapon. You may tell Nyxaris that. He's probably confused. The bolts were coated in an alchemical compound designed to penetrate dragon hide. A relic of my order."

"What fucking order?" I blazed. "What are you talking about?"

Nyxaris growled, but his voice was fainter than it had been. His massive body was trembling. *The Emberwatch. Dragon . . . hunters.*

Rodriguez knelt down by Nyxaris, yanking the lower bolt free. Blood spilled onto the frozen ground, dark and steaming. Tears blurred my vision as I watched.

"You're killing him," I cried.

"We're not killing him," Rodriguez answered calmly. "But we need his blood."

"For what?" I demanded. "What the hell are you doing, Rodriguez? Whatever it is, it's wrong. It doesn't take a genius to see that much."

"Wrong?" Rodriguez stood up, his eyes fiery. "I've never done anything more right in my life. It's the only way to protect you, to protect all of Sangratha. From him." He gestured to Nyxaris.

"He hasn't harmed Sangratha," I cried. "He hasn't harmed anyone. Except highbloods, that is. I thought you'd be a fan of that." I stared at the bolt in Rodriguez's hand. "What are you going to do with the blood?"

"Use it to return him to stone," Rodriguez said.

"No." I shook my head frantically. "You can't do that. He's been tortured for long enough." My eyes locked onto to Nyxaris's golden ones, his pain evident. For once, the dragon had no witty remarks. No scathing words. His face looked almost resigned. "This isn't happening." All the while I'd been struggling against Kage, trying to work my arm free.

His grip on my arms tightened painfully. "Medra, stop. Please. You're only making this harder."

I kicked him in the shins as hard as I could. "Go fuck yourself, Tanaka."

But Kage didn't even flinch. He was strong, as strong as Blake. This wasn't like going up against Regan or Quinn. Just like Blake, Kage was built differently—impressively, almost terrifyingly so.

"Nyxaris is a threat to the blightborn, Pendragon," Rodriguez snapped. "If he remains alive, the fragile balance we've had for a century will collapse. Do you know what will happen then? War. Chaos. The loss of lives will be immense. You don't want me to do this, but what's the alternative? Let a highblood soul-bond with you? Is that what you want?"

"No," I gasped, still writhing in Kage's grip. "But not this. What you're proposing is evil, Rodriguez. I thought you were a good man."

His face hardened. "A good man protects his people, no matter the toll it takes on his soul."

My mother's voice had been chanting in my head all this time, whispering words of bloodshed. Now I twisted and for just a second, Kage's grip on my right arm loosened slightly.

My fingers fumbled between the folds of my cloak, finding the hilt of the blade I'd strapped to my thigh in my room in the Avari tower before coming back down to the courtyard. I yanked it free and shoved hard against Kage's grasp. Then thrusting my wrist backwards, I drove the blade as hard as I could into what I hoped was his side. Blade met flesh.

Kage howled. The sound was raw, primal, furious. Hardly human. The hairs on my arms stood up. Still, I wasn't going to stop. I would *never* stop.

Rodriguez was shouting. Kage was growling. I ignored them both.

*Again, Daughter, again*, my mother encouraged me. *Do not stop until he is bleeding on the ground. Fight now, for your life, for the dragon.*

My fingers fumbled backwards for the dagger again, clutching its hilt and jerking it free. Then I wound my arm up as best I could and drove my elbow into Kage's stomach with as much force as I could muster. He grunted, his breath hot against my neck, but he didn't let go.

The hilt of the dagger was wet in my grasp. I twisted my wrist as Kage felt for my arm, trying to pin me against him again. With a feral snarl of my own, I slashed backwards but his reflexes were faster. His hand caught my wrist mid-swing, the dagger trembling in my hand.

"Enough," he growled, his voice low and guttural.

*He's in pain*, my mother murmured, sounding satisfied. *Good. I never liked him. Always thought there was something strange about a man who could stay so calm.*

I didn't have time to roll my eyes. I was too busy trying to break free, pulling against the confines of my own bones, muscles, body. Every ounce of my strength pushed against Kage's, but it was no use. He wrenched the dagger from my grip. The blade clattered to the stones, the sound ringing out like a death knell. Panic surged in my veins.

*You fight with a warrior's spirit*, Nyxaris rumbled weakly in my mind. *But I would not have them break you here today, little wingless one.*

"Don't you dare give up," I screamed aloud. "Burn them! Burn them both! Nyxaris, do it. Just do it, dammit." I was sobbing. "Don't let them turn you to stone. Nyxaris, please."

Kage's arms tightened around me, locking me in place. His breath was heavy in my ear. All I wanted was to be far away from him. I never wanted to see his face or Rodriguez's ever again. "Medra, please. Just stop."

"Never," I roared, my voice cracking as my tears burned hot against my frozen cheeks. "Let me go. Now!"

My scream was raw, torn from deep within me as Kage's iron grip held fast. The dragon's golden eyes flickered. They were dimmer than before. His wings dropped, the strength to lift them drained.

*Their poison*, he spat, *weakens me. I cannot summon flame. I am . . . sorry.*

*Don't you dare apologize*, I hissed back. *Don't you dare fucking give up either. You're stronger than this. You're stronger than all of us put together. Burn them, Nyxaris. I know you can do it.*

Nyxaris let out a low rumble but it was hollow. Devoid of his usual power. His head dipped slightly.

"Medra, you're not helping anyone," Kage grunted behind me, his breath ragged. I could feel his heart pounding against my back. "Just—stop!"

Instead I shoved against him even harder.

"Enough," Kage snarled, his voice tinged with frustration and pain. "I don't want to hurt you."

"You're going to have to fucking kill me when you let me go," I snarled right back. "Because otherwise I will kill you first, Tanaka."

Rodriguez was busy doing something on the ground. I watched as he opened his leather satchel and pulled out vials. Suddenly he glanced around. Then his eyes landed—not on me, but on Kage. "Where's Blake?" he called.

At that moment, something inside me cracked wide open.

CHAPTER 42

# FLORENCE

I t was half past midnight. The refectory turned ballroom had
emptied out. The festive energy that had been tangible earlier
in the evening had dimmed as the hours stretched on. The music had softened to a slower tune. Most of the remaining students
were paired off, dancing, or talking quietly at tables. Servants had
begun coming around to clear aside plates and centerpieces.

I stood near the edge of the dance floor, fidgeting with the edge
of one sleeve as I tried to hold back a yawn.

"You all right?" Theo had come up beside me.

I looked up at him, not bothering to hide my admiration. He
was very handsome this evening in a dark gray suit. He and Vaughn
made a striking couple.

The way Theo looked at Vaughn . . . What would it be like to
have someone look like that at you? I thought of Naveen briefly,
guiltily, then pushed the thought away.

Theo pushed a lock of dark blond hair off his face. "Would you
like to dance?"

I shook my head. "No, thank you. I was just wondering if Medra was coming back."

"Where did she go?" Theo asked.

I hesitated, then decided it wasn't really a secret. "She said she
had to meet Blake in the Dragon Court at midnight. Something to

do with Nyxaris. I thought she was coming back afterwards, but I must have misunderstood."

"Blake left to meet with our uncle in the keep," Theo said slowly. "He didn't mention anything about the Dragon Court."

Theo looked concerned, so I forced a smile. "Well, I'm sure it's nothing. They probably went off together somewhere, just the two of them."

He smiled slightly. "I'm sure you're right." Then his face darkened. "Though, I do wonder what the hell our uncle wanted to see Blake about, the old bastard. Couldn't even leave Blake alone tonight of all nights."

"He and Blake don't get along, do they?" I asked hesitantly. "Lord Drakharrow seems like a very hard man." I wanted to say something much worse, but Blake and Theo were Lord Drakharrow's family after all.

"Blake hates him," Theo said bluntly. "But he has to do whatever my uncle wants."

I thought of Medra. "Not everything, I hope."

"He stands up to him from time to time," Theo muttered. "He's shielded me more than once. I'm . . . grateful for it."

I glanced across the room where Vaughn stood talking to a group of House Orphos students, remembering what had happened with Coregon the year before. "That's good. Because you deserve to be happy, Theo."

Still, my thoughts were suddenly racing: something wasn't right. The longer Medra was gone, the worse the feeling grew. I wondered if I should go back to our room. Even if she were there with Blake . . . Well, I might be interrupting awkwardly, but at least then I'd know she was all right.

Before I could tell Theo I was leaving, Visha appeared, weaving her way through the dwindling crowd.

"Have you seen Lace?" she demanded.

I shook my head.

"No," Theo said, frowning. "Why? What's going on?"

"I don't know," Visha admitted, looking frustrated. "I can't find her anywhere. I thought maybe she'd slipped out for some air, but she's not on the terrace either."

I looked around the room, scanning for the dwarven girl Visha had stuck close to all night. "Kage is gone, too."

"Kage?" Theo echoed.

I tried to shrug lightly. "It doesn't matter. I just didn't see him leave, that's all." The other House Leaders were still there, though. Lysander Orphos was sitting morosely at a table alone. I caught Catherine Mortis moving towards the door, a group of House Mortis students trailing behind her. She'd been without her thralls this evening.

"I'm going to find Lace," Visha declared.

Theo shoved his hands into his pockets. "Vaughn has an Orphos party after this. I'm not invited." He shrugged. "I'll come with you."

"So will I." I couldn't shake the feeling something was wrong. "I want to find Medra. I think I'll check the Dragon Court once we've found Lace. Let's go."

We walked through the corridors. At this time of the night, everything was unnervingly quiet.

"I'm sure Lace is fine," Theo tried to reassure Visha. "She probably drank too much and went back to her room to be sick." He gave a half-hearted laugh. "Like you did last year, remember?"

"She wouldn't have left without telling me." Visha sounded on edge, her voice brittle. "We were supposed to leave together." She snuck a quick glance at me. "You know how some of these fucking highblood students get on Solstice, Theo. I want to find her."

Theo nodded. "All right. Fair point. Well, we'll find her soon. Don't worry about it. And then I'll walk Florence back to her room myself."

"Lace is House Avari," I said, speaking up for the first time since we'd left the ball. "Let's check there. We might save ourselves a lot of trouble if she went back to her room."

When we reached the entrance to the Avari tower, I went into the common room alone, leaving Theo and Visha waiting outside. I was mindful of the late hour. Most students had been drinking all evening. I didn't think bringing two Drakharrows in with me was a great idea, even if it were for a good cause.

A few minutes later, I slipped out of the tower, breathless and feeling a little more worried. "No one has seen Lace. I found out where her room was and checked there, too. No answer. I had a Warden unlock the door for me, but it was empty."

Visha was silent.

"Maybe she went for a walk outside?" Theo suggested.

I frowned. "In the cold?"

"Lace isn't exactly delicate," he pointed out. "If she was feeling sick, well, she might have thought the cold air would be bracing."

"I was going to check the Dragon Court anyway to see if Medra was still there," I said slowly. "I suppose we could look together." I glanced at Visha.

She nodded tightly. "Fine. Let's walk that way. Then we can check the grounds if we haven't found her yet."

I thought of the rocky cliffs and the treacherous sea surrounding us on all sides—not exactly somewhere I'd want a friend to walk if they'd had too much to drink. "That sounds like a good idea."

We walked through the school, following the quickest route to the Dragon Court. As we turned down a corridor, I froze.

"What is it?" Visha asked, already tense.

I pointed to the floor. A dark smeared streak marred the stones. I wasn't sure, but I thought it looked like . . . blood.

Visha swore and darted ahead. "Lace!"

"Visha, wait!" Theo shouted, but she was already disappearing around the next bend.

The sound that came next made my stomach twist. A wail of misery, piercing and raw. Theo and I looked at one another, then broke into a run. We rounded the corner and then skidded to a halt. Lace lay sprawled on her back on the blood-soaked stones. Her eyes stared blankly upwards.

"Oh, Bloodmaiden," I whispered, clapping a hand over my mouth.

Visha was already kneeling beside Lace, her hands hovering uselessly over her body as if afraid to touch her. Theo took a step forward but before he could take another, I grabbed his arm, my eyes suddenly locked on the far side of the corridor. We weren't alone.

There, crouched in the shadows farther along the hall, a small figure shifted.

A sound emerged from the darkness. A laugh. Light, like a child's giggle. But this didn't sound sweet or innocent. It sent a chill down my spine.

"Fuck," Theo breathed beside me as Aenia Drakharrow stepped forward.

Blood stained the young girl's mouth, her hands, even her wild tangled white-blond hair. Her eyes met mine and I glimpsed a feral, desperate hunger. I'd seen that look in Blake's sister's eyes before. My breath caught in my throat as I choked down a terrified sob.

"Florence!" Theo shouted.

But it was too late. Aenia lunged, moving faster than I'd ever seen, her hands outstretched, her nails sharp as claws. I screamed and threw up my hands instinctively, already knowing it was too late.

Suddenly Theo was there. He'd moved behind Aenia with unbelievable speed, as only another highblood could move. I heard Aenia scream. The scream turned to a gurgle. The highblood girl seemed to freeze, mid-attack. I lowered my hands, watching as she stumbled backwards slightly.

Theo yanked something out of Aenia's back: a blade. He gave a great, choking cry as Aenia's blood sprayed across him, across the stones, across me.

She crumpled to the ground.

For a moment, I couldn't move. The air was filled with the metallic scent of mingled blood. The corridor felt thick with death. I put a hand to my throat, feeling like I was going to be sick. Footsteps pounded against the stone behind me. I turned to see Blake coming around the corner, his face grim. He froze.

For a moment, all was silent. Then, slowly, I stepped aside, revealing the small lifeless form behind me. A keening sound came from Blake's lips. The world seemed to narrow to just him and Aenia. He moved forward like a man moving through water, slowly but deliberately. Kneeling beside his sister, he scooped her body into his arms, cradling her against his chest as if she might still wake. His hands trembled as he brushed blood-matted strands of hair from her face.

I wanted to say something, but the words caught in my throat. I looked at Theo, but his face had gone white. "Blake," I whispered, my voice breaking. "Lace." I wanted to say more, wanted to explain everything properly. To tell him that Theo had saved me. But those were the only words that would come out.

A choked sob pierced the stillness. Across the hall, Visha was on her knees. Blake didn't flinch. Slowly, he rose to his feet, Aenia in his arms, her hair spilling over his shoulder, blond and bloodied. As he rose, I gasped as for the first time moonlight streaming through the windows caught his face.

His left eye was gone. The socket was raw, surrounded by streaks of blood and jagged flesh, the wound exposed and unhealed.

But it wasn't just his face. Everything about him was wrong. The finery he'd worn to the ball was gone, replaced by the torn and blood-soaked remnants of some sort of guard's uniform. The stains on the fabric couldn't possibly all be from Aenia.

"Blake," I whispered, "what happened? Who did this to you?"

He didn't answer. He didn't even seem to hear me. His gaze was completely fixed on Aenia. With a careful, gentle movement, I watched as he adjusted her head against his shoulder, her bloodied blond hair spilling over his arm.

I felt frozen in place, torn between my terror and the desperate need to help somehow. I reached out but it was too late; Blake was already turning away. Still holding Aenia, he began walking in the direction of the Dragon Court.

"Blake, wait!" I called. My voice sounded so small.

I turned to Theo. His face was still ashen, the arm he'd used to thrust the knife hung slack by his side.

"I killed her," he whispered hoarsely. "I killed a child." His shoulders were shaking.

"You saved me," I said softly. But I knew nothing I said would comfort him. Not right now. "Come on." I grabbed Theo's arm, then glanced down at Visha and bit my lip. I didn't want to leave her alone, but at least right now, we knew she was safe. Meanwhile, something was horribly wrong and somewhere out there was Medra. "We have to follow Blake. Something horrible must have happened. You saw his face."

"Visha," Theo said, slowly, looking down at the highblood girl.

Visha didn't even look up at us. "Go. I'm not leaving her."

"We'll be back soon," I promised, trying to swallow my fear.

The air grew colder as we reached the open cloisters. My breath misted. Voices began to reach us, raised and urgent. I couldn't make out the words. Ahead of us, Blake had slowed. Kneeling, he gently lowered Aenia's body onto the ground along one wall. I took a step forward, following Blake as he entered the Dragon Court, Theo close behind me. I couldn't make sense of what I saw. Slowly, it started to come clear. Disbelief and shock flooded through me.

Nyxaris, his massive black body heaving with labored breaths.

Professor Rodriguez, kneeling on the ground, lifting a glass vial, his face tight with concentration.

Kage, his arms locked around Medra, restraining her as she thrashed against him. Her red hair was wild, her face streaked with tears.

"Medra," I gasped, already moving towards her.

But Blake grabbed my arm just as another figure emerged from the grove of trees across the courtyard.

"Hello, Brother."

Marcus Drakharrow stood on the other side of the court. Holding tightly to his hand was Lunaya Orphos. On his other side stood Catherine Mortis, mirroring Marcus's cold confidence.

I furrowed my brow. Lunaya looked strange. Her usually serene expression had been replaced by an almost vacant look, as if she wasn't fully there. Marcus tugged at her hand, pulling her forward and she moved in step with him, like a walking doll.

And then I saw them. Crossbows.

My breath caught.

Catherine's grip on hers was casual, as if the weapon were just an accessory. But Marcus was raising his slowly, deliberately. Like a man about to do something irrevocable.

"Medra!" My heart lurched in my chest. She turned towards me, startled, her green eyes meeting mine for a split second.

I didn't think. I moved. I started to shove past Blake, his shout of protest drowned out by the roaring in my ears.

I didn't feel the bolt at first.

One moment, I was moving forward, my arms outstretched. And then—fire. White-hot, tearing pain exploded in my chest. I stumbled, my hand clutching at my chest. Warmth spread across my fingers.

"Florence!" Medra screamed.

Her voice sounded as if it were coming from so far away. The world was blurring, colors smearing together like a child's messy painting. My knees buckled and I pitched forward, the ground rushing up to meet me. Strong arms caught me, stopping my descent. I looked up at Blake. I wanted to say something, anything. My lips wouldn't obey. The world was fading, Medra's screams dimming, Blake's desperate murmurs growing quiet.

The shadows rose up to greet me, swallowing me whole.

# CHAPTER 43

# BLAKE

I fixed my good eye on Marcus as he stepped out of the grove. In my periphery, I vaguely registered Pendragon dashing in front of me. She'd broken free from Tanaka's grip and, with Theo, began carrying Florence to the side of the courtyard. The blood on her hands made my chest tighten, but I shoved it down. I had to focus. Had to distract the sociopathic asshole better known as my brother.

"What the fuck, Marcus?" I said evenly, trying to keep my attention on me. "I knew you were a terrible shot. But really?"

Marcus shrugged. "She got in the way. You know damn well who that was meant for." He glanced back at where I'd left Aenia. "Carrying our baby sister's corpse around? Now, that's a new look for you, Blake."

Rage threatened to drown me but I bit it back, dodging as a second bolt hissed past my ear. My vampire reflexes pulled me toward Marcus in a blur, closing some of the distance between us. I wanted to tear him apart. Wanted to scream at him for his cruelty, his callous disregard. But above it all, I wanted her back. Aenia, my little sister, was gone. And I couldn't even afford the time to grieve.

"You don't get to talk about her," I spat. "Not ever."

"Why not?" Marcus feigned a pout. "She was family, wasn't she? Isn't that what you always wanted, Blake? For us to be one happy family?"

I snarled.

Marcus shrugged. "Fine. I won't mourn her, then. Not that she meant much, honestly. A feral brat with no leash. You should have put her down ages ago. Glad to see you finally grew a pair and did it." His voice was cool and mocking. His pale blue eyes were full of amusement, but there was something cold and calculated there, too. Marcus had always been unhinged. He'd never been much of a planner, too willing to follow Viktor's plans to ever come up with any of his own.

I didn't bother to correct him. Didn't bother to tell him I was pretty sure Theo had killed my little sister. It didn't matter. All that mattered was she was gone.

Gone. And I hadn't even had a chance to say good-bye.

Another bolt sped towards me. I sidestepped, the movement automatic, effortless. "You're a fucking monster," I hissed. "Aenia was more my sister than you'll ever be my brother. She was a kid. She didn't ask for any of this."

The words caught in my throat, a lump of raw grief and fury I couldn't swallow. She hadn't asked for this. She hadn't deserved any of it. And I hadn't been able to save her. When she'd needed me the most, I'd failed her.

Marcus shifted and this time I moved before he'd even fired, darting to the side. The bolt clattered harmlessly against the stones behind me.

"Let Lunaya go," I said, my voice low. The Orphos girl stood rigidly at my brother's side. Something was decidedly off about her.

Instead, Marcus tugged savagely on Lunaya's wrist. She didn't even flinch. He laughed, the sound grating on my ears. "Let her go? Not a chance. She's mine now. Look at her face. Can't you tell she wants to be here? She wouldn't miss this for the world." He lifted Lunaya's chin roughly. "Would you, darling?"

Lunaya said nothing, simply stared back at him, her face expressionless.

My jaw tightened. "What the fuck have you done to her?"

"I'd think it was fairly obvious," Marcus said disdainfully.

"Blood magic." No wonder he'd been visiting our class. "Why Lunaya? Did Viktor put you up to this? You've always been his puppet. Still running his errands? It's going to get you killed one day, Marcus."

If I had my way, today would be that day. But even that thought was hollow. Killing Marcus wouldn't bring Aenia back or undo what he'd done to Florence—nothing would. Those were my mistakes to live with. And I'd take the consequences.

"You'll find out soon enough," Marcus said, smiling. "She's been bound to me for weeks now. A useful fail-safe, among other things."

I looked at Lunaya and, for a moment, I saw Aenia's face instead. The way she used to look at me when she was small, her eyes full of trust and admiration. And then I saw her at the end, feral and wild, the sister I'd failed to save.

"You've been using her, twisting her. Walking in Viktor's footsteps, I see." My stomach churned.

"Speaking of the old man," Marcus smirked and gestured to my face, "I assume you finally snapped and tried to take him on." He gave a low, mocking whistle. "Looks like it didn't go so well for you."

My lips curled. "I wouldn't be so sure about that if I were you."

Marcus's expression became uncertain, but only for a moment. He chuckled. "Well, aren't you full of surprises? But it doesn't matter. I've already won."

"Won? Won what, Marcus? What the hell are you even doing here?" Out of the corner of my eye, I sensed Tanaka moving slowly across the court.

I risked stealing a glance at Nyxaris. The black dragon hadn't moved since I entered. He seemed listless. Had Rodriguez already completed the ritual to turn the creature back to stone? A chill went through my veins at the thought. I glanced over at where the professor still crouched over glass vials he'd arranged on the ground. His hand held one, full of a red liquid.

"Damned Rodriguez. He always was a hard-ass stickler. Worst professor at Bloodwing," Marcus said, following my gaze with an irritated expression. Lazily, he pointed his crossbow. "I don't know what the fuck he was up to here tonight and I don't want to know. But some blightborn prick isn't getting in my way."

He swung his aim toward Rodriguez.

"Marcus, don't—"

The bolt flew.

Rodriguez jerked, a strangled gasp escaping his lips as the projectile struck him high in the shoulder. The vial he'd been holding slipped from his fingers, shattering against the stones, red liquid spilling out.

Before I could move to help Rodriguez or to take on Marcus, Tanaka made the choice for me.

I'd seen impossible things in my lifetime. I'd become a fucking dragon earlier that same evening, after all. And yet somehow, what happened next was still beyond anything I could have imagined.

Kage growled. Then, before my eyes, his body began to ripple and contort. It started with his hands. Fingers elongating, nails becoming claws. His shoulders broadened, his neck thickened. And then the motherfucker started sprouting fur. Thick, snowy white fur, covering him in a gleaming coat.

Where the Avari leader had once stood, there now stood a massive white wolf, towering and muscular.

Marcus was looking at Tanaka, as slack-jawed as I felt. "Is that the fucking Avari?"

I didn't answer. I glanced at Rodriguez to see if he'd already known Kage's little secret, but he looked as shocked as I was. For a second, I felt myself reaching for the dragon within me. Could I summon it like Kage had just summoned the wolf? But when I reached deep inside myself, the dragon was silent, dormant. Part of me was kind of relieved.

Still, seeing Kage as a wolf was incredible. Someone else with a secret like mine. Someone who might understand what the hell I was going through. But I was a little jealous, too: Tanaka seemed to have full control. He could shift in a heartbeat. There'd been no ripping of skin or screaming in pain.

The wolf sprang across the courtyard, his massive form leaping onto Marcus with terrifying speed. As the two collided—man and beast—Tanaka snapped and snarled as he whipped the crossbow from my brother's hands, the weapon falling to the ground.

"Tanaka," I heard myself shout. "Be careful! If he dies, so does Lunaya."

Kage turned his head and I shivered. The wolf's pale eyes shone with fury. Then he growled—and I knew he'd understood.

I turned and sprinted towards Lunaya, who was standing frozen where Marcus had left her. I grabbed her arm, trying to pull her away. "Come on. You don't have to stay here."

Slowly, she met my gaze. But her eyes were cold and distant.

"Lunaya, please," I urged. "Let's get you back to your brother."

Without a word, she jerked her arm free and ran—not out of the courtyard towards safety but over to the golden dragon of stone at the edge of the court.

I froze for a split second before following her. As I came around the statue, my stomach dropped.

Catherine Mortis stood there. She had one hand pressed against the dragon's flank, her fingers smeared with blood. Her lips moved silently, chanting words too quietly for me to make out. Her eyes snapped open as I approached and I shivered. They were filled with something I'd only ever thought I'd see in my uncle's: a righteous zeal. "You're too late," she crowed, sounding gleeful and triumphant.

Catherine grabbed Lunaya, pulling her close. Then, with a quick motion she lifted a knife and ran the blade over Lunaya's hand. As blood welled up from the cut, Catherine shoved the girl's hand against the stone dragon's flank.

"Blood of a rider, blood of a master," the House Mortis leader chanted. "Blood of a rider, blood of a master. Let them be one. Blood of a rider, blood of a master. Bound by blood, rise to serve."

I fell back as the air around the two women seemed to shimmer and split with heat. The stone scales covering the golden dragon began to crack and splinter, revealing something that looked like tarnished gold beneath.

I was reliving the nightmare of Nyxaris's awakening. Stones began to rain down around me, each fragment falling with a baleful hiss, like the sounds of a trapped, angry spirit.

"Catherine, stop this!" I shouted, taking another step forward and stumbling as the courtyard shook. "You have no idea what you're doing."

The Mortis leader's eye snapped to mine, alight with fervent determination. "I know exactly what I'm doing, Drakharrow. You just aren't going to like it very much."

My gaze shifted to Lunaya. Her face was pale, her face twisted as if with pain. But she stayed where Catherine was holding her hand to the dragon's side, not even trying to resist.

"Lunaya, fight her! You don't have to do this!" I tried to press forward, to get to her, but the stones of the courtyard were shaking. I swayed as beside me the Luminthar of House Orphos began to stir.

I looked up at the golden creature as her head shifted, sending chunks of crumbling marble cascading to the ground. The dragon's once-regal features were emerging from beneath the stone. But something was wrong. They were twisted and misshapen—a cruel parody of the wisdom and serenity she had once been known for. Her scales, which should have been bright and golden, were tarnished and uneven, too—streaked with sickly black veins that pulsed like a corrupt infection. Her jaws parted, unleashing a sound harsh and guttural, nothing like Nyxaris's glorious, terrifying roar.

My heart twisted. This wasn't Molindra. Not as she had been. This was a perversion. A monstrosity.

Catherine and Marcus weren't just using blood magic to bring the dragon back. They were using necromancy.

The Luminthar's eyes opened and her head swiveled towards me, her eyes unfocused and full of rage. For a moment, I froze. Then Molindra's gaze swept past me.

I turned to see Marcus and Kage in the center of the courtyard. The wolf's snowy fur was streaked with crimson as he lunged and snapped, forcing Marcus to dodge and stumble. My brother had blood running down his temple and across his jaw. His once-pristine black-and-red armor was now ripped and smeared with dirt. He'd regained his crossbow but couldn't seem to aim it quickly enough to shoot the wolf.

Tanaka snarled, circling him, claws scraping, teeth bared. As they fought, something about the way Marcus moved—his stance, the way he dodged the wolf's snarling jaws—triggered a memory. Recognition struck. My breath caught as fragments of the day of the carriage attack rushed back. One of the attackers had moved just as Marcus was moving now.

It had been Marcus all along. He and Catherine must have staged the attack. Not Viktor. Not a rival from another house. Them.

I felt sick as it all came together. That was how Catherine was doing it. Pendragon's blood was the key. They'd gotten it from the knife she'd been stabbed with that day. They hadn't been trying to kill her—though, I was sure they wouldn't have minded if she'd died. What they'd been after was her blood. Blended with Lunaya's Orphos blood it had allowed them to somehow bring the Luminthar back to a semblance of life.

But they still didn't have a dragon rider. They couldn't control Molindra. My heart sank. Or could they? If Molindra wasn't truly alive but simply . . . reanimated . . . then, could Catherine control her with necromancy?

Why awaken Molindra at all? Why not the Drakharrow Infernus? Or House Mortis's own Silvrayne?

I thought of Lunaya. She was soft, pliable, easy to control. She'd been susceptible to Marcus's seduction. No doubt he'd begun to control her with sanguimancy early on. If Marcus and Catherine weren't using their own house dragons, there had to be a reason. And I knew it couldn't be a good one.

I started to move towards Tanaka to support him, but movement from the gold dragon made me pause. Molindra's immense head began to lower, and I realized with a jolt what Catherine must be commanding her to do.

The dragon inhaled, her chest expanding. I knew what was coming next.

"Kage! Move!" I bellowed, diving to lie flat on the ground just in front of the dragon's paws.

The wolf sprang to the side just as a column of golden flame erupted from Molindra's jaws. Marcus had rolled away, barely avoiding the flames himself. Now he staggered to his feet and made a mad dash towards the dragon.

"Shit," I hissed as I watched Marcus begin to scramble up onto the Luminthar's back. Catherine was already perched above me, feeding the massive beast her commands. I saw Lunaya reach down to help Marcus climb, her movements slow, almost mechanical. What the hell had they done to that girl? Was there anything left of the real Lunaya Orphos even in there?

I glanced around, realizing what they must have planned. This was bad. Very bad. "Tanaka," I yelled, "we can't let them take off."

Kage, still in the wolf form, gave his fur a shake and growled, his eyes locking on Marcus and Catherine. The flames had singed him, but he seemed more furious than hurt. I turned and sprinted towards Rodriguez who had crawled over to a column and sat slumped against it, clutching his wounded shoulder and looking as if he were about to pass out.

"We need to move," I said, grabbing him beneath the arms.

His head lolled slightly. "Molindra," he rasped. "She's—"

"She's still fucking dead, that's what she is," I said grimly. "But somehow she's back. And I doubt we can take her down now."

I glanced over at Nyxaris. I knew Rodriguez had shot the black dragon with some kind of a toxin so he couldn't fly away, but it wouldn't last forever. Surely it must be wearing off by now.

"Theo!" I yelled across the courtyard, to where he stood beside Pendragon, who sat on the ground, cradling Florence Shen's head in her arms. I knew Pendragon wouldn't want to leave Nyxaris, but she had to. "Get them out of here! Get them somewhere safe!"

I watched as Theo said something to Pendragon and bent down as if to lift up Florence. But even as they started to pull back, the courtyard erupted into chaos again.

Molindra roared, the sound sending the cloister pillars trembling. The corrupted Luminthar spread her wings wide, blowing aside fragments of stone. She turned her head towards Nyxaris, who was still crouched on the other side near Pendragon.

His massive body still seemed sluggish as he tried to rise and lift his wings.

"Shit," I muttered under my breath. Nyxaris was helpless and we were responsible.

We'd done this. Rodriguez, Tanaka, and I. We'd sabotaged our only chance of stopping Molindra. I glanced at Pendragon, wondering if she'd figured out the part I'd played in all of this yet. I'd let Rodriguez convince me I was helping her, protecting her. But the truth was, I knew she would never have wanted me to make the choice that I had. Because keeping her life wasn't worth it—not if it meant harming Nyxaris. And deep down, I guess I'd known that all along. Now Florence was wounded and that was my fault, too. The girl would never have been here if she hadn't been following Pendragon.

I'd been stupid and selfish, and I'd made the worst mistake of my life.

Again.

CHAPTER 44

# MEDRA

Florence's breathing was too slow. Too shallow. Each rise and fall of her chest was fainter than the last.

"No, no, no," I whispered, keeping my hands pressed against the wound in her chest. Blood slicked my palms, hot and persistent. "Stay with me, Florence. Please. Just keep breathing. You're all right. You're going to be all right."

But even as I repeated the words, doubt clawed at me. Her face was pale, her eyes closed. Panic surged, sharp and cruel. I was losing her.

*How is the fledgling?* Nyxaris's resonant voice was laced with something uncharacteristic.

*Not doing so well,* I said shortly. I tried to keep the tears from my voice.

I pressed my hands harder against the wound, but blood seeped through no matter how much pressure I applied. "Stay with me. You're not dying, Florence. You're not allowed to die. Just keep breathing."

*You waste time.* Orcades's voice broke into my thoughts, sharp, insistent, unwanted. *I know you care for her but the wound is deep. You can do nothing. Act before it's too late for all of you.*

*I am acting,* I hissed back at her. *I* will *save her.*

*You're wasting time,* she insisted. *The fight isn't here. It's there. They'll kill you all if you sit idle. Even Florence. Don't you see? The golden one. She's awake.*

My head snapped up, my pulse roaring in my ears as I looked across the courtyard. My mother was right. The Luminthar . . . She'd come back to life. But this . . . this wasn't how I'd expected to see her. Molindra's scales were faded gold stained with black. Her eyes glowed in a strange, unfocused way, full of rage but with none of Nyxaris's fierce intelligence or wisdom.

Kage was attacking the Luminthar's hindquarters, still in his wolf form. His huge sharp canines tore at the dragon's scales, though it seemed to have little effect. Still, he snarled as he jumped and clawed at the beast, trying to scrape her hide, grasping for purchase.

I glanced over at Blake. He crouched beside Rodriguez, the professor's crossbow in one hand, as he rifled through the professor's satchel with his other. He must have been searching for more bolts. My heart leaped with hope. If he found one that was tipped with whatever toxin had affected Nyxaris earlier, we might just stand a chance.

Whatever he was going to do, I hoped he'd do it fast.

A low rumble shook the ground. Molindra lurched forward unsteadily, straight towards Nyxaris.

The realization hit me like a blow. Catherine and Marcus didn't just want Molindra—they wanted her to destroy Nyxaris while they had the chance.

I looked over at Nyxaris. His wings twitched as he tried to rise fully to his feet. He wasn't ready for this. He could hardly even stand up.

"Get up," I whispered under my breath. *Nyxaris, get up. She's going to kill you. You have to move.*

*I cannot,* he growled. *The poison still lingers. My strength returns but slowly. Get the fledgling away. Save yourselves.*

*Is this the great Nyxaris I'm talking to or some weakling impostor?* I snarled, refusing to give him any leeway. *You're too stubborn to give up this easily. Don't you dare fucking die on me here. You're going to let two bolts bring you down when you spent a century trapped in stone? No. You're better than that. You're stronger than that. Now, prove it. Show them all.*

Nyxaris gave a weak rumble, but I could sense him bristling under the challenge. I'd wounded his pride.

*You've never let anyone best you before, Nyxaris. Don't let her be the first,* I goaded him.

He groaned—aloud and audibly, and I quivered. *She was once the best of us. Beautiful. Wise.*

I could feel his pain, his horror at what they'd done to Molindra. *There will be time for sorrow later. We'll destroy them for what they've done to your friend. But first, you need to get on your godsdamned feet this instant.*

His claws scraped against the stone as he struggled, his wings spreading, shaking off their sluggishness. Slowly, Nyxaris staggered to his feet. Pride surged through me as his immense black body swayed upright.

*That's it,* I encouraged. *You're the fiercest dragon in all of Sangratha, remember?*

*Don't forget the most beautiful,* he replied testily. *You may cease your empty platitudes now.*

I grinned through my tears. He could be as cranky as he wanted after this. As long as he lived. I glanced down at Florence. As long as they *both* lived.

*She's about to strike,* Nyxaris snapped suddenly. *Brace yourselves.*

Then, with a roar that echoed through the Dragon Court, Nyxaris snapped his wings outwards, the force of the movement sending debris flying everywhere. Across from him, Molindra snarled, her jaws parting as she unleashed a wave of fire. Instinctively, I threw myself over Florence, bracing for the flames as I shielded her. Theo had crouched down, too. I felt his arms go around me as we formed a ring, protecting her.

But the fire didn't touch us.

Nyxaris raised his wings, fanning the flames back towards the golden dragon, shielding the three of us from the inferno. The fire hit his obsidian scales, rolling off them like water against stone.

*I can shield you,* Nyxaris growled. *But that is all I can do. My fire . . .* He gave a roar of frustration.

"Forget the fire for now," I yelled aloud. "Just keep her from killing us."

Nyxaris gave a rumble I knew for a laugh. *Very well. I shall do my best.*

Molindra snarled, her head darting forward. Nyxaris gave a pained groan that tore at my heart. I knew he didn't want to have to fight his friend, but this wasn't Molindra, not anymore. He snapped at her throat, trying to put her off, but she was faster. Her teeth sank into the side of his neck and an agonized roar erupted. Blood spilled from the wound, dark and steaming as it slid over his ebony scales.

"No!" I screamed. Everything in me was screaming to go to him, to help him—but I couldn't leave Florence.

Molindra shook her head, releasing her grip as Nyxaris stumbled back. He sank down against the stone, his wings trembling as he struggled to regain his footing.

I looked frantically across the courtyard. Kage was still doing his best to distract Molindra—but a distraction was all you could call it. There was no way the wolf could bring the dragon down alone. He'd wounded her; she was bleeding a little from one of her back legs, but not enough to really be impeded.

Meanwhile Blake had found something. He was fitting a bolt into the crossbow he'd scavenged. I could see his lips moving as he cursed under his breath, fumbling to load the weapon. There must have been something wrong with it.

"Take over," I barked at Theo. "Put your hands here. Keep pressure on her wound."

Theo was already shrugging off his jacket. He folded it up quickly to make a bandage. "Thought you were never going to ask."

"Don't let go," I said quietly. "No matter what."

He nodded firmly, his jaw set.

I stood up, wiping the blood on my cloak. Coregon's dagger lay a little ways away. I swiped it, tossing it back and forth between my hands. I had no other weapon. It would have to be enough. I wasn't going to let Nyxaris die. I wasn't going to let any of them die. If I fell trying to stop Molindra, so be it. If that was the price of friendship, of love, then I'd pay it willingly.

"Medra!" Blake's voice rang out across the courtyard. "No! Get back!"

I ignored him, my gaze locking onto Molindra. She was terrifying. A corrupted creature of tarnished gold, black veins pulsing with unnatural energy. When her gaze swept across the courtyard and landed on me, I felt a chill go down my spine.

But my feet carried me forward before I could think better of it. I wasn't even sure what I was going to do, exactly. The knife in my hand felt pitiful against a creature of such might and power—more suitable for slicing apples than slaying dragons.

*You are the bravest child I ever bore*, my mother's voice suddenly murmured. *Have I ever told you that, my darling?*

*I'm the only child you ever bore*, I pointed out. *Unless there's something you'd like to tell me.*

*Very true*, she said with a sigh. *I should have raised more daughters. Warriors to stand by your side.* She paused. *That girl—she is like a sister to you, is she not?*

I didn't hesitate. *She is. I love her with all my heart.*

*Good. Protect her, then.*

Adrenaline surged as Molindra's massive head came swinging down towards me. Her jaws parted and I knew she would snap me in half if she could. I ducked, diving to the ground and rolling just as her jaws clamped shut where I'd just been standing. Then I saw it: a patch of skin between the claws of her foot. The spot was exposed, unprotected, nearly devoid of the scales that armored the rest of her body.

Without thinking, I rolled forward and plunged the dagger

downward with all my strength. The blade sank into the vulnerable flesh and Molindra let out a deafening screech, her entire body jerking back and away from me.

I scrambled forward to retrieve my knife and gasped. The dagger was pulsing with a dark energy. I pulled it out and the glow vanished.

*Finally*, Orcades hissed, her voice sharp. *Let me in, you golden bitch. That's it, let me in.*

*Mother! What the hell are you doing?* I demanded. *Where are you?*

But part of me already knew.

*Saving you and your sister.*

Molindra reared back, her body trembling violently. I could hear Catherine and Marcus shouting commands from up above.

Marcus's voice rang out, shrill and furious. "Get her up! Take off! Get in the air! Now!"

I glanced back at Blake just in time to see him fire a bolt from the crossbow. Molindra let out a shriek of rage as the bolt penetrated her scales just above the knee.

"How many bolts do you have?" I screamed to him across the courtyard.

But he only shook his head grimly. My heart sank.

Orcades's voice filled my mind, calm and determined. *Get away from the dragon, Daughter. She is mine now.*

Molindra's screeches filled the courtyard, a symphony of fury and agony. Her body convulsed, claws gouging the stone. I stumbled away from the dragon, sensing that something was shifting.

*Let me in*, Orcades commanded, her voice still resonating in my mind. *She is not whole. She's twisted. Broken.* She sounded shocked. *My poor beauty, what have they done to you? This creature doesn't even know herself anymore.*

*You're inside her.* I looked down at the dagger in my hand. The tarnished blade was lifeless and empty. My mother was gone. *Can you heal her? Help her? Are you speaking to her?*

Speaking *is a generous word for it,* Orcades replied dryly. *She is barely holding on to thought. A terrible corruption has her.*

*But you're in there. There has to be a way. Can't you try?* I pleaded.

*No.* Orcades's voice was final. *I cannot save her. But I can save everyone else.*

I gasped as Molindra's body jerked violently, her head swinging low as if she were trying to shake off the voice in her mind. Above her, Marcus and Catherine were shouting frantically, clinging to the dragon's back, clearly panicked. I stumbled back, shielding my face from the gust of wind as the golden dragon leaped into the air. Her massive body rose, but her movements were wild and erratic. She was fighting the toxins. It was taking everything the dragon had left just to get into the air. On top of her, Marcus's and Catherine's screams echoed faintly as they clung on.

Only Lunaya was silent. She looked down at all of us as she held tight to Catherine's waist, her face empty and remote. I was filled with pity.

*Lunaya,* I called to my mother. *Can you look after her?*

But there was no response. As the golden dragon flew away, my mother went with her.

Orcades was gone.

The tension in the courtyard was thick as blood. Every breath I took felt heavier than the last as I looked across the stones to where Florence lay on the ground. Theo's eyes met mine, full of something terrible. Something I refused to accept.

"No," I whispered, stumbling forward. "No, no, no—" I could hear the sound of my own heartbeat pounding in my ears. My mother was gone. I couldn't lose Florence, too. I reached where Theo sat crouched over Florence. Her chest was still. I watched, refusing to even blink. But there was nothing. No movement.

She wasn't breathing.

"No!" The word ripped from my throat as I sank to my knees beside her, grabbing her cold hand in mine. "You're not allowed to die, Florence. Do you hear me? You're not *allowed.*"

Nyxaris crept forwards, his black wings half-furled. *The little fledgling deserved better.*

"Don't you talk about her like she's gone," I screamed, swiveling my head to glare up at him. "Don't you dare!"

The dragon didn't respond.

"Pendragon." Blake's voice reached me, rough and hesitant, pulling me back down to reality. "She—"

"No." I cut him off, refusing to even look at him. "Don't you dare. Shut your mouth." I was trembling.

"Pendragon," he whispered. "Please."

And then, for the first time since he'd arrived in the Dragon Court, I looked at Blake—really looked. He stood a few feet away, covered in blood. His face was pale and strained. My throat choked. One of his eyes was gone. The left side of his face was a mess of dried blood and raw flesh. For a second, I couldn't breathe.

"She still has a pulse." The calm, rasping voice snapped me out of my spiral. I turned to see Rodriguez kneeling beside Florence, his hands bloodied but steady as he held her wrist. His face was gray, his shoulder soaked with blood from Marcus's bolt, but his expression was grimly focused. "It's faint, but still there." He met my eyes. "Not for long, though."

"Can you heal her?" I demanded, my voice sharp with desperation.

Rodriguez hesitated, then shook his head. "She's too far gone for my abilities."

"Then, what is the point?" I shouted. "Why are you here?" I turned to look at Blake and Kage who had come up around us. "She wouldn't have even been here if it weren't for you. She was following me." The tears were running down my face. "You did this. You all did this."

Rodriguez was looking past me, up at Nyxaris, something unreadable in his bloodshot brown eyes. "There's one way. But it's dangerous."

"What is it?" I demanded. "Tell me. Now."

Rodriguez didn't take his eyes off the black dragon. "Dragon's blood. Mixed with the blood of a rider. It's an old legend. But my family has records. One of my ancestors witnessed it work once."

I stared at him. "Once," I repeated.

He nodded slowly. "It's a gamble. It could just as easily kill her. But she'll die anyway if we do nothing."

The silence that followed was suffocating.

*I will make the decision for you*, Nyxaris's voice rumbled in my head, colder than I'd ever heard it before. *I will spare you this burden. The answer is no. I will not allow my blood to be used to bind me to another rider.*

I turned to look up at him in disbelief. *This? This is what would bind you? This is how the bonding is done?*

He lowered his head in assent.

*But Florence isn't a rider. How is that even possible?* I demanded.

*As your teacher has already said, it could very well kill her*, Nyxaris replied. *But the point is irrelevant. I have been betrayed by your kind once tonight. I will not do this thing. I will not allow her to become mine. No, not even the fledgling.*

Yet I latched onto the faint reluctance I heard in his voice.

"Then, you're killing her yourself. She's *dying*." I jumped to my feet, my voice cracking as I turned to face him. "She's not asking for this. She doesn't want to bond with you. She never wanted to be a rider. She just needs your help. Please, Nyxaris."

Nyxaris's tail lashed unhappily against the ground. *And what of the others, if I do this thing? The wolf, your professor. He paused. Your . . . mate. They conspired against me. Would have all but killed me. They sought to return me to the stone.*

*I . . . didn't know that*, I said slowly. Around me everyone was very silent.

*No? And yet they used you to bring me here. They lied and they deceived. Shall I simply allow them to walk away unpunished?* His golden gaze shifted, pinning Blake where he stood. Nyxaris growled.

Blake didn't flinch. Instead, he stepped away from the rest of us, moving into the center of the courtyard and raising his hands, as if he were surrendering.

"Do it," he said softly, to Nyxaris, not to me. "If you want to kill me, do it. I won't stop you. I know I deserve it."

"Blake," I gasped, my heart racing.

He turned slightly to me, his single eye meeting mine, and I saw something there that silenced all my protests. Shame. Deep, unrelenting shame.

Blake turned back to Nyxaris, bowing his head to the dragon. "I was wrong. I have done you a great wrong tonight, Nyxaris. I betrayed you and Pendragon both. I can't take it back. But if killing me will balance the scales and save Pendragon's friend, then I beg you—please do it."

I couldn't breathe. Nyxaris's chest began to heave. Smoke curled from his nostrils, rising into the cold night air. His massive body seemed coiled, ready to spring. I could feel the heat rising off him.

In a flash I was there, standing in front of Blake, my hands raised, palms out. "Stop! Nyxaris, stop." I took a deep breath. "If you're going to burn him, you'll have to burn me, too."

Nyxaris's amber eyes met mine. *Move aside. Do not test me. He is not worthy of you. Deep down, you have always known this to be true.*

"I'm not testing you," I said steadily, though my knees felt weak. "But he's mine. Right or wrong, he's mine. I won't let you harm him."

Blake's head jerked up, his face shifting to shock and surprise. The weight of my words hung between us. I hadn't forgiven him— not yet. All I knew was I couldn't lose him, too.

Nyxaris growled, but the fire in his chest receded. He snapped his jaws open and shut and I tried not to flinch. *You protect him. Why?*

*Because I believe there's good in him,* I answered. *And because right now, this isn't about him. It's about Florence. Will you help her or not?*

Nyxaris lowered his massive head until his golden eyes were level with mine. *You ask too much of me.*

*I know. I always have. It's not fair. Believe me, I know that. But I'm not asking you to trust me right now.* I took a deep breath. *Trust her. Florence is good, pure. She's nothing like the highbloods you hate. She's better than I am. If you're going to take a chance on anyone in this miserable, corrupt world, Nyxaris, then take a chance on her. I will never ask you for anything again, I swear it.*

Nyxaris regarded me in silence. His eyes narrowed as he looked down at Florence, his massive chest rising and falling as he pondered.

The courtyard felt deathly still. No one moved. No one spoke.

I held my breath. He was going to say no. I knew he was going to say no. There was nothing else I could do and now Florence was going to die.

A small, insistent sound broke the silence. A yipping noise that shifted into a soft trill—like the hum of a lullaby sung in a foreign language.

Neville.

The fluffin raced out from the shadows, his tiny paws pattering across the blood-soaked stones. His tufted ears were back as he fixed his large owllike eyes on where Florence lay. He trotted up to her, sniffing her face, his whiskers twitching, then let out another melodic hum—a sound so mournful, so achingly beautiful, that I felt it deep in my heart.

Nyxaris froze, his body going still as stone. His great eyes widened in disbelief as he looked down at Neville. *What is this? I know this creature. I know its kind.*

As if he had heard Nyxaris, Neville turned and padded over to one of the dragon's massive clawed feet. Then, without hesitation, he climbed up onto it. The fluffin looked absurdly tiny sitting there against the dragon's ebony talons. But he sat as if he belonged there, still trilling softly, his eyes glowing brighter.

*This . . . this cannot be*, Nyxaris murmured.

Neville simply hummed louder, the sound wrapping around us like a warm embrace. As the fluffin sat there on the dragon's foot, for the first time Nyxaris didn't look like merely a creature of vengeance and fire. He looked . . . more at peace.

*What is he doing?* I murmured.

Nyxaris inhaled sharply, in a loud puff somewhere between a growl and a gasp. *He is . . . reminding me. These creatures—they cared for us once. Tended our eggs. Helped heal our wounds. They soothed us. My last rider . . . She had one. The three of us were . . . very close.*

I stared at the black dragon, shocked that he had finally shared something about his last rider.

Neville pressed his tiny head against Nyxaris's scales and the dragon seemed to shudder.

*They were bonded to us as much as our riders were,* Nyxaris continued, a tremble in his voice. *When we burned too hot, they calmed us. When we bled, they sang us whole. They were . . . true companions.*

Neville suddenly leaped from Nyxaris's foot and returned to Florence. Gently he stepped up onto her body, curling up on her stomach below where Theo's hands were still placed. His hum deepened as he pressed his tiny form against hers.

Nyxaris's head tilted abruptly. *You dare to scold me, little one?*

I blinked. *What? Can Neville speak to you?*

*Neville?* Nyxaris sounded amused. *Is that his name? No, he does not speak to me. Not in words like you do. But his thoughts are clear enough. He thinks me stubborn.* The dragon's tail lashed the ground and I jumped. *He calls me heartless.*

Neville let out a soft trill that could only be described as reproachful.

The dragon sighed, the sound rumbling through the courtyard. *I am stubborn. But loyalty and sentimentality do not change the facts. You understand nothing of the consequences.*

Neville yipped, almost like a reprimand. His wide eyes never left Nyxaris's face, but his tiny form seemed to puff up.

*The audacity of this small thing,* Nyxaris grumbled.

*Surely if anyone understands the risks, a fluffin would,* I said cautiously. *After all, you said—*

*I know what I said,* Nyxaris snapped. He let out a heavy sigh. *The creature is loyal to the girl.*

*He is*, I agreed quickly. *He loves her.* I decided not to risk mentioning Neville's attachment to Blake. *Neville is telling you that Florence is worth saving. Please, Nyxaris. Listen to him.*

Nyxaris huffed, smoke curling from his nostrils. *She may well still die. If this goes awry, it will be on your head.*

I couldn't tell if he was talking to me or to the fluffin. I held my breath.

Nyxaris's gaze seemed to soften, ever so slightly as he gazed at Neville and Florence. *Very well. So be it.*

Relief and fear sped through me in equal measure. I turned to Rodriguez. "Do it."

★ ★ ★ ★ ★

**The dragon riders are coming . . .**

Medra, Blake, and Florence's story will continue in

THE
WINGS
THAT
BIND

**Coming from HQ in 2026**

**Welcome to Bloodwing Academy.**
**Expect magic. Expect competition. Expect blood.**

**Don't miss the unforgettable beginning**
**to Medra and Blake's epic story.**

# Join My Street Team:
# Briar's Rose Court

If you'd like to discuss my books, meet other romantasy book lovers, share pictures or quotes about your favorite characters, vote on character names and book titles, get sneak peeks at covers and other art, and enter exclusive giveaways, then I would love to have you over in our private Rose Court Street Team Facebook group!

**Come join in the fun!**
**Sign up for the Street Team:**
**rosecourt.briarboleyn.com**

ONE PLACE. MANY STORIES

Bold, innovative and
empowering publishing.

FOLLOW US ON:

@HQStories